The Phoenix Glove

(Book two in the Through the Portal trilogy)

NORTH LINCOLNSHIRE

ISBN-13: 978-1479398119
ISBN-10: 147939811X

TABLE OF CONTENTS

CHAPTER 1:
THE CAR

Jem had no idea where he was. He was running down a corridor, smacking into a wall, and turning down the other corridor. It was freezing in here, but he was sweating. Why was he running?

BOOM!

Something exploded behind him and bits of debris showered him. He threw a glance over his shoulder to see a massive black dragon with piercing red eyes tearing the corridor apart. With every swipe, it knocked away more of the corridor; it was twenty times the size of it.

So that's what he was running from. Suddenly, the ground gave out and he was falling... falling... falling...

He heard the ferocious dragon give out a violent roar and saw flames shoot over his head where he had just been. The fire had missed him—but he was in so much pain. He felt like he was on fire. Everything hurt. His insides were being torn apart. He saw the dragon poke its head down the hole he had fallen into, and its intense red eyes burned into him like lasers.

"Jem," said a soft gentle voice. He sat bolt upright in his bed. He was covered in sweat and all the sheets were saturated with it.

"You were having another dream," said the soft voice. "It's okay. Everything's okay."

Jem looked rapidly around the room, searching for the dragon, but it wasn't anywhere to be found. There was just Sierra, sitting on the side of his bed, stroking her fingers through his hair.

"It's not here?" he asked.

"No, Jem, it's not. You're safe," replied Sierra patiently.

He didn't understand why he still thought it might be here. He had had this dream a million times by now, about the black dragon, ever since he had realized that the Red Dragon was his friend, not his enemy. His dreams had seemed to accommodate for this and instead presented him with an even larger and more ferocious dragon to wake him every night.

He also didn't understand why Sierra was still here. For months, they had lived together with Aubrie and Edner Kuznet, the sweet couple in Luria City, and he must have awoken almost every night with nightmares or pains from his dragon bite, but Sierra was always there to comfort him.

He lay back down on his bed. He was so red with embarrassment at the moment that he was surprised his cheeks weren't illuminating the whole pitch-dark room. He hated when this happened. He felt weak. He felt gross, drowning in his own sweat.

"Relax," whispered Sierra. "It'll be okay, Jem." She continued to stroke his hair and lull him back to sleep. When he finally fell asleep, she stood up to return to her room, but as she stepped out of the room, a familiar figure was waiting for her in the circular second floor of the Kuznet Café.

"You can't keep doing this," said Aubrie. "You need your sleep too."

"I can't sleep when I hear him—you know that," replied Sierra firmly. There was nothing Aubrie could say that would convince her that sleep was more important than taking care of Jem.

"He'll be okay, Sierra," said Aubrie, giving her a motherly touch on the cheek.

Sierra grabbed the warm hand against her cheek and let the tears fall that she hadn't realized she had been holding back. Aubrie pulled her close and allowed her to cry into her shoulder, while she herself silently wept. Neither of them said anything; there was nothing to say. They both knew that Jem was stuck like this due to the poison from his dragon bite. Sierra knew she couldn't help him, and while Aubrie knew she couldn't help him either, it pained her doubly that she couldn't even help Sierra.

"Go get some rest, honey," said Aubrie after a moment. "You need it."

Sierra nodded, wiping tears from her eyes, and headed for her room. Aubrie gave one last fleeting look to Jem's room and then went back to her own room.

"Sierra was in his room again?" asked Edner as she stepped inside.

"Yeah. It was just a nightmare tonight, though," replied Aubrie as she snuggled into bed with her partner. "No pains."

"That poor boy… I wish we could help more, Aub."

"You know that what he has is irreversible, Ed. We've taken him to every hospital not under Regime control."

"I know, I know. But still…"

"I know how you feel, babe," said Aubrie, a note of true sadness prevalent in her voice.

***

Jem awoke the next morning feeling no more rested than when he had collapsed onto his bed the night before. He stepped out of bed groggily and accidently landed right on Snovel's tail. It yelped and jumped away quickly.

"Sorry," grunted Jem.

Snovel had been glued to him ever since they had fought Atychis and the Dragon on the North Island. The thing that Jem found strange, though, is that—as he had been told by the Dragon—some dragonets can communicate with humans telepathically, but Snovel didn't talk to anyone, not even Jem. Jem didn't mind; he liked the silence that came with Snovel's company anyway.

The two of them wandered out into the circular second floor room, and Jem saw that the doors to both Sierra's room and Aubrie and Edner's room were closed; they all must have still been asleep. He felt his cheeks getting red. His nightmares must've been keeping them up.

Oh well, he told himself, *it could've been worse.*

And it definitely could have been. There were nights where he had sleepwalked and had done terrible things. For some reason, one night, he had gone into Aubrie and Edner's room and had begun screaming until Edner slapped him awake. That was a particularly embarrassing night.

But sometimes he was violent. He can recall one night that he was strangling Snovel because he thought it was the black dragon from his nightmare, and Sierra had to pry his hands off Snovel's neck. He was surprised that Snovel continued to spend nights with him, but there it was every night just beside his bed.

And then there were the nights that he got physically ill. Those could go on for minutes, hours, or even days at a time. They came at random, making Jem completely immobile and useless. He would vomit until nothing came out and then dry heave for the rest of however long it lasted.

This night had been relatively painless compared to all the other scenarios Jem could think of off the top of his head, but he still felt terrible. The only reason that Sierra, Aubrie, and Edner were sleeping in is because he must have kept them up with his screaming. He vaguely remembered Sierra's soft voice comforting him last night and the familiar feeling of her fingers through his hair, but that was it.

He mindlessly wandered through the crowd of people downstairs in the Café. It got pretty busy in the mornings and he had taken to just ignoring everyone and heading straight for the door. He threw on all the warm gear he had stored in a locker by the door and ventured out into the cold Lurian landscape with Snovel right behind him.

The summer here in Luria was pleasantly chill. It never got very hot, no matter what time of year, but it was a comfortable kind of cold now. Certainly not the freezing bitterness that was present in the winter.

Jem had been taking some classes in Luria City, but eventually stopped attending all of them. An education seemed like something distant and tiny when the entire planet was at war. Not to mention that he had to keep leaving class when he would suddenly become violently ill.

So instead of taking classes, he spent most of his time wandering through the Earth, Callisto, and Kelados Organization Headquarters. ECKO HQ had become like a second home to him. He would visit Farouche, his friend from Ilios, and see how his inventions were going; he would visit Sam and Henry, the two pilots and engineers that Afflatus had introduced him to, and see what they were working on; and of course, he would catch up with Afflatus himself to stay updated on the status of the war.

After Jem had defeated Atychis, the assassin that Veroci had sent after him, Veroci and the entire Veroci Regime had declared war against Jem himself. It was the scariest day Jem could remember. It was back when the ECKO HQ was still in Neora, the day after he'd returned from the North Island. All the Regs in Neora had attacked the HQ, but Afflatus and the soldiers of the ECKO militia had been able to hold them off. Jem, Farouche, and Sierra had been made to stay hidden deep within the building, but of course, they hadn't listened.

They had ventured to the window to watch what was happening and had watched as hundreds of people died before them: Regs and militia. There were people whom they had spoken to at some point in the HQ, even people who had congratulated Jem on defeating Atychis. They probably weren't too grateful now that they were dead because of it.

Sierra had broken down crying, and while Farouche had tried to comfort her, Jem had stared out the window, unable to comprehend what he was seeing. Afflatus had been thrashing mystical, dark blue blurs around him like whips, knocking several Regs to the ground at once. Many soldiers of the ECKO militia had been armed with special knives that shot blue lasers from the blade tips, and they had cut and swiped professionally at the Regs, but the Regs had been well-armed too.

Each had a giant scepter like Jem was accustomed to them carrying, and from those, they could shoot deadly red lasers. He had watched from the window as an ECKO soldier had sliced a Reg across the chest, killing him, only for another Reg to hit the soldier square in the chest with a red laser. Jem had felt his eyes well up with tears. A sharp pain had struck his gut every time someone died. Each death was his fault. This whole war was his fault.

Then, somehow, a Reg had looked up to the high window of the HQ and had spotted Jem. He had shot a laser and Jem had fallen to the ground just in time—it had broken through the window and exploded the piece of ceiling above them. They had crawled through the debris and retreated deeper into the building.

Eventually, ECKO had driven the Regs out and relocated the HQ to Luria. Now the Regime controlled all of the Western Regions: Argo, Ilios, and Xena, while ECKO controlled the Eastern regions: Neora, Luria, and Radeon. But almost everyone had relocated to Luria, since they were down to only one Soul now. The Regime controlled the other five.

Souls were essentially the only source of magic. A person could only perform magic if they were near one. One Soul usually covered a Region, about a sixth of the whole world, but the Lurian Soul expanded slightly into both Neora and Radeon because there were no borders to hold it back anymore. Because of the strong magical border running through the center of the planet, though, all the magic from the five Regime Souls was contained in the three Western Regions. Jem imagined that everyone in the West must have great magic, but then he remembered that the Regime liked to control and sell magic for a profit. Most likely, all the Regs had extremely powerful magic and the citizens had none.

Jem had once transformed into his dragon form and flown to the border between the East and West territory. It had been a strange sight: the icy ground of Luria suddenly ended at the point where there was a large, semi-transparent wall jutting up into the sky. It had looked kind of like a wall of water. On the other side, Jem had been able to make out factories and cities in the distance, but not much else besides the barren dry land of Ilios.

When he had tried to stick his hand through the wall, it had bounced right off. Breathing fire was futile. Even banging his massive dragon tail against it was useless; the wall was impervious. The Regime really didn't want them coming in.

As Jem wandered up the stairs through the HQ, he still couldn't think of what the Regime might be doing behind those walls. Why hadn't Veroci just attacked ECKO already and tried to get Jem? What was he waiting for?

The first floor he got to was the engineering floor. He passed a room where Sam and Henry were working on some sort of massive engine hanging from the ceiling on chains. He didn't feel like talking to them right now, and they seemed busy anyway.

He decided to wander this floor; he had never really gotten a good tour of this area. Snovel strode on beside him, just as curious as he was.

They passed a set of windows through which Jem could faintly see a sort of arena that looked like it was used for training or testing. The next door was just a boring office space. But the one after that was more interesting, entirely because it was locked.

Jem looked to Snovel, and Snovel gave a cute sort of sneeze that shot fire out of its nose.

"Good idea, Snov," said Jem. He leaned down to the handle of the door and let out a small breath of fire. The handle immediately melted and drooped down the door. Jem turned one of his fingers into a dragon claw, set it into the molten metal, and pulled the handle straight out of the door. Snovel growled at him suspiciously.

"Hey, it'll teach them to lock doors, won't it?" said Jem.

He quietly pushed the door open and found himself inside a giant, dark room. He searched around for a light switch, but when he found it, the room was nothing like he had expected.

In the center was a broken down old car that was clearly from Earth. It was a barely recognizable silver Mazda Protégé that was rusted from top to bottom and thoroughly bashed in as if it had fallen down a mountain. Jem paced around it a few times and noticed that it was missing a rim. He leaned down to one of the wheels that still had a rim and pulled it off. It looked familiar, but he couldn't put his finger on it...

"I see you found our car," said a stern voice from the doorway.

Jem jumped suddenly and dropped the rim, which made several loud metallic *dings* as it hit the ground.

"Oh, s-sorry," he stammered. Snovel lowered its ears and backed away from Jem as if to say, "Not my fault."

"You didn't think we'd notice the melted handle?" asked Sam.

"Didn't really think about that..." confessed Jem.

"Bet you didn't expect to find an Earth car, did you?" asked Sam conversationally as he strolled into the room.

"Huh? I'm not in trouble?"

"Nah, it's no big deal. You knew we came through the portal in the lake anyway."

That's when Jem suddenly realized why the rim looked familiar. He picked it up and pointed it at Sam.

"So you drove your car into the lake?"

"Pretty much," replied Sam, folding his arms and staring at the car. "It's a shame. I really liked that car."

"So why'd you do it?"

"We had to get away. We were being chased."

"By who?"

Sam sighed. "Let's go back to the engine room and discuss this with Henry."

He guided Jem back to the room with the giant hanging engine that he and Henry had been working on.

"Jem found the car," Sam said to Henry.

"So we gonna tell him?" asked Henry, setting down his tools.

"Yeah. We have to, I think."

"But, Sam, he's from Earth."

"So?"

"So what if he—?"

"I think better of him than that," interjected Sam.

The three of them sat at a table towards the outside of the room.

"What do you mean?" asked Jem. "Why's it matter if I'm from Earth?"

"People from Earth," explained Henry seriously, "tend to have a very strong dislike for a certain kind of people. We haven't run into that sort of hate or discrimination here in Callisto, and that is why we like it here."

"However," insisted Sam, "we must assume, Jem, that even on Earth you are not the type to discriminate unjustly against people."

"Well, no, I don't think so," said Jem, now thoroughly confused about what this had to do with the rusty car.

"Alright then," continued Sam. "So the story begins like this: Henry and I began a project at our science research facility in Redmond—you know where Redmond is right? Just north of Sammamish? Anyway, our project was to create a wormhole generator capable of transportation to the moon or other planets. Would save a lot of traveling time if you just had a portal right?"

"We spent years on this," said Henry. "I eventually developed a way of locating and inputting universal coordinates, and Sam hacked into the NASA databases to discover the proper location and coordinates of the moon."

"So that's why someone chased you? 'Cause you hacked NASA?"

"No no no," laughed Sam. "They never would've found out that that was me."

"Anyway," continued Henry, "Sam actually found the coordinates of a couple planets that we had never heard of or observed. So naturally, we programmed those into the wormhole generator to see what would happen."

"But before we could test it out," interjected Sam, "we were fired from the project."

"You were fired from the project?" gasped Jem. "The project that *you* started? Why?"

There was a moment of tense silence before Henry said bluntly, "Because we're gay." Sam nodded, and the two of them grasped hands.

"Oh—oh!" stuttered Jem, a little surprised but not at all offended. "Well how could they fire you for that?"

"They found some loophole," muttered Sam. "Said we weren't living up to expectations or something, which is ridiculous because our wormhole project was done ahead of time."

"I think they kept us around just long enough for us to finish it," said Henry. "But they never asked for the commencement codes before they fired us."

The two of them laughed. "So they couldn't use it!" said Sam, clarifying for Jem. "And besides, the only coordinates programmed into it were the ones for a couple of planets we didn't even fully believe existed. We hadn't gotten to input the moon's coordinates yet."

"So where is the chase?" asked Jem.

"Ah, right," said Henry. "So here is the best part. We stole our generator back."

"What?" gasped Jem.

"Damn right!" said Sam. "We invented it and did all the work. We weren't gonna let them take credit. So we busted in one night and stole it. But genius over here—"

"Hey, it wasn't *all* my fault!" cut in Henry.

"—forgot to disable the exit alarms, so on our way out, the alarms sounded. The police were called and they began to chase us."

Jem's face was frozen in shock.

"And we went through Sammamish," explained Henry. "'cause we didn't know where else to go. But we just couldn't shake them, so I had the idea to use the wormhole generator."

"But we hadn't tested it out yet," interjected Sam, nudging Henry. "And we didn't have any coordinates for anywhere on Earth, just those mystery planets. We didn't have any other options, though."

"So as we drove down the Plateau towards the lake," said Henry. "I began to input the commencement code. And since we needed to be far away from all people, I told Sam to go straight for the lake."

Sam nodded. "We broke through the railing and went straight into the lake. Just as the car filled up completely with water, the generator initialized and we were transported to Argo. Thankfully, the process shattered all the windows and allowed us to escape from the car once we appeared in the lake in Argo."

"From there," said Henry, "we joined ECKO as soon as we learned of the Regime's terrible oppression and had the car lifted from the lake to remove all evidence. Atychis did a good job of keeping the Regime out so that we could do that."

"He helped you?" asked Jem, surprised.

"Yeah," said Sam. "He wasn't a bad guy back when he was the Argonian Elder. He obviously changed a lot."

"What exactly happened to him?" asked Jem, remembering him ranting about Veroci back on the North Island.

"That's something you'll have to ask Afflatus, Jem," said Henry.

"Why?"

"Because Atychis was his brother."

CHAPTER 2:
AFFLATUS' SECRET

"Afflatus!" yelled Jem, pounding on the door to his office on the highest floor of the HQ. "Afflatus! Open this door right now! I know you're in there!"

He didn't really know that Afflatus was in there, but he really hoped that he was. It was possible that he was still back at his old cottage, but he spent most of his time at the HQ now helping out with everything.

Jem just could not believe Afflatus never told him that Atychis was his brother. Jem had killed Atychis by tackling him into the lava. He had killed Afflatus' brother...

The door creaked open slowly to reveal an old wrinkled face with a straight white beard falling from it. His head was still shiningly bald, but his eyes were heavier. Afflatus had been looking increasingly more stressed over the past few months, and Jem had just thought that was because of the war. Now he knew it had to do with Atychis.

"Can I help you?" asked Afflatus lightly.

Jem heaved a few deep breaths. He hadn't realized how worked up he'd gotten running the stairs all the way up here. The levitator (a magical elevator) was turned off to reserve magic for the rest of the East, so everybody had to use the stairs to get everywhere.

"I need to talk to you," said Jem.

"I'm busy," said Afflatus tiredly, trying to shut the door, but Jem pushed his hand against the inside of the door.

"It's important," insisted Jem.

Afflatus sighed and hesitantly opened the door for Jem. The inside of Afflatus' office looked like it belonged to a teenager. Bright posters were layered multiple times along the walls and up the domed ceiling. Small perches were attached to the walls with tiny yellow birds sitting on them. When Jem looked closely he saw that each bird had a thin, long beak that looked somewhat like a trumpet or a megaphone, but they were all asleep. As they breathed in and out, they let out soothing yet somewhat somber whistle noises.

"They're trinks," explained Afflatus, taking a seat in a large comfy chair in the corner. "They're capable of beautiful, vibrant songs, but lately, they have done very little except sleep."

Jem grunted acknowledgement as he sat down in the poufy chair across from Afflatus. The old Lurian Elder was dressed in loose, dark blue robes that became tight at the wrists and ankles. Jem always thought the Lurian clothing looked kind of funny, like a ninja with over-sized garb, but he knew it was practical: the robes kept in the warmth while the skinny parts allowed gloves and boots to be worn easily.

"What is it that you wanted to talk about?" sighed Afflatus as if this were the last place he wanted to be.

Jem quit looking around the office and concentrated on Afflatus' baggy eyes.

"I know that Atychis was your brother," he said plainly.

Afflatus didn't even flinch. "And?"

"And... well, how come you didn't tell me?" demanded Jem.

"It was simply not relevant information at the time, nor is it right now."

"I think it is."

"Why?"

"Because I *killed* him."

Now Afflatus flinched slightly. He tried to cover it by rubbing his eye. "You did what you had to do, Jem. You acted out of self-defense."

Jem nodded grimly. He knew it was true, but he still felt bad.

"You want to know more," said Afflatus emotionlessly.

Jem looked at him curiously, trying to think of how to ask his question. "Atychis said that Veroci took away all his magic and attacked him because he didn't let him put outposts in Argo."

"That's true," said Afflatus.

"But there aren't any outposts in Luria. Why didn't he do that to you?"

Afflatus gave a sad grin. "Because I chose the more isolated region." When Jem looked questioningly at him, he continued, "We both grew up to be Elders, Jem, but I chose Luria and he chose Argo. The only reason I am whole and he is dead is because Luria is geographically harder to reach than Argo. That's it. I just as easily could have had my brother's fate as he could have had mine."

Jem frowned. "Where did you grow up?"

"In Argo City."

"So how did you get to Luria? Wasn't there that whole myth about how crossing the borders would get you killed?"

Afflatus smiled his first legitimate smile. "Well I didn't think like an Argonian, did I? I thought like a Lurian, and a Lurian questions everything. I was quick to discover that I could leave to any other region in the world, and I picked Luria because there were more freethinkers, just like me."

"And Atychis didn't want to come with you?"

"No, he loved Argo: the sense of community, the togetherness, the hard work and dedication… it was just meant for him—but not me."

"And when he stood up to Veroci, he ended up permanently scarred for it…" muttered Jem.

Afflatus nodded. "And that affected him psychologically for the rest of his life. You saw him… in his state of anger and repulsion towards everything in the world. He lived a pitiful life, wandering the furthest nowhere lands of Argo. He refused my help. He did not want to come to Luria despite the fact that he was considered a disgrace to his whole region."

"Why was he a disgrace?" asked Jem. "Why didn't the whole region get mad that Veroci did that to him?"

Afflatus gave another somber, ironic smirk. "Because nobody knew that Veroci did that to him. Only I did, and that is because he told me and because I performed the tests on his wounds to prove so. The official story was that he performed a spell that backfired, furthering the Regime propaganda that magic is bad and dangerous."

Afflatus let out a large sigh. "The sad thing is not that he chose Argo," he continued. "What is sad is that when he stood strong and brave in defense of his region, he was punished for it. It is my biggest regret that I did not support him more. I was selfish, for I did not want to risk the safety of my Lurians to protect Argo, but I should have. My brother might still be alive today, working and fighting beside me."

"No, Aff, that isn't your fault," reassured Jem. "You did the right thing. If Luria had fallen to the Regime, we wouldn't have anywhere to go now. All of Callisto would be under Regime control. But since we have Luria, we can fight back."

Just then, a violent, sharp ringing noise penetrated Jem's ears with incredible force. He cupped his hands over his ears and managed to drown out some of the painful noise.

"What's happening!?" he yelled to Afflatus, who remained sitting calmly in his chair.

"Those are the border alarms," explained Afflatus loudly but stoically. "The Regime invasion has begun."

CHAPTER 3:
INVASION

Jem was in shock. All he could do was try to keep his ears covered because the alarm was so loud. He had been expecting an invasion for some time, since the Regime had so much more magic than they did, but the immediacy of it had him frozen.

Afflatus reached his hand under the table and pressed something. It must have been some sort of off switch because the alarm immediately ceased. Jem heard a quiet ringing somewhere deep within his skull, yet was amazed at the quietness of the room.

Then Afflatus' voice was loud and clear in his head. It wasn't that he was talking just to Jem; his voice was being projected to every inch of Eastern land. Sierra, Edner, and Aubrie, all of whom had been woken up by the alarm, heard his voice. The Neoran Elder, Tekkara, who was living in a refugee city to the north of Luria heard him. Snovel, Sam, and Henry, who were all still downstairs in the engine room heard his voice, along with Rimaya and Cyneal, who had been watching cartoons in the common room of the HQ.

"Citizens of the East," boomed Afflatus. "The alarm you have all just heard indicates that a large Regime force has just crossed the border. I urge you all to remain calm." There was a pause as Afflatus took a deep, controlling breath that he did not project to everyone. "Given the strength and numbers of our enemy, fighting back would be futile. I ask you all to swallow your pride and do not fight. Instead, get yourselves to Luria City as fast as possible. There is a portal on the east side of the mountains which will be transporting everyone to a safe location. ECKO members will be guiding and protecting civilians. Please, get to the east Luria City mountains as quickly as possible."

There was a tone of pleading in Afflatus' voice that Jem had never heard before. Jem let out a deep breath that he realized he had been holding throughout the entire speech.

"You have been training for this, I believe?" asked Afflatus.

Jem grinned. "As a matter of a fact, I have."

"Then let us hurry!" yelled Afflatus, suddenly jolting across the room with the youthfulness that Jem had used to expect from the old man. He bolted down the corridor and to the stairs with Jem right behind him. People from all the offices and rooms of the HQ were bustling down the stairs making it ridiculously crowded.

BOOM!

A massive explosion struck somewhere in the building and sent dozens of those running down the stairs toppling head over heels. Jem struggled to help a couple people up and then continued on his way down. Another explosion hit, but this time, the crowd was prepared and nobody fell over.

When they reached the bottom floor, lots of people stopped to get their warm clothes on, but those more trained in magic, like Afflatus, did not bother wasting the time. Jem didn't put his warm clothes on because soon it wouldn't matter; he wouldn't need human clothes.

Afflatus held his hands out to the side and pulled up like he was lifting invisible heavy grocery bags. Two blocks of snow then rose from the ground and covered his feet. Jem watched curiously as he kicked off with one foot and began to skate across the frozen Lurian ground with unnatural speed and agility. Magic really could do anything.

Shaking the thought out of his head that he wanted to try that later, Jem focused hard on his dragon form. He had been training daily for this, but it was never as easy to do the real thing. His heart was beating too fast, his mind racing too much.

He envisioned his training sessions: Sierra and Farouche yelling at him, trying to distract him while he transformed into a dragon and back into a human; Edner launching objects into the air for him to blow out of the air with his fire breath; Aubrie setting up obstacle courses for him throughout the city so that he could practice his flying; the countless professionals that Afflatus had arranged for him to run drills with.

Transform! he imagined Sierra saying, just like she had during training. *Don't let the distractions get to you. You have to do this! You can do this! We believe in you!*

With that thought, he felt the hardening of his skin across his entire body. The feeling of cold disappeared. Giant fangs formed in his mouth as his whole body expanded into its full-blown dragon form.

It only took seconds for him to transform, and immediately, he took off into the sky, searching around for the source of the explosions that were drilling the HQ. It didn't take long to find it: fireballs were shooting across the sky, headed directly for them. In the far distance, Jem could see machines on the ground and in the sky. They would have been invisible to a human eye, but his dragon vision was impeccable.

Knowing that fire couldn't hurt him in his dragon form, Jem flew directly towards the first fireball in the sky, colliding with it just before it hit the HQ. It shattered into fiery bits around him which fell to the ground and sizzled out in the snow. He set his sights on the next fireball and crushed it in exactly the same way. Within minutes, he had cleared every fireball from the sky, but those machines in the distance were advancing quickly.

He flew around the HQ to examine the damage from the fireballs. A couple sections of the building were on fire, and Jem's first reaction was to try and blow it out—but then he remembered that he breathes fire in dragon form. So instead, he simply landed on the ground and flapped his wings so hard that the powdery snow from the ground was blown onto the fires, extinguishing them thoroughly.

He took to the sky to try and get the best look around that he could. From every direction he could see, people were flocking to the east Lurian Mountains. He remembered the cave where the portal was located and found it quite lucky that Afflatus had just dug a tunnel a few weeks ago that led from the cave to the outer side of the mountains. Previously, it could only be reached from inside Luria City. If Afflatus hadn't extended the cave to reach outside Luria City, a lot of the people traveling from outside the city wouldn't have made it. Clearly, Afflatus had known this moment had been coming.

Jem could see them all: large masses of people migrating from the north, east, and south. Nobody came from the west except the Regs. Jem had to assume they had already annihilated whatever cities they had passed over, and it was sad to think that people may have died while Afflatus was giving his speech for people to remain calm. The cities to the west of Luria City were just in an unlucky location. It was amazing how much came down to pure luck.

Delay the Regs, thought Jem, trying to formulate some sort of plan. *I can't protect every individual person, but if I can slow the Regs down enough to allow the others to get through the portal, we might have a chance.*

He took off into the sky and headed west towards the Regime machines. They were launching fireballs again, and Jem flew right through them like nothing. As he passed over the west Lurian City mountains, he could see everything that was a part of the invasion force.

The machines on the ground were enormous—each bigger than a house. They ran on treads similar to Earth tanks and had multiple barrels sticking out from the front which Jem assumed they launched magic through, much like how they shot magic from their scepters. On the top was what looked like a massive spoon that dipped down inside the machine and resurfaced with a massive, fiery ball. They launched another wave at Jem and he destroyed them all out of the air.

Since they couldn't be holding that much ammo within the tanks, Jem knew that the fireballs must have been some sort of magic designed to incinerate and explode upon contact. They weren't just aiming to kill; they were aiming to obliterate.

The flying machines hadn't launched anything yet. They were massive circular saucers that were almost as big as the tanks and much like the alien UFO saucers Jem had seen on TV back on Earth. They were black, but the outside ring around them glowed red. Jem had never heard of any flying machine other than Farouche's vimana, the giant triangular flying ship with an orb at each corner. This must have been what they were working on for the months leading up to the invasion.

He had to fly for a while, occasionally crashing through fireballs, before he was within striking distance of the machines. His first goal was to disable the fireball throwers so that they wouldn't destroy the whole city before they even got there. That seemed doable. Maybe they wouldn't have to flee to Kelados through the portal after all. Jem had to admit that that didn't seem like a great option since Kelados was a world inhabited by zombies. He had learned from the Dragon that there was a single human civilization left, but would they even accept all these Callistonians?

Maybe it wouldn't even come to that, though. There were only ten of the tanks and ten of the saucers. That wasn't too many targets for Jem as a dragon.

He swooped down to the nearest tank and was immediately pelted with dozens of red lasers. He felt them almost like pinpricks. He released a breath of fire across the tank that was shooting at him, and the pinpricks ceased momentarily. As he skimmed over the roof of another tank, the arm of its fireball thrower was extended, so Jem clamped onto it with his claws and tried to fly away.

The result was that he ripped the thrower straight off the tank. With a massive heave, he turned and hurled the thrower back at the tank, impaling it in the backside and causing it to stop moving.

Easy enough, thought Jem, but at exactly the wrong time. Just as he acknowledged his triumph, a small saucer about the size of a car smashed into him, sending him spiraling down towards the ground. His vision was blurred and barely functioning as he saw the sky spinning and the landscape around him coming in and out of focus.

Not even knowing which way was up, he began to flap his wings to gain some sort of control. Judging by how the wind pulled him, he was able to level out of his dive just before he hit the ground, skimming his belly along the icy ground.

He looked frantically around for the saucer that had hit him, but instead of finding one saucer, he found many. Several small saucers were being deployed by the large saucers. As the small ones dropped down from the large ones, they shot off in every direction at once at an unmatchable speed.

Okay, this could complicate things, thought Jem as he flew up into the sky, trying to obtain the higher vantage point.

They shot across his field of vision before he was even able to identify them. He had no idea which one struck him in the head just a minute ago; he couldn't even keep his gaze on one for more than half a second.

BAM!

Another powerful strike, this time against his back. Jem lost his position in the sky for a moment but quickly dismissed the pain and resumed flying. If he could just take them out one at a time…

He tried to lock onto one. As it zoomed by, he took off after it and didn't let it leave his line of sight. It ducked and twisted and turned and flipped, but Jem stayed steadily behind it. No matter how hard he flapped, though, he could not catch the quick little bugger.

BAM!

One of the small saucers he wasn't watching drilled him across the side of his body, sending him toppling through the air. He lost his target completely.

As he reoriented himself, he realized that the tanks were back to launching fireballs at the city, so he refocused his energy on them. He dove down and landed on the nearest tank. More pinprick-like lasers struck him, but they didn't matter. This tank had a retractable thrower that had lowered back into the tank when Jem approached, but the metallic hull couldn't stop him.

He sank his claws into the exterior of the tank and ripped a large chunk off. Just as this happened, he caught a glimpse of a small saucer out of the corner of his eye. Out of instinct, he threw his claw up into the air in defense. The saucer smacked into it and broke apart into a million pieces. Jem heard the faint cries of a person's voice but did not see a body.

Resuming his work, he ripped the hull open further and found the thrower. He breathed fire over it to weaken it and then slashed at it with his claws, destroying it thoroughly.

Satisfied, Jem took off for the next tank but was cut short as a saucer flew by just inches in front of him. Then another hit his tail from behind him, and as he rolled to the side in a desperate attempt at evasion, he saw one come shooting up right beside him and barely miss his underbelly. All of a sudden, they were everywhere—left, right, up, down—each trying their hardest to knock Jem out of the sky, and it was working.

With each hit, he fell a little closer to the ground, and his body began to ache miserably. In between hits, he got a glimpse of the west Lurian City mountains and noted that they were getting very close, which wasn't good since he still had eight more tanks to destroy, not to mention all the saucers. Maybe this wasn't going to work after all.

He suffered hit after hit after hit from the small saucers, and eventually, his flight wasn't even making progress towards the next tank—he was simply trying to dodge. Apparently, this had made him a very easy target because the next thing he knew, a giant net was falling over top of him, ensnaring him completely. As he fell from the sky, he saw a giant saucer hovering above him and cursed himself for not anticipating that it may drop some sort of weapon.

He hit the ground hard—hard enough to create a crater around him and send up a plume of snow. He struggled as much as he could, blowing fire and swiping and whipping his tail around, but nothing could free him from the net.

One of the small saucers came and hovered just above Jem as if observing him. Jem quit thrashing. It was just floating there... watching him...

Then it began to open up. The top half began to slide back into the rest of the saucer, and a man's head was revealed. He had black hair that was gelled back and a perfectly trimmed goatee.

"So are you the Dragon... or the boy?" asked the man, hovering even closer to Jem's face. Jem lashed out and tried to bite him, but the net prevented him.

The man laughed haughtily. "Fool, that net was designed for dragons. You're going nowhere. Now tell me if you're the boy!"

With those last words, Jem saw the man point something at him and then he felt his whole body go rigid. He couldn't move. Weak and unable to continue holding his dragon form, he slowly melted back into his human body.

The man put the shocking device back in the saucer and hovered closer to Jem.

"Jem Surwae," he said tauntingly. "So the rumors are true... you do have the powers of a dragon."

Jem had nothing to say in reply to this. Inside his mind, though, he was freaking out. Was this man going to kill him? He could hear screams and explosions coming from Luria City. The saucers and tanks must have reached their destination. Jem had failed.

"Well, seeing as you won't be going anywhere," continued the goatee-man, "I think I'll go kill all your friends and family. Then I'll be back to take you to Veroci. How does that sound?"

Enraged, Jem—still in his human form—spat a vicious pillar of flame at the saucer. The goatee-man quickly ducked and avoided it; in response, he took out the shocking device and pointed it at Jem again, sending him into a world of pain. Everything hurt. Every inch of his body was screaming with pain.

"Fool! How dare you attack me!" bellowed the goatee-man.

Jem had thought it clever at the time. He had learned to transform just parts of his body to a dragon, and it turned out that he could transform just his throat and mouth enough to breath fire. But he didn't find it clever anymore as he writhed in pain. In retrospect, it was just stupid and pointless.

After the goatee-man had decided that Jem had suffered enough, he quit shocking him and said, "I'll be back for you, but don't get your hopes up. Veroci only wants you alive so that he can kill you personally."

With that, the top of the saucer shut and it shot off towards Luria City. Just out over the edge of his crater, Jem could see that the tanks were still trying—rather unsuccessfully—to climb over the west Lurian City mountains. However, he couldn't see what was happening at the City since the mountains blocked his view. He didn't have the energy to fight against his net or stay at the edge of the crater, so he slid limply to the bottom of the crater and lay there.

A few minutes—to Jem it was hours—passed as he lay in a confused gaze, slipping in and out of consciousness. The thing that finally woke him up was a girl yelling loudly, "JEM! JEM!"

He mumbled something incoherent.

Someone began sawing at the fabrics of the net with some sort of magic blade that Jem could only really see as a bluish blur.

"Are you okay?" she asked. Jem's eyes finally came into focus as he realized it was Sierra.

"Yes," he said dismally

"I got here as quick as I could," she said, sawing furiously at the net around him. "Why did that saucer guy let you live? He looked like he was in a position to kill you."

Jem pondered this for a moment. "He said that Veroci wanted to kill me personally."

Sierra eyed him worriedly.

"The City's lost," she said. "We just have to get through that portal."

"What about everyone else?" asked Jem weakly.

"We can't get everyone through, Jem. There simply isn't enough time. This attack was a surprise for a reason; they don't want us to escape. But if you can escape, Jem, we still have a chance. You know Veroci is afraid of you, and you have powers that none of us have."

"But everyone else…"

"Their survival is not as important as yours," said Sierra bluntly. "If you ever want to defeat Veroci and reclaim Callisto then we have to flee—for now at least. This isn't surrendering, it's simply relocating."

She finally cut through a big enough hole that Jem was able to crawl out from under the net.

"But if we can save some others, we should," said Jem firmly.

"Only if you don't waste time with it," she replied equally firmly. "I'll take my slider back to the portal entrance. You gather as many people as you can, but you better be there when I get there! Then we can hold off some of the attacks to let people through."

"Deal," said Jem. These goals gave him hope, and he felt the wings extending out of his back as he jumped into the air and transformed into his dragon form. He watched as Sierra mounted her slider and took off for the City.

Jem didn't want to attract the attention of the little saucers again, so he flew low to the ground until he was just behind the mountains, and then he flew around them. The tanks must have already penetrated the City because they were nowhere to be seen.

Everything he could hear from inside the City was horrible: buildings exploding and crashing, people screaming and crying...

He tuned it out and continued flying. On the other side of the city, just east of the east Lurian City mountains, he saw a single giant saucer shooting beams down at the people making a break for the portal. There were masses of people, some running, some on sliders, some in transport vehicles, but the saucer was spraying them all down like nothing.

He had to risk drawing the attention to himself, but he would do it as quickly as possible. He flew along the ground, dodging people and sliders until he was directly below the saucer. Then, he shot up directly into the sky, aiming for its belly. He found a weak spot where it had dropped the little saucers from, and he broke through it like a piece of paper. Once inside, he thrashed his tail and swiped at everything in sight, tearing down structural columns and ripping off cords and things. He felt the whole machine shift its weight, and he figured that he had done enough.

As he flew back down, he could hear the saucer losing altitude behind him. In an effort to keep it from landing on civilians, he estimated where it would land and he landed there first. He flapped his wings with massive force, launching all the people around him hundreds of feet across the slick ground. It wasn't the most polite way to move large groups of people, but it was effective and safer than having a giant saucer land on them.

He only had a couple of seconds to leap out of the way as the giant machine crashed into the ground. There was no time to rejoice, though; all around him, he saw saucers shooting at people who were trying to make it to the portal. There wouldn't be enough time to take them all down before the portal was compromised. Sierra was right.

Ignoring his instinct, he took off for the portal rather than any of the other saucers.

Far to the east, he saw something large moving. Looking closely along the horizon, he recognized more of the tanks and saucers in the distance. Then he looked north. He could vaguely make out more saucers. To the south was the same. They were surrounded.

He made it to the cave entrance on the outside of the mountains and immediately flew straight up to the saucer hovering above it. Hundreds of people were scrambling below to fit into the tunnel, and he had to take out this saucer at least. He tore through the bottom and shot out of the top, taking out a large chunk of machinery and wires with his mouth as he went through.

Without time to clear a landing spot for the crashing saucer, Jem continued over the mountains only to see Luria City in rubble. Most of the buildings were blown open or completely destroyed. The HQ that Jem had just protected moments ago was toppling to the ground on fire, utterly annihilated. A violent crashing noise came from behind him and he saw that, fortunately, the saucer he had attacked had crashed somewhere in the mountains where hopefully there weren't any people.

"JEM!" cried Sierra from the base of the mountains at the entrance to the cave. He wouldn't have been able to hear her except for his keen dragon hearing.

She was fighting several people on the ground who were dressed in complete Regime attire: full black suits with a purple V across the chest, heavy black boots, thick black helmets, and a magical scepter for a weapon. The tanks must have been carrying bunches of foot soldiers.

Above her, a saucer was trying to shoot at her but was being deflected by Afflatus. In fact, Afflatus was protecting all the people rushing into the cave by blocking several of the saucer's beams. A short way away from Sierra and Afflatus, Aubrie and Edner were deploying shields to protect the civilians as well and fighting some of the foot soldiers.

Aside from the people that Jem recognized, hundreds of others were all locked in battle across the city. Jem began to swoop down the mountain when he heard a gentle, flute-like noise loud and prominent in his head. He looked around for the source, and immediately his eyes locked onto the vimana—specifically to Farouche standing inside one of the orbs holding a whistle-type thing to his mouth.

I can't believe it, thought Jem as he took off towards the vimana, which was clearly losing the battle against the more advanced saucers. *That kid made a dragon-calling whistle.*

He landed on the ceiling near the orb that Farouche and some other people were in. After he broke through with his claws and dropped to the ground, he transformed back into human form and ran into the orb room where Farouche and a couple other ECKO members stood.

"Jem!" called Farouche. "You heard my whistle! You gotta get us all out of here! This thing is goin' down real soon!"

"Okay," said Jem. "Get on my back and I'll fly us out." He transformed back to a dragon, barely able to fit inside the room, and Farouche and the others climbed onto his back.

Jem punched through the ceiling with his claw and the whole orb shattered. Not expecting this, Jem plummeted for a moment before getting his bearings and flying back up to the top of the vimana. Those on his back did not stop screaming.

There was a click and then a beeping noise as Farouche threw something from his messenger bag at the nearest saucer. Jem didn't have time to look, as he was busy opening up the ceiling of the vimana searching for crew members, but he heard a very distinct explosion and then the sound of a saucer dropping from the sky. Moments later, a violent crashing noise confirmed that the saucer hit the ground. Farouche just took out a saucer with a magic grenade.

Jem's search for more crew members wasn't turning up well. The more of the ceiling he ripped off, the quicker the vimana fell. He was able to find a few people near the center of the ship huddled in a corner. They looked petrified as he grabbed them all with his claws and took off from the now crashing vimana.

He went straight for the portal, seeing as the rest of the city was being swiftly destroyed by all the remaining saucers and tanks. Farouche was still lobbing grenades relentlessly, though, and Jem watched as he took out another saucer and a tank.

At the entrance to the cave, Jem dropped the few people he'd been holding onto and allowed Farouche and the others off his back.

"Thanks," said Farouche as Jem transformed back to human form.

"Why the hell did you even take the vimana up?" blurted Jem.

"Hey, we took out a bunch of those saucers!"

"Jem!" cried a familiar voice. Jem spun around to see Rimaya caring to an injured child just next to the cave with her pink dragonet, Cyneal, by her side.

"You gotta get through the portal!" she cried while holding her shaking hands over the injured child's bloody leg.

"We can't yet! Not everyone's through!" Jem yelled back. He didn't wait for her to respond; instead, he transformed back into a dragon and took off towards Edner who was the closest ECKO member. The plump little man was fighting with three Regs, each of them sending burst after burst of red magic from their scepters. He returned by sending blue shots of magic from his hands, mostly deflecting their shots.

Jem flew low to the ground and took out all three of the Regs with his wings.

"Thanks," breathed Edner. Jem motioned with his big dragon head for Edner to get on his back and he did. Jem took off again and took out the four Regs Aubrie was fighting.

Aubrie climbed onto his back and then Jem searched around for Sierra, but as soon as he saw her, he felt a shock in his side. He turned to face his attacker and saw at least ten Regs shooting at him. Their combined shots actually somewhat hurt. Jem lunged forward and took out as many as he could with his claw.

More attacked him from behind, bashing on his tail with their scepters and sending spells at him. They had him surrounded, but his first priority had to be to protect the two on his back. He lifted his wings up to offer them cover and began to swipe and lash out at all the surrounding Regs. Their shots hurt the underside of his wings, but he couldn't put them down.

Jem was getting overwhelmed by the all of the attacks. He couldn't take it any longer; the Regs were advancing on him. In a last desperate escape attempt, he beat his wings down and shot into the air, knocking all the Regs onto their backs.

Knowing that he had to return to get Sierra and Afflatus, he flew quickly to the opposite side of the mountain and dropped Edner and Aubrie off. Almost all of the citizens from the City seemed to have made it inside; they now needed to protect those from outside the city. He transformed back to a human to explain this to Edner, and then went back to a dragon and took to the sky.

Sierra was fighting a ridiculous amount of Regs now. Afflatus had come to her aide and they were both completely surrounded. Jem swooped down and grabbed both of them with each of claws. At least a hundred spells hit him as he did this, but the pain wasn't enough to keep him from flying on.

Sierra was clinging onto his claw for dear life, but Afflatus was charging some sort of orb in front of him, concentrating hard. The magical, bluish-gray orb grew larger and larger as Jem flipped around and headed back for the mountains. Afflatus then dropped it over the group of Regs they had escaped from. Jem glanced back and watched as the orb imploded in the middle of the group, sending up a mushroom cloud of snow. At least those Regs weren't shooting at him anymore.

Farouche, Rimaya, and the injured child were no longer outside; they must've been smart enough to go inside the cave. On the other side of the mountain, a group of ECKO members was fighting off a single saucer that was attacking the last group of people. Jem dropped off Sierra and Afflatus and then went for the saucer.

He ripped through one side of it with his claw and then pushed it in the direction of the mountain. Within a moment, it went spiraling out of control and smashed into the mountain.

The tanks outside of the city were advancing quickly and launching fireballs at the entrance of the cave, so Jem had to take out as many of the fireballs as he could as the last group entered the cave. He was able to stop most of them, but a couple got by him and he was unable to look back and see if they had hit anyone—the thought alone made him sick. The saucers and tanks in the distance were closing in, and they only had a minute before they would be completely surrounded by a whole new arsenal of weapons.

BAM!

The small saucer was back. Jem dropped from the sky like a rock and broke through several trees as he crashed into the mountain.

He wasn't going to give the saucers the opportunity to hit him again. He took off back into the sky and began flying at random as fast as he could to avoid them. Distracted by the small saucers, he didn't notice as the tanks and larger saucers surrounded the cave entrance.

Soon, Jem, Sierra, Edner, Aubrie, and Afflatus were the only people left. The rest of the ECKO members had fled into the portal and all the civilians within a reasonable distance had too. Jem could still see saucers shooting lasers at places faraway, though. They must be destroying other cities, and not everyone was going to get through, but most of the people nearby had gotten through at least.

He managed to swat a small saucer out of the air and it fell to the ground and exploded. Unfortunately, the dozens of other small saucers continued to pound against him. He had to get out of there or those saucers were going to kill him. The others were struggling on the ground fighting so many tanks, saucers, and soldiers.

"EVERYONE GET TO THE PORTAL!" yelled Afflatus.

Below him, Jem saw Afflatus leading the others back towards the cave. He swooped down to the entrance and transformed back to a human.

"INSIDE!" yelled Afflatus as spells crashed along the mountainside, sending large chunks of debris everywhere.

The tunnel was narrow and dark, and Jem could hear the Regs running behind them. Afflatus was ahead of him, dragging Sierra by the hand, while Aubrie and Edner were running behind him. He could hear them shooting spells backwards to slow down the Regs.

When they reached the familiar cave with the large silver portal, Afflatus wasted no time jumping through with Sierra, but Aubrie grabbed Jem's shoulder before he could go through.

He stopped and turned around to face them.

"We're staying here," uttered Aubrie hurriedly.

"W-what!?" stuttered Jem. He looked to Edner, who only nodded.

The cave was quiet. They must have toppled in the entrances with their spells because all the screams and machinery Jem heard were heavily muffled. He could feel explosions shaking the ground, though; soon, the Regs would blow through.

"Why would you stay here?" spat Jem. "The portal is right here! Let's go through now!"

He made for the shining portal but Aubrie stopped him again.

"We have to," she said softly. She sounded on the edge of tears. "We had this planned out with Afflatus. He is the strongest with magic, and a leader to this rebellion. He had to go, even though he wanted to stay. He can close the portal from the Kelados side, but we have to destroy the portal here."

"Why do you have to destroy it if we can just close it from the other side?" Jem was confused and angry. They were right here... they didn't have to die.

"Because Veroci could open it again," said Edner gravely. "Aff told us that it has to be destroyed indefinitely to prevent the Regime from getting to Kelados. Jem, this has to be done."

Jem didn't want to believe it. "No!" he cried. "You can't die!" he hugged them both tight and let the tears run down his cheeks.

They both embraced him for a moment, but they didn't have a lot of time. The explosions were getting louder and soon the Regs would be on them.

"Go, Jem," said Aubrie delicately.

He looked at both of them, the closest people to parents he had ever known, and found it nearly impossible to direct his feet to the portal.

"We love you," said Edner. "Never forget that."

"I love you too," uttered Jem. He was walking backwards, unable to take his eyes off them. He saw them grip hands as his back leg sunk through the portal, and then they were gone. He was looking at a rock with a silver blur on it. In one direction the sky was blue, and in the other, red. There was a mystical blue shield hovering around him like a massive magical tunnel, and just outside of the shield were hundreds of zombies pounding against it trying to get in.

"They will not be forgotten," said Afflatus as he stepped up beside Jem and began to close the portal. He slid his finger down the silver blur and it disappeared completely.

Jem looked to Sierra who was standing perfectly still, staring at the ground. "They're not coming back," he said.

"Afflatus told me," she said, not moving her blank stare from that spot on the ground.

"Come," said Afflatus, ushering them both away from the rock. "We should get to the Fortress before the shield wears out."

***

"This is it," said Aubrie, pulling her partner into a tight embrace.

"The end of Luria City," muttered Edner, enjoying the last few seconds of her warm hug.

"Not for long," reassured Aubrie. She pulled away to look into his big, caring eyes. "ECKO will stop them. They'll reclaim Callisto."

"I know they will," smiled Edner.

The explosions at both the entrances to the cave were clear now. The enemy was about to break through.

Aubrie and Edner clasped both their hands together and stepped back. They closed their eyes and concentrated. Between them, a small light began to shine. Eventually it grew, taking on a misty bluish hue and growing larger and larger. Within seconds, it was a massive glowing orb, emanating a powerful whirring noise and almost pulsating energy.

They both opened their eyes, feeling that their spell was about to be complete.

"I love you," said Aubrie.

"I love you too," said Edner.

And with that, their bomb exploded.

CHAPTER 4:
THE FORTRESS COUNCIL

The walk to the Fortress was like a dream to Jem. Well, more like a nightmare. The magical tunnel they were in didn't muffle the zombies' disgusting noises and screams. The sky behind them was blood red, while the sky ahead of them was a clear blue. After a while of walking, Jem began to see the vague outline of something large in the direction they were headed. Apparently, this was the Fortress they were headed to, but neither Jem nor Sierra wanted to ask any questions. They were both still in shock from losing Aubrie and Edner.

Around them, the tunnel shuddered and flickered as if it were alive. Zombies surrounded it, biting and clawing at it, but it was obviously impenetrable. They were gross, horrid creatures that made Jem almost sick to his stomach just to look at. Each of them was several feet taller than him, with greenish, wart-ridden skin covered somewhat by pieces of torn rags. Matted, wild hair covered their heads and many of them had ferocious, crooked fangs jutting from their mouths.

When they got closer to the large shape, Jem realized that it was actually a city. At the very top was a circular, pointed building, and all below it were hundreds of houses and buildings that worked their way down a massive hill until they reach the bottom which Jem was unable to see due to the massive cement wall.

The entire city was surrounded by a tan-colored, cement wall that was at least thirty yards tall, if not taller. It had no distinguishable features. No carvings or towers atop it. It was just a plain, empty wall. Their tunnel directed them straight towards it.

As they approached the wall, a hole just big enough for the three of them simply dissolved away from it. Jem brushed his hand along the wall as they passed through it, just to be sure it was real, and sure enough, it was

29

rough and rigid. At the other end, all Jem could see was a large crowd of people, but he was unable to distinguish any faces.

When they exited the wall, which at been at least ten yards thick, it solidified behind them seemingly out of thin air. Jem pressed his hand against it, but it was as sturdy as could be. Magic continued to impress him.

"They're here!"

"Is that him?"

"Afflatus made it!"

"But is that who——?"

Whispers were rampant around them. Jem squinted in the bright light and was able to make out hundreds of people all squashed within a giant sort of pen. Another large wall surrounded them on the opposite side, although it looked much thinner and had visible doors and windows.

"Where are we?" Jem asked Afflatus.

"Let me explain," he muttered back, raising his hand for silence.

The crowd immediately went eerily silent. Afflatus spoke loudly and clearly.

"People of Callisto, welcome to the Fortress of Kelados. Many of you have known of Kelados before your arrival here, but many of you have not. For those who don't know, it is a world ruled by zombies: cruel, violent, humanoid creatures. The Fortress, which is the city we are currently in, is the last remaining human civilization on this planet. I and the rest of the Lurian Council have been in talks with the Fortress Council here for quite some time now, as we have been expecting that this day may come.

"I urge you all to be polite and grateful towards our Keladonian hosts. They have shown great compassion in allowing all of us here, especially considering their very limited space within the Fortress walls.

"You will meet people here who will identify by one of two things: either Draig or Fenic. If you are asked to choose one to support, please consider them both and then decide which you would prefer. I cannot stress this enough. You do not want to remain unaffiliated.

"Also, many of you know that Jem here——" he gripped Jem over the shoulder "——was infected by a dragon and therefore demonstrates some unusual traits… please do not mention this to anyone else. That is a secret that must remain amongst us.

"Now, I suspect that our hosts will be with us shortly. Please remain calm and listen attentively when they arrive. I am thankful that those of us who are here have arrived safely, and for those who could not make it, we will miss them dearly. Love to you all."

Jem was confused by the last comment but assumed it must be some ancient Lurian thing to wish love upon people. The crowd immediately went back to their whispers. Rimaya ran up and embraced Sierra.

"Why can't people know I'm a dragon?" snapped Jem sharply as Afflatus sat down, leaning against the outer wall.

"Calm down," he breathed slowly. "It is for your own good. The beliefs of these people are complicated and your powers would only cause turmoil for us all."

"How so?" retorted Jem.

"The Draigs and the Fenics I mentioned... they each believe that a Supreme Being created Kelados. Draigs believe it was a Dragon, and the Fenics believe it was a Phoenix."

Jem tossed this over in his head a couple times as he sat down beside the old man.

"I don't get it. Wouldn't the Draigs love me then if I were a dragon? I'd be, like, part god to them."

"Possibly. But the Fenics would hate you. And they would stop at nothing to destroy you."

"Oh," said Jem, dejected.

Afflatus seemed tired, and although Jem still felt he should be allowed to use his dragon powers, he didn't want to push it any further at the moment.

In front of him, he saw Sierra standing with Rimaya, Cyneal, Farouche, Sam, Henry, and Snovel. He could tell that she was explaining about Edner and Aubrie because of the shocked and horrified expressions on everyone's faces. Rimaya and Farouche began to cry. Sam and Henry just stood there, mouths agape. Cyneal and Snovel whimpered pitifully and leaned against each other.

It's real, Jem thought to himself. No matter how surprised or sad they were, it didn't change the fact that Edner and Aubrie were now dead... dead because Jem had started a war that caused them to flee their entire world. Now they were all stuck here, and who knew what was going to happen here?

Jem watched the crowd of people before him. He recognized a lot of the faces, but many he didn't. There were people in very different clothes—definitely not from Luria. Lots of people were in brightly colored Neoran clothes or the more Earth-like Radeon clothes. He didn't understand how they all had gotten to the portal so quickly from across the world.

Snovel walked slowly over to him and licked his face. Jem gave a meek smile and petted its head.

News of Edner and Aubrie's death spread quickly. All of the Lurians suddenly seemed heavily depressed and the whole area felt colder and more solemn. Even Neorans and Radeons kept their heads down quietly out of respect.

That's when Jem saw them: Leo Terello's friend, Rick, and his partner, Ella.

"They made it here?" burst Jem, smacking Afflatus on the shoulder.

"Apparently," grunted Afflatus dully. He seemed abnormally tired or maybe just concentrating really hard on something. Jem couldn't tell.

He had never liked Rick. They had only stayed at his house after escaping from the Regime some while ago because he was the only person that they knew in Radeon. Sierra had always avoided him, though, and avoided talking about him. Something about that gave Jem a bad vibe. But Ella was really nice; he liked her. It was probably a good thing that they had made it to the portal in time.

"How many people didn't make it, Aff?" asked Jem quietly.

"Too many," he replied darkly.

It was obvious that he wasn't going to get much out of Afflatus. He must've been really shaken up from losing Edner and Aubrie. They probably had been even more like family to him than they had been to Jem.

Now that he thought about it, though, he felt like a giant piece of his chest was missing. They were dead. Gone forever. His chest kind of ached at the same time that it felt hollow. He didn't understand, and he didn't like it. Why did they have to die? They were the nicest people he'd ever met...

"Attention, people of Callisto," boomed a powerful voice from somewhere. Jem looked around and saw a light-skinned man standing high atop the opposite wall on a balcony. He was tall and strong-looking. He had on a thick black robe with dark red trim and wore a golden crown encrusted with red and black jewels. His unshaven face was square and bold. All in all, he was a very intimidating man.

"Welcome to the Fortress of Kelados," he continued, his voice magically magnified across the whole area. "I am Council Spokesperson Forenzi. I realize that you have all gone through great strife as of recently, and I do not wish to make things any more difficult for you. I merely have some rules that you must all be aware of to live peacefully within our humble city.

"First of all, be respectful of our culture and customs, which may be very different from those in Callisto. Our worlds have had very limited contact since the beginning of time, and this is a historic moment. But I need not remind you that you are guests in our city.

"Secondly, you must all reside in the Refugee District which is just outside this Containment Area. As you leave, you may set up residence in any of our temporary homes. Feel free to wander the Fortress during the daytime, but during the nighttime, please remain within the Refugee District.

"If you feel strongly about either the Draig or the Fenic system, please do not fight about it. We do not encourage fights based on systems.

"Lastly, I require to speak to your leader, Afflatus, at the Fortress Council building. Afflatus, you know where it is. You have been indicted as a member for the time being so that your Callistonians may have some voice amongst us.

"Well, that is everything. You all may exit in an orderly fashion through the gateway below me. Commotion will not be tolerated. Be respectful."

With that, the man retreated back into the wall and disappeared. Then, below where he had been standing, a giant cement gate began to swing back.

Nobody was rushing. Commotion wasn't going to be a problem; everybody was too downtrodden. The Lurians likely lost more than just Edner and Aubrie, and the Neorans and Radeons certainly lost many people. This small group of a couple thousand people could not have been even a fraction of all the people on the east side of Callisto. They had undoubtedly lost many; the only question was whether they were dead or enslaved by the Veroci Regime.

Outside of the gate, Jem saw what he could only describe as a slum. What Forenzi had referred to as "temporary homes," could hardly be considered homes to Jem. They looked like they had been abandoned for hundreds of years. Some were cement boxes with a cut-out for a window and door—but no window or door. Others were wooden, but those had mostly fallen apart or rotted to the ground.

Garbage and debris had been so heavily littered across the ground that Jem couldn't tell what he was actually walking on. He stopped for a moment and pushed away some of the old pieces of wood, cement, metal, and paper to reveal a ground of brown dirt.

There were tents set up. Some of the tents looked better cared for than the homes, but others were torn up and falling apart. This wasn't exactly paradise, but at least it wasn't outside the walls with the zombies or back in Callisto with the Regime.

"We need to go back," said Rimaya firmly as she came running up beside Afflatus, Sierra and Farouche right behind her. "We need to go get our dad."

"Hm?" inquired Afflatus.

Jem knew that they had never been able to retrieve Sierra and Rimaya's dad, Leo, from Argo, since it was part of the Regime-controlled West. But now the whole world, East and West, was controlled by the Regime, and they were in another world. What made her think they could get Leo now?

"We have to get him back," said Rimaya, who Jem could tell was barely holding back tears. "He needs to join us here. We couldn't get to him before because of the barrier, but I bet there isn't a barrier anymore since ECKO isn't there. We can get him—can't we, Aff?"

Afflatus glanced at her. There wasn't a lot of hope in his heavy eyes. Cyneal then came flying up over them and landed between Rimaya and Afflatus, looking sorrowfully between the two of them.

"You will need to be a Draig," said Afflatus, disregarding Rimaya's begging. "And never let Cyneal out of your sight. The Fenics will be out for its head. And Snovel, you probably shouldn't leave the Refugee District at all."

Snovel growled lowly.

"What?" gasped Rimaya, patting Cyneal's head. "Why would they want to hurt our dragonets?"

"Because they don't have dragonets here. So they will be revered by the Draigs and hated by the Fenics."

"Oh…" uttered Rimaya. "Well, anyways, we have to go get my dad! You have to convince the Council to organize a retrieval group."

"I'll see what I can do."

"Thanks, Aff."

They walked in silence, aside from the crunching of debris under their feet, until they reached the end of the Refugee District. Despite all the damage, it was quite a large area. It was surrounded by the same walls that had surrounded the Containment Area. The occasional balconies and windows in the walls made Jem feel like he was constantly being watched.

Towards the end of the area were several archways through which Jem could see a real city. As they stepped under the giant arches, the debris seemed to clear from the ground and was replaced with smooth cement flooring.

It seemed that the citizens of the Fortress had all been going about their business as usual until they stopped to stare at the large group of foreigners pouring out from the archway. Afflatus stopped and all of the Callistonians stopped as well.

They were dressed in long robes, kind of like how Jem had seen used as formal attire in Luria. About half the people seemed to wear some combination of red and black, while the other half wore some combination of yellow and white. There was an awkward silence as the Keladonians and Callistonians had a sort of stare off.

"If your Council has not informed you, our world was overtaken by an evil Regime, and we have been offered residence in the Refugee District," stated Afflatus to the group at large.

"Oh, we were informed," said a random old woman dressed in yellow, white, and orange robes that resembled flames. "We just didn't realize how strangely you all dressed."

All the Keladonians burst out into laughter. Afflatus, clearly angered, drudged across the street and began up a set of stairs. Jem, Sierra, Farouche, Rimaya, and Cyneal took off behind him.

"Where are we going?" asked Farouche.

"The Council building, I guess," said Rimaya. "That's where the Spokesperson guy said they needed Afflatus."

"Well, where's that?" complained Farouche.

"How should I know!?" burst Rimaya.

Farouche's cheeks turned bright red. He was quiet after that.

The stairs went up for a while and then let out onto another street. There weren't any sylphquads or sylphcycles here—the Callistonian equivalent of cars and motorcycles—everybody just seemed to walk. Jem thought it was weird, not to mention that everybody that they passed stared at them. That was incredibly annoying.

Then more stairs came. They slowly ascended the hill towards the center of the city. In fact, the whole city seemed to be one giant hill, all pointing towards the center which is where Jem assumed the Council building was. It took them a really long time to walk that far.

"Hey, what's that?" Farouche asked Jem, pointing at some sort of vehicle in the distance.

"It... it looks like a monorail," said Jem, squinting to see it better. Monorail was the best way he could describe it; it was a train-looking vehicle that looked like it was made of cement, sliding along a rail that went over buildings and headed up the hill.

"What's a monorail?" asked Farouche.

"Like a train, but elevated I guess," said Jem.

"What's a train?"

"Um..." Jem couldn't think of how to describe it in Callisto terms. "It's basically a vehicle that sits on a rail and travels along that rail."

"So it can only go on the rail? It can't like hop off and go elsewhere?"

"Yes."

"That sounds incredibly limited," snorted Farouche.

"It seems to work for them," said Jem. "Remember what Forenzi said about being respectful of their culture."

"Well, that's just plain primitive technology!" complained Farouche. When Jem didn't reply, he continued, "Well why don't we just take a monotrain up the mountain then? Why're we walking?"

"I thought they were primitive?"

"It'd beat walking..." muttered Farouche.

"Then you go talk to Afflatus and convince him to take one of the monorails."

Farouche looked ahead of them at Afflatus. The old man was walking with such vigor, and yet he seemed so depressed. He wasn't exactly inviting to be talked to.

"No thanks," replied Farouche.

When they finally reached the top of the hill, they were outside of the circular, pointed building that Jem had seen in the distance. At the top of the building, hovering above the pointed tip, was a bright, star-like light. Jem assumed that it must have been the Soul that powered the magic here.

From this incredible vantage point, he was able to see everything on this side of Kelados... and yet there was nothing there, not even zombies. It was just an empty wasteland. Nothing but dirt.

Forenzi was standing at the entrance to the circular building.

"Hello, Afflatus," he said calmly. "You have brought guests?"

"They followed me," said Afflatus. "They are—"

"I need to find my dad!" interjected Rimaya. Jem glanced at her. This obviously wasn't the time to speak, but Rimaya seemed beyond reason. Her hair was in a fluster around her face, and her eyes were wide and crazy.

"What was that, little girl?" asked Forenzi, almost curiously.

"Our dad is still in Callisto. We need to get him back. You have to send a retrieval team!"

Forenzi was silent for a moment, examining Rimaya's insane appearance, no doubt. Then he let out a cold, boisterous laugh.

"No, that will not happen," he said as if it were an entertaining joke. "Come, Afflatus, we have—"

"AHH!" yelled Rimaya, taking two long strides and landing inches from Forenzi. Her hand was glowing blue and she held two fingers to the man's neck. His demeanor changed from amused to somewhat afraid, but only for a moment—then it went back to amused.

"You won't assault a Councilmember," he said.

Jem didn't fully understand what she could do with the magic hand, but it was probably like the Earth-equivalent of holding a knife to somebody's neck. She could probably kill him right now if she really wanted to. But she wouldn't. Jem knew it. Everybody there knew it, even Forenzi.

Rimaya's hand and her whole body trembled. "I need to get him back," she muttered, dropping her hand.

Forenzi didn't even offer her a response. He simply motioned with his head for Afflatus to follow him, and then he turned and went into the building. Rimaya stood there in disbelief of what she had just done as Afflatus passed her by and disappeared into the building.

"Come on, let's follow them," said Sierra, pulling Rimaya by the hand. Jem, Farouche, and Cyneal followed quickly behind them as they ducked through the building and followed the curved hallway.

Jem heard the sound of a door latching shut. In a moment they were beside a large wooden door that had "Fortress Council Center" engraved on it. The strange thing about it was that there was no doorknob or handle.

Rimaya tried pushing against it, but no matter how much she struggled, it didn't budge. She backed up as if to run and slam against it, but as she came at the door with her shoulder, Sierra caught her and pushed her aside.

"You can't ram the door down!" she yelled at her older sister.

"Who says I can't!?" Rimaya burst back. "We need to know what is going on in there! LET US IN!" she screamed in the direction of the room. "WE NEED TO SAVE OUR DAD!"

Silence. Jem couldn't even hear anyone talking inside the room. This felt very useless. Sierra and Farouche examined the wall, looking for who knows what, but Jem didn't see the point since they could just wait until the meeting was over, so he turned and wandered under an archway to the outside of the building.

They were on the opposite side of the mountain now, and the vast nothingness he saw was a very different nothingness from the other side. It was still a dreary, desolate wasteland, but in the distance, he saw the distinct shape of a volcano. Immediately, he had a flashback to when he had emerged from the volcano.

He heard the Dragon's voice as clear in his head as he had heard it that day: *The Phoenix and I are going to work to rid this world of the zombies, Jem. We may need your help in the near future.*

Would he need to rid this world of zombies before the Dragon and the Phoenix would help him reclaim Callisto? Knowing how powerful they are, he had secretly been hoping that they would help lead the rebellion. Were they living in the volcano now? He wanted to see the Dragon. He hadn't talked to it since that day months ago. He missed it. Although he had thought it was his enemy for the longest time, he now regarded it as a friend and an ally.

"Jem!" called Sierra. "Come here! Rimaya figured it out!"

Figured what out? wondered Jem as he walked back inside. But his question was soon answered as he saw Rimaya holding a finger from each hand against the wall, just a few feet apart, and in that gap the wall had become transparent; they could all see the Councilmembers sitting around a circular table. Jem counted eight members, plus Afflatus which made nine. Their conversation was clearly audible now, as if Rimaya's magic had allowed the sound to exit the wall as well as the image.

"They can't see us," whispered Sierra. "It's a one-way window."

"Technically, it's a single-pattern audio-visual physical transparency spell," corrected Farouche.

"Shut up," snapped Rimaya. "I can't hear what they're saying."

"—said this wasn't going to happen!" ended Forenzi's obviously angered voice.

"I said most likely it would not happen," stated Afflatus calmly.

"And we trusted you!" shot a scrawny Councilmember in light yellow robes.

"I could not control the circumstances which led us here," said Afflatus. "The Veroci Regime has become far more powerful than I had ever envisioned."

"How could you let it happen?" spat Forenzi. "Weak leadership."

"I don't believe this is something that any leader could have prevented," stated a portly old Councilmember with deep yellow robes and a red hood. "Not even you, Forenzi."

"Shut up, you filthy Draig," countered Forenzi.

"Hey!" interrupted another Councilmember with black robes that had two red stripes running down them. "I thought we moved to not use that language within the Center!"

"Thank you, Ikuuno," said the portly Councilmember. "My point is, Forenzi, that the question should not be, 'How could you let this happen?' but instead, 'What can we do now to help you?'"

"Agreed," said multiple Councilmembers at once.

Forenzi scowled but said nothing.

"Now, Afflatus," continued the portly Councilmember, "what is this Retrieval Team you were inquiring of?"

Afflatus sighed. "There is a man named Leo Terello, the father of two of our best ECKO members, who would be very useful in our efforts to reclaim Callisto, which we obviously plan to do as soon as possible. He had been held by the Regime when they locked down the West, as I had informed you they did. We were unable to retrieve him then because of the Great Barrier, but now that the Regime controls the entire planet and likely suspects that we are unable to return to Callisto, I believe that the Barrier will have been removed. This means we now have access to Leo, and I would like to request a Stealth Retrieval Team be sent to retrieve him."

"Why would you need a stealth team if Veroci doesn't suspect you can return?" questioned a Councilmember.

Afflatus stroked his beard, but showed no change in facial expression. "We must take all necessary precautions."

"And you cannot reclaim Callisto without the help of this man, Leo?" asked another.

"It would be exceedingly more difficult."

The room was silent before Forenzi spoke. "A waste of resources," he said. "Why put our people at risk for the life of one Callistonian?"

Several people hummed and nodded in agreement.

"We shall take a vote on it then?" voiced a kind-faced, plump Councilmember with long brown hair. Nobody objected, so she continued, "All those in favor of sending the Team, raise your hand."

Everyone was still. Then Afflatus raised his hand, and the portly man in the yellow robes with the red hood slowly raised his as well. But they were the only ones.

"Okka, you fool—"

"Quiet, Forenzi!" shouted the Councilmember with two red stripes down her robes. "Our members' opinions are not up for judgment. Moving on: All those who do *not* wish to send the Team?"

All seven other members raised their hands, Forenzi being the first to reach eagerly to the sky.

"It's decided then."

"NO!" screamed Rimaya, banging her fists against the wall. Nobody inside seemed to be able to hear her. "NO NO NO!"

"Maya! Calm down!" yelled Sierra, pushing Rimaya away from the wall. "Be quiet!"

"We can't let it just be decided like that!" screamed Rimaya, pushing back. "That can't be it!"

"Shh, shh," hushed Sierra, hugging her sister. "We'll still get him somehow."

Rimaya cried loudly over Sierra's shoulder. Jem and Farouche exchanged a scared look. Cyneal brushed up against the sisters' legs.

The spell had broken once Rimaya had let go of the wall, and they no longer had any idea what was going on inside the Center. Jem and Farouche were curious, but neither wanted to get Rimaya to do the spell again. So they just waited.

After a few minutes in an uncomfortable silence, the Councilmembers finally emerged from the room. Forenzi exited first with an all too content smirk on his face. The plump man who Jem understood to be Okka exited afterwards, looking regretful. All the other members left behind him, and Afflatus came plodding out last.

Without saying a word, he headed back towards the stairs they had come up.

"Hey! Wait!" called Jem as they all ran up beside the fatigued old man. "What happened?"

"There's no Retrieval Team. But we can send our own," grunted Afflatus.

"What do you mean?" asked Sierra.

"We can send Callistonians to go retrieve Leo."

"Who will go?" asked Jem.

"I want to go," said Rimaya firmly.

"Me too," said Sierra timidly.

"Two is the most we should send," said Afflatus. "More than that would begin to draw attention."

"Then we have our Retrieval Team," said Rimaya, gripping Sierra around the shoulder.

Cyneal whined and pressed its head against Rimaya's leg.

"Cyneal, I'm sorry. You can't go," said Afflatus. "It's too risky."

The little pink dragonet growled and continued to rub against Rimaya's leg.

Rimaya smiled and petted its head, but Sierra looked absolutely petrified. She and Jem made eye contact, and he could almost feel the fear reverberating from her.

CHAPTER 5:
THE REFUGEE DISTRICT

When they got back to the Refugee District, Jem was surprised to see that it actually looked a lot better. The dirt ground was visible and all the debris was piled off to the side where some Callistonians were working together to levitate it over the wall and throw it out into the zombie land.

"Wow," said Farouche. "They were productive while we were gone."

"No kidding," agreed Jem.

The homes and tents were still abysmal, though. As they walked through the District, they passed dozens of children who were curled up under boxes or small structures in blankets. A few adults were crying. But for the most part, people were cleaning up and repairing the structures. It gave Jem a warm feeling in his chest to see how the Callistonians were handling the situation. Maybe all hope wasn't lost.

But then a sudden thought appeared in his head as he watched the garbage get levitated out. "Afflatus," he said quietly so that no one else could hear, "what happened to the Soul?"

"It is safe, Jem," he replied stoically. "Don't worry yourself with it."

Jem opened his mouth to argue that he should be allowed to know, but he decided against it. Afflatus didn't seem in the mood for an argument.

"Afflatus!" called a woman who was standing down the street waving her hand. "We saved you a place to stay!"

"Thank you, Tekkara!" Afflatus called back.

That name, Tekkara, sounded familiar to Jem, and as they got closer to the woman, he realized why: she was the Neoran Elder. He didn't recognize her at first because she was no longer in her decorative purple robes; instead, she wore green Lurian robes. Her tiara was absent as well, and her long, thick gray hair was loose instead of in its usual bun.

"This way," she said, leading them off to the side and in between other structures and tents. Jem would've called it an alley, but it was hard to tell where roads, alleys, and sidewalks would be considered in this scattered, wild district.

"I'm glad to see that you made it alright," said Afflatus gently.

Tekkara smiled meekly. "But many did not," she said.

"We weren't properly prepared," said Afflatus gloomily. "I didn't think it would happen so quickly."

"Nobody did."

They walked on in an eerie silence and Jem suddenly became aware of how many people must have died. An entire half of Callisto definitely would not have fit in this tiny district, and even though it was crowded, it wasn't overflowing. Were the people left in Callisto all killed? Or was the Regime simply ruling over them like they had in Argo? He had no way of finding out. Maybe Sierra and Rimaya would discover something. Either way, he knew that hundreds—if not thousands—of people had probably died trying to get to the portal. This was simply unreal.

They then went up a small hill where the buildings were built on a slant and seemed to be somewhat falling apart. Bunches of people were camped out in these buildings, likely in an effort to claim their spot. Jem hadn't seen an empty building yet.

"Here we are," said Tekkara as they stopped outside a massive building that looked as if it were made out of cement or mud. Smelled like mud. The building had multiple openings on this end, but the back of it was against the wall between the Refugee District and the rest of the Fortress. "Afflatus, we have sleeping quarters for you inside—"

"That's okay," interjected Afflatus. "I appreciate your thoughtfulness, but I will prefer to sleep outside."

"Oh, okay," replied Tekkara, obviously surprised. "Well then, children, your sleeping quarters are right here."

She ushered them into a small room connected to the larger building by a little archway. In fact, the giant building was really several smaller ones connected by archways.

"Blankets and pillows donated by the Keladonians are being divvied up and some will reach you before nightfall," assured Tekkara.

"Wonderful," said Afflatus, forcing a smile. "You've been very kind, Tekkara, but I must escort our Terello girls elsewhere. I will return soon to help with the procedures."

"Where are you escorting them?" she asked, throwing a nervous glance to Sierra and Rimaya.

"They are going to retrieve their father."

"From Callisto?" Tekkara looked horrified, but Rimaya stared at her with such a definite intensity that she knew better than to object. "My best wishes are with you," she said, bowing slightly to them.

They bowed back. Jem had seen the Neorans use this as a sign of respect, but usually people bowed to Tekkara, since she was the Neoran Elder, and she bowed back. It really spoke to their desperate situation that she bowed first.

Afflatus motioned with his head for Sierra and Rimaya to follow him. Jem and Farouche stepped after them, but Afflatus held out his arm to stop them.

"You two stay here," he said. "Help Tekkara with getting everyone settled in."

"Where are you going?" asserted Jem. "Why can't they go through to Callisto here?"

"We need to get them proper attire so that they can work stealthily, and we need to scout out a heavily forested area so that they won't draw attention with their appearance. It may take a while. Your time would better be spent here."

Jem glanced at Sierra. Her big brown eyes were still full of fear, but she stood tall and seemed braver than the innocent little girl he had met almost a year ago. He couldn't think of a good reason to go with them, and he knew he would just have to hope for the best.

"Fine," he conceded. "Good luck, you two."

Rimaya came over and threw her arms around him. He felt her hot tears stream down her face and down his back. She didn't say a word. Then she moved on to Farouche.

Sierra walked up to Jem slowly and gave him a much gentler hug, but he pulled her in tight. Her whole body shook slightly, but she didn't cry. Snovel brushed against Sierra's leg, whining.

"We'll bring him back," she said, voice trembling ever so slightly.

They broke apart and Jem nodded. With that, Afflatus began to walk away and Sierra and Rimaya turned to follow him.

"Bye," said Sierra over her shoulder. Rimaya didn't look back.

"Bye," called Jem and Farouche.

Justin Dennis

CHAPTER 6:
THE RETRIEVAL TEAM

"Alright, this should work perfectly," said Afflatus, peering through a small portal to Callisto. "You both ready?"

After they had spent the entire day preparing for the trip, they had finally found a rooftop that corresponded to a forest in Callisto. Just in time, too, because the sun had just set for both worlds, allowing them enough cover to enter stealthily.

Rimaya bent over to tighten her special boots which were meant to soften her steps. Sierra was fiddling with the cloaking device on her wrist.

"I still don't get how this works," she grumbled.

"I told you," said Afflatus, irritated. "It's powered by magic. As long as it is in contact with the suit, it can help render you somewhat cloaked."

"And by somewhat cloaked," interrupted Rimaya, "you mean..."

"People will still be able to see you, but only if they focus really hard. In darkness or chaos, you're invisible. But don't leave it on all the time. It will drain your energy very quickly."

"Fair enough," said Rimaya, adjusting her cloaking device against her wrist. She looked at her little sister in the skin-tight black suit, and suddenly realized how grown up she had become. Rimaya could barely remember the days when she would tease Sierra for locking herself up in her room for hours on end just to write, draw, and paint. She may have been a shy girl before Jem and Oliver's arrival, but the hardened, battle-ready young woman beside her was not that girl. Even more tears welled in her eyes, but this time, they were tears of joy—she was so proud of her little sister.

"I'm ready then," said Sierra, tightening the edges of the suit around her face.

"Now we're lucky enough for you to have the cloaking devices," said

Afflatus, "but the Keladonians have not yet made a device for communicating between worlds. So once you step through this portal, you're on your own. Find Eltaes—I'm sure you can do that—and free your father, but only move during the nighttime. Anything done during the daytime is just asking to be spotted. If you are spotted, run, but do not run here. If Veroci finds the portal, he will be able to push through to Kelados. Understand?"

The two girls nodded.

"I will leave the portal open, but only just slightly," continued Afflatus. "So you must remember exactly where it is or you won't find your way back. When you return, touch the portal, and I will come to expand it for you." He smiled with the tiniest glimmer of optimism. For a moment, he seemed encouraged, even hopeful, but then his expression returned to fatigued. He grabbed the edge of the small portal—which was hovering at his eye level—and extended it downwards until it was big enough for a person to fit through.

Rimaya leaned through the portal and climbed out onto the tree in Callisto, and Sierra followed her. With one last look back, they each gave a weak smile to Afflatus. He whispered, "Good luck," and shrunk the portal to a small hole just about an inch wide. The last thing Sierra saw was Afflatus' dark green eye before she and Rimaya began to climb down the tree.

"Keep quiet," whispered Rimaya. "Don't snap the small branches."

"I'm trying," said Sierra.

The climb down was slow and tedious since they could barely see where they were going and were trying to be absolutely silent. The entire time, both girls were trying to engrain this trip into their memories so that when they found this tree again, they would know exactly where the portal was.

"Which way?" asked Rimaya once they reached the ground.

"Dunno," replied Sierra. "I can't see the moon or any stars here."

"Then let's just head this way and try and get out of this damn forest," said Rimaya, tiptoeing off in a random direction.

After a few minutes, Sierra became agitated with their silent walking. "There's obviously nobody around, and we have the special boots, I don't think we need to be so cautious," she whispered.

"We can't be *too* cautious Sierra. If we got caught, we may never get back to Kelados, and we'll definitely never reach dad."

"But no one is around! No one at all!"

"Hush," said Rimaya boldly, and the conversation was over. They continued for at least an hour at the pace of a slaethl. Jem would've called it a snail's pace, but Sierra—not knowing what a snail was—thought of the three-legged primate that jumps quickly from vine to vine but crawls slowly on the ground. She felt like a slaethl now.

Surprisingly, though, there were no animals around. Sierra didn't hear the noise of a single caylix or even a trink, but then again, she didn't know the animals of Neora very well. Still, she felt like there should have been more animal life than there was.

She knew that they must have been in Neora from the shape of the trees: large, leafy, almost comical things. That meant they needed to head either east or west to get to Argo, and that would be easy to determine once they got out of the forest and could see the stars since both Sierra and Rimaya could easily point out Cynosura, the star that always pointed north.

Finally, they escaped the confines of the forest.

"Remember this exact spot," said Rimaya. "If we're a single pace off, we'll never find that tree again."

Suddenly an idea hit Sierra. "Why don't we just mark the trees?" she exclaimed. But before she could begin to carve an X into the tree nearest her, Rimaya grabbed her wrist firmly.

"No!" said Rimaya. "We can't leave any marks. If the Regs find it, it could lead them to Kelados."

"Right…" said Sierra, dejected. "Sorry."

"It's okay," said Rimaya, releasing Sierra's wrist. "Now, Cynosura is over there, so we must be on the western side of Neora, which is lucky. If we head west and maybe a little south, we'll probably end up near Eltaes."

"Perfect," said Sierra. "Let's go."

They walked much smoother and quicker out in the open grass rather than in the uncertain forest. The only sound that was made was Rimaya's occasional yawn. The brisk air felt good against their skin. Their full-body suits did very little to stop the wind from cutting into them, but they welcomed it. They both missed the Callistonian air, even after only less than a day in Kelados.

Soon, they came by a city in the distance. It was brightly lit, but not by orbs; rather, there seemed to be a bunch of torches and campfires, which was unusual for any place in Callisto. When they got closer, they saw that it was a small town, and they could easily see right into the town center where hundreds of people were lined up before a stage with a large crowd. On the stage, one man stood beside a Reg. Words were being exchanged and magnified so that the whole crowd could hear, but they were still too far away to hear or see the whole scene properly.

"We can't go too close," cautioned Sierra. "It's too bright. If we get caught, we won't be able to escape in the darkness."

"But we need to see what's happening," protested Rimaya. Sierra didn't bother to argue with her. Rimaya rarely listened to reason; she simply followed her heart. Sierra didn't understand that attitude. She hoped that it wouldn't get her sister killed one day.

They ran quickly to the back of the largest building they could see. From there, they could poke their heads around the corner and see and hear the whole ruckus, all while remaining relatively well shadowed.

"Do you accept Veroci as your Ultimate Leader and the Regime as your Guardian?" boomed the thunderous voice of the Reg on stage.

The woman on stage—the man they saw before must have already answered the question—was crying heavily and her clothes were severely burned. She looked as if she needed medical attention, not to be put on a stage and asked questions.

The question repeated, "Do you accept Veroci has your Ultimate Leader and the Regime as your Guardian?"

She sobbed harder, and then let out a cry of pain as if she had been hit. Sierra and Rimaya didn't see anything hit her, but she continued to act as if she were being beaten.

"YES! YES I DO!" she screamed as if her life depended on it. Maybe it did.

Two Regs hauled her off the stage and she disappeared out of view.

"Do you accept Veroci has your Ultimate Leader and the Regime as your Guardian?"

This time, a small boy was on the stage. His clothes were burned as well, but he wasn't crying. He seemed surprised, maybe mildly perplexed, but not otherwise very perturbed to be there.

"No," he said, pushing his hands into his pockets. "I am my own leader, and my own guardian."

He barely finished the word, "guardian," before there was a flash of bright red light, and he collapsed face first onto the stage.

"They killed him," uttered Rimaya in horror. Sierra didn't have words to express what she had just seen.

Two more Regs dragged the boy's body, limp as a piece of cloth, off the stage.

"HEY! You two!"

A Reg, who was off the stage patrolling the crowd, had spotted them. Without hesitation, they sprinted away at full speed.

Flashes of bright red light lit up Sierra's peripheral vision, but she felt nothing. She could hear the heavy sounds of the Reg storming after them and the thick metal scepter swinging through the air.

There were no trees to take cover behind, but there were bushes. Rimaya, who had been leading the way slightly thanks to her longer legs, decided to dive behind the largest bush she could find. Sierra came skidding to a halt just beside her and both sisters crouched low behind the bush, ready to run at a moment's notice.

"Why'd you stop running?" demanded Sierra at a whisper. A flash of red light illuminated a few of the bushes to their side.

"If we kept running he'd eventually hit us with that," explained Rimaya, indicating the passing beams of red light.

"So what, we hide here until—"

"Shhh!" commanded Rimaya, putting her hand over Sierra's mouth.

The flashes of red light had stopped. There was the soft flattening sound of boots on grass somewhere beyond their bush. Sierra's eyes darted from the edge of the bush to Rimaya's eyes; she was fearful that the Reg would appear suddenly, yet she also wanted to see what Rimaya was going to do. Her sister's eyes were wide, but concentrated. Her breathing was silent. Sierra was trying to breathe quietly through Rimaya's hand, but her heart was thumping so loudly in her chest that she feared that it might give them away.

The sound of something brushing up against leaves was nearby. The Reg was getting closer—and prodding at the bushes. Fear was prickling at Sierra's skin, telling her to run, but she knew Rimaya had some other plan, so she remained crouched.

"I know that you're here somewhere!" called the Reg in a deep, threatening voice. "But where will you run to? We don't just own this city; we own all of Callisto. You have nowhere to run." A flash of red light, and Sierra heard a fire crackling a few feet away from them and knew that a bush had been set on fire. "Nobody escapes the Pledge," continued the Reg, as if enticing children with candy. "You might as well come out now before I have to kill you. Don't you want a chance to recognize the Ultimate Leader and Guardian?"

He was feet away now. Before Sierra's eyes, Rimaya's image began to fade away like she was dissolving. That's when Sierra remembered the cloaking device. *Hide me, hide me*, she thought. She didn't know if the magic cloaking device worked like that, but it was all she could think to do.

The outline of a large man stepped beside them. He brushed the edge of their bush with his scepter, the tip of it inches away from Sierra's nose, but he didn't look at them or take any notice of them. Their cloaking devices must've worked.

As the Reg began to walk away, Rimaya's hand left Sierra's mouth, and Sierra instinctively held her breath to avoid being too loud. With the moonlight shining down on them, Sierra was able to observe a Rimaya-shaped shimmer in the air as it tiptoed up behind the Reg.

Her steps were silent. The Reg didn't suspect a thing as Rimaya stalked directly behind him. She became visible again as—in one swift movement—she pulled his helmet off with her left hand and then thrust her right hand onto the top of his skull. He barely had time to swing his scepter around before he froze and his eyes rolled back into his head.

Sierra let out an audible gasp that she had not meant to as the man fell to the ground with a dull *thump*.

"What did you do to him?" blurted Sierra, standing up and becoming visible herself.

"Knocked him unconscious," said Rimaya flatly. "You can't do it through the helmets, though; I was afraid I wouldn't be able to get it off quick enough."

"Can you teach me how to do that?"

"Of course," smiled Rimaya, "but later. Come on, let's get out of here."

"What about the scepter?" called Sierra as Rimaya began her walk westward.

"What about it?"

"Shouldn't we take it? For defense?"

"Our mission is stealth. It wouldn't be doing us any favors to lug that thing around. Besides, you can throw stunners can't you?"

"Well, yeah, but—"

"The only thing that scepter does is channel magic into a lethal force—and it requires less energy than a regular killing spell. If we can be stealthy and stun, we have no need to kill."

"Okay," agreed Sierra. "You're right. Let's go." She hadn't really thought about the fact that the red beams could have killed her. This was an actual war. She said it over and over again in her head, trying to grasp the reality of it. People had died back in Luria City. That boy on the stage had died. This was far too real.

As the sisters continued west, Sierra was reminded of when she and Jem had journeyed for a few days across Neora. Of course, they had been traveling north to Neora City, but the terrain was very similar even in the dead of night. She suddenly felt a strange, hollow feeling in her stomach. It wasn't hunger, just a vague emptiness. She wondered what Jem was doing right then. Probably sleeping.

Come to think of it, she was actually very tired herself. She had already been exhausted, having escaped Luria City only that morning, but the few seconds of having that cloaking device on had almost drained her of everything she had left. It was a good thing that all she had to do now was walk mindlessly to the west because she wouldn't have been able to do much else.

Hours passed of silent walking in the dark until some faint yellow light could be seen peeking up over the horizon.

"Guess we'd better find cover to sleep for the day," suggested Rimaya, redirecting their path towards the nearest grouping of trees. Sierra dragged on behind her, every inch of her body aching for sleep.

Unfortunately, there were no wunla trees inside the forest. Sierra had been hoping for one of those trees since they create nice comfortable beds high among the rest of the trees, but they had no such luck. Neither were there the comfy pods that she had slept in one night when she and Jem were in Neora. Sierra and Rimaya had to settle for sleeping in a pile of giant loose leaves. Rimaya was able to enchant the leaves to clump overtop of them and hide them from any passersby—hopefully.

The leaves offered very minimal cushioning against the hard ground, but Sierra didn't even mind at this point. After constructing a small leafy pillow, she fell immediately asleep. Rimaya did the same after setting up magical detection points so that they would be woken up if anyone came too close.

When Sierra woke up, she was incredibly disoriented. She tried to roll out of her bed, but instead hit a tree. *What is a tree doing in my room?* she asked herself as she opened her eyes groggily and sat up. Her face brushed bunches of leaves that fell in a heap around her. She looked around, trying to piece together how she had gotten there, and then she remembered everything: the invasion, Kelados, the mission to save their father.

Rimaya then woke up because Sierra had knocked down the enchanted leaves on top of her.

"What is it?" asked Rimaya sleepily. "Is someone there?"

"No, no one's here," said Sierra. *Just you and me,* she thought.

The sun was just now setting, creating an orangish glow that filtered between the trees and cast them in a multicolored evening display of Neoran beauty. It made Sierra squint; it was too bright. She lay down to go back to sleep, but something wouldn't allow her to relax fully: her growling stomach.

"I'm hungry too," said Rimaya in response to Sierra's very audible stomach grumbles. "We should get food before we leave."

"Ugh," grunted Sierra, getting up once again. *There has to be some edible berries around here or something,* she thought.

Rimaya pushed a clump of leaves off herself and sat up on her elbows. "What about those?" she asked, indicating a tree several feet away that had round, bright red fruit hanging from it.

Sierra walked over to the tree. She didn't recognize the fruit, even from her last time in Neora, but she would eat almost anything at this point. When she plucked it off the tree, though, it felt incredibly light, like it was hollow or made of paper. She stared at it curiously, rolling it around in her hands gently.

"What's wrong?" voiced Rimaya.

In response, Sierra clamped down lightly on the fruit, and it broke apart into a million pieces, floating out of her hand as black dust. Rimaya's jaw dropped in shock. Sierra could not comprehend it.

She plucked another fruit. Same thing. She plucked another. Same effect. Again and again, the fruits were brittle as paper and crushed into dust at the softest touch. Angry, Sierra smacked the tree, causing dozens of these fruits to fall to the ground and explode in a dusty frenzy.

"Are they supposed to do that?" asked Rimaya.

"I don't think so," said Sierra. She had never heard of a fruit doing that—not even in Neora. As she looked around, none of the trees actually seemed quite right now that they had better lighting. They were all slightly discolored. Most of them just looked pale, but some were turning black or grey, and all of them were bent over almost like they were sad. "It's not just the fruit," continued Sierra. "It's this whole forest. Something isn't right... it's like it's... sick."

Rimaya got to her feet. "That's ridiculous," she said. "How can a forest be sick?" But as she looked around, she began to realize the same thing Sierra did. As Rimaya ran her hand over the blackened spot of a tree, the bark gave way and her finger broke a hole through the tree, causing black dust to crumble down the tree.

"The trees are dying too, not just the fruit," said Rimaya solemnly.

"Why?" asked Sierra.

"Who knows? But we need to find food soon."

"We can go to the next city."

"Oh yeah, great plan, Sierra. We'll just stroll on in to the nice Regime-controlled town and ask for some food. I'm sure that will go over splendidly."

"I'm sure we could take food without being noticed," retorted Sierra. "We don't really have many options."

"Fine," spat Rimaya. "Let's get going."

The sun had completely set at this point, but there was still a faint glow over the land that led them out of the forest. Not long into their walk, though, they were once again pitched in extreme darkness.

It didn't take them long to come across another city. This one was larger than the last town: they had buildings several stories high and the whole city expanded rather wide. There were some fires lit in parts of the city, but other parts remained relatively unlit. Sierra and Rimaya used this to their advantage as they crept into the city behind a dark, unused-looking building.

When people walked by, they simply ducked into dark alleyways. It was incredibly easy to stay amongst the shadows in this city with all the nooks and crannies.

It did not take them long to find a merchant's shop, closed for the evening, in a very poorly lit area. The lock on the back door was unaffected by magic, but Sierra's knife—the one that Farouche had given her and she had used to cut Jem out of the dragon net—was easily able to cut through the door just above the lock, and she slipped her hand through that hole and opened the door from the inside.

"I knew that would come in handy," she whispered as she slipped the magic blade back into her boot.

Quietly, they entered the shop and gathered just as much food as they knew they could consume: a loaf of bread, a few pieces of some kind of meat, and a few red fruits that Sierra recognized as solaces. Hopefully, they could find water in a pond because there were no jugs or bottles here. They tossed their food into a cheap knitted bag and exited the building. Sierra's conscience yelled at her that this was wrong the whole time, but the hunger in her stomach yelled louder.

They had no problem escaping the city under the veil of darkness, and soon, they found a small creek covered by bushes. They sat at the edge of the creek, concealed decently by the bushes, and ate and drank to their hearts content.

When Sierra bit into the warm solaces, she immediately had vivid memories of convincing Jem to eat them—along with the spicier solite. She smiled goofily as she ate.

After they ate, Sierra felt completely refreshed, but Rimaya still seemed as if something was nagging at her. She avoided conversation and kept scratching at the same place on her arm.

"What's wrong, Maya?" Sierra asked, gripping Rimaya's arm where she was scratching.

"Nothing!" cried Rimaya, shaking Sierra's hand off. "Nothing. None of your business."

Sierra didn't ask anymore.

The next few days went relatively the same. All the fruit in Neora they found was utterly useless except for what they found in the cities. Because of this, they became reliant upon stealing for their source of food. Sierra didn't like it, but she didn't have any other options. Rimaya didn't seem to approve or disapprove; she just went along with it. In fact, Rimaya stopped showing any emotion at all.

Sierra still hadn't seen any animals in the wild, even though she occasionally heard animal noises in the forest. Something must have gone vitally wrong with the land and the nature of Neora, and Sierra suspected that it had something to do with the Veroci Regime's invasion.

The only thing Sierra found really nagging at her was Jem. She wanted to know what he was doing, how life was going in Kelados. She was concerned for him, but more importantly, she wanted him there with her in Callisto. He had made such a great companion during their first travels through this region, even if he had been sick a lot from the dragon poison, and Sierra was sad that she couldn't be with him now. But she didn't dare show that to Rimaya—not big, strong Rimaya who never let anything get to her—no way.

Near to the border to Argo, they ran out of cities to steal food from. All of the border cities must have been abandoned long ago because they looked like ghosts towns without a single fire lit. Crossing the border into Argo was surreal; Sierra hadn't been back since she had left with Jem and Oliver almost a year ago. It was nice to walk in the long, comfy grass again. She only wished she could be barefoot instead of in her stealth boots.

Rimaya was getting irritable now that they had gone for a couple days without any food, only getting water from the occasional creek. When they had first come upon a forest in Argo, Sierra had ran to it in hopes of fresh fruit, and what she had found was fruit, but it was bitter and vile. The good news was that it hadn't crumbled like burnt paper, but it had hardly been edible. What had the Regime done to all the natural fruit?

They were now getting close to Eltaes. Both Sierra and Rimaya could tell by the way the trees were—the bushes, the rocks, the hills. They had lived there their whole lives; they recognized the terrain. But the sun was rising, and they had to make camp.

This time, as they wandered into the closest forest, Sierra was amazed to be staring directly at a massive wunla tree. After spending a week sleeping on the ground surrounded by leaves, the sight of a wunla tree was equivalent to a giant comfortable bed. She was ecstatic. She ran to it and climbed quickly, plopping down amongst its tall, comfortable branches that formed such a perfect, intertwined canopy.

Rimaya came up a moment later and sat beside her, tapping her foot and scratching at that same place on her arm. Sierra ignored her. She reveled in the comfort of being in a wunla tree. But when she thought about why it was so welcoming to her, the first thing that popped into her mind was Jem and the day she had taken him to her hideout. Her hideout was really just a wunla tree near Eltaes, but she had only ever shown it to Jem.

Pointing her finger out, she began to levitate a nearby konko—what Jem would have described as an acorn—and twirl it around in the air. It reminded her of him and, in a painful way, made her sad that he wasn't there.

"What are you doing?" snapped Rimaya. "Quit it."

Sierra dropped the konko and stared at Rimaya. "I can do what I want."

"It's annoying."

"It reminds me—" Sierra ended her sentence abruptly, realizing that she was about to admit to missing Jem.

"It reminds you of *what?*"

"Of... nothing," mumbled Sierra.

"No, really, Sierra, of what?" repeated Rimaya, sounding angry and yet concerned at the same time.

"Why do you keep scratching?" asked Sierra, pointing at Rimaya's hand which was currently scratching the opposite arm.

"I... I just itch. That's all."

"I don't believe you."

"Well, I don't believe you."

There was a long silence between them after that. The sun was rising in the distance and the wunla canopy glowed a warm yellow that was out of place in the tense atmosphere between the sisters.

"I miss Jem," said Sierra finally. "The konkos remind me of him. We were in a wunla tree when I told him about mom, and he told me about his parents."

More silence. Sierra didn't dare look over to see how Rimaya had reacted.

"I'm going through withdrawal," said Rimaya finally. She paused and then continued, "I was injecting a lot in Luria. It was fun, and there wasn't much else to do. But now I don't have it, and I'm miserable."

Sierra took the chance to glance over; Rimaya's eyes were all watery. Her tough, rebel sister looked weak for once. Unbelievable.

"I'm sorry," said Sierra.

"No, I'm sorry," choked Rimaya as they both fell together in an awkward sitting hug. Rimaya began to cry freely and her tears made Sierra cry as well.

"We shouldn't... have wasted... these days... not talking..." whispered Sierra into her sister's ear between choked breaths. "I love you, sis."

"I love you too," returned Rimaya. "And I shouldn't've let this happen to me. No more propo, I promise. It's just no good; it does nothing good! Only bad. So I'm done."

Sierra pulled back from their close hug just to smile at her sister.

"And I know you have a thing for Jem," continued Rimaya. "But you shouldn't let him have such control over you. This mission is about saving dad, not missing Jem. I'm sure he's fine. No matter what happens between you two, though, you have to remember that you have to be a strong person alone to be a strong person with someone. I know how independent and brave you can be, Sierra; I don't want to see you weakened by someone else."

"I guess Jem's my propo," frowned Sierra.

Rimaya laughed lightly. "Not exactly. He's a good kid. You just can't be dependent on him. You understand?"

"Of course," smiled Sierra. She still missed him, but the longing ache for his company that she had felt a few minutes ago melted into complacent indifference.

"Get some rest," said Rimaya, lying down on the comfy wunla leaves. "We definitely need it."

"I wish we had some food," complained Sierra, sniffling and lying down as well.

"Now that is definitely something we can both miss," said Rimaya.

"Well, we'll be in Eltaes tomorrow, right? Or I guess, tonight. Hopefully we can get food then before we find dad, or we won't have any energy to help him escape."

There was silence for a moment as they both stared up at the sky that was pink from the sunrise.

"What if we don't find him?" asked Rimaya, sincere worry in her tone. "Or what if something has happened to him?"

"I'm sure he's fine," lied Sierra.

"And if we don't find him?"

"I'm sure we'll find him," said Sierra, but in actuality, she was not sure of anything.

CHAPTER 7:
FORENZI'S DAUGHTER

The Refugee District hadn't turned out so bad. By the time Afflatus had returned that evening from sending Sierra and Rimaya on their mission, everyone had found a place to stay for the night and had been given blankets and pillows. Jem, Farouche, Snovel, and Cyneal were all in one room; their neighbors—under the same roof but separated by archways—were a couple adults with a young child, Afflatus, Tekkara, and a few other families.

Campfires had been set up all across the District. They could have used light orbs, but the warmth of the fire was welcoming. At Jem's building, which was one of the biggest and had an amazing view of the whole District, they had started a fire on the roof for all the residents to sit around and talk. Everyone had had a long, stressful day. Many had lost loved ones. There was a fair share of tears falling against the floor of the flat roof, only to evaporate from the warmth of the fire.

Ella and Rick must have been living in their building, or one of the small ones connected to it, because they were huddled close together on the opposite side of the fire from Jem. Ella was crying and leaning against Rick who was staring mindlessly into the fire. They both must have lost friends.

And that's when Jem began to look around for Edner and Aubrie... but he couldn't find them. *They're dead,* he told himself. But it just wasn't possible. He continued to scan the crowd of people around the fire, somehow expecting that he would come across their warm, smiling faces. They never appeared.

Jem wanted to cry. He wanted to let the tears speak for the loss of the closest thing to parents he had ever had, but they didn't come. His eyes became watery and blurred his vision, but no tears fell. Snovel, who was laying at Jem's feet, rubbed against Jem's legs and rolled over. It made Jem smile a little.

To his side, Farouche was picking up bits of dirt and rocks and things and tossing them into the fire, a dazed, lost look on his face. Edner had been even more of a father to him than he had been to Jem. Instead of pushing his greasy, long hair back behind his red headband like he usually did, Farouche just let it hang down in front of his face.

To Jem's other side, Afflatus was fiddling with the stitching on the end of his sleeve. His robes, at one point, had been white, but over the course of the day had become almost a dark grey. Jem was unable to decipher the emotions hidden in the old man's wrinkles, but considering how bubbly Afflatus usually was, Jem assumed that he was either incredibly sad or in deep thought.

Afflatus then rose to his feet slowly, and everyone stopped talking to look up at him. He reached inside the chest of his robes and pulled something out. His fist remained clenched around it as he extended his arm out, everything silent aside from the crackling of the fire. Then he slowly and carefully unraveled his fingers, unveiling a shining ball of light floating dutifully in his palm. It was so bright that everyone in the District could see it. Everything was suddenly silent, and Jem knew that everyone was observing what was happening at their building.

"For all of those who died today," spoke Afflatus, quietly and solemnly, and yet his voice was projected to everyone within the Refugee District, "we honor you. For all of our loved ones who have died, we will always love you. For every single person who made it here today, we are glad to have you. With our Soul intact, we will return to Callisto one day and reclaim our home from Veroci. For all of those who remain in Callisto and cannot hear me, we will fight for them—we will free them.

"For no matter the strength of our enemy, as long as we have love and the courage to stand up for what is right, we can overcome them. We are all in this together now: every Callistonian, every Keladonian. I would like to present our Soul to the Fortress for our time here. If you stand with me, raise your Light now."

Jem watched as all the people around their fire and the rest of the Refugee District simultaneously held up a single, glowing finger. Jem watched Farouche for guidance, and after pushing his hair back from his eyes, Farouche also stood up and held his magically glowing pointer finger in the air. Jem didn't know how to do that kind of magic, but he rose to his feet, last of all the refugees, and nervously held his right hand into the air with one finger extended.

The tip of his finger began to glow a bright, white light, and at that moment, he felt more connected to all the other refugees than he ever had while in Callisto. He felt as if they were all one entity, making one conscious decision. It warmed his heart slightly—the togetherness of it all.

"And if you disagree, speak now, please," spoke Afflatus.

The District was silent; not a single person objected.

"Then for all of those who died, and all those who could not make it to Kelados: We will make it right. We shall not let the deaths be in vain, and we shall not let our friends and family be enslaved by Veroci and his Regime. With this Soul, we fight for freedom!"

With that, Afflatus released the Soul and it went shooting across the entirety of the Refugee District. It flew up high and then swooped down low, visiting every campfire briefly. It visited all the people, and all the people felt the hope that the Soul represented, the hope that there was still a chance, that all was not lost.

Eventually, after crossing the whole District, the Soul shot up high into the sky and hovered momentarily, sparkling brightly. All the Callistonians' Lights—their glowing fingers—shone even brighter in response. Then the Soul went in a straight line through the sky and flew directly into the Keladonian Soul that was hovering above the very top of the highest building, the Fortress Council Center, in the center of the Fortress. Together, both Souls shone brighter than ever, and Jem himself felt a little more hopeful for the future.

The next morning, nobody quite seemed to know what to do with themselves. They couldn't leave the Refugee District, but there wasn't any food at all within the district. Gradually, a commotion began to build up as people got hungrier and hungrier. Jem woke up to the noise of some people banging against the wall that separated them from the rest of the districts.

He sat up groggily, throwing off the old, torn-up blanket he had slept in. Snovel, who was snuggled up beside him, got up as well and stretched out all its limbs, even extending its wings out as far as they'd go.

"What's going on out there?" Jem asked Farouche who was just now waking up as well. His headband had fallen around his neck while he had slept and his long hair was twisted and sticking up in a really hilarious sort of manner.

"I dunno," grumbled Farouche, sitting up as well. Cyneal, who had been sleeping at the edge of the room, got up too and stretched beside Snovel.

"Well, come on," said Jem, stepping through the archway and out into the bright daytime.

Dozens of people were lined up against the big wall that separated the Refugee District from the rest of the city. "Food! Food! Food!" they chanted.

Jem felt his back tingle as he prepared to sprout his dragon wings, but then he remembered that Afflatus had warned him not to reveal his dragon identity, so he stopped.

"Yeah, I'm pretty hungry too," said Farouche, rubbing his stomach and standing beside Jem.

Suddenly, there was the loud noise of rock rubbing against rock in the distance, and Jem and Farouche walked out to the main street area to see what was happening. Even those who were chanting and banging against the wall stopped what they were doing. Cyneal and Snovel flew into the sky to see what was happening, but of course, neither of them could communicate it to Jem or Farouche. Cyneal could only talk telepathically to Rimaya, and Snovel didn't talk to anyone.

Once out in the main street, they could finally see what was going on. A massive doorway had opened at the far end of the Refugee District that led into the rest of the Fortress, and hundreds of people were coming into the District now led by Council Spokesperson Forenzi, who Jem recognized from before, and a young girl walking beside him.

Forenzi walked boldly, as if he owned everything, and the girl, even though she was much smaller, walked with much the same attitude. She wore black shorts and a dark red shirt with sleeves to her elbows, along with boots that ran up her calves. She had light skin and straight, sharp blond hair that looked as if it cut the air as she walked. It was short in the back, longer in the front; Jem couldn't remember what that hairstyle was called, but whatever it was, it was intimidating. She was strikingly attractive, but at the same time, Jem feared her. She carried very much the same air of power that Forenzi did.

Behind them marched all sorts of other people. Some, Jem could tell, were handing out food to the refugees; others were distributing fliers. But whatever was going on, the refugees closest to the door seemed to like it because the chatter Jem could hear was friendly, not angry.

Afflatus came up behind Jem and Farouche to observe what was happening. Cyneal and Snovel landed beside them as well.

"Afflatus!" beamed Forenzi as the large group of Keladonians finally reached them. "Good to see you. Sleep alright?"

"Decent," grunted Afflatus, obviously not very delighted to see Forenzi. "What is all this?"

"Well, you refugees got to get to work! So we have people looking to hire some of you, that way you won't be such a burden on us while you're here."

"And they're delivering food," added the blond girl. "Because we know you must be starving."

"Yes, yes, that too," muttered Forenzi, brushing her aside. "What are these abominations?" he grunted, indicating Cyneal and Snovel. The two dragonets lowered their heads and tails and slowly backed away.

"Dragonets, Forenzi, you know that," said Afflatus.

"I find them offensive."

"Obviously they don't like you very much either."

Forenzi glared at him, as if deciding whether or not it was worth it to hit him. "This is my daughter, Avalon," he said finally, pushing the blond girl forward.

"Hi," said Avalon, bowing slightly to Afflatus. She turned to Jem and Farouche and asked, "And you are?"

"Uh, uh, Farouche," stammered Farouche. He gave an incredibly awkward bow.

"Jem," said Jem, refusing to bow. Avalon's gaze flickered to the scar running down Jem's arm that ended in a three-pronged flame symbol on the back of his hand, and she smiled widely.

"Nice to meet you," she said.

"Y-yeah," stammered Farouche uselessly. Jem gave Avalon what he intended to be a suspicious stare, because of her glance to his arm, but she merely grinned back mysteriously.

Cyneal poked its head forward between Jem and Farouche's legs and Avalon went to pet it, but her dad slapped her hand away.

"How dare you?" he demanded. "A Fenic, touching a filthy dragonet. Why don't you go put on yellow robes and sing some stupid Draig songs?"

"Sorry, dad," said Avalon, lowering her head. Her intimidating factor went away completely as she was reduced to a foolish child by her father.

"Let's go," he commanded, gripping her by the wrist. "Good to see you, Afflatus. I hope you all find appropriate jobs."

Snovel growled at Forenzi as he walked away.

"Bye, Forenzi," said Afflatus, who then turned to Jem after Forenzi was out of ear-shot. "You need to hide your scar," he said. "I'm afraid there may be some connection between it and the Fenic scriptures."

"Fine," agreed Jem, turning and heading back for the building that they had stayed in last night because he knew that Farouche had left his cold weather clothes there. It was sunny out and mildly warm, but there was a slight breeze. Jem wouldn't mind too terribly to have to cover his right arm and hand.

Beside where Farouche had slept were his heavy Lurian clothes, all in white but ridiculously filthy. Transforming one of his fingers into a razor sharp dragon claw, he cut off the sleeve of the heavy jacket. Then he cut the inner, softer layer out so that he wouldn't have a giant, bulky sleeve on his arm—just a thin cloth, essentially. He then took one of the gloves and cut the fingers off it so that he could have mobility in his hand while still covering his scar.

Taking the materials, he left the building in search of something reflective. Behind the building and past a couple others, he found a small pond against the giant wall to the rest of the city. He kneeled down beside it and stared at his own reflection. His first thought was that he needed a shower—badly. So he took off his shirt and splashed the water across his face and chest. It was pretty cold and stung each of the cuts across his face and body, but he welcomed it.

His hair, he noticed in his reflection, had gotten ridiculously long—especially now as it stuck up in all different directions and had various bits of debris and who knows what else lodged in it. His skin was paler than ever; Luria didn't help him there since he was always bundled up to stay warm whenever he went outside. He felt puny and weak. How was he, this scrawny little boy, supposed to reclaim Callisto?

He wanted to transform into a dragon to prove to himself that he was stronger than he appeared, but he knew that he couldn't. He just dunked his head in the pond and held his breath. When he came back up, he dried off almost instantly by heating his entire body. It was a strange warming sensation that he knew was a part of his dragon powers. All the water evaporated off him and steam floated up into the sky.

Then he took off his boots, stuck his feet in the water, put on his shirt, and went to work on his sleeve. He pulled it up against his shirt and slowly and meticulously weaved the fabrics together using magic.

"Hey, Jem," said a cool, calm voice.

Losing concentration on his sleeve, Jem looked up to see Avalon poking her head around the corner of a nearby building.

"Oh, hi," said Jem, utterly surprised. "What're you doing here?"

"I just told my dad I wanted to go explore the Refugee District a little… and, well, 1 just kinda wandered over here. Why are you here by yourself?"

"Um, just putting a sleeve on this shirt," he said plainly.

"Why?" she inquired, walking slowly nearer.

Jem tried to avoid her sharp, grey-green eyes by remaining focused on his sleeve. "Um," he stuttered, unable to think of a viable excuse, "Because I'm cold."

"Just one sleeve? Not two?"

"Uhh…"

"You're sure it isn't to cover your tattoo?" she said, close enough now that Jem could lightly smell her sweet scent drifting through the breeze.

"It's not a tattoo," said Jem, a little flustered.

"Oh, really? What is it then?"

Crap, thought Jem. *I probably should've gone along with the tattoo thing.*

"It's… uh… a birthmark," he replied meekly.

"A birthmark?" she repeated. She knew he was lying. Why could he not think of a better excuse? "It's a detailed birthmark," she said, tracing her finger around the fire emblem on the back of his hand. This sent shivers down Jem's spine.

"How far does it go?" she asked, pulling his sleeve up further.

"Just to my back," he said, finishing the stitching on his sleeve.

"They're like metal…" she whispered, rubbing her hand against the scales of his scar. "Take off your shirt," she said commandingly. "I want to see the rest of it."

Jem was a little taken aback by this, but he complied apprehensively.

"Oh my gosh," she said, seeing the Dragon's bite marks on Jem's back around his shoulder. "This isn't a birthmark."

She kneeled behind Jem and was running her hands across his shoulder, back, and chest. He felt like there was a dead weight in his stomach, but he couldn't explain why.

"How'd you really get this?" she asked quietly in his ear. "Because it's not a tattoo either, and I know it's not a birthmark."

"It's a scar," said Jem without thinking.

"A scar? From what?" she asked, stepping back to get a view of Jem's scar as a whole. Jem's heart started to beat rapidly as she circled around him, sizing him up with her laser-like eyes.

"I—I can't say," said Jem, looking down and averting his gaze. He was afraid that looking at her would make him tell her anything.

She sat beside him, took off her boots, and dipped her feet in the water too. Suddenly, Jem became aware of how stunningly attractive she was compared to him as their reflections glistened in the water side by side. Why was she here with him?

"It was the Dragon, wasn't it?" she asked absentmindedly, not even looking at Jem but, rather, at his reflection in the pond.

"Y—yeah," stammered Jem. "How'd you—?"

"The Phoenix can't bite," she explained. "It has no fangs. And that scar could only have been caused by something as powerful as the Dragon or the Phoenix. Plus the scales are something I've never seen before, and they must be dragon scales."

"Oh."

"So the Dragon is real?" she asked, turning to him, a big smile on her face.

"Well, yeah," said Jem, pulling his shirt back on. "Have you not seen it here?" He figured that the Keladonians would have seen the Dragon or the Phoenix by now since the legendary creatures were living here—as far as Jem knew.

"No," she said sadly. "No one has seen the Dragon or the Phoenix since the dawn of time when the Phoenix created it all."

"The Phoenix created it all?" asked Jem. It didn't seem realistic to him that the Phoenix he had met had created this whole planet.

"Well, that's what they tell us. My dad would swear by it—but I don't know. Maybe it did." When Jem didn't respond, she continued, "But you know what the Dragon represents, right?" She put her hand against his

63

cheek. "Pure evil. The absolute enemy of the Phoenix."

She said it with a certain relish in her tone, as if she enjoyed the fact that Jem was essentially a manifestation of pure evil.

"So I'm evil?" asked Jem, trying not to laugh at the absurdity of it. "According to who?"

"Fenic scripture," she said. "But that's okay; I don't mind." She stood up, brushing her hand against his chin and once again sending chills throughout his body. "Come on, let me show you the city," she said, offering him her hand.

Hesitantly, he reached up and took her hand. She helped him up with considerable strength and led him to the giant archway that went out of the Refugee District and into the rest of the Fortress.

"You're gonna love the Fortress," she said enthusiastically as they left the Refugee District behind them and ventured out into the city. Jem had already seen this initial area when they had gone with Afflatus to the Fortress Council Center, but she was taking him in a completely different direction around the outlying districts.

To Jem, the buildings seemed like something out of an ancient Chinese town. They were unique and undoubtedly the Keladonians own culture, but they seemed much like the pagodas Jem had learned about when studying Chinese architecture in school. The buildings had roofs which were mostly grey, red, or yellow; they had very steep roofs that curved out at the edges; and the walls were a smooth, dark wood.

The people, dressed in all sorts of colored clothes ranging from nice robes to shabby shorts and shirts, didn't take much notice of Jem, although lots of people greeted Avalon as she went by. The Council Spokesperson's daughter was obviously well known.

"Where're we going?" asked Jem as they passed by a market selling the strangest looking fruits he'd ever seen.

"Oh, I don't know," she said airily. "You must be hungry; let's find a place to eat."

"Okay," agreed Jem, just realizing how hungry he was.

"So why are you really here?" she asked, looking at him with those powerfully vivid grey-green eyes.

"What do you mean?"

"Well, all we were told," explained Avalon, "is that your world was temporarily uninhabitable and that you had to stay here for a while until the time was right for you to return. They said it was a part of the Phoenix's great plan."

Jem almost laughed at the last part, but he felt insulted by the whole comment. "Temporary uninhabitable? Really?" he said, more to himself than to Avalon. It made all the deaths seem pointless to coin it as simply *uninhabitable.*

"There was a war," he explained. "The Veroci Regime, which began in Xena—"

"What's Xena?" interrupted Avalon.

"It's a region of Callisto—that's the world I come from," he elaborated. He didn't want to bother with the whole backstory of him really being from Earth. "It's down in the south—"

"The south?" gasped Avalon. "Aren't there zombies?"

"Huh? Oh, no. No! There're no zombies in Callisto."

"No zombies…" repeated Avalon, as if it were some distant, foreign concept. "Wow. That's incredible. So if there are no zombies, why did you have to leave?"

"The Veroci Regime, they expanded from their one region, Xena, and began to take over the rest of the western regions. Then they attacked the East, where we are all from, and we escaped. Some of us," he added drearily.

"Why did that Regime take over? What was its goal?"

Jem thought about it for a moment. He didn't know Veroci's motivation behind taking over; all Jem knew was that Veroci was after him because of his blue eyes—because he thought Jem was somehow related to him. But that didn't explain why he was so eager to kill Jem himself. Why would he want to kill his own relative?

"I don't know," said Jem finally. "I guess they just wanted control over everything." That was the best explanation he could think of, and he didn't feel like explaining that Veroci was really out for him specifically. She didn't need to know that.

"Well, jeez, I'm sorry, Jem. That's got to be rough to have to come here after losing your entire world. I hope I've made you feel welcome."

"You have," smiled Jem, even though his heart still felt heavy when he thought about the destruction of Luria. She was nice company to keep his mind off it, though.

"Oh!" exclaimed Avalon. "We should eat here!"

She turned sharply and pulled him into a small building called Ignavio's Eatery. Light flooded in through the front door, but skylights also allowed light in at various points throughout the building. The tables were mostly a dark, knotted wood, aside from a few that looked like marble or some sort of rock. People were chatting away animatedly, taking no notice of them as they approached the ordering counter.

The menu, instead of being up on the wall, took up the entire surface of the counter. No person stood behind the counter, and Jem wondered how they would order their food.

"Do you like kibahl?" Avalon asked him.

"Umm, I've never heard of it," said Jem. "All the food here is probably different from anything I've ever had."

"Oh, well in that case I'll just order something that has a bunch of different stuff so that you can try it all."

She ran her finger across the menu, scanning across all sorts of words that Jem didn't recognize, and eventually pressed her finger against the "Combination Platter with Mewani Sauce." It glowed dark red for a moment and then went back to normal. She selected a few drinks that glowed in the same manner before pressing her hand against a blank part of the menu. Her handprint glowed dark red for a moment, an impression of it left on the menu, and then it disappeared too.

"Put your hand here," she said, indicating the blank space she had just pressed her hand against. Jem complied and it glowed dark red again and then faded away.

"Come on," she smiled, leading Jem over to a table.

"What was that?" asked Jem, perplexed as to what she had just done.

"I ordered food," she said matter-of-factly.

"Um, well… how?"

"Oh, you didn't have those in Callisto?" she laughed, touching his hand. "It's just a pad to order food. You press what you want and it sends an order to the cooks. When your food is ready, you'll feel a tingling in your hand."

"How do you pay for it?"

"Pay?" she replied, as if the word was foreign.

"Yeah… like, money?"

She tilted her head to the side and gave him a blank, confused look. "I don't know what you're saying. We just use our food credits."

"Food credits?" repeated Jem, now the confused one.

"Yeah, the Fortress gives everybody a certain amount of food credits per day. When you guys arrived they gave you food credits as well; that's why your handprint works too."

"How did they know what my handprint was?"

"They don't, but now they do."

Jem was still baffled. "But then how do they know it's me just from my handprint?" he asked.

"Because it's not *just* your handprint," explained Avalon. "It's your impression—your Magical Impression. It contains every identifying piece of information about you! No two MI's are the same."

"Hm." *That's incredible*, thought Jem.

"So tell me," she began, leaning across the table, "what was Callisto like?"

"Well, the region I come from is Luria," said Jem, leaning forward to mimic her. "It's always freezing cold there, but I loved it. The people we stayed with—the Kuznets—they were the nicest people…" his voice trailed off. *The Kuznets are dead*, he reminded himself.

"Jem? Is something wrong?" she asked, eyes big and worrisome.

They were dead. Really dead. Gone.

"No—no, nothing's wrong," he insisted.

She gripped his hand. "So is it nicer here, since it's warmer?"

His stomach seized up in a painful knot.

"I'm sorry," he uttered. "I need to use the bathroom."

"Oh, okay. Over there," she said, pointing to a door in the far end of the restaurant. "You okay?"

"Yeah, yeah I am," he stammered, clutching his stomach and walking quickly to the bathroom. There wasn't a men's or women's door, just a single door. He didn't have time to think about this anomaly; instead, he just threw the door open and ran to the nearest stall.

The stall was really more like a miniature room with a door that dissolved as he reached it and reappeared after he had entered. Jem fell to his knees right away and vomited violently into the toilet.

After a few moments of expunging any contents from his stomach, he sat back and wiped his mouth. The toilet was little more than a bowl—no body or flushing lever. It didn't even hold water; currently, it was only coated in his vomit. Mist then appeared in the bowl, swirled around, and it was shining clean again.

Jem had no time to admire the magic toilet before his stomach seized in violent pains again, and he fell to the ground in the fetal position. His scar, mostly on his back and under his ribs, hurt like he was being stabbed repeatedly, and his stomach was doing barrel rolls.

Get up, he told himself. *Avalon is waiting for you.* He tried to stand up but merely fell back to the ground again, too weak to stand.

It was no use. All he could do was lie on the floor and writhe in pain. Avalon would be sitting out there wondering what he was doing… thinking he was some sort of freak… but he couldn't do anything about it.

Pain was Jem's time; there were no minutes or hours. Just pain. Lots and lots of pain, and no light at the end of the tunnel. No comforting voice, no soft hand to stroke his hair. Just cold, disgusting bathroom floor.

After several minutes, he managed to get to his feet. His scar still felt like it was piercing through his organs, but it was somewhat bearable. He just needed to get back out to Avalon, and he should be able to hide the pain. It was bad, yes, but he could function, and that's more than he could usually do when the dragon poison got to him.

Carefully, he began to stand up but lost his balance and tried to catch himself on the door. However, the door dissolved to let him out of the stall and sent him stumbling into the bathroom where he had to catch himself against the sink. He rinsed his mouth out with water to get the vomit taste out and then headed for the door.

"There you are," said Avalon as Jem approached the table. "You sure you're alright?"

"Yeah," said Jem through somewhat gritted teeth. "I'm fine, really."

She smiled and indicated the food on the table which had arrived in his absence. "Dig in!" she exclaimed.

He was barely able to eat anything, feeling that at any moment it may just come back up again. Luckily, he held it all down and was able to maintain a conversation with her. She was very talkative, hounding him with questions about Callisto and then telling stories about her times in the Fortress. Jem appreciated the conversation and the normality of it all; if only he weren't having such pains, it would've been a really great time.

After they had eaten, she showed him around more of the city. His pains lessened throughout the day, and he was gradually able to relax around her. It was a beautiful city, and all the people were kind. Jem tried strange fruit from all the different street vendors and had a delicious purple ice cream-like treat. Avalon looked adorable when she smudged some of it—she called it violare—on her nose and giggled as she wiped it off, scrunching her face.

His favorite part was riding the sylphskates, which really weren't so much skates as just sylph wrapped around regular shoes. He was happy to know they used sylph here—that made it feel more like home. Small bits of his silver sylph wrapped around his feet and allowed him to slide around the ground as if it were ice. Avalon, who had dark blue sylph like everyone else, smirked at Jem's silver sylph as if she had expected it to be peculiar.

She was far more skilled than Jem, obviously having practiced before, and she literally skated circles around him as he struggled to gain a footing. Eventually, though, he got the hang of it and had a great time exploring the city with her.

As it started to get dark out, Avalon walked him to the entrance of the Refugee District and hugged him goodbye. Farouche was at their building talking with some of the other folks about highly technical stuff that Jem didn't understand, but he sat with them nonetheless because they were serving food around the new, giant wooden table. He ate silently and listened to how everyone else's day went.

"Well, did anyone here find a real job, outside of ECKO?" asked Farouche.

The room was silent for a moment before Afflatus spoke. "Good! We need all the assistance we can get."

"If you want assistance, you could ask me," piped up a younger girl from the other side of the table. She could only have been ten or eleven at the oldest.

"Teek!" exclaimed the grown woman beside her. "You know why you can't be involved with ECKO."

"But I want to help!" demanded Teek. She had dark skin and wild, curly hair that flew about her head as she protested. "My age doesn't matter!"

"If only it were so," said Afflatus. "But your mother is right, Teek, you are too young to be involved with ECKO. You're better off forgetting about it."

"I won't" she snorted, burying her face in her food.

Jem felt bad for the poor little girl. She was really young, but then again, Jem was only fifteen. What made him old enough to be a part of any of this? Or Sierra? Or Farouche? It seemed arbitrary to allow them to be a part of ECKO but not Teek.

"Anyways," began Farouche, "how're we gonna get by if none of us have real jobs here?"

Afflatus glared at him. "These are *real* jobs," he insisted. "You know that as well as I do. Heck, Farouche, you took out so many of those tanks and saucers back in Luria that you probably saved hundreds of lives. Tell me that isn't real!"

"I see your point, Aff," grunted Farouche between bites of food, "but we don't contribute to the Fortress directly by saving lives! We'll be a burden, like Forenzi said."

"Don't mind him," said Afflatus. "We'll all be taken care of here, don't you worry."

Farouche nodded. Afflatus seemed so much more serious recently, and Jem began to miss the eccentric old man from Luria.

"How was your day, Jem?" asked the Neoran Elder, Tekkara. "Did you find a job?"

"No," said Jem hesitantly. Truthfully, he hadn't even looked for one at all. "I'll just help at ECKO."

"Well, we can certainly use your assistance," she said kindly, beaming at him.

After dinner, Jem made his way to the blankets he had set up for a bed and stared out of the building at the stars and the giant moon. The same giant moon from Callisto... weird.

He didn't think too much about the stars, though, or the moon. All he could think about was Avalon. For some reason she had hijacked his thoughts and refused to leave. Her stunning grey-green eyes, her sharp blonde hair, and her intimidating demeanor kind of excited Jem for reasons he couldn't fully explain to himself. He soon drifted off into a content sleep, wondering when he would get to see her next.

Justin Dennis

CHAPTER 8:
LEO AND THE REG

When Sierra woke up, the sun had already set.

"Maya!" she yelled, rolling over and hitting her sister on the shoulder. "Come on! It's dark again!"

Sierra got to her feet and began to descend the wunla tree; Rimaya followed swiftly behind her. They were running across the Argonian fields, knowing that they must be close to Eltaes. Rimaya was yelling for Sierra to slow down, but she wasn't listening. She was eager to see her old home and find her dad, and she refused to stop no matter how much her older sister protested.

"Sierra! Slow down! Remember what Afflatus said about stealth!"

Sierra was deaf to her sister's yells as she ascended the hill that she knew overlooked Eltaes. Her home was right over this hill...

Sierra froze dead in her tracks. Rimaya almost collided into her from behind.

"Damn it, Sierra," panted Rimaya, clutching her side and bending over, "what got into you?"

Sierra didn't respond. The sight before her had wiped out her voice.

Finally lifting her head up to look around, Rimaya understood Sierra's shock. "No way..." she uttered.

Eltaes was a graveyard. Some houses were completely destroyed, others only partially. The town center looked like it had been a war zone—maybe it actually had been. From their vantage point, they could even see their home—the crumbled remains of it at least.

"Everything's... dead..." breathed Sierra, clenching her fists. She wanted to feel sorrow, but she only felt hatred—hatred towards Veroci. The side of her face stung where he had slapped her, but physical pain seemed trivial in comparison to the destruction of Eltaes. Everything she had ever known for the first fifteen years of her existence was now gone. And what about their father...?

"What's that?" asked Rimaya, indicating a massive rectangular building out in the distance past the city. Sierra hadn't even noticed it.

"It's Regime, definitely," said Sierra weakly.

"You think he's in there?"

Sierra turned to look her sister in the eyes. "I sure hope so."

Taking slow, sorrowful steps, they began to descend the hill into Eltaes. It was the strangest feeling Sierra had ever experienced: revisiting the ruined remains of what she had once called her home. The only thought that kept circulating in her mind was, *Just let him be alive... just let him be alive...*

They walked alongside what must have been Bert's Café. Sierra could tell because of the circular structure of the ruins, and the bits of tables that still stood. She had a quick flashback of them sitting at one of the booths last year when it exploded and they were blamed for it. They had thought it was the Regs at the time, but when they had faced Atychis at the North Island, he had explained that it had been him riding the Dragon that had caused it. In her mind, she saw the whole incident from an outsider's view, watching the Dragon bomb the Café with a powerful fire breath and fly off, leaving the Regs to ponder what had just happened.

It was strange, reliving scenes around the ruins. It was almost like they came to life with their haunted pasts. As they passed the town center, she watched Anne Tompkins die again in her mind's eye—the woman whom the Regime had killed to make a point: magic was not allowed.

Then came the strangest of all sensations: passing through the remnants of their home. Sierra stepped over the splintered, ash-covered remains of the wall and pictured everything as it had been. Her bed had been right where this large pile of ash was. There was no clue that her dresser had ever existed and certainly not a hint of any of her posters. All her drawings, writings, poetry... gone. Her eyes welled up, but she held back the tears well enough, instead grinding her teeth and clenching her fists.

Rimaya wasn't handling it so well. She was standing in what used to be her room, watering it with her tears as if they'd bring it back to life.

Sierra wandered out into center of the house, entirely aware that she was walking through where walls should've been. She felt like a ghost passing through things which should have been there.

Kneeling down, she rubbed her hand across the ground and coated her hand in ash. The grass under them was dead and shriveled, but its brown color contrasted against the black ash. She glanced around and saw that the whole floor was black with ash other than where she and Rimaya had stepped, leaving brown footprints. Nobody had been here except them, not even their dad. Sierra didn't want to consider that he might have been in the building when this had happened.

The moonlight drenched everything in an eerie silver light, and Sierra wanted nothing more than to leave this dead home and to quit replaying old scenes in her head. She remembered her dad fixing Oliver's broken leg. She remembered coming inside for water breaks after working the fields and laughing with Jem, Oliver, and Rimaya. The normalness of her memories was painful considering how much had changed.

"Let's go," said Sierra quietly. "Dad has to be in that building."

Rimaya nodded her head from a few yards away, still sobbing lightly. Sierra turned and headed for the intimidatingly large Regime building without looking back, but she could hear Rimaya walking behind her.

The metal building loomed ahead of them at least five stories tall, much bigger than anything that had ever been in Eltaes. There didn't seem to be any windows or doors, but in pure black, Sierra reckoned that they would be hard to spot approaching the building at this time of night even if the Regs were watching them from some hidden window. The moonlight was bright, but their suits didn't reflect it, and Rimaya had tucked her blond hair into her hood. Starving and not wanting to waste their energy, they didn't use their cloaking devices.

Upon approaching the side of the building, it became clear that there was no way in on this side, so they began the trek around the metal behemoth. On the other side, sylphquads and sylphcycles were lined up against the side and there was a massive metal door near to them. Lights from the building overlooked the vehicles, meaning that they had to be careful to stay in the darkness.

"Can we get in here?" whispered Rimaya.

Sierra felt her way around the edges of the door, at least twice the size of a regular door, but didn't find anything loose or movable.

Sierra shook her head. "Any other entrances?"

They both knew that there weren't. No windows, no other doors. This was their only option.

Rimaya began to feel around the sides and bottom of the door just as Sierra had. "How do you think it opens?" she asked.

"What d'ya mean?" replied Sierra. "Like a door, I suppose."

"I don't think so," Rimaya whispered back. "There's no handle on the side, the handle is down here." She gripped a protruding handle from the bottom of the door. "I think it opens upwards, not sideways like a regular door."

This perplexed Sierra, although Jem would've recognized it as like a garage door. "So?" she said, uncaring of which way the door opened if they couldn't open it.

Rimaya grinned at her, the moonlight reflecting off her teeth, and then she began to wriggle her fingers at the bottom of the door. Blue sparks began to jump from her fingers to the edge of the door, and gradually, it lifted up.

Sierra's jaw dropped as the door rose even higher. Rimaya was concentrating hard, and the complicated maneuvers with her fingers to keep the door up looked too complex for Sierra to ever master. Knowing the draining feeling of magic, Sierra knew Rimaya wouldn't be able to keep that up much longer.

"Go," grunted Rimaya, not taking her eyes off the work she was doing.

Sierra did as she was told and lay flat against the ground, sliding swiftly under the door and into the building. Rimaya followed immediately after.

The door slammed shut behind them much louder than Rimaya had intended.

"Crap! Rimaya!" yelled Sierra as quietly as she could. "We can't stay here! They had to have heard that!"

Rimaya was breathing hard and her eyes weren't focusing on Sierra. It was darker in here than outside, but there were dim lights in the distance and more were turning on as footsteps made light metallic noises from somewhere within the building.

"Rimaya, I'm serious; I know you're drained, but we gotta move!"

Sierra half-dragged her sister away from the door and hid them behind a collection of crates. Just in time, too, as several Regs came down the steps and stood in front of the main entrance. Sierra peeked between two crates to get a good view.

"Somebody got in."

"Who would've got in? We've got everybody from the towns near here."

"Maybe we missed somebody."

"The only people we missed are dead."

"Well, *somebody* got in."

"Right. Don't wake up the prisoners. We don't need a riot on our hands. But wake the other guards and get everybody patrolling right now."

"Yes, sir."

With that, footsteps went off in all directions. One Reg even walked directly past their crates, but didn't glance over the edge to see them. Sierra let out the breath that she finally realized she was holding and turned her attention to Rimaya.

"Maya," she uttered, "you gotta get up. They're patrolling—they'll find us soon. We gotta get moving and find dad."

Rimaya groaned uselessly but gave no other response. That magic had really drained her. Sierra didn't have any choice but to leave her. If Sierra stayed, they would both be found and they would never find their dad, but if she left, maybe she could find her dad and get them all out. She had to.

"You're gonna be safe," Sierra told her sister, pushing her lifeless body into the most discreet corner of the crates. "I'm gonna find dad and we'll get you outta here."

Rimaya didn't have the consciousness to acknowledge her, and Sierra didn't have time to wait for a response. She slinked away from the crates quietly. Most of the guards had gone to check other areas of the building. Most of the lights were still off, aside from some very dim yellow lighting in the metallic rafters of the ceiling.

The bottom floor that Sierra was on only seemed to have empty rooms with hospital-style beds. What were they doing here with the prisoners? Obviously, though, this floor had no prisoners. Not wanting to risk the stairs, which were lit better than the rest of the area, Sierra climbed the piping along the wall to the second floor. The floor was a rigid, metallic mesh, easy to climb but rough on her hands.

She had a better view of the building here; she saw all the way to the other end at least a hundred yards away, if not more. Down the center was an empty drop to the bottom floor, but the metal flooring she was standing on wrapped around the walls to give access to the cells. A cold wave of despair crashed over her as she realized that she could never check all the prison cells before somebody found Rimaya behind the crates. She was trapped. She couldn't even get out with Rimaya semi-unconscious since she couldn't magic the door open. In fact, even if she found her dad she didn't know how they would get out. Her situation seemed hopelessly futile.

Just find dad... she thought. *He'll know what to do.* Why she believed that, though, she didn't know. Her dad was always reluctant to rebel and never used magic. How could he help them escape?

Just then, a guard came up the nearby stairs, and without any cover to hide behind, Sierra was forced to cloak herself magically for a moment. He walked by the section of the wall that she was pressed flat up against without even looking over. Just as he passed, she lost the energy to hold her cloaking and all she could do was hope he didn't look over his shoulder. The shadows weren't cover enough at that close distance.

With the guards patrolling everywhere and the multiple floors of hundreds of cells, she knew she had to find a quick way to get her dad's attention without checking every single prisoner. She examined every inch of her mind to think of something, but it was like trying to find her way through a thick fog without any idea of where she was going.

Suddenly, she felt a tugging in her mind, an almost physical force, like a headache but somehow different. She felt around her head with her hands, but there was nothing there. Whatever it was, it was distinctly in her mind, but she had never felt it before. It almost felt like it was clearing her mind, helping her to think straight, and yet forcing her thoughts towards one direction.

Her eyes began to scan the building. One floor above hers and about a third of the way across the building, her eyes locked on one cell. She didn't know why, but the force in her mind told her that something was there. She didn't have the time to question this phenomenon. Instead, she took off running across the metallic grate. Above her was another Reg, but he was oblivious to her thanks to her stealthy boots that silenced her steps. Without those boots, she would've made a distinctive *clank* against the metal with every step much like how the Reg was doing right then.

Around the corner was another Reg, but this one was on her level. Without options, since there was no piping nearby to climb, she clambered over the handrail to her side and gripped onto to the grating below for dear life. Her fingers fit within the grating and the sharp metal dug into them, causing a great deal of pain. Thankfully, she was able to sink her toes between the handrail and the grating on the other side, keeping her body flat against it grating. She tried to force herself to cloak, but it flickered on for a moment and then went out. She was drained, and it was taking everything she had just to hold her body against the grating.

The Reg walked by slowly, his boots sounding as if they came within inches of crushing her fingers. Her eyes were closed, so as not to give away her position, and she was attempting to hold her breath, but it wasn't working. She was beyond lucky that he did not look down or accidently step on her fingers. Seconds after the Reg had passed, she let her legs drop and pulled herself back over the handrail and onto the grating. She took off at a sprint away from the Reg, breathing heavily and hoping that he wouldn't look back.

After she turned the corner, she saw a set of stairs up to the next floor, but it was too well lit. Luckily, there was some piping nearby that went through a large opening in the grating. She swiftly climbed up the piping to get to the third floor and crouched low to get by the bright lighting near the stairs. There were no Regs in the nearby vicinity, and the lighting was dim from here to the cell that she was trying to reach. Perfect.

She sprinted quickly across the metallic grating, sights locked on the cell that was pulling at her mind, and stopped abruptly in front of it. Through the bars, she saw a man sitting on the edge of a small bed, holding his fingers to his temples with his eyes closed. Even in the terrible lighting, Sierra could make out the image of her father.

"Dad!" she called, clanking her hand against the metal bars. Wrong move.

"HEY! THERE THEY ARE!" yelled some Reg. Immediately, the metallic chiming of their boots was descending upon Sierra.

Leo looked up from his concentrated position, and it took him a moment to realize who was standing before him.

"Sierra!" he called, so much love and affection in his voice. But then, in a much more serious voice he yelled, "Get back!" He stood from his bed and planted one leg firmly in front of the other, holding his arms back at the ready. Sierra had never known her dad to do magic, but as his hands began to glow, she got out of the way of the cell door just in case. Seconds later, the bars of the cell door went rocketing out with a blue flash and clanked and crashed all the way to the bottom floor. Immediately, all the lights went on and blaring alarms sounded.

Leo came sprinting from the cell, swiftly picked up Sierra in one arm, and leaped over the handrail. Sierra thought they were going to plummet to the ground and die, but her father expertly shot sylph from his hand like a rope and it wrapped around an overhanging rafter to swing them down to the ground safely. Red lasers of magic whizzed by them as this happened, but he spawned a sort of blue bubble around them that was absorbing the shots that should have hit them. Sierra had never seen such magic.

He sprinted across the ground at full speed, headed straight for the door. Multiple Regs appeared from a nearby room and all shot lasers straight at him. The combination of their hits broke the protective bubble, and Leo covered Sierra with his body as he leapt over the guards and dodged the rest of their shots. His shield then flickered back into existence just as he came screeching to a halt.

A Reg was standing directly before them, holding his scepter against Rimaya's neck. All the other Regs had stopped firing as Leo faced his eldest daughter and her captor. The only noise came from the prisoners protesting the ruckus that had woken them up.

Then there was a slow clap. Just one person clapping. "Bravo, Leo," came a strong voice from somewhere above them. "I didn't think you would make it that far."

Leo released Sierra from her protected position at his chest and she was able to stand beside him. She looked up to see the snide-looking Reg from Eltaes, the one who had used the lightning whip to kill Anne Tompkins, floating down from the highest floor on a red, misty cloud. His whip hung from his belt and flicked around like a snake's tongue. (Although, not knowing what a snake was, Sierra associated it with a cuorl—an armadillo-like creature with only two legs and a snake-like head that lived in northern Ilios and southern Argo.)

As the cloud touched the ground, it dissolved away, and he stepped forward menacingly to stand off to the side in between Leo and the Reg holding Rimaya. Leo couldn't seem to decide who he needed to look at: the lightning-whip Reg or the hostage-taker Reg.

"Give up, Leo, and drop the shield. Nobody is going to shoot you," said the Reg with the lightning whip.

Leo complied, and the magical blue bubble around them dissipated. Sierra, as drained as she was, still felt like she had enough energy to take the lightning whip man. All her anger and hatred towards the Regime, it was all directed at him. Who cared about Veroci? This man had killed Anne. He had started it all in Eltaes, and he obviously ran this—this prison or whatever it was. But despite her hatred, she stood still. They were vastly outnumbered, and she knew the damage that whip could do.

"I think you should be happy, Leo," continued the Reg. "Now your daughters will be here to join you. You won't be so… lonely."

This got snickers from some of the Regs. Leo's expression remained stoic.

"My daughters won't be staying here, Gurant," said Leo, his voice rougher than Sierra remembered it.

Gurant laughed a false, hardy laugh. "Don't be a fool. They are in my possession now. Tachel," he added, turning to the Reg who was holding the barely conscious Rimaya. "Don't release the girl until Leo is safe in his cell. And if he resists, kill her."

Tachel the Reg nodded and turned his gaze towards Leo. Sierra's dad merely stared back at him. "Tachel…" he said, his voice uneasy. "Remember who you are…"

"Shut up," spat Gurant, brandishing the lightning whip and snapping it in front of Leo. "Tachel, follow him to his cell. Leo, move!"

But neither man moved. They just stared at each other as if trying to communicate wordlessly.

"I said MOVE!" screamed Gurant, snapping the whip directly at Leo. But in one elegant move, Leo avoided the tip of the lightning whip, grabbed the length of it, and jerked it from Gurant's hand. It went sliding across the cement floor, snapping and twitching like a dying bug.

At the same moment that that happened, Tachel removed his scepter from Rimaya's throat and smashed it against the back wall which exploded outwards. With one arm, Leo sprayed a thick fog from his hand, and with the other, he lifted up Sierra and tucked her under his arm.

"STOP THEM!" bellowed Gurant from somewhere within the fog, but before anyone had the chance to even try to stop them, Leo was leaping through the hole in the wall and following after Tachel who had Rimaya under his arm. Tachel put Rimaya's limp body onto the nearest sylphcycle, stowed his scepter on his back, and hopped on. He peeled out just as Sierra and Leo were able to mount a cycle. Leo's sylph flowed from his feet and took its place around the wheels, spinning rapidly and throwing them backwards as they accelerated powerfully away from the building, only a couple red lasers flying behind them.

Leo pulled up beside Tachel, and the two made eye contact for a moment. Sierra, absolutely confounded as to why a Reg was helping them, could only watch as her dad and Tachel each swung one of their arms in a melodic rhythm. It didn't make any sense to her until, with one massive swing of their arms, a huge chunk of ground behind them went shooting up.

All Sierra saw was a wall of ground come tearing up like a mountain being born in an instant. It extended for miles out to the sides and reached higher than the prison building. Unless the Regs could do magic like that, they wouldn't be catching them anytime soon, and it also stopped the red lasers from shooting by them.

Leo then whistled three short notes and held the fourth for a few seconds. From a nearby forest, a small gray dragonet came flying above them, moonlight glinting off its scales. *Ryelox*, thought Sierra. *He survived.*

Ryelox swooped down and flew at the same speed as the cycles just beside Leo. With a joyful laugh, the dragonet tossed its head to the side and licked Leo up the whole side of his face. Leo laughed in return and petted Ryelox's head. They didn't say anything, but Sierra knew that they could communicate telepathically, and she was happy to see them reunited.

Though Ryelox had been weak and slow the last time Sierra had seen it, it now seemed stronger and flew with much more confidence. It likely had been living alone in the forest, fending for itself for a long time now. With a big, toothy smile, Ryelox ascended and flew above them, keeping watch.

Leo and Tachel nodded to each other and then looked ahead. They drove by the edge of Eltaes, passing the backside of the town center. Leo didn't look at any of it; he only looked forward.

Finally, they were headed home.

Justin Dennis

CHAPTER 9:
OKKA'S SURPRISE

Jem had a good time over the next few days, his favorite part being the nights spent with Avalon. They often ate dinner together and then either skated around the Fortress or just lay on rooftops and watched the stars.

In the mornings, he usually stayed around with Afflatus and Tekkara to help with the plans for ECKO. From what he was able to discern from their conversations, he understood that the different branches of ECKO had been very separated ever since their inception; this was the first time that the Callisto and Kelados branches had come together in a long time.

This was evident at the meetings when the Keladonians refused any attempts by Afflatus or Tekkara to prepare an army for reclaiming Callisto.

"We gave you our Soul," said Afflatus.

"A kind gesture, undoubtedly, but it holds us to no commitment," sneered Forenzi.

Jem watched quietly as the exchanges went back and forth in the large, circular Fortress Council Center. Farouche had been invited, but he had chosen to stay in the Refugee District to work on more inventions. Jem, knowing that Avalon would be free later after she got out of school, gladly spent his day with the ECKO members.

All of the Fortress Councilmembers were the Keladonian representatives of ECKO. Afflatus and Tekkara became the ECKO representatives from Callisto since they were the only Regional Elders who made it to Kelados. Some other City Elders from the outlying Lurian, Neoran, and Radeon cities had made it, but they didn't have as much authority as Afflatus or Tekkara. Unfortunately, nobody knew what had happened to the Radeon Elder.

In an effort to keep a tally of all the ECKO members, Jem had memorized all of their names and whether they were a Draig or a Fenic. It was easy to tell by their robes: Fenics all had some combination of red and black while the Draigs wore mainly white and yellow. Also, the Draigs all had a yellow, three-pronged flame emblem (almost identical to Jem's, except his was blood red) somewhere on their robes, whereas the Fenics wore a red, two-pronged flame that kind of looked like a claw.

Afflatus sat to Jem's right with his bald head shining and his long, white beard falling under the table. He wore neutral blue robes so as not to be associated with the Draigs or Fenics. Tekkara was beside him wearing all green, her long grey hair pulled up into a bun. She sat tall and listened attentively, her brown eyes focusing intently on whoever was speaking. While all the Councilmembers treated Afflatus and Tekkara fairly within the Center, Jem noticed that they wouldn't associate with them outside of it. They both always returned directly to the Refugee District after the meetings. Jem wondered if it was because they hadn't yet sided with either the Draigs or Fenics.

To his left was Lenro, a scrawny, light-skinned, argumentative Draig in light yellow robes. Then there was Harcos, a skinny, hawk-eyed woman with dark red hair. Beside her, Okka was currently making his case for why they should reclaim at least a portion of Callisto. Mualano, the plump, kind-faced Draig woman beside him, was smiling and listening dutifully.

Forenzi wasn't even looking at Okka, but Ikuuno, the tall, dark-skinned woman with two red stripes running down her black robes, was listening with a stern expression on her face. Beside her, Zenska, an attractive man with shoulder length dark hair, was fiddling his thumbs together. In between Zenska and Tekkara was Fey. She was a small, quiet woman with short, spiky black hair.

Okka was finished making his case for reclaiming Callisto. They took a vote, but again, it was only Okka and Afflatus who voted in favor of returning to Callisto.

"I think," began Zenska, "that the zombie issue must be addressed before we address Callisto. Our own Kelados should be safe first."

"With all due respect," said Mualano, "our world hasn't been free of zombies for two thousand years, and it won't be free until the Dragon—"

"Mual, you remember the agreement," cut in Okka.

"Right, sorry, Okka," she said politely. "Until the Legendary One comes back to destroy the zombies."

Jem looked to Afflatus confused, and the old man explained quietly, "The Draigs believe the Dragon will return to save them; the Fenics believe that Phoenix will, and each believes the other spawned the zombies. So to encompass both beliefs, they say 'Legendary One' or 'Evil One' instead of Dragon or Phoenix."

Zenska didn't seem satisfied with Mualano's answer. "Well, maybe it is time we take matters into our own hands instead of waiting around for the Legendary One."

This comment got Zenska dirty looks from pretty much everyone in the room.

"And who are you to say that you know better than the Legendary One, Zenska?" scoffed Forenzi.

"I simply think we've been waiting long enough, that's all," said Zenska, biting his lip and leaning back in his chair.

Jem made a mental note to find the Dragon and the Phoenix when he could. He was very sure that they were at the volcano, unless something had happened to them.

"Well, until the Returning," began Ikuuno in a bold, confident voice, "what do we do with the Refugees?"

"Have them assimilate, get used to life here, 'cause we aren't doing anything anytime soon," declared Forenzi.

There seemed to be a general consensus of nodding heads.

"Sorry, you three," said Ikuuno solemnly, looking at Jem, Afflatus, and Tekkara.

"Moving on," said Forenzi. "The fourteenth quadrant has requested revisions to the building spacing protocol..."

"Excuse us," said Afflatus, standing and motioning for Jem and Tekkara to follow him. "Thank you for including us in your meeting, but we'll be going now."

"Goodbye," said the Councilmembers in unison.

"I'm gonna stay here, Aff," said Tekkara. "Make sure no decisions are made without at least one of us present."

"Good," smiled Afflatus. "Thanks, Tekkara."

"Thanks," Jem said to Afflatus once they were outside the Council Center. "I didn't want to have to sit through that."

"Not a problem. Now, Jem, I remember distinctly that you told me that you came here and communicated with the Dragon at that volcano." He pointed to the distant volcano that Jem had spotted before. "Can you communicate with it now?"

"No," said Jem truthfully. He hadn't been able to bridge any sort of mental connection with the Dragon since the battle at the North Island.

"Then it's not there..."

"What do you mean?"

"Your mental connection should reach that far, Jem. The Dragon must be elsewhere, too far away for you to reach."

"Then how do I contact it? Obviously, we need to have it return before they will help us get back to Callisto."

"I don't know," mumbled Afflatus, biting his lip. "I feel that we are in quite a bind. I really do."

Jem patted Afflatus' shoulder reassuringly. "We'll figure out something, old man."

Afflatus half-smiled and began the walk down the stairs to the Refugee District. At the entrance, Avalon was standing there waiting for Jem.

"Hi!" she called to him in the distance.

"Are you seeing Forenzi's daughter?" whispered Afflatus.

"No—I mean, well, we've been hanging out, yes," stammered Jem. Afflatus gave him an unreadable glance before walking alone into the Refugee District.

"Come on, Jem," smiled Avalon, taking his hand and leading him into the city.

They got something to eat in a distinctly Fenic part of town—Jem could tell from all the black and red, as well as the sharp corners and more minimalist design. Draig areas incorporated a lot of white, yellow, and some orange, and they were much more decorative and elaborate. Those two styles never seemed to combine much—one area simply morphed into the next as the city went on.

As they were finishing up their food, the sun low in the sky behind them, Avalon said to Jem, "I have some people I want you to meet tonight."

He came close to spitting out his drink. The last thing he wanted to do was meet people; he was just fine being with Avalon. But he didn't want his worry to come across so blatantly.

"Who?" he asked.

"Some other Fenics, the ones I hang around with. I think you'll like them. But first, we need to get you a proper haircut." She smiled brightly and took his hand to lead him away from the restaurant.

"What's wrong with my hair?" asked Jem as they approached an open, grassy field.

"Well, it's gotten a little mangy, Jem, if you haven't noticed. Look." She spawned a circular disk of blue sylph that hardened into a mirror-like surface and Jem was able to see himself in it. His hair was long, down into his eyes, and covered his ears completely.

"I guess it is too long," he said, turning his head to the side and running his hand through his hair. "What're you gonna do to it?"

"Oh, you'll see," said Avalon, beaming. "Sit down."

Jem sat on the grass, legs crossed, and Avalon stood behind him. She began to run her hands inches above his head, and he could feel hair being cut off with magic. He had had one of these magic haircuts back in Luria once, and the feeling tickled almost as much now as it had then.

After a few minutes, she was done and she made another mirror out of sylph for him to look into. "What do you think?" she asked. He stared into the sylph and saw himself, but he looked much older now. His ears and forehead were visible, and his short bangs were sticking straight up. The rest of his hair was relatively short and well-kept.

"I like it," he said, smiling. "Thanks, Av."

"Aw, I'm so glad!" she said, throwing her arms around him, tackling him to the grass. The two of them rolled a couple times, giggling and smiling. Jem thought for a moment that they might kiss, but then Avalon stood up and offered her hand to Jem, helping him up.

"Come on, my friends are waiting to meet you," she said, smiling and blushing slightly.

After a couple minutes more of walking, they came to a small building squished in between two larger ones. Jem wouldn't have even noticed it if Avalon hadn't directed him down the stairs to the front door.

She pulled open the rickety old door and grinned as Jem stepped hesitantly forward. The interior was smoky and warm; candles and incense were lit abundantly around the cozy room. A fireplace crackled in the corner where five kids sat around in a circle playing some sort of game. Large, comfy-looking chairs and sofas were placed around the room along with a big table that looked like a pool table without pockets. Lights orbs floated along the walls beside a few paintings of phoenixes and a dartboard-looking thing.

"Welcome to the Nest," smiled Avalon, gripping Jem's arm. She pulled him past the table and around one of the sofas to the group of kids by the fireplace.

"Hey, Av."

"What's up, Av?"

"Who's he?"

The air was tense, and Jem was nervous as they all stared at him.

"Everyone," began Avalon, "this is Jem. He's one of the refugees."

Immediately, the tension loosened. Four of the kids greeted him warmly and fist bumped him—the Keladonian equivalent of a handshake. One kid, however, with curly black hair and a square jaw, eyed him suspiciously and remained quiet.

"Is he a Fenic?" spat the suspicious kid.

"Hey, Baiz, chill out," said a curvy girl with multi-colored hair. "Y'ain't gotta be all rude to the kid. He just lost his whole world!" Jem liked her already.

"Shut up, Tyyni," he retorted. "You know the rules. Only Fenics."

"Rabaiz," said Avalon loudly. "He isn't a Fenic, but he isn't a Draig, and he's with me. You can get over it."

"Whatever…" grumbled Rabaiz.

Avalon smiled. "So, FI?"

"Mhm," grinned Tyyni, flashing her brown eyes at Avalon.

Jem was confused about what FI was, but said nothing as they all sat back down and began to concentrate on something in the center of the circle that he couldn't see.

Avalon explained in his ear, "They're playing a game called Fortress Invasion. It's based on if zombies invaded the Fortress, and you play as a skilled magic soldier who has to kill them all. It's really fun."

"Hm," said Jem, looking around at all the kids who were flicking their fingers at random through the air. "I don't see any screen, though, or anything like that."

"A screen?" she questioned, scrunching her nose in confusion. "Like the mav?" She indicated a screen against one of the walls that looked to Jem like a TV, or what the Callistonians called a reedee.

"Yeah, you don't need one? I don't see them doing anything."

"It's magic, dufus," said Rabaiz.

"Shut up," yelled Avalon, kicking him. "Here," she said to Jem, grabbing his hands, "let me show you how it works."

She directed his hands in a particular motion in front of them until a map of the Fortress appeared in front of them in such startling quality that Jem could've sworn they were floating above the city. Controlling his hands, Avalon pinched out to zoom in on the map until they were watching a virtual Tyyni send a powerful spell at a fast-moving zombie that had the name "Rabaiz" floating above it. Jem laughed as the zombie exploded into several different pieces.

Rabaiz glanced up from what he was concentrating on and glared at Tyyni who giggled.

Jem watched the rest of the events unfold from his sky view. The soldiers, Tyyni and two others, were eventually able to hold off the zombies for the required time and save the city. They cheered as the last zombie, the skinny, greasy-haired boy who had introduced himself as Jario, was caught in a trap set by Tyyni and catapulted over the Fortress walls out into the nowhere land. Tyyni was apparently very good at this game.

"Another one?" she suggested, smiling around at her friends.

"I've had enough," grunted Jario.

"Me too," grumbled Rabaiz. "But hey, it's dark out now," he said, glancing through a narrow window near the ceiling that looked out into the sky. "What d'ya say we hit up Okka's place now?"

"That dirty Draig?" laughed the frizzy-haired girl who'd introduced herself as Naoyla. "I'm down. Let's hit it."

They all jumped up in unison, Avalon taking the hand of a confused Jem. "What's happening?" he asked as she pulled him behind her while the group went out the front door.

"Going to prank Okka," said Avalon casually.

"Why?"

"'Cause he's a Draig, of course."

"So?"

"So, we prank Draigs. That's how it works."

Sounded stupid to Jem, but he just stayed quiet and went along with it. He didn't have much other choice; it was true that he technically could leave—but he didn't want all these people to dislike him, especially Avalon.

After walking in the darkest parts of the city, through tight alleys and up a secluded staircase to the top of a building in an obviously Draig part of town, they were facing Councilmember Okka's home.

"There it is," said Rabaiz. "Everybody ready?"

All six of the Fenics nodded, Jem just looked around trying to figure out what was going on. They all sat crouched at the edge of the building watching the street.

"We're waiting for Okka to return," explained Avalon. "He usually leaves the Council Center just after dark."

"What's gonna happen when he gets here?" whispered Jem, not wanting the other Fenics to hear the worry in his voice.

"You'll see," she smiled mysteriously.

"What if we get caught?" voiced the chubby boy who had introduced himself as Ennui.

"Shut up, En," spat Rabaiz. "You always were lame."

"Cool it, ya'll," said Naoyla. "I don't think you're lame, En," she added, patting Ennui on the shoulder.

Some people passed by on the street since it really wasn't too late out yet, but it was obvious when Okka got near because all the Fenics simultaneously crouched even lower. Jem was down low and behind everyone, so he could not see Okka but could hear the man's light footsteps just beyond the building.

He wanted to jump up and warn the kind man who had been his only advocate during the ECKO meetings, but he didn't even know what to warn him against. Not to mention that ruining the Fenics' plan would mean Avalon would never want to see him again, and he liked seeing her. Curiosity got the better of him, though, and he peeked over the shoulder of Tyyni to see Okka approaching the door to his home.

The door began to shimmer like Jem had seen doors do here, just before they disappear to allow the person to walk through, but as it shimmered away, a reflective liquid began to materialize above him. It was almost as if the door had melted into water and moved above him. When the door completely disappeared and Okka was directly in front of the doorway, the large pool of water released from its position above him and drenched him.

The Fenics burst out into laughter. Rabaiz jumped to his feet and blew a powder from his hands before turning and running back down the stairs behind the building. The others ran too, but Jem watched as the powder Rabaiz had blown turned into a bright, flaming phoenix and flew overhead of Okka's home in circles.

"Jem!" yelled Avalon. "Let's go!"

But Jem was torn; Okka was down there, watching the phoenix circle above him, with the saddest look on his face, and the poor old man must have been freezing now in his robes.

"Jem!" Avalon grabbed his arm and tugged. "We gotta go!" He complied, allowing himself to once again be dragged by her, this time away from the area. They descended the same staircase and took off for the Nest.

Before they could catch up to the rest of the Fenics, however, Jem stopped Avalon.

"Wait, I'm actually gonna go," he told her. "Lots of stuff to do with ECKO tonight, but thanks for having me."

He didn't know why he added that last part. He certainly was not thankful for watching his only ally in the Fortress Council get drenched in water.

"Okay. Thanks for coming, Jem. It meant a lot to me," she said softly, wrapping her arms around his neck.

Jem didn't have time to react before she was pressing her lips against his. It was only for a moment, but time had this weird way of freezing as he considered what was going on. When she released him, she was blushing and smiling, and Jem was sure that he looked dumb as a post.

"Bye," she said lightly, turning and following after her friends.

"Bye," he uttered stupidly as she left. He was completely speechless.

Snap out of it, he told himself. *You had a reason for leaving now.* He jolted himself back to reality and turned to go back to Okka's house. He could think about the kiss later. The kiss... he had had his first kiss!

Okka was still outside by the doorway of his home, but he was pointing his hands up at the phoenix that was still fluttering around and moving his hands in a fluid, wave-like motion. Slowly, the phoenix got dimmer and dimmer, and then went out. Okka made to enter the house, and Jem ran out from his cover of darkness.

"Wait, Okka! Can I talk to you?"

"Why, sure, Jem," said Okka, obviously surprised at his appearance, "but you have chosen a strange time to arrive. I was just ambushed by a good bit of water."

"I saw," said Jem as Okka ushered him inside.

"Ruuna!" called Okka, peeling off his yellow outer robe to reveal just a thin, sleeveless white shirt and orange pants. He kicked his soaked sandals off and they slopped noisily against the wall. "Ruuna? You home?" he called again.

"Is there any way I can help?" asked Jem. "Magic the water off maybe? I never really learned how to evaporate water, though..."

"No need, Jem," smiled Okka. "This is enchanted water. It can't be magicked away."

Wow, thought Jem. *They really tried hard to make this miserable for him.*

"Poor Fenics," continued Okka, "don't hardly know what they're doing."

"Oh, Fenics did this to you?" asked Jem, trying to sound as surprised as possible.

Okka looked at Jem for a moment, perhaps to see if he was lying, or—as Jem felt it—to give him another moment to tell the truth. Jem glanced away momentarily and then back to Okka's eyes.

"Yes," said the old man finally. "Yes, Fenics did this to me. You could tell by the Phoenix flying in the sky. They leave it as their mark. Plus, I'm a Draig, so there is no need for any Draig to do this to me."

Jem grinned uneasily. Did he know that Jem had been a part of this? *No,* Jem told himself, *you weren't a part of it... you just... didn't do anything to stop it. And that's not your fault, is it?* He wasn't sure. It felt like he had done something terribly wrong.

"Yes, hun?" came a voice from the nearby room. A man then walked in of about the same height as Okka, but with grey hair instead of snow white hair, darker skin, and a larger nose. "Oh my gosh, what happened to you?" he gasped, waving his hand to evaporate the water.

"No use, Ruuna," explained Okka. "Enchanted water."

"Damn Fenics," grunted Ruuna. "I'll be right back, hun; let me grab you some dry clothes."

"Thanks, love," beamed Okka.

Ruuna left the room in a hurry and Okka turned to Jem who had an unintentionally surprised look on his face.

"That is my partner, Ruuna, if you hadn't picked up," explained Okka. Jem felt the same minor shock he had when he had learned of Sam and Henry, but it quickly subsided into acceptance. Okka seemed happy, so why should it matter if Ruuna were a man or woman?

"Is he a Draig?" asked Jem, attempting to make some sort of casual conversation out of it. He knew the answer, though, since Ruuna had been wearing yellow and orange pajamas when he had entered.

"Yes, of course, Jem. Intersystem relationships have been attempted, but they rarely work out. The two systems, Fenic and Draig, clash far too much on the most vital of topics. Their disputes are unavoidable. Please, have a seat," he added, motioning for one of the wooden chairs by the warm fire.

"Thanks," said Jem, sitting down. "So why did you put out the phoenix as it was flying around?"

Okka had his back turned as he hung his robes up to dry, but he answered, "Because, Jem, if I hadn't put it out, it may have flown into someone's home and set it aflame. We wouldn't want that!"

"But if it did, that would be the Fenics fault, right? And they'd get blamed?"

"Does it matter who was at fault if a home is burnt down?" asked Okka, turning and staring Jem in the eyes. "We may have our disputes, but I respect my fellow Keladonians: Fenic, Draig, or whatever else they may be."

"Are there other options, other systems?"

"No," laughed Okka. "But many don't truly believe it. I've tutored many students who laugh at the idea that our world was created by the Dragon, just as I've met Fenics who don't believe the Phoenix made it. And as I see both Draigs and Fenics behave in ways outside our respective scriptures, I know they don't truly follow and believe it."

"Here you go!" called Ruuna as he came stumbling into the room with fresh pajama-looking clothes. Okka waved his hands and his wet clothes were replaced with the fresh ones. Jem had to stifle a laugh because Okka looked hilariously out of place in the bright pajamas, and his big plump belly made him look somewhat like a Santa Claus who had trimmed his beard.

"Ruuna, this is Jem, by the way," explained Okka as Ruuna wrapped a blanket around him. "He is one of the refugees from Callisto."

"Oh, pleasure to meet you," said Ruuna, fist bumping Jem.

The couple sat down together on the couch across from Jem, and Ruuna floated in a plate of tea from the kitchen.

"So, Jem, have you decided on a system yet?" asked Ruuna. "The Draigs are a large, welcoming community and—"

"Ruuna!" interjected Okka. "There is no need to indoctrinate him. I'm sure he will make a wise, informed decision on his own, whether it be Draig, Fenic, or neither."

Ruuna flinched at the word "neither," and Jem was starting to get the feeling that not being Draig or Fenic meant being ostracized from both sides.

"But, Jem, if you do ever have any questions, about the Draig or Fenic system, feel free to approach me," smiled Okka, sipping on his hot tea.

"Thanks, Okka," said Jem. This man was too nice. "Well, I'm gonna head out, I just wanted to make sure you were okay after I saw the water."

"Well, as you can tell, I'm very well cared for," said Okka, brushing up against Ruuna. "Have a wonderful night, Jem."

"Thanks," said Jem.

"And nice meeting you!" said Ruuna.

"You too!"

"Oh, and Jem," said Okka, as Jem was walking out the door. "Don't let the people you are around dictate who you are."

"Right," said Jem, giving a weak smile and shutting the door behind him. He walked quietly back to the Refugee District, now quite unsure about everything.

Justin Dennis

CHAPTER 10:
MISS ARGO THE GREAT

Sierra was clinging onto her dad's back so tightly that she had long ago lost feeling in her arms. They were moving fast, trying to put as much distance between them and that prison as possible, and the rushing ground below her didn't look very inviting.

She still hadn't received an explanation for why a Reg was helping them. They hadn't stopped yet for anything, but they needed to soon because Sierra's mouth was painfully dry and her stomach was roaring for food.

Rimaya had woken up eventually, and at first, she had tried to fight Tachel who was behind her holding the handles to the sylphcycle, almost causing them to crash. But she was too weak to do any real damage and Leo rode up beside her and reassured her that it was okay. She relaxed hesitantly and rested her head forward on the front of the cycle.

"We need to stop soon," yelled Sierra in her dad's ear. "Me and Rimaya are both too weak and hungry and thirsty."

Leo nodded and motioned Tachel towards a small forest. They had just passed the Argo-Neora border a few minutes ago, and Sierra had been shocked to see that her dad had willingly crossed the border. She remembered the horror stories he had used to tell her about the people who had crossed the border. She herself had been apprehensive when Jem and Oliver had tried to get her to cross into Ilios all that time ago.

But when they had switched from the long, luscious Argonian grass to the shorter, vivid green Neoran grass, Sierra had only felt her dad tense up, as if expecting to possibly hit an invisible wall, and then relax moments after they had passed. But he didn't slow down or hesitate in any way. Something had changed. Sierra knew that. Ever since he had blasted open the door to his cell, she knew something had changed. The dad that she remembered never would have rebelled.

When they reached the forest, Leo and Tachel slowed down and carefully maneuvered their cycles around the skinny, awkward trees. The large, funny-looking leaves skimmed over their heads as they went through, dripping light dew over them. They found a clearing and set up a small camp. Leo started a fire while Tachel cast spells around them to alert them if Regs got close.

Leo removed his large, dark red shirt and gave it to Rimaya who was shaking violently while lying beside the fire. Sierra cuddled close to her, trying to keep warm too, but she was in much better condition than Rimaya at least. Tachel eventually came and sat across from them in his pure black Reg outfit.

"They need food," said Tachel matter-of-factly.

Leo glared at him. "I know," he said, "but you know what Veroci did to the crops."

"I know I can reverse it too," grunted Tachel, dropping his scepter in front of him.

"You can?" gasped Leo, jumping to his feet. "Well, what are you waiting for?" He ran over and began to pick all the dead, shriveled fruit from the trees and bushes surrounding them. In a moment, he returned with his arms full of them and dropped them in front of Tachel.

Tachel took his scepter and, as it glowed an eerie red, touched it against the cluster of blackened fruit. The first fruit slowly became colorful and then plumped up until it was a full, ripe fruit. Gradually, the fruit around it began to do the same until they had a smorgasbord of Neoran fruits. Tachel picked one up and smiled, tossing it over the fire to Sierra.

She wanted to be suspicious of it—a recently dead fruit restored by a Reg she wasn't fully sure she trusted—but her hunger overcame her suspicion, and she bit into the delicious, juicy fruit. Leo took one and fed it to the barely conscious Rimaya was soon a little more lively and able to eat by herself. Within minutes, both girls were stuffed full of fruit and felt a thousand times better.

"Alright," said Rimaya, finishing the last of her fruit and holding her hands out by the fire, "you said you'd explain: who's the Reg?"

"I've got a name," spat Tachel.

"You're all the same," retorted Rimaya.

"Hey! I saved your life! You could be a little more grateful."

Rimaya glared at him from across the fire.

"Tachel befriended me," explained Leo. "After Veroci took over Eltaes—it wasn't that long after you both left—they set up that prison. Everyone was forced into it and the ones who refused—"

"Killed 'em?" cut in Rimaya.

"Yeah," said Leo solemnly, tossing a stick into the fire.

"Yeah, they tend to do that," grunted Rimaya, glaring again at Tachel who shook his head and looked away.

"They got Stan," said Leo in an empty, quiet voice.

"Stan?" repeated both Sierra and Rimaya. There was silence as they let the name float in the air for a moment, the tragedy of it sinking into their skin. Sierra remembered her dad yelling for Stan as Stan's partner, Anne, was killed by Gurant and his lightning whip. Stan had given in then and had allowed Anne to die because he had been afraid of the Regime. Sierra found it ironic that when Stan had finally stood his ground, he had been killed.

"So then what?" asked Rimaya, breaking the silence and stirring Sierra back into reality. "How'd you meet *him*?"

"I wanted out," sighed Tachel, before Leo could respond. His voice sounded older than he looked, but also immature in a way—like a scared child in a twenty-something's body. He snapped a twig into pieces and flicked them into the fire.

"I wanted out," he repeated. "So I tried to find a rebel—any rebel who had survived the takeover. Then one day, I caught Leo practicing magic—" Rimaya perked up at this, giving her father a curious, proud look. "—and so I asked him to teach me. As a Reg, I never learned magic aside from this damn scepter. I never wanted this... any of this. I understand your hatred towards the Regime, Rimaya, I do, but I hate them too. That's why I got out."

Rimaya gave him a weak nod, as if unsure whether or not to believe him. "Thanks, I guess," she said, "for saving me."

"Hm, anytime," he smirked.

"We rehearsed that whole escaping scenario a lot," explained Leo. "The final wall to block them from chasing us was the most difficult. I didn't think we'd get it, but we did!" Silence for a moment. "What happened to you two?" continued Leo, his voice now full of worry.

"I left Eltaes," explained Sierra, "with Jem and Oliver—"

"I knew it!" growled Leo. "I'll kill 'em!"

"Dad, no! I chose to. I wanted to stop the Regime; you saw what they did to Anne! I went all over Callisto with Jem. Oliver had to go back home..."

"To Kepler?" interjected Leo.

"Not exactly," said Sierra. She and Rimaya glanced at each other, deciding to share everything with their father for the first time. "Jem and Oliver are from Earth—another world," began Sierra. "The Ilian Elder opened a portal for Oliver to go back because his family was sick. After that, the Regime captured us, but Farouche—a kid we met in Ilios—helped us escape."

"That was you guys?" interrupted Tachel. "I was in Xena—in a small town in the northeast—when they sounded the alarms alerting everybody of the escaped fugitives."

Sierra smiled. "It was us. We went to Radeon and stayed with Rick. Dad, you remember Rick."

"Yeah, I remember him," grunted Leo. "Ran off with some girl, damn bordercrossers."

"Hey, you're a bordercrosser now too," shot Rimaya.

Leo laughed lightly. "I guess so. Anyway, Sierra, continue."

"Right, well we stayed with him and then went north to Luria to join the rebellion. Jem was attacked by the Dragon. You remember the Red Dragon from the cave? It bit him, but it gave him dragon powers. Then we flew to the North Island, and we fought Atychis."

"The old Argonian Elder?" gasped Leo. "You fought him? Sierra!"

"Dad, relax. Obviously, I'm fine. Him and the Dragon had been tracking us, trying to kill Jem because Veroci had ordered him to. Veroci is still out for Jem. We don't really know why." She didn't want to freak out her father by telling him that Jem may be related to Veroci.

"And I escaped prison," explained Rimaya, "with help from ECKO—it's an organization that's helping to fight the Regime. Then we flew in a flying machine called a vimana to get Sierra and Jem from the island. Since then, we've been living in Luria. We couldn't get to you because of the barrier separating the East from the West, and when the Regime took over Luria, we fled through a portal to a world called Kelados."

"But we came right back," said Sierra, "to get you."

Leo gave a shocked smile. "Wow. Quite the adventure."

"So we goin' to Kelados?" asked Tachel.

"Yeah," said Rimaya. "We've got a portal open in a forest near central Neora. We can make it there in the next few hours."

"So we should get going?" asked Tachel, getting ready to stand up.

"No," said Sierra, louder than she had intended. "I have a question, dad."

"Yes?"

She watched the fire crackle for a minute, trying to get the emotion out of her voice before she spoke. "Why now?" she blurted. Her attempts to hide the emotion in her voice failed.

They all looked confused at the sudden outburst, even Rimaya. "What do you mean?" asked Leo.

"Why now?" repeated Sierra, throwing her hands up. "Why are you rebellious *now*? We had all these years at home where we were suppressed, told not to use magic for this or for that. Rimaya never listened, that's why I admired her, but I looked to you for guidance, dad, and you never questioned the laws, the stupid magic rules. Until all of a sudden, we come to rescue you, and you blast the cell door with magic, break out of a Regime prison, and use a sylphcycle. Why are you rebelling *now*? Why not before, when we needed it?"

She was almost in tears. Her eyes were red and watery, but she kept any tears from falling. The anger and confusion in her voice, though, had been apparent. For a moment, Leo didn't know how to respond.

"I... I'm sorry," he said finally. "I was... I just..." he looked around nervously. Rimaya and Sierra were both staring at him, eagerly waiting for an answer. Even Tachel seemed interested. Leo picked some of the leaves off the twig he was holding and fidgeted with them nervously.

"It was... your mom," he said finally, avoiding both his daughters' eyes.

"Mom!?" they both blurted, completely shocked.

Leo nodded grimly. "Ari was a rebel—oh yes, she was a rebel. Loved magic! Couldn't stand Veroci's oppression."

Sierra and Rimaya's jaws were on the floor. They had never discussed their mom with their dad; it was just an unspoken rule. It was incredible to hear him talk about her in such a loving tone, especially since she herself had been a rebel.

"I know of ECKO," he continued, pointing his twig at Rimaya. "In fact, your mother founded the ECKO division in Argo."

Rimaya and Sierra stared at him in complete disbelief.

"Sadly, though, I haven't heard from any ECKO members in thirteen years... since Ari died."

Silence.

"What... what happened?" asked Rimaya before Sierra could open her mouth. They both had always wanted to know the truth about their mother.

"We were both active members of ECKO. Actually, that was how I met your mother was at the first meeting for all of Argo. ECKO already had bases in the other five regions, but it was your mother who organized everything in Argo. It was fantastic, really. She was such a leader, such an activist.

"And so we regularly worked at the Argo base in Kapina, a city not too far from where I grew up, Eltaes. She lived in Kapina, but eventually, she agreed to move with me to Eltaes, which was not an easy decision for her. Leaving her hometown to come to some small farm town with me must have been hard... but we were in love and we thought Eltaes would be a better place to raise a family. We still went to Kapina everyday on a sylphquad to work at the ECKO base, though.

"But after we had you two, we started spending less and less time there, since we had to be home to take care of you both. It was mostly my responsibility; your mom was so wrapped up with her work. But she loved you both, very much." His voice snagged again.

"She was fighting for a better future for you two, for all of us. She managed to bring three worlds together. She accomplished amazing things in her lifetime, and all she wanted to do was open the doors for cooperation between Earth, Callisto, and Kelados. The leaders from the other worlds, although they agreed to be a part of ECKO, refused cooperation except in the case of a world threatening emergency, but she insisted on working together.

"One day, she had a very important meeting: she was to meet with the leaders from the five other regions. Her goal was to get them all to work together better and agree to try and improve our relations with Earth and Kelados. I had wanted to attend, but, Sierra, you had gotten very sick, and I stayed to tend to you. Our neighbors offered to babysit, but I wouldn't have someone else caring for my children when I should be. So I stayed home and took care of you. Rimaya, you were very helpful that day, helping me take care of your sister."

Leo gave a weak smile to his daughters as tears welled up in his eyes and his voice became shaky.

"But your mom never came home that day. I learned later that Veroci's Regime had attacked the base and killed everyone inside." He paused. "When the Regime finally came to Eltaes... you can imagine my fury. I wanted to kill every Reg I saw because I knew what they had done to my love, your mother. But I couldn't bring myself to fight them. You two needed at least one parent, and if I were taken to prison, you would be alone. I chose you two over rebellion.

"You see, it was never that I sided with Veroci; I just needed to ensure that I was going to be around to raise you girls. I've always been a rebel at heart, and I will always loath Veroci and his Regime with everything I have."

Rimaya and Sierra dragged themselves closer to their father and leaned into his chest. They all sobbed lightly, and Tachel pretended to be occupied by a very interesting twig.

"Dad," said Sierra between sobs. "I threw out mom's doll, the Miss Argo the Great doll."

This made Leo laugh slightly. "Good. I always hated that doll."

Sierra looked up at him, confused. "Huh? Then why'd mom give it to me?"

"Because it shut you up when you were crying," smiled Leo. "You used to nibble on its little head and throw it across the room to have it walk back to you. Could entertain you for hours! She never liked the doll, though, either; she hoped you would grow up to be so much more than just another Miss Argo and, well, you've certainly lived up to her expectations there, sweetie."

A warm feeling of comfort lit up Sierra's insides. By being herself and not obeying the path Argo had set out for her, she had lived up to her mother's ambitious expectations. The gratification was incredible.

"I can't believe you're a rebel, dad," voiced Rimaya, nuzzling against him. "I'm so proud of you."

"Well," said Tachel after a few moments, "you've all had your moment. Can we get headed for this portal now? I don't feel like waiting around much longer for the rest of the Regs to catch up with us."

The others agreed, so they put out their fire, mounted their sylphcycles, and took off to the east. Sierra couldn't wait to get back to Kelados.

Justin Dennis

CHAPTER 11:
THE RAID

Jem woke up that morning somewhat hoping that the night before had been a dream. He pushed Snovel away from him and threw off the old blankets. Rubbing his eyes, he tried to recall everything that had happened. Avalon's friends—the Nest Fenics—had pranked Okka by pouring enchanted water all over him, Avalon had kissed Jem, and Jem had been introduced to Okka's partner, Ruuna. That was definitely real, not a dream. He could still feel that last hint of Avalon's lips on his and smell her light, flowery scent.

But, said a voice in the back of his mind, *what about Sierra?*

He shook his head and rubbed his eyes once more, trying to get some clarity; his head felt foggy and heavy. He stood up, ignoring Snovel's light growls, and tiptoed by Farouche and Cyneal who were both fast asleep. Everyone, in fact, was still asleep; he must have been up pretty early. This was confirmed as he stepped outside the building and saw that the sun was just barely rising. He considered trying to find some food, but he really wasn't hungry; instead, he tried to find a place to be alone.

As he walked along the giant wall dividing the city and the Refugee District, he dragged his fingers along it. For a split second, he let one of his fingers become a dragon claw, and he scraped the wall a couple inches deep. It felt good to use his dragon powers, and he wished that he could push out his wings and take off, but he knew that would send the city into a riot if a dragon was spotted.

Soon he came to the pond where Avalon had originally found him. It was strange to think that a week ago he had not even known her. He had probably been in Callisto having pains and having Sierra take care of him. Sierra... where was she? Had she found her dad yet? He panicked for a moment, worried for her safety, but then he recalled her fighting the Dragon and Atychis on the North Island, and he realized that she had handled much tougher things. She would surely comeback unscathed.

He plopped down against a large boulder and faced the wall. Delicately, he began to spew sylph from his fingers. The magical substance had always fascinated him, but he still found it strange that his was silver and everybody else's was a misty blue. He couldn't understand why; his magic was certainly no better than anybody else's, and it had been silver even before the Dragon had bit him.

He swirled it around his fingers, twirling it in intricate loops for a moment before combining it all into a ball about the size of a tennis ball. Then he tossed it against the wall and had it come back to him—it bounced like a tennis ball too. He did this over and over rhythmically. It helped him clear his mind.

Avalon had kissed him. He had had his first kiss and had it in a new world with someone he only met a few days ago. For some reason, he had always pictured his first kiss being with Sierra, but now everything was upside down. He had been very close to Sierra for almost a year after venturing across Callisto and living in Luria for a few months, and they had never kissed. With Avalon, it only took a few days. Did that mean anything? Did that mean that Avalon was who he should be with?

How would Sierra feel, though? He couldn't imagine. He tried to picture Sierra with another guy and his stomach clenched up disapprovingly. Maybe he shouldn't be with Avalon; maybe his heart really was with Sierra. She did seem to care about him a lot, especially caring for him all those months when he was sick from the dragon poison. He was still sick—he still had the vomiting and the terrors that kept him awake at night. Would Avalon be just as helpful and understanding?

He threw the ball with force against the wall and it almost hit him in the face as it rebounded back.

He wanted Oliver back. Oliver would've known exactly what to do in this scenario. Farouche said he was working on making another set of rendomuffs so that Jem could talk to Oliver, since the others had been lost in Luria, but they still weren't ready. He would have so much to tell Oliver when they could finally talk. Heck, Oliver didn't even know that they were living in Kelados now. The only time Jem had ever mentioned Kelados was when he had told him that he had been able to manipulate the portal to Kelados that Afflatus had made.

That's right... he had been able to manipulate a portal. And maybe if he had been able to manipulate one, he could actually make one. Afflatus had sounded very surprised when Jem had told him what he had done, and he had even told Jem later on that his portal ability was unique. In fact, if his memory served him right, Afflatus had even said that it would be a "useful skill" in the future.

Well, what better time to try that out then right now? thought Jem.

Jem allowed the sylph ball to disappear back into his palm and then focused his hands ahead of him. He put two fingers from each hand together and concentrated all of his energy there. Silver mist began to swirl around his fingers and hands, but as he pulled his fingers apart, there was nothing there except more silver mist.

He lost concentration and the mist disappeared. This time, he tried putting out all of his fingers in an attempt to grab the edges of the portal he wanted to form. Silver mist began to form around his fingertips, and he could feel the physical ledge of something invisible. He tried to grip harder, but that forced it to slip away. His hands smacked against his legs below, and the mist disappeared.

Frustration almost got the better of him, but he closed his eyes, took a few deep breaths, and tried again. He put his fingertips together so that his nails were touching and began to feel for the edge again. Within a couple minutes, his fingers nestled into a certain groove, and he felt a definite physical touch on something. There was no mist; instead, his hands almost gave off a slight glow.

He slowly and carefully began to pull apart the invisible thing that he had a grip on. It took all his energy and strength to bring it apart, but he was able to do it. Between his hands grew a small space that was a hazy combination of the wall ahead of him and sparkling water. As his hands got a couple inches apart, the wall behind faded away, and he saw only glistening blue water.

When he had stretched the portal out to about the size of a grapefruit, he paused for a moment to admire what he was seeing: endless water without land, buildings, or civilization in sight. It was gorgeous and captivating. He gently let go of the edges of the portal, suspending it in midair, and moved to put one hand through it.

"Jem!"

The voice threw him off, and the portal dissolved away into the air, leaving only the dull city wall to stare back at him.

"Jem, there you are," said Avalon, sauntering on over to him from behind a nearby building. "I couldn't find you anywhere."

"Yeah?" said Jem, not really wanting her company right then.

"What're you doing out here all by yourself?" she asked, smiling at him and tossing her hair.

"Nothing really, just... thinking."

"Hmm," she said, coming to stand beside where he was sitting. She put one leg over him and sat down, straddling him. "I wanted to apologize for last night," she said lightly. "I didn't mean to make you uncomfortable."

"R-right," stammered Jem, slightly enamored by her scent and closeness.

Was she talking about the prank? Or the kiss?

"That's just how things are done around here," she explained. "We mess with Draigs; Draigs mess with us. It's a constant cycle."

"Isn't that a little…" he turned his head away from her, avoiding her intense grey-green eyes, "pointless?"

"No," she whispered in his ear, "that's just the way it is, and the way it will always be."

"You could change it, if you wanted," he whispered back. "You don't have to be a part of it."

"No, Jem, I do," she said with more vulnerability in her voice. She drew her head back but remained close. "Those are my friends."

"Are they really your friends if they wouldn't support your choice to stop pranking Draigs?"

"I have responsibilities to the rest of them, Jem, and so do you. You're a Fenic now."

"I'm not—"

But his words were cut short as Avalon pressed her warm lips against his. Jem pulled back, but she remained firmly glued to him for several seconds. In this time, Jem heard rustling coming from nearby and then a light gasp.

He finally wrenched out of the kiss and opened his eyes just in time to see Sierra's shocked face before she turned and ran away from him.

"Sierra! No, wait!" he yelled, attempting to get to his feet, but Avalon kept pulling him back.

"Don't worry about her, Jem," she insisted, grabbing his arms and torso in an attempt to keep him there. "She'll be fine. Stay here with me."

"Let go!" demanded Jem. "No, I have to go after her! Do you realize what you've done? SIERRA!" he added, yelling towards where she had disappeared. He finally shook off Avalon's hands and took off after Sierra.

He continued to yell her name as he zipped past building after building, almost knocking over a few people in the process. He would just barely see her heels as she disappeared behind each building, but it was enough for him to keep after her. She was zigzagging through the randomly sprawled out buildings and was headed right for the entrance to the city.

They finally made it past most of the buildings and into the small open area just before the major archway leading into the city. Jem, panting hard, tried to call her name once more. She didn't even look back.

Suddenly, a deafeningly loud alarm sounded. It didn't even seem to have a source—the noise just exploded from everywhere, wailing a painful shriek similar to that of a fire alarm. The entire Fortress darkened as a shimmering, dark blue, magical force field shot up from the outer walls and began to encapsulate the entire city, partially blocking the sun's light.

Sierra continued to run despite all of this, but the only entrance from the

Refugee District to the rest of the city was closing, its massive stone doors gradually swinging shut. The alarms made Jem want to lie down and cover his ears, but he ignored this instinct and continued to run after Sierra.

He wasn't quick enough, though. Sierra slipped nimbly in between the closing doors, but Jem smacked right into them just as they locked into place. He banged his fists against them violently, but that merely bruised his hands and did nothing to reopen the doors. He didn't care anymore about people knowing he was a dragon. Whatever those alarms were going off for couldn't be good, and Sierra could have been in serious trouble over there where she didn't know anyone. Even if she hated him now, he had to make sure she was safe.

Jem braced his feet and began to sprout the dragon wings from his back, but just as he felt them emerging from the center of his back, a strong hand pushed against them, and he receded them back in.

"She's safe," Avalon yelled in his ear over the noise of the alarm. "It's only a drill. Don't risk it."

***

"How much longer is Avalon gonna be?" groaned Jario. The gang was standing just outside the entrance to the Refugee District waiting for her.

"Who knows?" grunted Rabaiz. "Too busy snogging that refugee scum."

"What's wrong with Jem?" asked Tyyni, smacking Rabaiz on the arm. "Seemed like a nice kid to me."

"There's something wrong with anyone who ain't a Draig or a Fenic. I mean, what does he believe in?"

"Who cares? It's none of your business."

"It's all of our business," defended Rabaiz, "if he's a thing with Avalon."

"She wouldn't go for him," said Ennui. "Too funny-looking."

"Agreed," said Naoyla, "not the most attractive option out there for the Council Spokesperson's daughter."

"Well, maybe he makes her happy," said Tyyni shyly.

"How could she be happy with someone who ain't a Fenic?" spat Jario. "We all know she'd only love a Fenic—just like any of us."

"Well, if there are entire other worlds that have no Fenics or Draigs, what if neither of us are right?" asked Tyyni, but immediately she regretted asking it as they all lashed out at her.

"Of course Fenic is right!"

"How could you question it?"

"Don't be stupid, Tyyni."

"You know in your heart that the Phoenix looks after you."

"Alright, alright, sorry I asked…" she said wearily.

Just then, the all too familiar sound of the zombie invasion alarm went off. They had been prepared for it—after all, everyone in the Fortress outside of the Refugee District had been notified that a drill would be taking place today—they just didn't think it would happen while Avalon was in the Refugee District. They all clasped their hands over their ears to wait out the noise. They saw the doors closing to the Refugee District, but knew there was nothing they could do to stop them from shutting; they would reopen in a few minutes anyway.

As they began to walk away to find a bunker to stay in, a short, brown-haired girl came flying out from the Refugee District just as the doors were shutting and crashed into one of them.

Sierra felt really bad. She hadn't been looking where she was going and had completely fallen on top of this person. She rubbed her eyes to get the tears out and smiled at the cute boy beneath her.

"Well, hi," said Rabaiz.

CHAPTER 12:
REMEMBRANCE

What was this place?

Jem was wandering through the jungle, tripping over roots and pushing apart vines. It was a distinctly Earth-like environment—chimpanzees grunted in the distance, birds chirped—but at the same time, it was very alien. He had never seen or been to this place, and the enormous trees were intimidating.

"Oliver!" he called. "I know you're in here somewhere."

As if his words had summoned all the animals in the area, flocks of birds began to fly above him and a stampede of chimps came from every direction. Some deer ran by and even a lion. Jem was pretty sure lions didn't belong in rainforests.

"Hey! What are you doing?" he demanded of the chimps as they lifted him up as a group and began to carry him through the forest.

"Could you please be quiet, sir?" requested the chimp nearest his head in an eloquent British accent. "We are merely performing the task that was asked of us."

Jem, too confused by the fact that a chimp had just spoken to him, didn't respond. Soon, they emerged from the forest and the chimps lowered him onto the bright yellow, sandy ground. Ahead of him was a single palm tree before a massive, crystal blue ocean. At the top of the palm tree was a comfy looking chair with a boy sitting in it. The boy stood up and dove off the palm tree as if into a pool, but then began to fly back up and gradually floated to the ground before Jem.

"Bit of an improvement since the last time we talked," laughed Jem. "Monkey servants, really?"

"We're chimpanzees, sir," said the chimp nearest him in a polite tone.

"Exactly," laughed Oliver, hugging his friend. "Don't insult my chimps."

"The British accents may have been overkill," said Jem. "But how'd you pull off the flying thing?"

"It's a dream, Jem. I can do whatever I want. So can you!"

"Really? How?"

"You're the one who can transform into a dragon," laughed Oliver. "I'd think you'd know how to fly."

With that, Oliver kicked off the ground and flew back up into the clear blue sky. He did a quick backflip and took his seat at the top of the palm tree. Jem also kicked off and followed him, but didn't even attempt the backflip. It wasn't like being a dragon where he felt in control and powerful; it was more like his body had lost all of its weight and he was floating uselessly. Oliver handled the dream-flight much better.

"So what gives?" asked Oliver after Jem finally sat down beside him at the top of the palm tree. "We haven't talked in like three weeks!"

"Well, a lot's been going on," sighed Jem, and he told the story of how the Regime had invaded Luria and forced them all to flee to Kelados. He mentioned that he was only able to talk to him now because Farouche had finally made another pair of rendomuffs. Then he described Sierra and Rimaya's mission to get Leo back. Rimaya had explained it to him, since Sierra wasn't talking to him. Then he explained about Avalon and how she had kissed him in front of Sierra.

"You're kidding!" exclaimed Oliver. "That sucks! Did you try explaining it to Sierra?

"Of course, but she wasn't going to listen to me after that. She found someone else too, this prick named Rabaiz who's one of the kids Avalon hangs out with."

"I think your life just became a soap opera," laughed Oliver. Jem threw a coconut at him, almost knocking him out of the tree.

"Shut up," said Jem. "She hasn't said a word to me since she's been back, and it's weird not having her around."

"But you have Avalon, right?"

"Yeah, so? It's not the same."

"Yeah, I know what you mean. Those Terello girls…"

Jem eyed his friend suspiciously. "What do you mean *those* Terello girls?"

Oliver's eyes went wide like he'd been caught in a lie. "Um…" he began. "Well, when you all were back in Luria, me and Rimaya would talk a lot. Like more often than you and me did. She would borrow the rendomuffs too and we would coordinate times to meet up. It was really cool 'cause it was like we could actually hang out even though we're in different worlds."

"You're in love with Maya!" yelled Jem.

"Hey! I didn't say that. I just like talking to her."

"You seeing anyone from Earth?"

"No, but—"

"You looooove her!"

"Shut up!" yelled Oliver, this time throwing several coconuts at Jem and successfully knocking him out of the tree. Thankfully, Jem was able to use his awkward dream-flying ability to get back up to the top.

"You could've killed me!"

"It's a dream, Jem, you'd've woken up if you hit the ground."

"True, but knocking your friends out of dream-trees isn't how you deal with your denial," teased Jem.

Oliver crossed his arms and scowled. "Well, you love Sierra!"

Jem bit his lip and looked across the crashing waves on the shore. "Maybe," he said, the seriousness taking Oliver by surprise.

"What about Avalon?"

"I dunno... I like her too, I guess. She definitely cares about me. What if I love two people?"

Oliver shrugged. "Can that happen?"

"I dunno," said Jem. "Feels like it."

There was silence for a minute while the wind whistled the leaves.

"So what is next, with Callisto and ECKO and everything?" asked Oliver.

"I don't know exactly. I still need to talk to the Dragon, because it said that it was going to rid Kelados of the zombies, and I know that is what the Council wants. I don't know how to contact it, though, since I can't transform into a dragon and fly outside the Fortress—Aff says the Keladonians can't know I am a dragon."

"Why not?"

"Because they have these two groups, the Draigs and the Fenics, that make all the decisions for the Fortress. He says the Fenics would want to kill me just for being a dragon 'cause they believe the Phoenix is like the Ultimate Good and the Dragon is the Ultimate Bad, or something like that, and the Draigs believe the opposite."

"That's stupid," grunted Oliver. "But are you gonna take back Callisto?"

"The Council doesn't want to, and we don't have enough Callistonians to go back and fight the Regime. We need help from the Keladonians and they aren't willing to until the zombies are gone. So who knows? Maybe somehow we'll rid the whole world of zombies."

"I'm jealous; I'm still stuck here. When do I get to come back?"

"Whenever we can figure out how to get a portal to Earth. Afflatus says he can't do it, which I don't really understand since he can make them so easily to Kelados and Callisto, but Sam and Henry are working on another generator right now. They said it could be a while, though, before they finish since they don't have the same materials as they did on Earth."

"That sucks! I want to help. You know that."

"I know," sighed Jem. "How is your family holding up?"

"A lot better. Mom's getting that new liver she needs."

"Oh, you found a donor?"

Oliver laughed. "In America? Of course not. Too many people, not enough livers. But dad has a connection in Sweden at a medical hospital that has figured out how to grow a whole liver. We're lucky; this isn't exactly something that is available to most people. We leave tomorrow."

Jem smiled. "That's great. Well, we'll get you back when we can. I promise."

"Thanks, dude," said Oliver. "But I wanna get some sleep now. Real sleep. Good talking to you."

"You too," said Jem, standing up to leave.

"Oh, and Jem, could you give the rendomuffs to Maya next?"

Jem smiled. "Sure. Talk to you soon."

"Bye," smiled Oliver. And with that, Jem jumped from the palm tree and dissolved out of the dream, falling into a deep sleep.

When Jem woke up that morning, he had no motivation to go to the Council meeting with Afflatus. He knew it would be the same stubborn members arguing over the same pointless stuff. Instead, he went walking throughout the Fortress with Snovel by his side. He intentionally avoided areas where he knew Avalon liked to frequent and did his best to remain in purely Draig areas.

He passed by Rimaya and Cyneal once, as Rimaya had quickly declared herself a Draig and fell right into place with the other teenagers there. She was surrounded by too many people Jem didn't recognize, so he didn't bother to say, "Hi." Besides, he had already left the rendomuffs for her on her bed back in the Refugee District.

When he did pass through Fenic areas, many of the folks glared at him and Snovel. One old man even tried to kick Snovel as they went by, but it dodged the kick and flew quickly to the nearest Draig building. *How do these people all live together without killing each other?* thought Jem.

"Sorry, Snov," said Jem when he caught up, petting the dragonet on the head. "I wish we could fly away from here."

He really did. He had had enough of this stupid city. Avalon had destroyed his relationship with Sierra, and the bickering between the Draigs and Fenics was irritating. Actually, that was unfair. Avalon hadn't destroyed his relationship with Sierra; he had destroyed his relationship with Sierra. He couldn't blame Avalon for his own decisions. She was just being nice and doing what felt right, he supposed.

He still cared about Avalon very much; she made him feel more at home than anyone else did. That is why he continued to see her—but not today. Today, he had a lot on his mind and didn't want to deal with her. His pains had been more frequent too, and it was getting difficult to hide them from her. He also missed not having Sierra to comfort him on the nights when the pains got really bad.

There was a dinner planned for that night, though, a large feast between his refugee building and some of the others around it. He was hoping that maybe in the friendly atmosphere, he'd be able to talk to Sierra finally, but he knew the chances of that were slim.

Eventually, he had explored probably every Draig region of the city and had wound up on the outskirts against the giant wall. Being so close to the outside gave him an idea. He went behind a medium-sized stone building that looked like some sort of clothing store so that the outer wall was to his back, and he transformed his fingers into dragon claws. Together, he and Snovel scaled the side of the building and clambered onto the roof. From there, Jem retracted his claws, and it was only a short jump (helped with a little burst of magic) for him to land solidly on the outer wall. Snovel flew over swiftly and sat beside him.

"Wanna play fetch?" asked Jem.

Snovel nodded eagerly, dove down to the ground below, and scooped up a stone. It brought it back to Jem who made a slingshot of sylph and shot it far away for Snovel to fetch. It caught it swiftly in its mouth and brought it back for Jem. They did this for at least an hour, Jem's mind racing with thoughts of Sierra, Avalon, Oliver, and Callisto.

"You know you're not allowed to be on the wall."

Jem jumped to his feet and turned to see Afflatus standing on the building he had scaled earlier.

"Sorry," he said, rubbing the back of his head.

Afflatus kicked at the claw marks that were in the wall, and they magically mended themselves. "And what did I tell you about transforming?"

"Nobody could see me. It was just a short climb."

Afflatus half-jumped, half-floated from the building to the wall. His magic was much more refined and majestic than Jem's.

"Still, no dragon magic at all, Jem. I'm serious."

Jem sat back down on the edge of the wall, dangling his feet over. Afflatus sat beside him.

"I don't like it here," said Jem, gazing out at the sky where it turned from blue overhead to red far in the distance. In between it swirled in a captivating display of colors. "I want to go home. I want things to go back to normal."

"Whose normal?" asked Afflatus. "Your real normal is back on Earth, but that changed when you arrived in Callisto. Now you have arrived in Kelados, and this is normal, is it not?"

"I meant normal like…"

"Your few months in Luria?"

Jem nodded.

"Why is that normal?" continued Afflatus. "It was a very small portion of your life."

"Yes, but I felt at home there, Aff. I just want that back."

"Well, I am glad that you consider it your home. I consider it my home too."

"Don't you want to go back?" asked Jem, turning and looking at the old man's dark green eyes.

"Of course. Of course I want to go back, but it is important not to dwell on the past; instead, we should focus on the present and prepare for the future. That is not to say the past is not important—it is where we learn all our lessons from—but if we only miss what once was, we may never have it again."

Jem smiled. Snovel then landed beside him and dropped the rock in his lap. It laid its head down on his leg and looked up at him with its big black eyes.

"You seem to be in a much better mood, Aff."

Afflatus let out a big, toothy grin that reminded Jem of the eccentric, spirited old man he had originally met back in his cottage in Luria.

"I had a very enlightening discussion with Tekkara," he beamed. "That woman is brilliant and insightful, let me tell you."

"Glad to hear it," said Jem.

"Will you be attending the dinner tonight?" asked Afflatus.

"Yeah, I guess," said Jem. "Sierra will be there, right?"

"She does live in our building, so yes, she will be there," laughed Afflatus. "Why the nervousness?"

"Sierra hasn't said a word to me since she's been back. She saw me kissing Avalon," he admitted. Although he had been expecting shock, Afflatus merely let out a sly grin.

"That made her upset?"

"Apparently!" cried Jem. "But I don't get it, because me and Sierra never kissed."

"That doesn't matter. Feelings of love and attachment can go far beyond physical contact, Jem, and jealousy can be a powerful poison."

"I know," sighed Jem, thinking of how much he hated the fact that Sierra was hanging around Rabaiz now.

"So have you stopped seeing Avalon?" questioned Afflatus, raising one eyebrow at Jem.

Jem's face went red and he said embarrassedly, "No… I like seeing her. She really cares about me, and I care about her."

"But as long as you are seeing her, I don't imagine that Sierra will be very fond of you."

"Well, that just doesn't seem fair! Why can't I like Sierra and Avalon?"

Afflatus laughed lightly. "The same reason you wouldn't like for them to be with other people."

Jem immediately thought of Rabaiz. "That's confusing," he said, trying to justify why he could like Avalon but Sierra couldn't like Rabaiz. "What if I didn't mind them being with other people?"

"Then I guess that could work," said Afflatus, "if they didn't mind either."

"Hm," grunted Jem, swinging his legs idly and staring out across Kelados.

"Life is always going to be confusing, especially relationships, but as long as you are mindful of your feelings and the feelings of those around you, you should come out just fine."

Jem grinned weakly. That was possibly the vaguest advice he had ever been given. "Thanks, Aff," he said meekly.

"We should get going to prepare for tonight's dinner," said Afflatus after a moment.

"Sounds good," said Jem, and with that, they headed back for the Refugee District.

By the time they had organized all the food and everything, the sky had grown dark and the air had gotten slightly chilly. They had prepared a giant fire in the center courtyard between many of the buildings and used magic to contain it in a bubble so that it wouldn't spark on them or spread outward. The visual effect was magnificent as the flames licked the insides of the bubble and curled in on themselves.

Different foods that Jem didn't recognize were skewered on metal rods that hung across the fire, cooking. Each person used magic to cut their share and bring it to their plate. Bowls of vegetables and plates of sweets also made their rounds. Chairs had been set up all around the fire and people from the five surrounding buildings were invited. Not everybody had come, but enough had that it was very crowded around the fire.

Jem sat between Afflatus and Farouche, with Tekkara on Afflatus' other side. Sierra and Rimaya were a few seats away, both chatting animatedly with some of Rimaya's Draig friends. Sam and Henry were sitting beside Tekkara and talking to her about something too technical for Jem to understand. Some people were here, though, that Jem hadn't been expecting. Rick and Ella were seated across from Jem on the other side of the fire, and Bert was sitting beside Leo opposite Sierra and Rimaya.

He knew Rick and Ella had made it, but it surprised him to see Bert there. He didn't understand how the man had made it from Eltaes to here with the giant barrier being put up between the East and West of Callisto. Had he somehow gotten to Luria before the barrier went up?

The dinner was pleasant, though, despite Jem not talking to Sierra one bit and the surprise of Bert being there. Jem talked with Afflatus, Farouche, and the few kids his age that Farouche had befriended within the Refugee District. The food was also very good, whatever it was.

"Jem, do you see that?" asked Afflatus, pointing his shish-kebab across the fire at Ella.

"See what? Ella?"

"Yes, but do you see how she is acting and who she is looking at?"

Jem watched her for a moment. Her hands were shaky; she dropped her food several times and kept glancing about nervously. Jem watched her eyes and saw as they flickered to somewhere near Leo and Bert, to Rick, and then to Jem himself. He looked away as soon as they made eye contact.

"I don't get it," said Jem.

"I've been around Ella for a while now, Jem, and she hasn't acted like that until Bert showed up tonight—she keeps looking at him."

"But... that doesn't make any sense? She lived in Radeon with Rick; Bert lived in Eltaes in Argo."

"But you have relayed to me this story before, and you said that Rick used to live in Argo and that he left with Ella to start a new life in Radeon. Something happened with Bert before that."

Jem thought of Bert, sitting on the stage at their trial and refusing to attest to the fact that they had been inside his café on the night it burnt down. Bert's hideous cackle rang in his ears, and he thought that if Ella was remembering Bert, it couldn't be anything good.

"What are you gonna do?" asked Jem.

"Talk to Ella. I think we need to figure out what this is before it really gets to her."

Jem nodded. "When did Bert get here? I haven't seen him around."

"You know, he's been keeping a low profile until now. He stays in that hut over there," said Afflatus, indicating a smaller of the structures that was wooden and falling apart. "But Leo says that Bert disappeared right as they were rounding up people to go to that prison. Everybody thought he'd been killed, but turns out he must've made it to Luria somehow and gone through the portal with us."

"Hm," grunted Jem. He didn't know if he really believed that, but he couldn't think of any other way that Bert would've arrived here.

After a moment of chewing his food, Afflatus said, "Jem, when you're done with your food, go wait in the sitting room of sixty-four."

A little confused, but nonetheless willing, Jem nodded and downed the rest of his juice. He knew sixty-four to be the name of their refugee building since they had recently numbered all of the buildings in an attempt to give the district some sort of organization. Quietly, he stepped away from the fire and went to wait inside the building, spawning a few light orbs to light the room.

Within a couple minutes, Afflatus came striding in accompanied by Ella. She glanced at Jem nervously.

"What do you need, Afflatus?" she asked.

"Rick didn't seem very happy to allow you to come with me," said Afflatus quickly. "Why is that?"

"I—I don't know," she stuttered. Her eyes bolted between Jem and Afflatus. "Why is he here?" she asked, nodding towards Jem.

"You remember him from somewhere," said Afflatus accusingly.

"Of course I remember him. He stayed with us in Radeon before all this."

"But more than that. You remember something about him that you don't fully understand, much like you do with Bert and Leo."

Her jaw dropped and her voice caught in her throat. "I—but I—they…"

She turned and stared Jem in his eyes. He watched her oddly glowing brown eyes as they examined him like an animal in the zoo.

She turned back to Afflatus. "It was Bert. I saw him, and I remembered something—I don't know what. Something from long ago. It feels like a blur on the edge of my mind that I can't fully reach." She glanced at Jem's eyes again. "And now looking at Jem triggers the same memories, but I can't tell you what they are—I don't know what they are."

Afflatus gripped her shoulder reassuringly. "We can help you. Will you come with me to an amnesiast?"

"What—what is that?"

"Someone who can help you remember what may have been hidden from you."

She looked between the two of them, as if hoping one of them would answer the question for her. Finally, she nodded. Afflatus then led them from the building and into the city.

Ella tripped several times on her way there. She was dressed in thick robes, and yet, she began to shiver and her teeth chattered loudly. Jem was confused at what the point of all this was—why he was being brought along. Ella's memories surely didn't concern him.

Eventually they made it to a circular Draig building that was spaced just a couple of feet from the other apartment-style homes. It had a steep, pointed roof with etchings of dragons that ran down it and ended in flame sculptures around the edge of the roof. The building glowed yellow from the light orbs inside that emanated light out from a few small, circular windows. The front door was a thick, black wood with a massive metal knocker. Afflatus raised the knocker and swung it down three times.

A tall woman slowly peeled the door open, revealing only her eyes which were black as night. "Who?" she asked promptly.

"Tulevik," smiled Afflatus, "I had a favor to ask of you."

The woman's eyes lit up and she pulled the door wider. "Ah, Afflatus. Good to see you. Please come in."

She ushered them inside quickly. Jem saw that she was dressed in dark red robes with yellow cuffs and accents. Her hair was straight and black with a single blond streak running through it, and she had tied pieces of yellow and black cloth around her head. She walked slowly for how old she looked, maybe only forty or fifty.

"What can I do for you, Afflatus?" she asked, motioning to the large, poufy chairs around them. Jem sat in a beanbag-type chair that almost enveloped him completely. The room was strange with so many paintings hung on the walls and so many different colors swimming about. Multiple chandeliers hung from the ceiling despite the small size of the room; that couldn't be very safe. A small wooden staircase in the back led up to a second floor that Jem felt must've been where she lived.

"I would like you to remove a memory modification I feel may have been made to my friend Ella here."

"Hmm," said Tulevik, eyeing Ella up and down with her large black eyes. "Erasure, or addition?"

"Both, possibly," said Afflatus.

She nodded, continuing to examine Ella. "And who's he?" she asked, tilting her head towards Jem.

"Trigger," said Afflatus.

"I see, I see."

Trigger, thought Jem. *Since when did I become a trigger? That doesn't even make sense.*

"Well, come sit at my table, Ella. Let me see what I can unlock," said Tulevik, standing and walking over to a small circular table draped in a dull yellow tablecloth. Jem admired the rest of the room as Ella took her seat across from Tulevik. Light orbs circled the ceiling and danced about in a particular pattern. He noticed that some of the paintings moved occasionally too. He didn't like it here so much, too hectic.

"Close your eyes," said Tulevik. Ella did as she was told, but her hands continued to shake as she rested them on the small table. Tulevik rose from her seat quietly and strolled around the table to stand behind Ella. She hovered her hands inches from Ella's head, and they began to glow.

Jem watched with amazement as the woman twitched her fingers slightly here and there as if working her way through an intricate puzzle. Ella had her eyes shut tight and was gritting her teeth as if bracing for an impact. Tulevik, on the other hand, was concentrating hard.

"Relax," she said to Ella. "I'm only here to help you."

Ella's expression softened slightly, but she gripped at the tablecloth as if she were going to fly away and needed something to keep her grounded. Tulevik continued to manipulate the space around Ella's head, her fingertips glowing and sparks of magic dancing from them.

"It was a skilled amnesiast who did this to you," she whispered softly. "But nothing I haven't undone before."

Afflatus' expression remained stoic as the minutes passed. Jem was intrigued but also kind of worried for Ella because she looked as if she were in pain. She didn't protest, however, and continued to grip the tablecloth as Tulevik's twitching fingers grew nearer and nearer to her skull. Eventually, Tulevik's fingers were tracing distinct patterns around Ella's head, and Ella's expression began to loosen. She released the tablecloth and her jaw fell open as if she were sleeping. Her eyes slowly closed, and her head began to droop to the side.

Minutes more passed, and Tulevik was beginning to break a sweat. She was biting her lip hard in concentration, and the glow of the magic was becoming brighter and sparking more.

"Almost there..." she uttered.

With that, she gripped Ella's head on each side and both of her hand's glowed brightly as Jem watched the magic course through one hand, go into Ella's head, and come back up through the other hand. Ella jolted awake and sat stiffly upright, her eyes glowing the same electric blue as Tulevik's magic. Then, Tulevik released her and stepped back. Ella's posture slackened and her eyes stopped glowing. Both women were breathing heavily as if they'd been running for hours.

"I couldn't do it..." muttered Tulevik, examining her hands. "I couldn't break the second level." She turned to Afflatus and put one hand to his cheek. "I'm sorry, Afflatus, I have failed you. I removed one layer of amnesia, but there is something there that I cannot unblock, that I do not know how to unblock. I apologize. I have never before met an amnesia spell I could not break."

"It's okay," replied Afflatus, gripping her arm reassuringly. "You did what you could. Thank you."

He then turned and walked over to Ella.

"What do you feel?" he asked her.

She turned to him, face blank and inquisitive like a young child, and said, "I remember."

After that, Jem was sent to retrieve the Terellos and Bert from dinner so that they could all meet. He ran back to the Refugee District as quickly as he could and poked Leo on the shoulder, asking him to get Sierra, Rimaya, and Bert. He didn't think that Bert would listen to him if he tried, and he knew Sierra wouldn't.

As Jem waited for Leo to talk to the others, Bert eyed him suspiciously from across the fire. Jem put his head down and pretended to be very interested in picking at his fingernails. Out of his peripheral vision, though, he could see Rick standing up and walking over to him.

"Have you seen Ella?" Rick asked Jem bluntly.

Jem glanced up at the man with the unshaven face and slick black hair. "I haven't, no, sorry," he said.

"What the hell," spat Rick, sitting beside Jem in an empty chair. "That old fart, Alfalfa or whatever his name is, said he needed to talk to Ella for a minute and she's been gone for a while."

"Sorry," said Jem, trying to avoid Rick's eyes. "I dunno where he'd've gone."

Rick grunted in frustration and then was quiet for a moment, rubbing his chin and staring at Jem. Jem was nervous that Rick might suspect that he knew where Afflatus and Ella were, and he was hoping with everything he had that Rick wouldn't try to beat the information out of him. The man seemed outraged enough to do it.

"I knew I shouldn't've let that prick take Ella," he grunted finally. "I'm gonna go look for him." With that, he stood up and left Jem alone. Jem let out a heavy sigh of relief. He then saw that Leo had the others and was motioning for him to come along. He stood up and went over to them, constantly checking over his shoulder for Rick.

Somehow, they made it back to Tulevik's house without being spotted by Rick. Now they were all gathered around a large circular table, yellow light falling down on them.

"I have gathered you all here," began Afflatus, sitting tall and commanding beside Tulevik, "to discuss events that have taken place many years ago. Our friend here, Ella," he motioned to his other side where Ella was, "has recently been able to recall a bit more of her memory thanks to Tulevik, our gracious host and skilled amnesiast. If you'll notice, Ella's husband, Rick, is not here. That's because I think that he was the one who altered her memory."

Ella's eyes widened at this, but she maintained a somewhat glazed, thoughtful expression.

"As such, none of what is spoken in this room will be uttered in the presence of Rick. I want Ella to feel safe telling us what she remembers. Can we agree on that?"

Afflatus scanned the people around the table as they all shook their heads in agreement.

"Alright then," said Afflatus, "Ella?"

Ella looked up at them with her big, pitiful eyes. They glowed the same strange brown that Jem remembered seeing when they had met in Radeon.

"I don't know you," she said, staring directly at Sierra. "At least, I don't know you how I thought I knew you."

Sierra looked in shock as Ella stumbled to search for more words.

"When we met in Radeon, I had a memory of you as a little girl... but I know now that that wasn't you. I remembered babysitting you. I remembered you laughing and smiling, rolling around in your crib. But those memories… they were fake. I remember, now, what life was actually like in Argo. I wasn't close to you, Sierra, was I?"

Sierra shook her head.

"But I had that memory!" yelled Ella, clearly letting her emotions get the best of her. "And I remembered all sorts of things until just now that were lies. Most of my life has been a lie!"

There was a minute of silence accompanied by her heavy breathing before she turned to Leo and continued, "Me and Rick weren't close to your family, were we?"

"No," said Leo, looking at her sorrowfully. "You two mostly kept to yourselves."

"That's what I thought…" she whispered. "But I had all these wonderful memories of Argo—memories that I know now weren't true! They were fabricated, made-up lies. After Tulevik removed the memory spell, it was as if a curtain was raised from my mind. I am finally able to see what is really going on in my own mind, and it's a relief, but it's saddening as well. I had thought life had been wonderful in Argo and I know now that me and Rick weren't happy there.

"That's why we moved to Radeon. I thought it had been a move of spontaneity, something to satisfy the adventurer in both of us, but it wasn't. It was a move of desperation to find somewhere happier. I can't understand why my memory was altered to make my life seem happier than it was."

She looked to Afflatus after this, and he responded, "I think Rick may have been hiding more than just a sad life."

Ella looked absolutely offended at this. "He loved me!" she yelled. "How do you know he wasn't just looking out for me? Trying to make me happier?"

"I don't pretend to know the inner workings of Rick's mind," said Afflatus forcefully. "But there is something you haven't spoken about yet. Look at Jem. Look at Bert."

Cautiously and suspiciously, Ella turned her head and her eyes locked first with Jem and then with Bert. Her gaze stayed hooked with Bert, and Jem couldn't tell what either of them was thinking. Bert's face remained expressionless, but he had his head tucked down like a sad puppy and his beard and hair were as mangy as ever. Ella stared him down as if she was trying to find some answers within him.

"I remember you," she said to him. "And you," she said, looking at Jem. "But I don't know why. I know you were the bartender at the Café in Eltaes," she said to Bert, "and I know I met you in Radeon," she said to Jem, "but I remember something before that…"

Bert laughed a little bit. A deranged, maniacal kind of laughter, but he said nothing.

119

"Do you have something to say, Bert?" asked Afflatus.

Bert swayed a little in his seat. "No, sir," he said, smiling a creepy, toothy smile.

"Ella, continue," said Afflatus, glaring suspiciously at Bert.

"I... I don't know," she stammered. "I just know that I know you both... from... somewhere..."

"I see," said Afflatus. "Can you tell us any more about Rick?"

She was quiet for a moment, staring at a spot in the center of the table.

"He loves me," she said finally.

"What do you remember of him now?" asked Afflatus.

"That he loves me," she said heatedly, slamming her fists against the table. "That is all."

While Ella and Afflatus stared each other down, Leo spoke up. "My partner..." he began, "do you remember my partner?"

Ella turned and looked at him blankly, cocking her head to one side.

"Her name was Ariomeda Terello," said Leo, more emotion in his voice than Jem had ever heard from him. "She was at the Peace Meeting in Southern Argo in a large ECKO base. You were the only survivor they found there. That was how we met you."

Suddenly, Ella's face was in complete shock. Her eyes stared through Leo into nowhere in particular, and Jem could only imagine the sea of memories that must have been flooding back into her mind at the moment. She looked overwhelmed and horrified.

"That's... that's as far back as I can remember," she said finally, speaking slowly as if each word might be her last. "I had that memory, after Tulevik removed the memory spell, but I couldn't make any sense of it. Now it all falls into place."

Jem noticed here that Afflatus gave a slight grin. It was a somber grin, and Jem recognized that Afflatus was probably not happy about the news Ella was about to bring, but he knew that it had to be told. Maybe that is why he had gathered these people here; each of them was a trigger, but maybe Afflatus knew that the Terellos could learn about Ariomeda this way.

"My earliest memory..." continued Ella, "is being in that building. You said it was called the Peace Meeting? I remember seeing that sign on the door when the explosions began. The entire place erupted in fire and deafening noises. I had no idea where I was, and I tried to run but... but everything was falling..."

She swallowed to try and recover her voice which was thick with emotion.

"And one of the walls toppled in, and I was trapped under it. I was positive that I was going to die... the smoke was everywhere... people were screaming... but then... that woman—you said her name was Ariomeda—

she blasted the debris off my legs with the most powerful magic I had ever seen."

Ella began to cry gently at this point and dabbed the tears away with her sleeve. Leo, Sierra, and Rimaya all seemed on the verge of tears as well.

"But it drained her, that magic. It exhausted her, and I watched her collapse. My savior—the reason I'm alive today—I watched her fall to the ground as the rest of the building collapsed on her. I wasn't able to do magic; I was too overwhelmed and weak at that point. I tried to pull the debris off her by hand, but it was useless. The next thing I knew, an explosion sent me flying off the side of the building and into the grass.

"I watched as people from the nearby town sprayed water on the building... and I watched as some of them were killed from explosions too—explosions that were raining down from the sky. I learned later that it was an attack by the Veroci Regime, but at that point, all I knew was how lucky I was that none of the explosions hit me. I was taken in an ambulance to a town called Thysia. That's where I met Rick; he was one of the brave paramedics in that ambulance. We must've lived together in Thysia for about seven years before we moved to Radeon.

"I can't remember who I was before that, though—before that attack. I had thought, just earlier today, that I had lived my whole life in Eltaes. I had this whole fictional, wonderful life in my head. A life that was a lie. I don't know who I really am, or who I was before that day."

Ella was full on crying now, burying her face in her arms. Leo, Sierra, and Rimaya were all in tears too after hearing about Ariomeda. Jem, Afflatus, and Tulevik had the only dry eyes in the room, but Jem was still feeling the utmost sadness gripping at his insides. It made him wonder what had happened to his parents, how they had really died...

"That woman, though," continued Ella, looking at all three Terellos, "is a hero. She saved my life. And I know that she was your mother, Rimaya, because she looked just like you... I don't know why I didn't make the connection sooner."

Rimaya was absolutely balling now.

"I think," interjected Afflatus, "you may not have made the connection before because your memory was altered to erase that traumatic experience. You say that you thought you had this whole life in Argo, but it was fabricated. If you had made it to Eltaes before your memory was altered, I bet you would have noticed that Rimaya looked strikingly like Ariomeda."

"What are you saying?" replied Ella, obviously not too happy with what Afflatus was implying.

Be careful, Aff, thought Jem. *He's being painfully blunt towards someone who just recovered her whole memory...*

"I'm saying that Rick likely altered your memory before he took you Eltaes."

"THAT IS NOT TRUE!" screeched Ella, standing up violently and throwing her chair back. "He loved me! He still loves me!"

Afflatus remained in his chair, leaning forward on his elbows, calm as ever. "I never said he doesn't love you. I only said—"

"Shut up! I heard what you said," howled Ella. "Why did you bring me here, Afflatus? Just to make false accusations about my partner?"

"No, you know that isn't true, Ella," replied Afflatus. "I'm not accusing anyone of anything, I'm only looking at the possibility that—"

"It's not a possibility!" yelled Ella, pointing her finger at Afflatus' face. "Rick loves me and would never do that to me!"

"But, Ella, you must see—"

"HE LOVES ME!"

And with that, Ella went running furiously out the door, slamming it loudly behind her. All was deathly silent in Tulevik's home except for Bert's quiet cackling.

CHAPTER 13:
THE NEST

Things after that became exceptionally awkward. Ella did not talk to any of the Terellos, Jem, Afflatus, or Bert. She spent all her time with Rick, usually secluded away from the rest of the refugees, and the two of them stopped coming to the community dinners.

It didn't make any sense to Jem because, after all, they had only tried to help her. Tulevik had given her back a good chunk of her memory. Sure, Ella still wasn't able to remember anything before appearing at the Peace Meeting, but that was more than she had remembered before. If Jem's memory had been altered, he would have been thankful to get it back; he wouldn't have yelled at those helping him and then stormed away.

Ella's problems were her own, though, and Jem soon stopped worrying about her. He had enough stuff on his mind. He had fallen back into the habit of spending most of his time with Avalon, and Sierra was spending most of her time with Rabaiz. For some reason, the Nest Fenics had accepted Sierra even though they still disliked Jem. He would see her in passing, holding hands with Rabaiz and heading to the Nest. Sometimes, Jem and Sierra would both be in the Nest at the same time, although they never said a word to each other or interacted in anyway, and Rabaiz was very good at complaining loudly about Jem and Avalon. Gradually, Avalon and Jem spent less and less time actually in the Nest, instead spending their time on the roof or out in the city.

For Jem, it was strange that he and Sierra still hadn't talked since she had left to retrieve her dad. Jem had had a few conversations with Rimaya and Leo, neither of whom seemed too upset with him, but Sierra continually avoided him, and soon he learned to avoid her too.

But on the nights—and now sometimes, days—when he would have excruciating pains from the dragon poison, he would miss having someone there to take care of him. He knew it was a selfish reason to miss her, but her presence had always been comforting to him, even when she couldn't lessen his pain. Now he suffered by himself, and it seemed a hundred times worse.

Although he shared a room with Farouche and Snovel, (Cyneal now lived with Rimaya in a nearby room) he would crawl or limp away at night and have his fits of pain in the privacy of the alleyway outside their building. He did his best not to scream in pain, so as not to attract any attention to himself, but sometimes he didn't know how successful he really was at that. He just hoped that he never woke anyone up.

Bert was almost nowhere to be seen. He kept to himself a lot and had moved to a part of the Refugee District that was as far away as possible from building sixty-four. Jem didn't mind, though; he found the old bartender exceptionally creepy.

Within their own building, people had been moved around to make room for the three Terellos who had returned from Callisto, plus Tachel, the Reg they had brought back. Upon first seeing a Reg in Kelados, Jem had leapt behind a building and had considered transforming into a dragon just to quickly breathe fire on him. Thankfully, Afflatus had seen Jem and stopped him. Then he had introduced the two.

"He's an ally," Afflatus had said as Jem had scanned the Reg with his eyes, searching for some reason not to trust him. "He helped the Terellos escape."

"Name's Tachel," the Reg had said, offering his hand for a fist bump.

Jem had bumped his fist and said, "Jem." He had already known that a Reg had helped the Terellos escape, but he hadn't met the person until then.

The Reg had been abnormally tall and strong. Although he no longer carried his scepter as he walked with Afflatus, he had still looked as if he could kill Jem if he had needed to. His arms had bulged out of his Reg suit and his thick, square jaw had been locked in an indefinite scowl. Not the friendliest-looking person around. He had removed his helmet and Jem had noticed that he had incredibly pale skin, probably from being covered in that full suit all the time, and bleach blond hair cut short against his skull.

Tachel had given a weak smile and continued on his way with Afflatus. Jem still didn't trust him. He wasn't sure if he could ever trust a Reg.

Jem also had something new to fret over: Decision Day. Almost two weeks after the incident at Tulevik's, Afflatus informed everybody that every refugee would have to pick a system, Fenic or Draig, in about a month at a giant ceremony. Most of the people didn't find this to be such a big deal.

"Well, I'll be a Draig, of course," said Rimaya at the dinner table after

Afflatus had made this announcement.

"Me too," said Leo, patting Ryelox on the head beside him. "Gotta stick with my buddy here."

"I wanna be a dragon!" yelled Teek, the feisty little girl who lived in their building a few rooms down. "Fly around all whoosh—" she stuck her arms out like wings "—and breathe fire all fwaaa—" she used her hands to symbolize fire coming from her mouth, "and just be awesome!"

"Sweetie," said her father, a round-faced, gentle fellow with short curly hair, "you don't actually get to be a dragon. You're just a part of the Draig system where they worship the dragon."

Teek looked up at her dad as if he had just told her that her puppy had died. "I can't be a dragon?" she asked pitifully.

"No, I'm sorry," said her dad, petting her on the head. "But you can definitely be a Draig!"

"Hmph!" she pouted, crossing her arms and sinking lower in her chair.

"Then I think we should be Draig too, Saai," said Teek's mom to her dad. "It doesn't matter a whole lot to me."

"Me either, Tylsa," agreed Saai. "Draig it is."

Some of the other people then went around announcing what they would choose, including Farouche, Sam, and Henry who all declared that they would be Fenics. For the most part, everyone had made a clear decision already and the building was pretty evenly split.

"What about you, Sierra?" asked Tekkara after the other families had finished. Sierra pushed some of her food around on her plate with her fork before answering.

"Fenic," she mumbled, almost too quiet to hear.

"Sorry?" questioned Tekkara. "What was that?"

Jem thought that Tekkara had to have been able to hear that. After all, Jem was further away from Sierra than Tekkara was, and Jem had never known the Neoran Elder to have trouble hearing.

"Fenic," said Sierra louder without looking up from her food. "I'm gonna be a Fenic."

Rimaya rolled her eyes at this, and Leo cringed so slightly that Jem was positive that he was the only one who saw.

Tekkara smiled. "Very nice," she said, ignoring Sierra's blushing. "And what about you, Aff?"

Afflatus smirked as if expecting the question. "Me?" he laughed. "I do what I want, Kara."

Tekkara shoved him jokingly. "You do," she laughed. "But you're no fool, and I think I know what you'll pick."

"Oh do you?" mocked Afflatus lightheartedly. "Please enlightenment me then."

Tekkara smiled and took a big drink from her cup. "Fenic," she said, smiling wide.

Afflatus narrowed his eyes suspiciously. "You're good," he said, stealing some of her food with his fork. "But what are you going to be, Kara?"

She scraped her food back from his fork, flipping it up and catching it in her mouth. "Draig," she spat through a mouthful of food.

"Perfect," said Afflatus, admitting defeat and eating his own food. "What about you, Jem?" he asked, turning and pointing his fork at him.

"Um, uh," Jem stuttered. He hadn't really thought about it at all. The first thought that came to his mind was becoming a Fenic for Avalon, but then Snovel nudged his leg from beside him and he thought he should be a Draig to stay close to Snovel.

"Haven't decided yet?" asked Afflatus airily. "No matter, plenty of time! But be sure to have made up your mind by Decision Day!"

Jem occupied himself with his food again, keeping his head down as everyone else resumed talking happily. Snovel growled at him.

"I'm sorry," he whispered to Snovel. "I just don't know."

Snovel nibbled on Jem's pants legs a little bit, but otherwise didn't bother him anymore. Jem didn't eat much after that; he just pushed his food around while worrying about which system he would choose.

A couple weeks later, Jem was sitting on the roof of the Nest with Avalon, staring up at the stars like they so often did. They had just finished playing a racing game on Avalon's mav—a small, thin screen that she carried around that could be expanded into a larger screen for watching movies, reading books, playing games, and all sorts of stuff. She had explained to Jem that it was also used as a communicator and that every citizen of the Fortress had one. Jem thought it was a really cool invention, and it certainly provided them with a lot of entertainment when they hung out alone together. The mav was far from his mind, though, as he stared up into the dark night sky. The air outside was comfortably warm, and a slight breeze blew across his face. He cherished these bits of calm among all the chaos.

"Do you ever feel like you don't belong?" Avalon asked, lying beside him with her hands behind her head. Her body was warm against his side.

"What do you mean?" asked Jem.

"I don't know. I just… sometimes I feel like I don't belong here. But I don't know where else I would belong." They lay in silence for a few moments before she spoke again. "Maybe one of those stars. Do you think other people are out there? Do you think maybe we all belong *somewhere?*"

"I sure hope so," said Jem. He wanted at this point to tell Avalon about Earth, but he knew that after hiding it from her for so long, she might be mad at him. "Have you heard of ECKO?" he asked.

"Yeah, it's where you are all day," she replied, "with my dad and the other Councilmembers. I know that."

"So you know about the other worlds?"

"Huh?" she asked, sitting up and looking at him. "There are other worlds?"

"Yeah," he said, surprised that she didn't already know this. "It's the Earth, Callisto, and Kelados Organization. What did you think ECKO stood for?"

Avalon looked absolutely astounded—her jaw dropped as far as it would go. "I didn't think it stood for anything," she said. "I don't know... I just thought it was a word..."

"Well, yeah," said Jem, laughing slightly and leaning up on his elbows. "There are two other worlds; you know all the refugees came from Callisto."

"Yeah, that's true, but dad said not to talk about Callisto..."

"He told you not to talk about Callisto? Why?"

"Well, really, we aren't even supposed to talk to the refugees," she admitted, blushing slightly and looking away from Jem.

Jem put his hand lightly on Avalon's shoulder. "You aren't supposed to talk to us? Then why do you spend so much time with me?"

"I don't know," she said, still not looking at him. "I just like to be with you."

She cuddled up against Jem, the two of them lying back down with his arm around her. Jem stared up at the stars wondering if any of them could be Earth, his home that seemed so far away.

"Have you ever been to the other world—what'd you call it? Earth?"

Jem opened his mouth to talk, but paused before he said anything. He couldn't lie to her. Avalon had obviously been lying and sneaking behind her father's back to see him, and that meant something to him. But he had already told her that he was from Callisto. Oh well, he had no other choice but to be honest.

"I'm actually from Earth," he said finally. "I only arrived in Callisto like a year or so ago. Me and my other friend from Earth just fell through this portal, but he has already gone back to Earth."

She didn't react the way Jem had anticipated, with anger at him for not telling her sooner. In fact, she seemed so calm that Jem almost thought she might have seen his answer coming.

"How come he went back to Earth, but you didn't?" she asked nonchalantly.

"There was this Elder there—a leader of a city or region who's really good with magic—and he was only able to send one of us home, so he sent my friend home 'cause his family wasn't doing well."

"And there is no way for you to get home?" asked Avalon.

"No," said Jem. "Apparently, portals aren't very easy to make."

"Would you go home if you could?"

Jem thought about this for a minute. It was actually something he had stayed awake thinking about before. Would he? The first answer that came to his mind was no, but he kind of missed the normality of Earth. Ever since being in Callisto, everything had been nothing but chaos. The scar from his dragon bite pulsed painfully in his shoulder and arm.

"No, no, I don't think I would," he said finally. "It's not my home anymore."

"Hmm," hummed Avalon, squeezing up tight against him. Jem felt comfortable and safe, for once, in this crazy world of Kelados. The air around them was peaceful and quiet.

"Hey, Draig filth!" yelled an angry voice from below in the street. "What do you think you're doing on our roof?"

Jem and Avalon jumped up and leaned over the ledge to see who was yelling at them. Rabaiz stared back up at them, red-faced and pointing at them.

"Get the hell off there!" he yelled. "Y'ain't welcome here anymore!"

"I'm a Fenic, you dragon-blooded nitwit!" Avalon shouted back. "And Jem's with me!"

Jem leaned further over the edge, trying to see down to the entrance of the Nest. Sierra was just barely peeking her head out, and when she saw Jem, she disappeared back into the Nest.

"We decided you're out, Avalon," Rabaiz yelled back. "You know that."

The rest of the Fenics slowly walked out of the Nest, Ennui pulling Sierra along by her wrist.

"You're serious? We can't even be on the roof?" called Avalon, her voice only subtly choking.

"Scram," spat Rabaiz.

The rest of the Fenics kept their heads down but nodded. "Sorry Av," said Tyyni. "I still—"

But Tyyni's voice caught and she never finished her sentence.

"What the hell, everybody! We're family!" yelled Avalon, losing her cool completely.

"We *were* family, Avalon," sneered Rabaiz. "Now leave."

Avalon gripped Jem's hand and led him away quickly. He got one last glance at the group of Fenics, all of whom were staring at the ground uncomfortably aside from Rabaiz who made eye contact with Jem and glared viciously at him. Sierra avoided his eyes completely, and the last thing Jem saw before he and Avalon disappeared beyond the edge of the building was Rabaiz putting his arm around Sierra.

Whimpers came from Avalon has she led Jem over the rickety bridges that connected some of the edges of the buildings. With one hand, she gripped Jem's hand, and with the other, she wiped her sniffling nose as they ran along. Jem felt horrible. He felt as if everything that had just happened was entirely his fault, but he had no idea what to say to her.

Avalon was rushing too quickly for them to talk anyway, so Jem just allowed himself to be led wherever they were going and figured he'd think of something to say when they got there.

Soon they were through the gate into the Refugee District and Avalon took him to the same pond where she had originally found him stitching his sleeve. She collapsed against the huge wall between the districts just at the edge of the pond and Jem sat beside her. She buried her head in his chest and cried heavily, tears streaming down her face.

Jem held her while she cried, a sick feeling of guilt weighing in his stomach. The Refugee District was quiet tonight, and there weren't many lights around them. The only light came from the moon, glittering above them and reflecting off the pond, while Avalon's crying was the only sound breaking the eerie silence.

After maybe half an hour there, Avalon stood up and wiped her face with her sleeve. "I have to go," she muttered. "I need to be home or my dad will be mad." She hugged Jem tightly and kissed him on the cheek. "Thank you for putting up with me."

"Of course, Av, you know I'm here for you," said Jem, cringing a little bit in an effort to hide his own pains that were beginning to originate from his scar.

Avalon smiled and stood up. "Thanks, Jem." And with that, she walked away back towards the rest of the Fortress.

Jem sat there for a minute, trying to suppress the pain enough to stand up. When he thought he could handle it, he stood up quickly and stumbled forward, only to slip and fall down halfway into the pond. Spitting out water and sand, he rolled over onto his back to get out of the water. The cold water reminded him just how pitiful and weak he really was, causing him to shiver violently as he writhed in the sand.

Just get back to your room, he told himself. *That's all you have to do. You can't spend the night out here. People will know something's wrong.*

He gripped into the sand, dragging himself away from the pond and eventually making it to where the sand became dirt. Half-crawling, half-walking, he almost made it back to his room. He gave up just outside the side entrance and collapsed onto the ground, unable to move himself any further. However, this entrance was where Sierra usually entered and exited building sixty-four, so Jem knew that she would have to come back here at some point in the night. He didn't want that to happen; the last person he wanted to see now was Sierra, but he couldn't move.

He lay there all night, though, and not a single person passed by.

CHAPTER 14:
DECISION DAY

In the morning, just as the sun had begun to rise, Jem had managed to crawl into his room and collapse onto his pile of blankets before anyone else had awoken. He slept well into the afternoon and came out from his room to join some of the others for lunch.

"Something wrong?" Farouche asked him.

"Nah, I was just really tired," Jem reassured him.

Teek was being exceptionally annoying at lunch, and Jem kept glancing nervously at Tachel as if he would attack at any moment. Sierra was still nowhere to be seen; she was still probably with the Fenics out somewhere. He hoped that she was okay. It wasn't like her not to come back for the night.

"Has anyone seen Sierra?" Jem asked the group at large.

"Yeah, she was here for breakfast," said Leo. "You were asleep."

Judging by Leo's calm tone, Jem inferred that Sierra must've gotten back to the Refugee District just after the sun had risen and just before breakfast. If Leo knew that she hadn't spent the night at building sixty-four, he likely would have been much angrier. Afflatus probably would have been angry too since the Refugees were supposed to remain in the Refugee District during the nighttime. She must have timed her return perfectly so that everyone believed she had spent the night here.

Jem wanted to be mad at her for it, but he quickly realized that he was just jealous. He wanted to be out with friends all night instead of writhing in pain by himself. He wanted to be friends with the Nest Fenics, play FI, and spend time with Avalon. But Sierra was now in that group, and he and Avalon were not. He thought about revealing to everyone that Sierra hadn't spent the night in the Refugee District, but he couldn't do that to her.

A month later, Decision Day came around, and Jem still wasn't sure what system he was going to choose. He and Avalon were so far estranged from the Nest Fenics that he really didn't feel like he wanted to be a Fenic, but he wasn't sure how upset Avalon would be if he were to be a Draig. Seeing as she was the only person who seemed to care about him recently, though, he really didn't want to upset her.

But then there was Snovel who was spending more time flying around the Refugee District and less time with Jem. It made sense; Snovel was safe in the Refugee District, and it would be dangerous for it to be traveling throughout the Fortress with Jem and Avalon. Jem missed the days when he and Snovel would walk around Luria playing fetch. He thought about becoming a Draig just to prove to Snovel that he still cared about it.

The morning of Decision Day, a loud trumpet sounded just after breakfast. It played a short tune, and then Forenzi's voice could be heard across the District: "All refugees, please report to the stage for Decision Day. We hope you have chosen wisely."

And then his voice clicked off, and everyone around the breakfast table was silent. That last line seemed to make everyone question their pre-made decision. Jem, having still not decided, just sat quietly and hoped that no one would ask him what he planned to declare himself as. He was hoping something would pop into his mind on the way there.

Afflatus had them all dress in long, silky grey robes. Jem's robe was soft and cool, falling over his skin like water. The hood was so large that when he attempted to put it on, it covered his face entirely. Teek began running around the house with her overly large hood on yelling, "Rawr! I'm invisible!"

"Teek, you're not invisible, I can see you, sweetie," said her dad calmly, picking her up.

"No!" cried Teek, keeping her hood pulled over her face. "I can't see you, so you can't see me!"

Afflatus laughed and continued to dispense the robes to people. When everyone had finally changed, they began the march over to the stage with all the rest of the refugees. The entire District, it seemed, was out in the main street headed for the stage. Jem looked around and saw everybody else wearing the same silvery robes, some wearing hoods and some not. Jem kept his on to try and avoid conversation with those around him. He needed to think.

As they were led out of the Refugee District, they turned left and followed a specific path to the stage. Jem had never been this way before. The other roads, paths, and alleyways were all blocked off and people were lining the streets to watch the refugees march. They wore similar robes to the refugees, but either in white and yellow (Draigs) or black and red (Fenics). They were all clapping and cheering like this was some great celebration, but Jem didn't feel that way. He felt like they were being forced to pick sides in a war that he didn't want to be a part of. He remembered what had happened to Okka, and he didn't think it was fair to attack people just based on what system they were in. Whatever side he chose, though, he could only please half the people, and the other half would hate him. It seemed like a lose-lose situation.

Their pathway finally ended in a large square with a stage on one end. The tall buildings around them made Jem feel like he was trapped in a bowl that could be filled up with water at any moment. Around them, fiery decorations and posters were strewn about announcing Decision Day.

Up on the stage, eight chairs were set up—four on one side and four on the other. Above the chairs on the left was a black flag with a red, two-pronged flame. Above the chairs on the right was a white flag with a yellow three-pronged flame in the center. Jem recognized them as the Fenic and Draig symbols respectively. In the center was an empty space with a cannon-like thing protruding from the top of the building directly behind the stage. People were gathering on the roof and around the square, all dressed in their system's colors, although now they were divided: Fenics on the left and Draigs on the right.

Once all the refugees had filed into the square and everyone was packed tightly together, the Councilmembers came out from behind the buildings and walked up onto the stage. The four Draigs sat in the chairs to the right, and three of the Fenics sat in the chairs to the left. The fourth Fenic, Forenzi, stood in the center wearing black robes with red flames across the chest and projected his voice across the square.

"Thank you all for joining us on this lovely Decision Day," he announced, throwing his hands into the air in a celebratory fashion. The people lining the square on rooftops yelled and clapped in joy; some of the refugees clapped.

That's funny, thought Jem. *Thanking people for attending a mandatory event.*

"As you all know, we are here today to give the refugees the privilege of joining one of our two great systems: Fenic and Draig." More cheers. "It is an honor to be a part of one of our systems, and we will gladly accept whoever decides to join us. The process works like this:

"First, we will begin calling refugees up by name. We have you sorted by the building you are living in. Second, when your name is called, you will walk up the center stairs here—" he motioned to the stairs directly in front of him "—and stand exactly where I am standing now. You will then declare, loudly so that everyone can hear you, what side you will be choosing. You must choose either Fenic or Draig.

"Upon decision, this canon—" he pointed above him at the canon jutting from the building "—will shower you in the colors of your chosen system. Then you will exit to your chosen side. Fenics will pass by me and the other Fenic Councilmembers before exiting behind the building, and Draigs will pass the four Draig Councilmembers on the other side of the stage before exiting.

"Once everybody has chosen a system, a celebratory luncheon will be held for each system so that you can get to know your peers, and you will be led by a Councilmember to your respective luncheon. Any questions?"

Somewhere in the crowd, a voice called, "Can we choose not to choose?"

Forenzi let out a bold laugh. "And why would you want to do that? Our systems will lead you to greater happiness, greater inclusion in our society, and the ultimate truth about our world. You need not do yourself the harm of not choosing. You must choose either Fenic or Draig."

There was silence for a few moments before Forenzi yelled, "Great! Then let the decisions begin!"

Forenzi left center stage and sat next to the rest of the Fenic Councilmembers. Almost immediately, a robotic voice began shouting out names from seemingly nowhere.

The first person who went up was a short old woman who staggered up the stairs cautiously. When she reached center stage, she yelled, "DRAIG!" at the top of her lungs and was promptly showered in white, yellow, and orange confetti from the canon. Her silver robes shone bright white light, and when the light dulled, she was wearing brilliantly white robes with a yellow stripe running down one side. She laughed and smiled giddily before fist bumping all of the Draig Councilmembers and hurrying off the stage.

A few more people announced that they were Draigs and the same process happened. Then a young man, probably about Jem's age, declared that he was a Fenic and was showered in black and red confetti. The silver of his robes began to darken to a pitch black and a red stripe appeared down one side. He punched the air triumphantly and ran off towards the Fenic side.

This all went on for a while, and Jem was getting incredibly tired of standing still in one place for so long. His feet hurt from the cheap sandals they had been given, and he still hadn't decided what side he was going to choose. He bounced the pros and cons of both back and forth in his head over and over again, but couldn't seem to make a conscious decision.

He felt like his best choice would be Fenic since Sierra, Afflatus, Farouche, Sam, and Henry were all going to be Fenics. Plus, Avalon was a Fenic, and maybe if Jem was too, her dad would be more accepting of him. But he knew that being a Fenic would isolate him from Snovel, Cyneal, Ryelox, Rimaya, Leo, Tekkara, and Teek. He didn't know what side Tachel was choosing, but if Tachel was called up before him, he would likely choose the opposite. He still couldn't trust a Reg.

But it also didn't make sense for him to be a Fenic when he was actually part dragon. He slipped his left hand into his right sleeve momentarily and felt the rough scar on the back of his hand in the shape of the three-pronged Draig flame symbol. He felt the tingling going down the scar from his shoulder to his hand, and he could almost feel the spot where his wings would protrude from his back if he were to transform. He stayed in human form, but his thoughts began to lean towards being a Draig as he recalled memories of flying around as a dragon.

"Teek Erasmus" called the robotic voice over the murmuring crowd. Jem watched as Teek hugged her parents and disappeared into the crowd, only to reappear leaping up the stairs and standing proudly on the stage.

"Draig!" she shouted exultantly. She was then showered in confetti which she proceeded to dance around in until her robes had fully changed into white and yellow. The Draig Councilmembers had to call her to walk over to them because she was so distracted with the white and yellow pieces of confetti that would magically disappear when she caught one.

"Saai Eras," called the robotic voice. Teek's dad kissed her mom, went up on stage, stood under the canon, and declared that he was a Draig. He stood patiently as the confetti showered him and then walked silently off to the side.

"Tylsa Mus."

Teek's mom went up and followed the same procedure.

"Elder Afflatus."

Afflatus released Tekkara's hand and went up.

"Does Afflatus have a first name?" Jem asked Tekkara.

"No," she whispered back, "and neither do I. Upon becoming an Elder, one must give up their birth name and accept an Elder name."

"Fenic," said Afflatus proudly, puffing out his chest.

"Elder Tekkara," called the voice.

Tekkara smiled at Jem and approached the stage.

"Draig," she declared, smiling widely.

"Tachel Avayos," called the voice.

Tachel, who was standing alone, walked up quietly to the stage. "Fenic," he said so quietly that Jem barely heard it. Confetti showered him and his robes changed colors as he sauntered off without shaking anybody's hand.

"Leo Terello."

Leo hugged Sierra and went up to the stage. Rimaya wasn't near them; she had walked with some of her other friends who were planning to be Draigs. Up on stage, Leo shouted, "Draig," but Jem saw him watching Sierra in the crowd, and he wondered how it would be to choose a different system from your daughter, knowingly alienating yourself from her. Or maybe Sierra was alienating herself from the family.

"Rimaya Terello."

Rimaya came sprinting up to the stage from somewhere in the crowd and happily shouted, "Draig!" She twirled as the confetti fell and her robes shone brightly and changed color. She pranced jubilantly off stage.

"Sierra Terello."

Jem watched as Sierra walked up without looking back at him. She reached the stage and kept her head down, not looking up at the crowd. Jem was waiting for her to speak; she seemed to be frozen. He saw Forenzi whisper something, and Sierra looked up. She made eye contact with Jem briefly, and then said, in a choked voice, "Fenic."

The confetti fell, and she grudgingly shook all the Fenic Councilmembers' hands.

Up on the rooftop, on the Draig side, Jem could see Rimaya with a group of other Draigs. She was laughing about something.

"Farouche Rendo."

Farouche ran up to the stage, looking funny without his signature red headband. "Fenic!" he declared, over-sized hood almost falling over his face. The confetti canon didn't shoot for a second, and then just a few bits of confetti came out and trickled down on him. Farouche looked disappointed, but his robes changed color regardless and he headed off the stage.

"Sam Collins."

Sam kissed Henry briefly on the lips before walking up to the stage. He stood tall and declared, "Fenic!"

The canon made a gurgling noise and shook a little bit, but nothing came out. Jem's eyes darted around the audience. Everyone looked confused, except for Rimaya and her friends who were still snickering and trying to control their laughter. What were they finding so funny?

Sam looked up, expecting confetti, but it never came; his robes did change color, though. The Councilmembers, looking as confused as everyone else, motioned for him to exit the stage anyway.

"Henry Willard."

Apparently, the robotic voice didn't care if the canon was malfunctioning. Henry looked back and nodded at Jem. Jem nodded back. He felt alone in the crowd of strangers as Henry left him to go stand on the stage.

Henry looked up at the canon and then turned to face the crowd, slight nervousness present in his expression. "F-Fenic!" he declared, peeking over his shoulder at the canon.

The canon made the same gurgling noise, but this time shook more violently and finally spurted out flame red confetti. Henry's nervous face broke into a small smile.

Good, the canon is working again, thought Jem. But he was quickly proven wrong.

The smile on Henry's face lasted no more than a second; just as the confetti floated down and touched him, he howled in pain. Jem then realized that the confetti looked flame red because it was literally flaming. The canon was raining fire down on Henry.

He screamed in pain, running away from the canon and falling to the ground at the same time. His cries echoed throughout the entire area, sending shivers down everyone's spines. Jem went bolting through the crowd, shoving people aside violently on his way, in an attempt to help Henry. His eyes momentarily darted up to Rimaya and he saw that she and her friends looked as stunned as everyone else. They then turned and disappeared behind the building.

"Henry!" yelled Jem, pushing through the last people in the crowd and clambering up onto the stage. The Draig Councilmembers were all waving their hands in rhythmic motions at the canon and the remaining confetti. The canon had stopped firing, and the flaming confetti was reduced to ash by the Councilmembers. The Fenic Councilmembers were standing around Henry. Jem went up beside them and kneeled over Henry.

He probably should have kept his distant, though. The side of Henry's face that was visible was so grossly burnt that Jem wouldn't have otherwise recognized him. He was still howling in such excruciating pain that Jem could almost feel the screams reverberating within his own bones. Zenska and Fey were both performing spells above Henry, probably to ease the pain, but it certainly didn't seem to be working. Ikuuno was blocking the other Fenics who were behind the stage from entering. She wasn't able to stop Sam, however.

"Henry!" he screamed, running up beside his partner and kneeling beside him. "What happened? What burnt him? I wasn't able to see from back there!"

"The canon! It shot fire," explained Jem. "I don't know why—it just did."

Sam frowned at Jem and then turned his attention to Henry. "It's gonna be okay, babe, it's gonna be okay," he said over and over again. If Henry could hear him, he certainly didn't show it as he continued to writhe and scream in pain.

"You said it wouldn't burn!" yelled Rimaya from somewhere over near the Draigs. Jem looked over and saw her and her friends entering the stage from the Draig side.

"It shouldn't have burned!" one of them shouted back at Rimaya. "I don't understand."

"That wasn't the spell we used!" cried another.

"You did this!?" yelled Lenro, the hawk-eyed Draig Councilmember.

"We didn't mean to—" began Rimaya's friend.

"Look what you did!" screamed Lenro. "Look!"

Rimaya's face couldn't have been more horrified as she covered her

137

mouth with her hands and stared at Henry's mutilated body. "It shouldn't have…" she muttered.

"The spell wasn't a burning spell—it was just a prank!" shouted another one of her friends. "Just a harmless prank!"

"Does that look harmless?" bellowed Lenro. "You're all under arrest." She promptly shot blue sylph from her hands and it tied itself around all of their wrists, joining at a single point and connecting like a rope around Lenro's wrist.

The other Draig Councilmembers and Forenzi were all trying to keep people from rushing the stage. Zenska and Fey were levitating Henry and moving him towards the Fenic's exit.

"Where're you taking him?" demanded Jem, who hadn't been listening to the discussion over Henry's body. The loudness of the crowd and the commotion of Rimaya getting arrested had distracted him.

"The hospital," explained Zenska in a smooth, calm voice. "The quicker he can see professionals that have the proper tools and medicines, the better he will heal."

Jem nodded, and Zenska, Fey, and Sam left the stage with Henry's body floating between them.

"Jem Surwae," rang the robotic voice. It really didn't stop for anything.

The chatter amongst the crowd died down a little, and then Forenzi shouted, "Silence! The decisions must continue," and the crowd fell completely silent.

Jem immediately looked to the canon, and Okka, who was standing beneath it, said, "Don't worry, Jem, we've blocked it completely. It's safe."

Jem was frozen, though, in a state of panic. He glanced from the canon to Okka to Forenzi to the crowd. He still hadn't reached a decision.

"Jem Surwae," repeated the robotic voice, although with a tinge of annoyance.

"Choose, boy," commanded Forenzi. "We're waiting."

As the entire crowd watched in silence, Jem looked at Rimaya and her friends in the sylphcuffs and made his decision.

"Fenic," he said quietly, so that only those on the stage could hear. Then he repeated himself loud enough for the crowd. "Fenic!" he declared. He couldn't be a part of a system that could have killed Henry.

Maybe the crowd cheered a little, or maybe they were silent. The robotic voice might have called for the next person to make their decision, but all Jem could hear was the thumping of his own heartbeat as he walked off backstage and his robes changed to black and red.

CHAPTER 15:
THE OR'LIDI

Thankfully, Henry was able to recover fully. After three months in the hospital being cared for daily, he was finally released and didn't have any scars to show for it. Jem was amazed at the skill of the medical professionals here to be able to heal him so thoroughly. But at night, he would still have nightmares where Henry's scarred face would pop up, reminding him of what happens when the two systems collide.

Rimaya and her group of friends had been released from prison the day following their attack on Henry. They had all insisted that the confetti was supposed to catch fire, but that the fire wasn't supposed to be dangerous and shouldn't have hurt Henry, and they must have accidently used the wrong spell. Jem wasn't sure if he fully believed their story, but it was enough for the judges, apparently. They were sentenced to many hours of community service and warned not to pull anything like that again or else their punishment would be much more severe.

When Jem had returned back to the Refugee District after Decision Day, Snovel had been waiting in his room. But when it had seen his black and red robes, its head and tail had drooped down disappointedly, and it had walked slowly out of the room. Jem had chased after it, of course, but it had flown away as soon as it had gotten outside the building. Jem had felt more alone than ever at that point when he had sat outside building sixty-four and watched Snovel fly away.

For the next three months, Snovel became more independent. Jem didn't know where in the Refugee District it slept at night, but during the day, he sometimes saw it with Rimaya and her friends or Teek and her friends. Jem even saw Teek try to ride Snovel at one point, but Snovel couldn't hold her and they both went toppling down on top of each other, laughing.

Being a Fenic somewhat helped his relationship with Forenzi. He was still treated with hostility, like an outsider, but at the few Council meetings that he attended, he noticed that Forenzi was more likely to agree with him. He also allowed Avalon to be with Jem, although he didn't allow Jem to their house, wherever it was, and had given Avalon a strict curfew that she almost never obeyed.

Avalon was really the only person who Jem felt was there for him. Sometimes he saw Sierra with Avalon's old group of friends, the Nest Fenics, and sometimes he saw her around meals at building sixty-four, but they didn't talk or associate with each other at all. Occasionally, Jem was able to have a good conversation with either Afflatus or Tekkara, but it wasn't the same as having someone his own age to relate to. Jem had been able to spend more time with Farouche and Sam since they were Fenics, but they both spent a lot of time working on developing new technologies for ECKO, and Jem didn't have a whole lot that he could contribute to that, so he felt like he just got in the way.

At night, he sometimes transformed his fingers into dragon claws and played around with little droplets of fire. He missed being in dragon form and wanted more than anything just to transform and fly away—fly as far as possible and hopefully find the Phoenix and the Dragon. He wished that he knew where they were, or why they hadn't shown up yet. He wanted to help them, and he wanted their help. Their absence didn't do anything but add to his loneliness.

And that is how the three months after Henry's attack wore on for Jem, just weeks and weeks of the same dull days: Council meetings, hanging out with Avalon, exploring the Fortress by himself, pondering what the Phoenix and the Dragon were doing, and wondering what in the world Veroci could be doing back in Callisto. Even the New Year's celebration and Rimaya's 18th birthday passed by without anything eventful happening.

One morning, however, all this monotony was upheaved in an instant for Jem. A few days after Henry's release from the hospital, Farouche shook him awake violently yelling, "Jem! Jem! You need to transform right now!"

***

Farouche woke up with a slight headache. His vision was blurry as he pulled his head up from the desk and looked around.

Crap, he thought, *I fell asleep in the office again.*

He went to push his long hair back from his eyes and his hand hit something off his head. He looked down to see the rendomuffs lying on the ground. He must've fallen asleep with them on. He bent down to pick them up and put them around his neck. He then looked back at his desk, and his body was still there. He was asleep with his head down on the desk, drooling, and his big pink Rendomuffs over his ears.

Farouche tried to poke his sleeping body, but his finger went right through it. Freaking out a little bit, Farouche looked down at his hands and body and saw that he was transparent. He waved his arm a few times and it left a misty impression where it just was as if it was made out of light.

Am I dead? he thought. *Am I ghost? What's going on?*

He looked around for some sort of answer, but it was just his plain old office where he always worked. He headed towards the door and it didn't open automatically as it usually did. Instead, Farouche reached his transparent hand forward cautiously and it went straight through the door. He then put his leg through and stepped completely through the door.

I can go through doors, he thought. *This is so cool.*

What had at first been panic was now semi-elation. The power to move through solid objects had limitless possibilities if he could figure out how to harness it. But how was he even doing this?

He took off the rendomuffs from around his neck and examined them. They were the only invention he had been working on last night; they had to have something to do with it. He poked his head back into his office and watched his sleeping form drool with the rendomuffs on. Some tweak he made in it must have caused his mind to leave his body without entering a dream. Maybe this was a dream.

Well, might as well go explore while I can, he thought. He headed for the stairs, but just before he got there, he had a better idea. He approached a window and poked his head through it. Hardly able to contain his excitement, he slid his body through the window and was standing on the outer ledge of the window sill. He put one foot out into the air, feeling for some sort of traction. It didn't float entirely, but he didn't feel like he was going to fall. Besides, even if he fell, he would probably just wake up back in his body.

So he stepped off the edge of the window sill, and his stomach dropped, but he quickly gained control of his fall and drifted down slowly to the ground, landing gracefully. He was in a Fenic part of the Fortress, just outside the technician's building that had been designated for ECKO use. He had been spending most of his time here with Sam—Henry had just joined them a couple days ago when he had been released from the hospital. They both had gone home, though, when it got dark. Farouche had been too intrigued with the work he had been doing on the Rendomuffs, trying to get them to work while the wearer was awake rather than asleep. Well, he hadn't succeeded in that, but maybe he had found something more useful.

As he began to walk alone in the dark city, looking for something to do in his new ghostly form, a foreign object in the sky caught his eye. Something was glowing a dull, yellowish color up in the clouds. He squinted to try and get a better look, but he couldn't make out anything clearly.

When he turned back to his path, though, he almost walked right into a little child.

"Oh, I'm sorry," he said aloud, but it only took him an instant to realize that this was no normal child. She looked up at him with big, sad eyes. She was transparent, glowing a dull yellow, and wearing robes that only went over one shoulder.

"What—who are you?" stammered Farouche.

The little girl opened her mouth as if to speak, but then covered her mouth with her hands shyly. She motioned for him to follow her, and she began to float upwards.

"I can't fly!" called Farouche. "Come back! I can't follow you like that!"

But she had turned her back and was drifting away as if she were caught in a breeze. Farouche jumped up and expected to hit the ground afterwards, but he didn't. He began floating just like the little girl.

"Oh this is too freakin' cool," he said aloud, swirling around and flapping his arms in an effort to control his floating. It felt like swimming, but instead of being subdued by the water, he felt light and weightless.

"Where are we going?" he asked the little girl ahead of him, but the answer was obvious. They were headed straight for the glowing yellow thing in the sky that was hidden behind the clouds. Farouche looked back down to see the Fortress fading away and almost panicked from the sheer height.

"Can we speed up this flight a little bit?" he asked. "I think I'm going to pee myself."

The girl didn't turn around, though, so Farouche waited patiently until they had reached the cloud. Once there, they floated through the clouds and came out in a large open area with bunches of other people who were glowing yellow. They were all naked, however, and only the puffiness of the clouds covered anything. Farouche also noticed that they were all bald as well.

He followed the little girl as she landed on the clouds and the two of them were able to walk along them. The clouds were so light that Farouche almost felt as if he were hovering or flying rather than walking. He felt like he could melt into the cloud and become a part of it, if he wanted to.

She led him past several people, all of whom were talking casually as if nothing was wrong or different. Farouche was bursting with questions, but knowing that the little girl wouldn't talk to him, he decided to hold them until they got wherever it was that they were going.

Eventually, they reached a man and a woman who were standing side by side and talking, wearing similar plain white robes. The woman had a necklace with a key on the end hanging around her neck. The little girl approached them and then scurried behind them, hiding behind the man's legs.

"Ah, thank you, Minosa," said the man, patting the little girl on the head. "You did well."

"Um," said Farouche, "who are you two?"

"I am Ontam," replied the man, "and this is my partner, Benya."

"But we," said the woman, holding her arms out to indicate all the people in the clouds, "are the Or'lidi, the Sky People. And you are?"

"I am Farouche Rendo," he said, holding his fist out. They both bumped it. "I am one of the Humans, the Ground People."

They both laughed. "We know who humans are. We used to be them."

"You did? What happened? How are you here? What is this place?"

"One question at a time," said Ontam. "Relax. But first of all, we need to know how you entered our dimension."

Farouche took the rendomuffs from his neck. "These," he said. "I don't know how, but I tweaked the magic in them and I ended up here. I'm still not entirely convinced that this isn't a dream."

"A dream?" repeated Benya. "Well, you can decide that for yourself when you return to your physical body. But if you have any reason to believe us, we can assure you that this is not a dream. We are very much real, and we can help you in the fight against the zombies. If you are willing to accept our help, that is."

Farouche rubbed his chin for a moment. "Okay, well first tell me what is going on. How did you find me?"

"We can sense when someone enters our dimension," said Benya. "It is a power we are endowed with. So we sent our daughter to come find you and bring you here, else you may never have found us. We felt that if one of us went, we may have scared you away."

Farouche nodded. "How did you get here if you used to be humans?"

"Ah, now that is a long story," said Ontam. "And it begins a long, long time ago. You see, there weren't always zombies in Kelados. When humans first arrived here, the world was vast and empty. The only occupant, they thought, was the mighty Phoenix. It soared majestically overhead every once in a while, never landing near humans, never coming close enough for them to know much about it.

"So they spread across the planet, from the north to the south, taking advantage of the natural beauty of Kelados. Soon the humans began seeing a dragon flying alongside the Phoenix. Immediately, there was a division amongst them. Some thought that the Phoenix must have created everything because it came first, and others thought that the Dragon must have created everything and that it had merely been in hiding until then."

"The funny thing about that," interjected Benya, "was that the Dragon and the Phoenix got along perfectly. I might go so far as to say they were in love, and yet, we fought over which one was the Creator. It seems silly in retrospect."

Ontam smiled. "Indeed," he said. "So that is when the humans became divided: the Draigs and the Fenics, as I'm sure you've heard of by now."

Farouche nodded. "I'm a Fenic."

"Are you? Are you?" questioned Ontam. "Hmm. Well, as I was saying, humans became divided. But that isn't what ruined us. What ruined us was one unfortunate experiment. We had been testing the ability to enter other worlds, because there had been rumors that our own kind, and even possibly the Dragon and the Phoenix, had come from another world. These rumors gained little traction, due to the popularity of the Draig and Fenic claims that we were created in Kelados, but we wanted to test the other world hypothesis regardless.

"We engineered magical devices capable of creating windows into other worlds. We saw beautiful, unique, magical lands when we looked through these windows, but we were unable to enter them. For some reason, we couldn't get the magic right to allow the transport of living matter— humans. And before we were able to... something worse entered our world.

"We hadn't properly prepared for anything to enter our world through the portal. Our expectation had been that the other worlds wouldn't have intelligent life capable of finding our portal and entering Kelados through it, so we hadn't set up proper safety measures to ensure Kelados would remain safe. If something could enter through the portal, it could infect all of Kelados, and it did."

Farouche was shaking his head, anticipating what was coming next. *Always prepare for the worst*, he thought to himself. *That's how science works. Even I know that safety should be the first priority. And why in the world would they assume that they were the only intelligent life? As vast as the universe is, there must be something else out there.*

"The Zombie Virus entered Kelados one day," continued Ontam. "It was microscopic—so small that no one knew it had entered our world until people starting transforming. Their skin would rot and they would attack their friends and family. It was horrific. The three of us were all infected, as well as everybody you see around you.

"Today, the zombies you see are not humans who have been taken over. All the humans who were bitten are here in the sky. In a last act of desperation, many of us were able to magically preserve our minds and allow them to survive up here. But our minds are not stagnant. We have all learned much in our two thousand years in the sky. Minosa may look young, but after so many years here, she is relatively the same age as the rest of us.

"And that is how we got here, Farouche. We are the ones who were infected with the Zombie Virus. And while we are unable to communicate with the humans who live today, you have somehow found your way into our dimension, and because of that, we would like to help you as much as we can, to enlighten you about the workings of this universe. Is there anything you would like to know?"

Farouche's mouth opened, but he was unable to think of which question to ask first. He had a million questions swimming around in his head, each fighting to be the one to come out of his mouth.

"What's with the multiple worlds?" he asked finally. "I mean, I'm from Callisto, I know a person from Earth, and now I'm in Kelados. How does that all work? What world is the Zombie Virus from? How many worlds are there?"

Ontam laughed lightly. "Slow down, young one, we can only answer so many questions at once. But to start, we don't know where the Zombie Virus came from. I think that will be a mystery forever unsolved. As to how many worlds there are, we don't know that either. There could be an infinite number of worlds for all we know, and there most likely are. I know of the other two you speak of, though, because they are not so far away: Earth and Callisto."

"What do you mean they aren't so far away? Aren't they as far away as any other world?"

"On the contrary, they are quiet close. Would you like to see them?"

Farouche, still skeptical, nodded slowly.

Ontam smiled. "A curious one we have here, Benya." Benya smiled too. "Come," continued Ontam, "I have more to show you before Callisto and Earth—information which I feel is more pertinent for you to know."

He then began to drift slowly below the clouds and so did Benya. Minosa sat atop the clouds, waving at Farouche as he seemed to fall beneath the clouds as well. He kicked and flailed his arms and legs, feeling as if he was falling, but it was a very controlled fall and he stayed level with Ontam and Benya just below the clouds.

"Don't fly often, ground dweller?" teased Benya as the three of them soared through the sky, skimming the bottom of the clouds.

"Not in a while," joked Farouche.

As they headed south, the sun appeared to rise extremely quickly. In his few months in Kelados, though, Farouche had learned that the sun rises first in the south and then in the north. The Keladonians referred to it as rising in the southeast and setting in the southwest, even though all directions from the Fortress were technically south. Farouche had made the assumption that Kelados orbited its sun differently than Callisto did. What this meant for him now was that the zombie settlements were out in broad daylight when they arrived. The weird thing about broad daylight there, however, was that the sky was red, painting everything below them in an eerie glow.

"You see that?" said Ontam as they stopped and hovered above a massive zombie city. "These are the Rastvo. These are the zombies that the Keladonians know of—the ones that attack the Fortress sometimes. They have grown to be much taller than humans and have sickening green skin. Technologically, they are very advanced, as you can see. But they are incapable of magic of any kind."

Farouche stared down at the city in awe. Massive metal towers were constructed, factories were churning out black and red smoke, and zombies were driving about in giant metal machines that looked like a combination between a car and a tank. There was not any vegetation or trees; even the brown dirt was covered in a layer of black soot, and the red tint on everything only made it creepier. Farouche looked back the way they had come and couldn't even see the blue sky on the horizon anymore. They were far into zombie territory.

"Why do they attack the Fortress?" asked Farouche.

Ontam grinned. "Good question. Our best guess has been that they lust for fresh blood. After so many years of not having any humans to feed on, the Fortress must look like a giant dessert to them."

The zombie city seemed to extend to the east and west for as far as Farouche could see. It was like a massive winding snake, spurting out smoke and crawling with green zombies that looked like parasites among the terrain. The buildings were tall and intimidating; they wrapped around each other as if they were wrestling and were interconnected by all sorts of extravagant tunnels. It was horrific and astounding to Farouche at the same time. For zombies, they had an incredible civilization, but it was a scar on the side of Kelados.

As they flew on south, the city went away and a vast wasteland with small, scattered buildings was revealed. The area appeared war-torn: buildings were blown apart, huge craters were visible in the ground, pieces of the bodies of zombies were all around, and living zombies were firing weapons and fighting each other hand-to-hand. The zombies on the other side, though, looked different.

Farouche flew down closer, leaving Ontam and Benya up in the sky. Closer to the battlefield, he was able to get a better look at the zombies fighting from the south. They were smaller, had dark purple skin, long skinny tails, reptilian faces, and sharp blades along their forearms. As Farouche floated just above them, zombie body parts flew by him and blood splashed right through him. Luckily, in his current form—whatever it was—they weren't able to see or touch him.

The scene was horrific. Zombies were screaming violent, shrill cries as they ran across the bloody ground, slashing and hacking at each other and shooting large black guns with sharp edges. Farouche watched as a small purple zombie jumped up behind a large green zombie, ripped its metal helmet off, and sliced its throat with its arm-blades. The green zombie fell to the ground headless, shooting off its gun into the sky and killing a purple zombie that was jumping high overhead. The purple ones seemed to leap extremely high and glide slightly, while the big green ones tried to shoot them down with their huge guns.

Unable to watch the bloodbath anymore, Farouche ascended back into the sky beside Ontam and Benya.

"What are the purple ones?" he asked, gazing down at the creatures.

"Djimota zombies," explained Benya. "Small, but vicious. Today's Keladonians don't know of them; they have only ever encountered the Rastvo. The Djimota live at the southernmost point of Kelados and are at constant war with the Rastvo. This war land in between their two regions is never calm."

"That's unbelievable…"

Farouche couldn't take his eyes off the battle as they continued on south. An unending war seemed like the most horrible thing imaginable to him. All he wanted was for the war against the Regime to be over and to get home to Callisto, but these zombies were at home and still fighting each other.

"Why are the two kinds of zombies at war with each other?" asked Farouche.

"Because of something they both want control over: the Sacred Portal. They call it the Sacred Portal because it is where they came from; it is their origin, their beginning, and they are willing to fight to the death to possess it. The Djimota currently have it, but they have only had it for the last few hundred years. Before that, the Rastvo had it. It's just a never ending cycle because both sides will always be willing to kill the other for it, which is ironic since they both come from there."

Farouche nodded. The irony was saddening.

In the middle of the wasteland they were passing was a single building. It was circular and extended up as a tower, a bright white among the rest of the blackened and bloody battlefield. It glowed slightly blue in parts as if it was electric. Djimota clung to the top of it and jumped off, gliding down to attack the Rastvo. Several Rastvo hid behind the base of the tower and fired their guns at the attacking Djimota. When stray bullets—lasers, whatever they were—hit the building, they just glanced off, not damaging it in the slightest.

"What's that?" asked Farouche.

Ontam was silent for a second before he replied. "The Holy Tower," he said finally. "A tower that has been sealed shut since the zombies arrived. It is completely indestructible and unable to be opened."

"What's inside?"

"That is a good question," replied Ontam. "If only we knew. But we do know that the zombies fight over it just like they do the Sacred Portal, only the Tower changes possession every few seconds. They think that because it is so indestructible, it must be holy—a building that came directly from the Sacred Portal."

Further south they went until they were finally out of the battlefield. Now they were above the Djimota city. Farouche had thought the Rastvo city had been extravagant, but the Djimota city was a million times more complex and awe-inspiring. Tall, lean towers stood around the city like stalagmites, and curved roads rose from the ground and whipped around the towers like elevated racetracks. The small, purple creatures were out in abundance, gliding from roof to roof, racing small vehicles through the streets, and many were marching out to the battlefield.

The buildings here were much sleeker, all made of silver or gold, but the air was still heavily polluted and the sky was still red. As they passed over an empty part of the city, Farouche saw two Djimota fighting with a crowd of other Djimota surrounding them.

"What are they doing?" he asked.

"It's called an Unekai," explained Benya, "a duel. When one Djimota challenges another Djimota to an Unekai, they must accept, and then they must fight to the death."

"Why would they do that?" Farouche wondered aloud.

"For any of the same reasons that humans fight," laughed Ontam, as if it were obvious. "Over partners, over jobs, over misunderstandings, to prove that they are stronger, anything really. An Unekai is just a way for them to have a fair one-on-one battle. But don't try challenging a Rastvo to an Unekai; they could care less about a fair fight."

"And what's that?" asked Farouche, pointing to a massive castle in the distance.

"That is where the Djimota Leader lives, and where the portal rests."

"The portal that brought the Zombie Virus?"

"Yes," said Ontam solemnly.

"Can I see it?"

Ontam exchanged a quick look with Benya before saying, "Okay, follow us."

They descended from the sky and approached the front gates of the castle, flying just overhead of a bunch of Djimota roaming the streets below. The castle was the biggest building by far, and its many towers splayed outwards like guns pointed in every direction. The outer buildings and towers were made from a dark brown while the center dome, the largest part of the castle, was a shiny gold. Even knowing that he was in some bodiless form and couldn't be harmed, Farouche was intimidated by the formidable building.

The three of them flew through the giant main gates with ease, and after passing through several outer buildings and the golden dome, they were standing in a vast hall before an enormous purple zombie on a golden throne.

"That's the Leader," said Ontam. "Nir name is Loph."

"Nir?" repeated Farouche.

"Nir," said Ontam. "Like his or her, but without gender."

"Oh, they don't have gender-neutral pronouns, hun," said Benya, grabbing Ontam's arm. "That is something we learned from the Dragon and Phoenix. Humans don't have it."

"That's right," agreed Ontam. "We have much to teach you, Farouche. You see that?" He pointed to a giant black disc hovering above Loph. It looked big enough for a full-grown human to walk through, but maybe not a Rastvo. Although the hall was brightly lit, the disc seemed to be void of any light at all; in fact, the area around it looked darker. Farouche didn't know why, but he felt a very ominous force emanating from it, as if it were spewing noxious gases into the room.

"That's the portal the Zombie Virus came through, the Sacred Portal," continued Ontam. "Loph had nir throne put directly under it so that ne could guard it."

"So that's what has to be destroyed," reasoned Farouche.

"Indeed. If they are to be stopped, that portal needs to be shut somehow. Without a source of virus, they will die out very soon. But we have never met someone with the power to shut a portal."

"Afflatus can open and close portals," said Farouche. "Maybe he can do it."

"Then good luck getting Afflatus here alive. The Djimota won't just let you stroll into their Leader's castle that easily."

"I like a challenge."

"And you will have one," smirked Ontam. "Do you see that diamond in the Leader's crown?"

"Yeah, why?"

"The second Soul of Kelados is trapped within it. Unlike Callisto, which has six Souls, Kelados only has two. If your fellow humans wish to retrieve it, it will have to be snatched off the head of the strongest zombie to ever walk Kelados."

Farouche gulped.

"Come now," continued Ontam. "We have spent enough time in this forsaken land. Let us return to the sky."

With that, Ontam and Benya begin to drift upward, but Farouche took one last look at Loph. The forceful-looking Leader was at least twice the size of a regular Djimota and had massive fangs hanging from nir mouth.

Nir claws looked razor sharp, along with the blades protruding from nir arms, head, and back. Ne even had a long, pointed tail that dragged behind nem as ne walked. Golden armor plated nir body everywhere that blades were not protruding, and ne paced in front of nir throne as if waiting for something.

Farouche knew that they needed to rid Kelados of the zombies to even have a chance of saving Callisto. Somehow, they needed to infiltrate this castle, get past Loph, and shut that portal. He gulped as he floated up through the roof and into the sky, following the two Or'lidi.

"You have a plan for getting past nem?" asked Ontam, indicating Loph. The weird pronouns continued to throw Farouche off.

"Oh, um, no, not yet," stammered Farouche, "but I will."

"Mhm," said Ontam.

"So, those funny pronouns, what are they again?"

"Ne—like the knee on your leg—instead of he/she," explained Benya. "Nem instead of him/her. Nir instead of his/her, and nirs instead of his/hers. Think of it like: ne smiled, that is for nem, that is nir hand, that hand is nirs. It's simple once you get used to it."

"Got it," said Farouche. "And you said the Dragon and the Phoenix taught you that?"

"Yes, because they are genderless as well—they use those pronouns."

"Speaking of them, do you know where they are?" asked Farouche, knowing that Jem had been trying to reach them ever since they arrived in Kelados.

"Indeed," said Ontam. "They are being held captive by the Djimota. See that silver dome over there?" He pointed to a building just beyond the golden castle, a smaller silver dome that was splotched in black dust. "That's where they are kept. If you ever infiltrate this far with your humans, you should free them. They are your friends."

Farouche nodded, and they flew higher through the red sky, dipping in and out of clouds once and a while, headed for the north where the sky was blue once again. When they had finally reached blue sky and were almost back to the Or'lidi's home, Farouche asked, "Can I see Callisto and Earth now? You said they were close."

"Ah, I did. Yes. Let's do that now. Follow us, Farouche."

He and Benya then took off straight up into the sky, leaving the clouds far below them. Farouche threw his arms to his sides and shot up right after them, moving as fast as his form would allow him. Above him, the blue sky turned to black, and stars were visible throughout the sky. Were they going into space? Was that even possible?

But his questions were answered soon enough as they cleared Kelados' atmosphere, and Farouche was able to look down at the planet in all its strangeness. The north was so blue, so friendly, and the rest so dark, so infected. When he returned his gaze back to the night sky, several things were immediately clear which he hadn't seen before.

His first sight was the moon, larger than ever and shining brightly. Then there was a small planet beside the moon with blue poles, a white center, and brown everywhere else. He had to have been looking at Callisto: the blue was the oceans, the white was Luria, and the brown had to be Neora and Radeon. He had always pictured Neora and Radeon as being green, though; the Regime must have destroyed a lot of the greenery.

The other strange sight in the sky was a planet Farouche had never seen before. It was huge and mostly blue, with splotches of brown and green land here and there. White clouds swirled around it in a beautiful display of nature. That had to be Earth.

"It's... amazing up here," muttered Farouche.

Ontam and Benya only smiled and nodded, allowing Farouche to soak up everything he was seeing. It was like a dream come true for Farouche who had always dreamed of designing and flying in a spaceship. It also made everything on Callisto and Kelados seem incredibly insignificant. People weren't even visible from here—only planets. Their actions meant almost nothing out here in space. He looked out to the other stars and wondered how many other planets could be out there.

"Why couldn't I see them before?" asked Farouche. "Callisto and Earth aren't visible from the ground."

"That is true," answered Ontam, "but we don't know exactly why that is. Some spell was placed on the planets at least a thousand years ago. If you are within the atmosphere of any of the three planets, you cannot see the other two. We don't know who did it or why, but that is how it is."

"Wow," said Farouche spinning around and trying to look at everything at once. But then, something caught his eye. Something was moving towards them, coming right from Callisto. Farouche squinted and saw that it looked a lot like what he would imagine a spaceship to look like.

"Um, Ontam, Benya, what's that?"

They both squinted too, staring at the same place.

"Well, it looks like some sort of ship," said Ontam. "Do you think someone from Callisto could have sent a ship here through space?"

"Veroci..." uttered Farouche. "I've got to tell Jem!" And with that, he went rocketing back down to the surface, ignoring Ontam and Benya's calls behind him, and landed directly in his body, waking up instantly.

He ran down the stairs of the technician's building as fast as his legs would take him, feeling so energized by what he had seen that he crashed into several walls on his way down. He sprinted out of the building and went straight for the Refugee District. Not even trying to be quiet, he went running past all the homes and tents and finally found Jem lying asleep in building sixty-four. He didn't bother being gentle; he grabbed Jem by the shoulders and shook him awake yelling, "Jem! Jem! You need to transform right now!"

CHAPTER 16:
THE TRANSPORT SHIP

"No," grunted Jem sleepily. "No, Olive, I don't want to go to the lake… go home…"

"Jem, it's not Oliver; it's me, Farouche."

"Hm?" Jem sat up rubbing his eyes. "What're you doing here?"

"You need to transform! You need to be a dragon right now!"

"What? Why? You know I'm not allowed to transform here—"

"But you need to!" cried Farouche, not paying attention to the volume in his voice and almost certainly waking up some of the neighbors. "The Regime has sent a warship over here through space!"

"Space? The Regime? What are you talking about? And keep your voice down!"

"Jem, this isn't the time for that. We have to act quickly. In space, Kelados, Callisto, and Earth are actually really close but we can't see them because of some spell placed on the planets a long time ago. Veroci must've figured that out and he's sent a spaceship to Kelados. If you don't stop it before it gets here, Veroci could have the Fortress under his control too, and then it's all over."

"Okay, okay," said Jem, getting to his feet and trying to comprehend everything he had just been told. "So you want me to just transform and fly into space and stop the ship? I can't just go into space, Farouche! Even dragons need air."

"Right, right. I'm sure there's a spell around that. But I don't know it. You'll need to see the Or'lidi…"

"The who?"

"The Or'lidi. They're these people who live in the sky—long story. I was able to go see them because of a glitch in the rendomuffs. But I bet they can do something. I'll need to communicate with you, though. Follow me back to the technician's building and I'll hook you up. Come on."

With that, Farouche grabbed Jem by the wrist and dragged him out of building sixty-four and down the street towards the city. The sun was just beginning to rise, and the Keladonians were beginning to awaken. The cold air prickled Jem's skin as he ran down the street in just a one-sleeved shirt (enough to cover his scar) and a pair of shorts that he had been sleeping in. Farouche hadn't given him time to put on any more clothes.

When they reached the building, Farouche went sprinting up the stairs, not even bothering with the levitator. He threw open the door to his small office space and began rifling through the drawers, searching for something. Jem stood there and looked around at the incredible mess. Giant pieces of crumpled paper and pieces of half-attempted inventions were scattered about the room at random. There was a chair hanging from the ceiling for some reason, and he had painted a fake door at one end of the room. Strange place.

"Ah, here it is!" shouted Farouche suddenly, holding up a tiny metallic object. "Here, put this in your ear."

"Tell me what it is first," said Jem, taking the little thing in his hand. It looked like a silver grain of rice with little circles etched into it.

"It's a communication device—a rendocom. I haven't fully tested it yet, and I definitely don't know what will happen when you transform into a dragon, but it's the best thing we got. Just stick it in your ear."

Jem eyed him skeptically, raising one eyebrow. "You expect me to just shove this in my ear?"

"It's that, or you'll be alone up there. At least with this, you can communicate to me, and I can see what's going on. Now put it in."

"Is it safe?"

"I have no idea," said Farouche, completely serious.

Jem swallowed hard and shoved the rendocom deep into his ear. Immediately, he felt it latch onto something in his head, and his vision went blurry for a second as he dropped to his knees and threw his hands over his ears.

"Ahh!" he cried in pain, hitting himself in the head, trying to get it out.

"Jem, relax! You'll be okay!" insisted Farouche. "Just give it a minute!"

Jem was not able to relax. The excruciating pain in his skull seemed to last forever, and the blindness was terrifying. When he was finally able stand up again, his head felt light, like it was filled with helium. Farouche was holding a small tablet in his hands, poking away at it furiously.

"What are you doing?" asked Jem. "Am I okay?"

"You're fine," laughed Farouche. "Now look at this." He held up the tablet and Jem saw, in the tablet, Farouche holding up the tablet. This image repeated itself until he couldn't see any smaller.

"I don't get it," said Jem. "What am I looking at?"

"It's what you're looking at! It's what you're seeing. I can see what you see in this tablet. And with this…" Farouche picked up a small earpiece from his desk with a thin, long microphone extending from it. He placed it in his ear and held the microphone to his mouth. "Hear me?" he said, and Jem heard the words clearly within his own head.

"That is freaky," said Jem, pushing his fingers into his ears, trying to discern where Farouche's voice was coming from.

"It works! It works!" cried Farouche. "Alright, we gotta get you up there to that ship. Come on." He grabbed Jem by the wrist again and took him back down the building and outside. The sun had risen now and plenty of people were out walking the street. Terrible timing for needing to transform discreetly into a dragon.

"Okay, where do I find these Or'lidi?" asked Jem.

"There," said Farouche, pointing to the spot in the clouds where he had found them just a short while ago. "I had to be in some weird dream dimension to see them, but I don't know how to get back there. You try to find them normally, and I'll examine the rendomuffs in case that doesn't work. Just talk to me in your head, and I should be able to hear you. Got it?"

"Got it," said Jem, even though this seemed like a terrible plan to him. He stepped away from Farouche and stood in the center of the street, but he was too nervous to transform. There were so many people around…

"What are you waiting for, Jem? Transform!"

Jem looked back over his shoulder and gulped. "I can't, Farouche. Can you imagine what would happen if a Fenic transformed into a dragon in broad daylight?"

Farouche bit his lip and looked upwards. "Jem… look up," he said.

Jem looked up, and he saw a small dot gradually growing larger in the sky. He transformed one of his eyes into a dragon eye and used that to zoom in on the small object. Up close, he clearly saw that it was a large silver ship, much like an airplane but without the wings. Hundreds of windows lined the ship, and hundreds of helmeted faces were visible through them. Soldiers, no doubt. Veroci really had sent an army to Kelados. This was real.

Immediately, wings shot out from Jem's back and his transformation began. Some people nearby dove out of the way and others stared in amazement as Jem grew rapidly into a massive silver dragon. He flexed his wings wide and stretched his long neck upward as high as he could. It felt good to be back in his dragon form.

He roared as he kicked off the ground, pounding his wings hard and kicking up a storm of dust in his wake. The feeling of flying—that exhilarating, heart-pounding, absolute sense of freedom—he had missed it immensely. Soaring through the sky felt so good that he almost forgot where he was going, but Farouche was quick to remind him.

"To your right," said Farouche inside of Jem's head. "They're in the cloud up to your right."

I forgot you were there, thought Jem, unable to speak aloud in his dragon form.

"Apparently the rendocom even works for dragons. Go figure. Anyways, you gotta get to the Or'lidi. I hope you can talk to them somehow."

We'll see.

Jem turned to his right and headed for the cloud that he remembered Farouche pointing out. Below him, he could feel the gaze of all the Keladonians on him, but he wouldn't have to deal with them until he landed again. He kept his attention focused on the Or'lidi's cloud.

As soon as he broke through the cloud, he heard Farouche's voice, "Can you see them?"

Yes, replied Jem, staring at a bunch of naked, bald people who were so transparent that he couldn't tell if they were real or just a part of the cloud.

"Can you talk to them?"

Let me try.

Jem opened his mouth to speak but only a roar came out. All the Or'lidi suddenly stopped what they were doing and stared up at him.

I am a friend of Farouche, said Jem, hoping that they could somehow hear his thoughts telepathically. *And I need help to stop an attack on this planet.*

"Ask for Ontam and Benya," said Farouche.

Are Ontam and Benya here?

"We are here," said a man, walking up to Jem. "But how are you here?"

I flew. You can hear me?

"Yes, although I couldn't tell you why. Dragons must have the ability to view and communicate in our dimension, unlike humans. We have spoken with the Dragon nemself, at times."

Nemself?

"It's a pronoun," explained Farouche in Jem's head. "They use these weird gender-neutral pronouns for zombies and the Dragon and the Phoenix. Just roll with it."

I see. Well, we can discuss the Dragon later. For now, I need to be able to survive in space. Do you have any spell to make that possible?

Ontam stared at Jem for a minute, rubbing his chin.

"We could try a helmet," said Benya finally. "A magical helmet to hold in air. But it means you won't be able to breathe fire while you're out there."

That's fine. I just need to get out there and stop that spaceship before it gets here. I'm sure I can do that without fire.

"Okay then," said Ontam. "Let us give it a try. Benya, take the left side; I'll get the right." The two of them then stood by Jem's sides and waved their hands in a melodic motion up towards his head. He began to see a shiver in the air as if his head was in a bubble.

"Done," said Ontam. "But please return here when you are done, we have more to discuss with you that we weren't able to discuss with Farouche before he left."

Deal, thought Jem. *Thanks.*

He began flapping his wings and gradually took off from the soft, cloudy surface. The ascent was difficult, but he was eventually able to gain some speed, and before he knew it, he was in space. His scales felt tighter, as if they had been vacuum sealed around his body all of a sudden. Only his head felt normal, but he could still see the slight shimmer indicating that he had a helmet of air around his head.

For a minute, he was caught gazing in awe at the distant Earth. It looked so far away and so tiny, yet huge compared to Callisto. He thought about all the fighting, all the wars that were going on back on Earth, and how insignificant they all seemed when he saw the Earth from there. It would do everybody a lot of good, he thought, to see how tiny they all really were and to see that they are just one planet.

"Focus, Jem," said Farouche. "You need to stop that ship. Can you see if it's carrying weapons? The Council is down here along with Afflatus and some other ECKO members. They're monitoring what's going on through your view alongside me, but I'm the only one who can hear you. Keep me informed, okay?"

You got it.

Jem tried flapping his wings to change direction, but it did nothing. He flapped harder and harder, but he kept drifting at the same pace away from Kelados.

Farouche! Farouche! Why can't I fly out here?

"You're in space, genius; you can't just flap your wings to get around. There isn't any air to push around. Use magic."

Jem took a deep breath through his nostrils and felt a tingling extending down his wings. This time, when he flapped his wings, they propelled him forward thanks to the magical energy he was sending out through them. He was lucky that that worked; otherwise, he would've been plummeting deep out into space.

"You never paid attention in science class, did you?" laughed Farouche.

Shut up. I'm nearing the ship.

It only took Jem a couple minutes to reach the ship, and at the speed it was going, it would enter Kelados' atmosphere in even less time.

"Hurry, Jem, y'ain't got much time. The Council is ordering you to destroy that ship ASAP."

Farouche, thought Jem. *It's not a weapons ship. It's a transport ship. Do you see what I'm seeing?*

Jem was flying alongside the vessel which was very plain aside from the purple V imprinted on the front. Through all the windows, he gazed upon the faces of the soldiers. Many of them were shaking their guns at him, taunting him, but one face caught his attention. Towards the end of the ship, one soldier had her visor up so that her face was visible.

Sanyee, thought Jem.

"Sanyee?" repeated Farouche. "Who's that?"

Sanyee is the doctor who healed me in Luria after I was bitten, Farouche. She's on that ship. She doesn't look like she wants to fight.

"Yeah, but all the others do."

Doesn't matter. I won't destroy this ship as long as she's on it.

"Jem, the Council is ordering you to destroy it. They're saying you'll receive harsh punishment if you don't."

What's Afflatus saying?

"He's silent."

That's a first. Alright, Farouche, give me some options, 'cause I'm not destroying this thing.

Jem swooped around the back of the transport ship, feeling the heat coming from the thrusters on the back, and looped around the other side of the ship. They were getting extremely close to Kelados now.

"Alright, alright. I bet that the ship is on a closed trajectory—meaning Veroci probably didn't install thrusters that adjust if the course is altered, they are just set to get to one place."

So?

"So move the ship. Nudge it."

Nudge it where? thought Jem, but he was already pushing up against the side of the ship. It was many times larger than him, and it was taking all his energy to move it just a few degrees.

"Point it back where it came from, I guess. Otherwise the people onboard are as good as dead when they drift off to space."

Got it, thought Jem as he heaved with all his might against the ship. He could feel the gravity of Kelados pulling them in, but he was just barely able to get the ship turned around soon enough for its engine to pull it away from Kelados. After that, Jem just had to nudge it so that it was headed directly for Callisto.

"Mission accomplished, captain. Head on home."

They'll be back. This isn't over.

"I know."

I have to stop and talk to the Or'lidi before I come back to the Fortress.

"No worries. The Council doesn't seem too happy right now anyway. You might be better off taking your time."

Got it. Thanks. See you soon.

"See you soon."

Jem watched the transport ship as it hurtled back to Callisto, and he saw Sanyee put her hand against the window. He may have saved her life now, but what would happen when she returned to Callisto? He hated knowing that people were over there suffering at that very moment. He needed to fix it. It was his duty, given that he could transform into a dragon.

The trip back down to Kelados was much easier than the one going up had been. He simply dove down headfirst using his wings as brakes—the air helmet dissolving away once he entered the atmosphere—and landed upright on the Or'lidi's cloud. He almost transformed back into a human before remembering that he was on a cloud.

"So you sent it back the way it came?" asked Ontam, standing just as Jem had left him.

Yes, replied Jem. *I didn't want to destroy a transport ship with possibly innocent people on it.*

"Wise decision, young one."

Thanks, thought Jem. *So why am I here? Who are you all?*

Ontam then went on to explain to Jem about their origins. He told him that a portal was opened that allowed in the Zombie Virus; he told him about the two kinds of zombies, the Rastvo and Djimota; he told him that they lived in a dimension layered over Kelados, unable to interact with humans but apparently able to interact with dragons.

If you can communicate with dragons, Jem thought to Ontam, *have you heard from the Dragon?*

"Yes," replied Ontam. "But ne and the Phoenix are being held captive by the Djimota."

Captive? You mean they were captured by zombies? How could that have happened?

"They cornered themselves. They tried to attack the portal through which the Virus came, and in doing so, they had to get inside the Leader's castle. The castle is large, but not large enough for either of those legendary creatures. They attacked the portal with incredible amounts of fire, but it continued to exist. When the Djimota armies caught up to them, they had nowhere to escape from in the giant golden dome."

I can't believe it, thought Jem. *This whole time, I thought they were unbeatable. I thought they were out there somewhere and would come help us defeat the zombies. But we'll have to do it without them, and we'll even have to rescue them. This just keeps looking more and more impossible.*

"Do not think that just because something is difficult, that it is impossible," reassured Ontam. "We know of a secret weapon that may help you to get past both the Rastvo and Djimota and close the portal for good."

And that is?

"The Phoenix Glove."

What is that?

"A glove made from one of the Phoenix's feathers back before the Dragon arrived in Kelados. A human, one of the first to arrive in Kelados, stole one of nir feathers and forged it into a Glove that harnessed all of the Phoenix's powers. At first, this person became consumed with power and fought with the Phoenix, but they must have come to their senses at some point, because they eventually surrendered the Glove to the Phoenix. Unable to destroy it, ne hid it—hid it so well that no human was ever able to find it."

Then how do you expect me to find it?

"If you are clever enough to deserve the Glove, then you will find it."

And if I could find it, it would help me defeat the zombies and close the portal?

"It would give you the powers of the Phoenix; the rest would be up to you."

Jem nodded his giant dragon head. *Got it.*

"You should return to your people. I am sure they are anxious to greet their hero."

I'm not so sure that I should be called a hero.

"Well then, maybe you can become one," smiled Ontam. "Return to us if you ever need our help. We are capable of great magic, as you saw with the helmet. You need only ask for help, and we will provide what we can."

Thank you.

Ontam and Benya smiled. "Good luck," said Benya, before the two of them turned and walked away. Jem swallowed hard, nervous about what was waiting for him back down at the Fortress.

"I don't know if you want to come back here," came Farouche's hushed voice inside Jem's head. "The Council doesn't seem very happy."

It's the Fortress or the zombie cities.

"Right. You should come back then. But be careful."

Careful as a dragon can be, thought Jem as he went diving down through the clouds and headed directly for the Fortress. From the sky it looked incredible, the circular city with the lowest buildings on the outskirts and the highest buildings at the center. The Council Center was the highest, of course, with the Soul shining brightly above it—Luria and Kelados' combined Souls. It really was an unforgettable sight.

He returned to the technician's building where he had left Farouche and slowed his flight considerably, coming to a soft landing just in front of Farouche who was sitting cross-legged at the entrance to the building. All the Councilmembers were gathered around, as well as many citizens and civil servants—Kelados' version of police which they referred to as servs.

As Jem's feet touched the ground, he transformed back into his human form. His clothes were somehow still on, but they were stretched and ripped to the point of barely covering his body. His shoes had fallen apart completely and the scar along his shoulder and arm was clearly visible, not that that mattered anymore.

"Arrest him," said Forenzi, before Jem even had a chance to speak, "for refusing to defend the Fortress and possibly aiding a dangerous foe."

"Aiding? I didn't aide Veroci!" shouted Jem. "I just prevented his transport ship from landing here!"

"Yes, but you didn't destroy it," sneered Forenzi, "and now he will only come back harder and stronger. You have put everybody on this planet at risk, and you must be detained."

"No!" cried Jem, flailing about as the servs grabbed his arms. "I did everything I could! There were innocent people on that ship!"

"Innocent people who were on a ship meant to come attack us. We saw Farouche's feed; we saw the soldiers in the ship. Those were not peaceful negotiators—that was an army!"

"Not all of them! Besides, I stopped it from getting here anyway! Now we have time to prepare—"

"Enough!" yelled Veroci, whipping his hand through the air. The air rippled in front of him, and suddenly, Jem couldn't open his mouth. He screamed as loud as his lungs would allow, but his lips were sealed shut and only a muffled scream was heard as the servs tied his hands behind his back.

Some people cried out in protest as this happened, Farouche yelling the loudest, but Jem had everything blocked out except for the servs he was struggling against desperately. They clasped what felt like a metal chain around Jem's wrist and he lost it; he began to transform into a dragon. A tail sprouted from his lower back, knocking the servs over, and his head began to transform too, but then a powerful shock was delivered through his body and he fell to the ground, unable to move and completely human.

Somebody kicked him in the stomach and the crowd went, "Oooh." Jem tried to look around but his neck was stiff and his vision blurry. The last thing he saw was someone in a red headband jumping on the back of whoever had kicked him in the stomach.

Justin Dennis

CHAPTER 17:
THE GREAT SCRIPTURES

"He did what he judged to be right," said Afflatus calmly, despite the lividness of some of the other Councilmembers.

"That is irrelevant," roared Forenzi. "His judgment was wrong."

"He did save innocent lives," defended Okka.

"No Regime life is an innocent life," said Forenzi. "They are clearly aggressors looking to take over our planet. We showed them mercy; that is unacceptable."

"We showed them compassion," said Okka.

"We showed them weakness," interjected Ikuuno.

"Jem showed them weakness," corrected Zenska. "But the Regime will see it as representative of all of us. I guarantee you that when they come back, there will be many more spaceships, and this time they will be armed, and Jem won't have the chance to gently nudge them back home."

"Then we will deal with that when it comes," said Mualano. "But if you had to choose between killing a group of people and sending them away, which would you choose?"

"I kill my enemies," sneered Forenzi, "because I am not a coward."

"I don't think Jem is a coward," spat Lenro. "I think he was only trying to do what was right. He is not a danger to anybody here, and therefore he should not be jailed."

"Not a threat?" laughed Forenzi. "He's a dragon! The only thing stopping him from eating everybody is the shocker on his wrists!"

"Don't be stupid," gawked Afflatus. "He would not eat anybody. He has incredible control while in his dragon form. If he did not, he would have destroyed that transport ship and then eaten you when he returned."

"Regardless of his control," said Zenska, recognizing that Forenzi had clearly been defeated, "he failed to protect the Fortress. End of story."

"That's not the end of the story," spat Harcos, talking as fast as his mouth would allow. "He saved innocent lives on that transport ship, he still protected us from an attacking army, and he didn't commit any crime other than not murdering a whole army of people you think should have been murdered. I think the real reason you want him locked up is because he can transform into a dragon, and that scares you."

Immediately, the room erupted with Forenzi, Ikuuno, and Zenska's shouting. Fey remained silent.

"Don't you bring systems into this!"

"You are only protecting him because he is dragon scum!"

"I won't tolerate this bias in the Council!"

"ENOUGH!" shouted Okka, silencing everybody in the room. "This deliberation has gone on long enough, and it is obvious to me that nobody's mind is going to change. Let us have a vote. Those in favor of keeping Jem imprisoned?"

Forenzi, Ikuuno, and Zenska all raised their hands into the air. Fey stared at the center of the table, but did not raise her hand.

"Fey, what are you doing?" shouted Forenzi. "Raise your damn hand!"

Fey did not answer him; she just continued to stare at the table.

"Those who wish to let Jem go free?" asked Okka.

All four Draigs, Okka, Harcos, Lenro, and Mualano, raised their hands. But, to everybody's surprise, Fey also raised her hand.

"How dare you?" cried Forenzi.

"Traitor! Draig sympathizer!" shouted Ikuuno.

"I can't believe you," said Zenska.

After they stopped yelling at her, Fey took a moment before she replied without looking at them. "Jem broke no laws," she said calmly. "That is why I made my decision. I believe this session is adjourned." And with those words, Fey stood up and walked out of the room.

***

When Jem opened his eyes, the first thing he saw was that red headband. As his vision came into focus, he saw that it was Farouche wearing the headband, sitting against the wall in a small gray room. Jem picked his head up and looked around; it wasn't just a room—it was a jail cell.

"Morning, sunshine," laughed Farouche. "Sleep well?"

"What happened?" asked Jem, remembering shouts and yelling and chaos just before he had passed out.

"Forenzi attacked you when you landed. Remember, you went to the Or'lidi and saved the Fortress from that Regime spaceship?"

"I remember that," said Jem. "But Forenzi attacked me?"

"Yeah, dude. After you freaked out and started transforming into a dragon, Forenzi went up and kicked you in the stomach. I thought he was going to kill you, so I ran up behind him and jumped on his back trying to strangle him. It became chaos after that, but Afflatus did some spell and everyone went flying away from each other. Then they took you and me to this cell and, of course, let Forenzi go free."

"I can't believe that," gasped Jem.

"Yeah, real crap, ain't it? Forenzi said he thought you were losing control and he had to subdue you. But that's a lie. You had stopped transforming when he kicked you, and you looked like you were about to pass out. Those shockers can be a doozy."

"Shockers?"

"That thing around your wrists. Electric. Try to use magic or transform into a dragon and they'll deliver a shock so powerful that you lose concentration immediately. Apparently, if you really fight them, they'll knock you out cold," he added, laughing lightly. "It's about time something interesting happened around here."

Jem faked a smile and tried to reposition himself to be more comfortable. His ribs ached painfully as he sat up and leaned against the wall, keeping his bound wrists behind his back.

"How long have we been in here?" asked Jem.

"A few hours."

"You think they're gonna let us live?"

"I know they'll let you live," smirked Farouche. "You're the best weapon they got. And hopefully they'll let me live, considering I design and engineer most of ECKO's tech. The real question is whether or not they'll set us free or keep us locked up in here until they really need us."

"I vote for the first one," said Jem.

"Me too. But we'll see what the Council decides. Either way, I don't plan on letting them own me."

"What would you do if they kept us locked up in here?"

Farouche looked at Jem with his brown eyes and said, "I don't know exactly, but it wouldn't be pretty. Nobody controls me."

Jem smiled. He admired Farouche in moments like these. Calm, collected, light-hearted, but dead serious. In the dark cell, Farouche's face was difficult to make out, but Jem could tell his features were sharper, more defined, and more handsome than they had been when they had first met over a year ago. They both must have grown a lot, but Jem just now gained a certain respect for Farouche and the way he handled himself. He smiled, and Farouche smiled back.

A few minutes passed in silence before a light flicked on down the hallway. A woman in a serv uniform unlocked their cell door and swung it open.

"Council says you're free to go," she grunted.

Jem wondered if she was one of the servs who had attacked him. He studied her face carefully, searching for any emotion.

"Can I get these off then?" asked Jem, indicating the shockers holding his two wrists together.

"Sure," grumbled the serv, fiddling with the device. Jem heard a *click* and then the pressure lifted from his wrists, bringing with it a completely rejuvenated feeling to his body. He felt like he had just taken off a heavy coat as magic coursed happily through his veins once again.

"Thank you," he said, rubbing his wrists and proceeding outside, Farouche walking along beside him.

"Hey, Jem," said Farouche, pricking the shoulder of Jem's torn, stretched, filthy shirt. "You might want to find some new clothes."

"Oh, right," said Jem, changing the direction he was walking to head for the Refugee District.

"So what now?" asked Farouche. "What do we do?"

Jem was quiet for a second, looking up at the sky and trying to figure out which cloud the Or'lidi could be hiding in.

"Um," said Jem finally. "I think we need to visit Okka."

"Okka? That Draig? Why?"

Jem could hear Okka's voice clearly in his head: *If you do ever have any questions, about the Draig or Fenic system, feel free to approach me.*

"Because I have a question for him," said Jem vaguely. "Did you hear the stuff about the Phoenix Glove when I was talking to the Or'lidi?"

"Yeah, of course," said Farouche. "Listening the whole time."

"Good, because we need that thing."

"But how are you gonna get it? Ontam himself said that the Phoenix hid it so that nobody could find it."

"He said you had to be very clever to find it; you and me are pretty clever."

"Cleverness seems like a weird thing to determine who should wield such a powerful weapon," said Farouche. "I mean, Veroci is probably pretty clever."

"Then I guess it's a good thing he's not on Kelados, isn't it?"

Farouche laughed. "I guess so."

Eventually, they passed into the Refugee District and made for building sixty-four. To Jem's surprise, however, Avalon was sitting at the entrance to the building.

"Ooh, I see how it is," said Farouche teasingly. "Why don't you go get changed then? I'll catch up with you later. Let me know what Okka says."

"Oh, Farouche, you don't have to—"

"Nah, it's cool," smiled Farouche, patting Jem on the shoulder. "I've got stuff to work on anyway. Go be with your girl."

"Thanks," grinned Jem. "See ya later."

"See ya."

Farouche then peeled off behind a random building and headed back for the city. When Avalon caught sight of Jem, she jumped to her feet and ran out to greet him.

"Jem! Jem! I'm so glad you're okay! Oh my gosh, I was so worried!"

She squeezed Jem so tight that he yelped in pain, forcing her to let go.

"What's wrong, baby?" she asked worriedly.

Jem gripped at the spot on his abdomen where his ribs were bruised. "Your dad gave me a pretty good kick in the ribs," he said. "But I'm sure you heard about that."

"I did..." said Avalon sympathetically. "I'm so sorry, Jem. He got out of control. He'll be disciplined for that, I'm sure."

"I don't think so," replied Jem. "But it's whatever. I'm fine now."

"Good, good," said Avalon, throwing her arms around his neck and being careful not to press against his ribs. She kissed him on the lips for a few seconds, and he held her tight, relishing the comfort she gave him even in the dreariest of times.

"Come on, hun, we need to get you into some better clothes. Apparently, they can't handle your transformation very well."

Jem followed her into building sixty-four where she picked out fresh clothes for him. She didn't leave the room for him to change, but he felt surprisingly relaxed in front of her and didn't mind.

"So tell me all about it," she said. "I want to hear your take on it. All I've heard are rumors and what people saw."

Jem then went on to explain to her about the Or'lidi, the zombies, the other planets, and the Regime transport ship. He finished his tale by telling her about the Phoenix Glove.

"Wow," she said. "I think I may have heard of that somewhere before..."

"Like in Fenic scripture?" asked Jem. "I was planning on going to Okka's to ask him about that. I figure that the key to finding the Glove must be in the scripture somewhere."

"That's a great idea, Jem! Can I come with you?"

"Oh, um, sure," replied Jem, surprised. "But are you sure you're allowed to be in a Draig's house?"

"If Okka allows it, then I'll be fine. I don't care anymore what my dad thinks I should do with my life. He crossed the line when he kicked you. He can kick me out for all I care, and I'll live in the Refugee District before I let him control my life. Draig or Fenic, I don't care anymore. It doesn't matter. Who knows what's real and what's fake and why does it matter? Okka seems like a nice person, and I don't care what he believes in. And I know that you can turn into a dragon, but I know that doesn't make you evil like all the other Fenics think. I think we should judge people by their character, by how they act, not by their beliefs or their lack of beliefs. I don't even know what I believe, but I know I don't believe in hating for no reason."

Jem smiled widely. "I understand."

Avalon laughed happily. "So let's go to Okka's then?"

"Yeah, yeah, definitely," said Jem, still thinking about everything Avalon had just said. Her eloquence and compassion made her that much more attractive to him.

On the way to Okka's house, Jem noticed that people were looking at him funny. Draigs said nothing, only staring with their mouths agape as he passed by. He didn't know what to think of them. The Fenics, however, made their opinions very clear. Some glared at him, but others shoved him roughly as they passed by and muttered things like, "Dragon spawn," "Filthy dragon scum," and "Evil scaly prick."

Avalon's hand stayed gripped tight in his, and she walked close to him. It comforted him, having her beside him, but he knew that doing so was going to make a lot of people hate her. She was a Fenic walking down the street with someone who had just revealed himself as a dragon; that would only isolate her further from the Fenics, and the Draigs already disliked her. Jem knew of the sacrifice that she was making by staying with him, but her presence was too comforting for him to tell her to leave.

When they finally reached Okka's house, Jem knocked a few times on the door and then waited. Ruuna answered the door with a big smile on his face.

"Well, hello there!" he said, beaming. "How nice of you to stop by, Jem. I'm glad you're okay; I heard about the incident. And who is your friend?"

"This is Avalon," said Jem.

"I'm his partner," Avalon said, fist bumping Ruuna. Jem was a little shocked at the word "partner," but it kind of made sense. There didn't seem to be boyfriends, girlfriends, husbands, or wives here, just partners. And Avalon basically was his girlfriend.

"Oh, so nice to meet you," said Ruuna. "Please, come in. Let me go find Okka. OKKA!" he hollered upstairs. "JEM AND HIS PARTNER ARE HERE!"

Ruuna then disappeared up the stairs, leaving Jem and Avalon to sit down on the couches in the living room. The word "partner" ringing in his head, Jem looked at Avalon for what felt like the first time. Her bright blond hair, longer towards the front and very short in the back, swayed as she took her seat. She had a black shirt on with a unique kind of collar that Jem had only seen in Kelados; an unzipped, dark red jacket with the sleeves rolled up; and tight-fitting black pants that tucked into her dark red boots with multiple buckles across them.

That was Jem's partner: bright grey-green eyes, soft pink lips. He couldn't help but wonder why she had been so willing to give up everything for him. He wasn't that special, was he? Would he have been willing to give up everything for her? Well, he kind of did already. He gave up Sierra and Snovel, the only ones who he had always been able to rely on back in Luria. But now he had Avalon, and he was happy with her. Right? Why shouldn't he be?

"Jem?" said Avalon, waving her hand in front of his face. "Are you okay?"

"Yeah," said Jem. "Yeah, I'm fine." He smiled at her, and she smiled back. His chest felt a little bit warmer.

"Hi, Jem," said Okka as he came down the stairs, Ruuna right behind him. His tone sounded much more somber than Ruuna's had. "It's good to see that you are no longer imprisoned."

"Thanks," said Jem, standing up to hug Okka.

"And you brought your partner?"

"Yes, my name is Avalon," she said. "Nice to meet you." Okka and Avalon hugged, and the four of them all sat down. Jem noticed that Okka looked surprisingly tired and sad, especially compared to cheerful Ruuna.

"So what brings you to our home?" asked Okka, looking at Jem.

"Well, I would like to know why I am free," said Jem. "What went on in the Council Center?"

Okka sighed heavily. "A lot of bickering, a lot of division, not a lot of progress. We are very lucky that Fey is such an intelligent, thoughtful individual because without her, you may not have been released."

"Fey voted to have me released? Why?" asked Jem, surprised that any Fenic would have wanted him to be free.

"She said you did not break any laws, and this is true. The other three Fenics were thinking through their system, not through logic, and that is a dangerous place to be caught in. As Councilmembers, we all need to be careful to keep our beliefs out of our decision making. They are very separate things, and some of our members seem to forget that from time to time. I'm just thankful for people like Fey."

Jem smiled meekly. "Me too."

"But," continued Okka, sighing heavily once again. "Your legal freedom is different from your social freedom. As I'm sure you have noticed in your short time out in the city since your release, Fenics are not going to be particularly kind to you. And while Draigs may be in awe of your power now, they will not forget that you chose to be a Fenic. You are essentially a social outcast from both systems."

Jem nodded.

"And you, Avalon, in being his partner, have accepted much of that too. Do you realize that?"

"I do," said Avalon. "But it's worth it for me to stand by Jem's side."

Okka smiled his first genuine smile since they had been sitting there. "That's just delightful to hear. But, Jem, tell me, there must be more of a reason why you are here."

"There is," said Jem, leaning forward, his arms on his knees. He paused for a moment, and then asked, "What do you know about the Phoenix Glove?"

A sly grin crept up Okka's mouth, and then he chuckled lightly. "Now where did you hear of the Glove?" he asked.

"The Or'lidi," said Jem. "Do you know of them?"

"The Or'lidi…" said Okka, pressing two fingers between his eyes, deep in thought. "The Sky People. I have heard rumors of them, but I never thought them to be real."

"They are real," said Jem. "Farouche saw them through an invention of his, and when I transformed into a dragon, I could see them. They are the humans who were around when the Zombie Virus entered Kelados. They are trying to help us destroy the zombies."

"And they told you that the Glove could do it?"

Jem nodded.

"Well, if they are real, then it is just as possible that the Glove is real. Avalon," he said, turning to her, "as a Fenic, raised by a severely devout Fenic, I imagine that you must know about the Glove."

"I… well, I, uhh…" stuttered Avalon, blushing and rubbing the back of her head. "I never really read most of the Fenic scripture. And I slept through Gathering a lot."

"What's Gathering?" asked Jem.

"When a bunch of Fenics get together and read scripture and talk about it and stuff," answered Avalon. "It's really boring."

"Mhm," said Okka. "We've all had to sit through plenty of boring Gatherings, trust me. Even Draig Gatherings can be dull at times. But anyway, about the Glove. There are hints of it, just minor mentions, in both Fenic and Draig scripture, but the real key is a very significant line from the Great Fenic Scriptures: Your greatest weakness is your only defense."

Jem stared blankly at Okka. "What does that even mean?" he asked.

"I've heard that before," said Avalon. "They said it a lot at Gathering. It's supposed to mean that by overcoming your weaknesses and your fears, you build yourself stronger. The more fears you conquer, the better you can defend yourself from the world. It's meant to inspire people to work to overcome their weaknesses and become better through the Phoenix."

Okka smiled. "Exactly. But it also has another meaning that not many Fenics pay attention to. What do you think would be the Phoenix's greatest weakness?"

Jem thought it over for a minute. "Water," he said finally.

"Exactly. And if the best defense is in a weakness, then—"

"The Glove is underwater..." said Jem.

Okka nodded. "And in Draig scripture, there is a tale of a Draig who was never seen again after he went swimming in a river—the river that wraps around the center of Kelados. It is a part of Draig scripture which forbids swimming, although I don't know of a Draig today who doesn't swim. Regardless, the story is significant—I think—because the boy's body was never found. Now if that boy had drowned, his body would have washed to shore. But it didn't. That means one of two things: he was either trapped in a cave he never escaped from, or something ate him—something that was guarding the Glove."

"That's a bit of an assumption, don't you think?" asked Jem.

"Yes, but you have nothing better to go off of," said Okka. "The tale even includes a location: just to the east of the island with the rock—the one you came from when you entered from Callisto. I bet you that there is a cave under there with the Phoenix Glove in there. What else is in that cave, though, I don't know. And it would be a deathly risk to try and find out."

Okka then summoned a piece of paper with his hand and wrote that information down on it, using the tip of his finger and a bit of magic to etch the words. He even drew a small map of where he thought the cave to be relative to the location of the island. When he finished, he handed the map to Jem who stuck it in his pocket.

"Do your own research," said Okka, switching his gaze between Jem and Avalon. "But if you dig around enough, I'm sure you will come to the same conclusion that I have. If anyone else has discovered this before, they dared not venture out of the Fortress, and I am not encouraging you to. But if the time comes when you need this Glove, then you know where to look at least."

Jem smiled. "Thanks, Okka. You have been very helpful."

"I do what I can," said Okka.

"How come you never went after it?" asked Avalon. "If you know so much about it."

"I have no need to," said Okka as if it were the most obvious thing in the world. "I am content here. Why risk my life venturing into zombie territory for more power that I don't need?"

Avalon shrugged.

"Well, thanks for stopping by, you two," said Okka, standing up. "Let me know if you ever need anything else."

"Will do," said Jem.

The four of them fist bumped each other goodbye and then Okka and Ruuna let them out the front door. Walking down the street, Jem had one hand in his pocket gripping the map and the other hand holding Avalon's.

"What do you think?" he asked. "About all that?"
"I think we need to get that Glove," said Avalon.

CHAPTER 18:
OUTSIDE THE WALL

Despite Jem and Avalon's desire to get the Phoenix Glove, they never actually made the plans to do it over the next few weeks. It was too risky to leave the Fortress with all the zombies roaming around out there, and they had no way of getting deep underwater, much less finding a cave there. So the goal of obtaining the Phoenix Glove kind of became a vague, distant dream to them.

Avalon continued to attend school regularly but now spent even more time with Jem since she was completely friendless due to her loyalty to him. Jem often skipped Council meetings since he felt betrayed by all the Fenics there, aside from Fey. They were merely talking in circles now, never getting anywhere and constantly arguing back and forth. It was pointless to listen to.

He did do a lot of research about the Phoenix Glove, though. He spent hours each day at the library, searching through books and scrolls and stories that were saved on a computer-type thing. Basically, the library had several large frames just inside the entrance that behaved like holographic screens. When Jem first encountered one, he stuck his hand through the frame and suddenly, words and images were dancing around inside of it: "Touch here to search by author," and "Swipe here to view our most popular books."

The magical system was intuitive, though, and he got used to it quickly. It helped him a lot by allowing him to search for the word "Glove" in all the Draig and Fenic scriptures. It turned out that the word "Glove" was mentioned a lot, so he had quite a bit of homework cut out for him.

While all the Great Scriptures had hard copies, some writings had "cloud copies," which were basically texts that had been saved digitally on the library's servers. Jem could then read those cloud copies on the frame things or the library would lend him a small tablet to read them on if he wanted. It all reminded Jem a lot of technology he remembered from Earth, but he had to keep reminding himself that none of it was electric—it was all magic.

Unsurprisingly, everything Okka had said was spot on. Jem found the tale of the boy who drowned in the river in the Great Draig Scriptures, and he found countless tales in the Great Fenic Scriptures involving the "Your greatest weakness is your only defense" line. Whatever reservations he had had about the location of the Glove, however, were squashed when he read a Fenic story about someone who died trying to retrieve a fiery hand from the depths of a frozen cave. An island was even mentioned in the description of where the cave was.

Avalon had researched through archives at her school too and had found similar things. Together, they decided that Okka had to be right and that the Glove was in an underwater cave near the island. Neither of them could think of a way to retrieve it, though, so they didn't.

Then there was a day in which Avalon was going to be busy the whole day with school and political events that her dad had lined up that she had to attend. Jem didn't mind; he could use some time alone to think anyway. His pains had also been getting worse the last few days, and he didn't feel like putting on a comfortable mask around anyone.

So to spend his day alone, he decided to go to the small pond in the Refugee District. The weather had been very cloudy recently, but today was bright and sunny. He took deep breaths of cool, fresh air as he walked through the district, enjoying the slight warmth of the sun's rays on his face. When he turned the corner around a building near the pond, though, he saw a girl sitting at the edge of the pond with her feet in the water. And it wasn't just any girl: it was Sierra. Since she hadn't yet seen him, Jem almost turned around and left, but he couldn't bring himself to do it. He missed her too much. So after an awkward moment of standing frozen, watching her kick light ripples in the water, he decided to walk up beside her.

"Hey," he said.

She turned her head and looked at him without smiling. "What are you doing here?" she asked.

"I wanted to be alone."

"Well, sorry, I was here first."

"That's okay," said Jem, pushing his hands in his pockets and looking down at her. "I don't mind your company."

"Maybe I mind yours," she spat back, not looking at him but rather at somewhere in the shining blue water.

Jem was a little dumbstruck at this, and it took him a minute to think of something to say. "Look," he said finally, "I miss you."

"Better not let your partner hear you say that."

"She's not—" But Jem didn't finish his sentence. They both knew that Avalon was his girlfriend or partner or whatever it was called. "Well, so she is my partner. Why does that mean that we can't be friends?"

"Because… because, I don't know," stammered Sierra. "I guess because… I just thought we were something. That's all."

"You mean, you thought we were like, boyfriend and girlfriend?" asked Jem, sitting down beside her and taking off his shoes. The water felt like ice as he stuck his feet in it, and he wondered why Sierra was doing this in the middle of winter.

She looked at him puzzled, clearly not knowing what a boyfriend or a girlfriend was. "I don't know what I thought we were, but I just didn't expect you to be kissing *her*."

"You mean Avalon? Why did you say *her* like that?"

"Because she's such a—ugh, I don't know. I just don't like her."

"She's a nice person," said Jem defensively.

"I'm sure she is," retorted Sierra with as much sarcasm as she could muster.

"I don't see why you and me can't be friends just because I'm dating Avalon. You're dating Rabaiz and he seems like a real prick."

"He's not a prick!" cried Sierra. "He's a nice guy."

"Sure," laughed Jem, matching Sierra's previous sarcasm.

They both sat in silence for a few minutes, letting the waves from their kicking splash over the edges of the pond on all sides. On the side of the pond where the water touched the large wall that separated the Refugee District from the rest of the city, the waves hit the wall and fell back on themselves, disrupting all the other smooth ripples. It was rhythmic to watch.

"Can we at least try to be friends?" asked Jem, breaking the silence. "I don't like not talking to you."

Sierra turned and looked him in the eyes, the water reflecting off her big brown eyes. "I don't know, Jem. I—"

"HEY!" came a voice from behind the two of them. Jem whipped around to see Rabaiz storming towards them. "What are you doing with my girl, dragonfreak?"

Jem stood up to face Rabaiz, ready to fight, and Sierra stood up just after, putting her arm in front of him. "Relax, Baiz. We were just talking," she said softly, as if she were trying to tame a wild animal.

"I don't care what you were doing; he's a DRAGON! Do you understand that? He is everything that is wrong with this world! Everything! He brought the zombies here!"

"Are you serious?" laughed Jem. "You are legitimately that stupid that you honestly believe that?"

"Of course I believe that!" shouted Rabaiz, stepping so close to Jem that Sierra had to stand between them. Short as she was, however, Jem and Rabaiz were still able to glare at each other over top of her. "Gathering teaches me all sorts of stuff about you filthy Draigs and your corrupt magic that brought the zombies upon us all."

Jem laughed loudly. "You are so right! Now why don't you walk away before I summon some of my zombie buddies to come eat you, huh?"

Rabaiz lunged forward at Jem and Sierra pushed him back. Jem stood his ground and didn't flinch. Sierra then put on her shoes, took Rabaiz by the arm, and led him away. "Come on, Baiz," she said. "We don't need to be fighting."

"Watch yourself, dragonfreak," spat Rabaiz. "Y'ain't safe anymore."

For laughs, Jem quickly transformed his throat to its dragon form and breathed a puff of flames that went straight for Rabaiz and made him scream like a little kid. The flame disappeared before it hit him, though, and then he disappeared around the corner.

Later that night, after spending a day alone with far too much to think about, Jem found himself sitting on the edge of the Fortress wall looking out over the Keladonian landscape. It really wasn't much to look at. On his far left was the volcano that he had once popped out of when he had tackled the Dragon through the portal into Kelados before. He knew that the island where the portal to Callisto used to be was to his far right, but he was unable to see it from so far away.

Some patches of dead, leafless trees hung about the brown, lifeless dirt. There were a few boulders here and there, and even a couple hills. There were no zombies in sight, though, which was nice.

Jem was bundled up in several layers of clothes and enjoying the fresh evening air. No longer needing to hide his dragon powers, he occasionally blew fire from his mouth to warm his hands. He thought about sprouting wings and flying around outside the Fortress walls for a bit, but his pains had been increasing in intensity all day and he didn't feel like risking it. At that moment, his scar was burning pretty painfully, and he felt like he had been stabbed in the side. So it wasn't as bad as it could be.

As the sun began to set, Jem heard a rustling behind him much like someone was climbing the side of a building. He looked over his shoulder only to see Rabaiz's head poking up over the edge of the nearest building.

"What do you what?" Jem called, not wanting to deal with him right now. Rabaiz pulled himself up onto the building and began walking over.

"I want to know why you're bothering my partner, Surwae."

Jem stood up slowly while gripping his side in pain. The sudden movement almost made him vomit, but he did his best not to show his pain.

"I wasn't bothering anyone," he said. "I was just talking to her. And if you don't mind, I really don't feel like talking to you right now. So you can leave."

"I'm not going anywhere," laughed Rabaiz. "Not while you're still alive."

Alive? thought Jem. *Is this kid serious? Is he actually going to try and kill me?*

"Have you ever fought a dragon?" asked Jem, growing his wings out from his back and allowing them to stretch out to their full, massive wing span. He grinned, almost daring Rabaiz to come at him.

"Nope," said Rabaiz. "But I don't plan to."

In an instant, Rabaiz whipped out a small black object from his pocket and hurled it at Jem. The projectile came flying at Jem with four long arms outstretched. Jem had no time to react as the device clamped down onto him and the mechanical arms seized him tightly. The impact knocked him backwards off the wall and he flapped his wings vigorously, but they shrunk away as he fell, and when he smacked hard against the ground outside the Fortress, a puff of dust rose up around him and his dragon wings were completely gone. The device on his chest was squeezing him and sending electrical shocks throughout his body, making him unable to transform or use any magic.

He writhed in incredible pain as he watched Rabaiz descend the Fortress wall. Rabaiz was using his dark blue sylph as a sort of grapple to lower himself slowly down the enormous wall. Then he walked up to Jem and laughed boisterously.

"Not so tough are you now, huh?" spat Rabaiz, kicking Jem hard in the ribs. "Thought you could be all powerful as that dragon beast, but you can't do that with electricity coursing through your veins, cleansing you of your accursedness." This time he delivered a whopping kick to Jem's head, sending Jem rolling across the ground and screaming in pain.

Jem coughed violently and his blood splattered against the dirt beside him. Just above that, in the horizon, he saw something coming—a lot of somethings that were moving very quickly. He wasn't able to see or think clearly enough to piece it together, but it didn't seem good.

Rabaiz kicked him several more times, laughing and enjoying his pain. Jem couldn't even tell where his pain was coming from anymore. He felt like he needed to throw up but the electric shocks kept his muscles so tight that he couldn't. His back felt broken from the fall down, and every inch of his body was in furious pain. He was in far too much pain to move, much less put up any sort of fight. Rabaiz was almost certainly going to kill him.

Rabaiz stepped closer to Jem and stood over top of him wielding a large rock. "Well, you're gonna stay away from Sierra now," he said, smiling sadistically and tossing the rock up and down in his hand. Behind him, Jem could see the figures in the distance getting closer, only now he could tell that they were Rastvo zombies, the giant green ones. "And I'm sure the Phoenix will be very happy with me for wiping a heretic off the face of this planet," continued Rabaiz. "For the Phoenix!" he cried, hurling the rock down at Jem's head.

In what was more of a convulsion than a dodge, Jem rolled to his left and the rock struck against the arm of the device that was gripping his right shoulder. It made a loud metallic *clink* as the rock broke through the device's arm and hit Jem's scar. Jem howled in pain as the rock shattered into several pieces and the device's broken arm flailed about uselessly. The device stopped shocking him momentarily during this, and in his extreme pain, he kicked his legs about ferociously, accidently knocking Rabaiz to the ground.

Jem heard Rabaiz scream, but Jem's eyes were shut tight, trying to block out the pain long enough to transform. It wasn't working. He glanced behind him and saw the zombies were very close and running very fast. Rabaiz stood up to run but tripped over Jem's body. Jem managed to slip out of the electrical device and stumbled past Rabaiz. The war cries of the zombies were right behind them, and the Fortress alarms signaling that it was going into lockdown were blaring.

Jem looked up and saw the dark blue force field shooting up to cover the Fortress. There was no way back in now, not even for Rabaiz with his sylph grapple. Jem knew that the only way he might survive was to transform into a dragon and fly away, but he was just in too much pain to do that. Rabaiz yanked him back and went running alongside the Fortress wall away from the zombies. Jem went running after him as fast as he could, gripping his shoulder that felt like it was dislocated.

Running much slower than Rabaiz, the zombies caught up to him first. One massive creature swung its hand out and struck Jem right in the head. He managed to stay on his feet and keep running, but the long-legged zombies were much faster than him. Another zombie grabbed at Jem's left shoulder and tore off a piece of his clothing, leaving a bloody gash on that shoulder.

Before the zombies could catch Rabaiz, he shot sylph from his hand and tried to latch it onto the top of the Fortress wall like a grapple a few yards ahead of them. It managed to catch on the very edge of the wall, and Rabaiz swung forward and began to pull himself up.

As Jem ran by, he was close enough to reach up and grab onto Rabaiz. He threw his hand up, thinking about either trying to latch onto Rabaiz so that they could both be saved or pulling Rabaiz down and preventing him from escaping at all, but he quickly withdrew his hand and kept running. The risk of them both falling to their death if he tried to hold on was too great, and there was no point in dragging Rabaiz down to his death if he had the chance to escape this terrible end.

After he passed Rabaiz, though, Jem no longer heard the zombies right behind him as he ran on. Looking over his shoulder, he saw that all the zombies were gathered underneath Rabaiz, reaching up and jumping and trying to grab at him. Rabaiz had just barely managed to get out of their reach, and he was gradually pulling himself up. It looked like he would be safe, but Jem didn't have much time before the zombies would refocus on him. He was headed towards a hill straight ahead that he could hopefully hide behind if they didn't see him go there.

Just as he reached the top of the hill, he heard Rabaiz screaming at the top of his lungs. Jem dropped to the ground on the opposite side of the hill and peered over the top. He saw one zombie standing on another zombie standing on another zombie; they had basically made a three zombie ladder to be able to reach Rabaiz. The zombie at the very top was swiping at Rabaiz's feet, and Rabaiz was howling in fear, apparently unable to drag himself up any higher. The zombie then leaped up so high that it was level with Rabaiz and it grabbed him easily around the chest with both its hands. It then went toppling back to the ground with Rabaiz, and Jem heard screams mixed with the sound of breaking bones and tearing flesh as the zombies devoured Rabaiz.

I'm next, thought Jem. *There's nowhere to go after this hill. If they see me, I'm dead.*

"Hey!" came a gruff voice from behind him. "Over here!"

Jem turned around to see a person in full black poking their head out from an apparent door in the Fortress wall.

"Get over here!" the person yelled in a hushed tone. They sounded familiar, but Jem couldn't think of why.

Jem shook his head and muttered, "I can't," but he doubted that the person could hear him. He was in too much pain and his vision was beginning to lose focus and fade. Unable to move from his position near the top of the hill, Jem watched as the stealthy person ran out quickly from the doorway and came to his side. The person hooked their arms under his shoulders and dragged him back towards the door.

Just as Jem was being pulled into the wall, he saw a few zombies come running over the hill. A cement door then came sliding down in front of him, safely blocking the zombies from reaching him. He wanted to breathe a sigh of relief, but he could barely breathe. He felt his rescuer let go of his shoulders and rest him on the ground.

"Will you be okay?" the voice asked.

"I... don't... know..." breathed Jem, hardly able to speak at all.

"I'll go get medical help. Don't move."

Jem then heard footsteps as the person left him in a dark chamber somewhere within the Fortress wall. Just outside the wall, he could hear the zombies pounding against it, and bits of dust fell from the ceiling onto his lips. A sharp pain shot throughout his abdomen, and he vomited against the wall beside him.

Medical attention won't help, he thought. *Doctors can't help me. Not with this poison. I need to leave.*

So he began to crawl out of the dark chamber, and he knew where he needed to go. He needed to find the Or'lidi.

CHAPTER 19:
ANYELA

The chamber was narrow and almost lightless as Jem crawled his way through it. He saw a dim light coming from somewhere, and he just went towards that. The chamber turned to the right, went on a while more, then turned left and opened up to the rest of the city. Light was streaming in from this opening—bluish light because the lights around the city were reflecting off the blue sphere protecting the Fortress. The bright light made Jem's eyes hurt. He managed to crawl out of the entrance to the tunnel, which was cleverly concealed behind some building, and find his way to a nearby alley.

As soon as the tunnel was out of sight, he collapsed onto the ground and just lay there for a few minutes. The alarms signaling the zombie invasion were blaring in the background and drilling their way into his skull. He threw up a couple more times and then just lay there and waited. Eventually, the alarms stopped, and Jem could tell that the shield was lowered because the piece of ground he was staring at was no longer blue from the reflection.

Slowly, he was able to pull himself up by leaning against whatever building he was beside. Concentrating all of his effort into transforming, he began to grow wings. Then his legs grew, and within seconds, he was fully transformed. He didn't feel fully transformed, though. He felt like a weaker version of the dragon he could be. He didn't attempt to breathe fire, roar, or do anything. He just dug his claws into the building and climbed up it.

Once on the roof, he beat his wings a couple times and started to take off, but then crashed back down again. *Focus*, he told himself. *Focus*. He tried again, this time thinking to himself that if he could just get to the Or'lidi, maybe they could take the dragon poison away. Maybe they could stop all of this once and for all. He needed that, and that motivated him to get his wings flapping and to take off into the air.

He flew slowly, losing a few feet of altitude every time he had a sharp pain, but he continued on regardless. He could see the Or'lidi cloud ahead of him, and he was hoping with everything that he had that they could help him. There was no way he could take this pain any longer. He couldn't keep putting up with it; it was too much.

Immediately when he broke through the clouds, he quit flapping. His huge dragon body fell down onto the clouds, and he began to transform back into his human form but caught himself just in time and remained in dragon form. *Humans can't see the Or'lidi or stand on the cloud*, he told himself. *Don't get yourself killed.*

"Jem?" came Ontam's voice from somewhere. "What brings you here? Are you okay?"

Jem lifted his big dragon head up to see Ontam, Benya, and Minosa looking down at him. They were all naked, but the puffiness of the clouds and the dark night sky concealed most of them anyway. Minosa came walking forward cautiously and poked Jem's nose. When he didn't react, she began to pet it, and then she hugged his head which was probably bigger than her whole body. This made Jem smile.

I need your help, he said, looking between Ontam and Benya. *Please. There is poison in my body from the Dragon. That is why I can transform into a dragon. But I need it gone. It gives me unbearable pain and it almost just got me killed. I can't handle it anymore.*

Benya looked at him slowly and came up to crouch beside Minosa. She examined his eyes and then turned and called to Ontam to come closer.

"I can feel it in him," she said.

"We could remove it," replied Ontam.

"But then… would his powers be gone too?" asked Benya.

"Almost certainly," said Ontam. "You can't take away just the bad parts of the poison and leave the good. Once poisoned, it's all or nothing."

Jem's heart sank. He felt like all his organs had fallen through the cloud and crashed down on the ground below. Give up his dragon powers to be freed from the pains… could he do that?

Using all the energy he had left, he slowly managed to pull himself up to a sitting position. *So that's it?* he asked. *You can help me, but then I can't be a dragon anymore?*

"That is correct, Jem," said Ontam. "I'm sorry. I wish I could help you more, but the pains are interconnected with the powers. That bite was both a gift and a hindrance. If I could take the hindrance and leave the gift, I would. But unfortunately, it is not so."

Jem stared long and hard at Ontam and Benya, too many thoughts spinning around in his head. Minosa curled up against his neck, petting his scales. His pains persisted as strong as ever, but the little girl's touch was soothing.

"If you ask us to, we can remove the poison from your body," said Benya. "But considering what an asset you are to the humans, I think—"

Weapon, interjected Jem. *I'm a weapon for them.*

Benya looked a little flustered. "Well, yes, I guess you are. But, unfortunately, that is necessary in these circumstances. Without you, there is much that can never be achieved."

You don't understand what I go through every day, retorted Jem angrily. *You don't understand the pain and humiliation of being crippled completely for hours or days at a time. You can tell me that I'm useful all you want, but that doesn't change the fact that it is torture for me to continue on. I could let go whenever I wanted. I could let the pains take me and I could die, but I haven't yet. I don't know if I can keep fighting that fight. Eventually, you just get tired.*

Both Benya and Ontam stared at the ground, looking embarrassed.

I know that a lot rests on my shoulders, continued Jem, *but this is just too much for me to handle. It's just too much.*

"I understand," said Ontam. "But before you make your decision, please allow us to show you something."

Jem nodded and then watched as Ontam and Benya stepped aside and held their arms up together. In the space between their arms, an image began to take focus.

"This is a recording from a couple of days ago," explained Ontam.

Different colors all came swirling around in the air and began to align themselves into what looked like a person sitting down in a metallic chair. Gradually, the image became more vivid. The room was empty aside from the person in the chair who had jet-black hair and was wearing black pants, black shoes, and nothing else. A bright light illuminated the room and made his skin look sickeningly pale. His eyes were a piercingly bright blue.

A woman then came strolling into the room wearing robes that were infused with all sorts of colors: crimson, scarlet, dark purple, dark brown, and black. Her hair was long, black, and intricately woven in a delicate pattern that fell down her back. She walked slowly, her boots clicking against the hard floor as she did, echoing throughout the quiet room. She was carrying a tray with five vials: four were glowing white and one was glowing a deep red.

"You know," she said, her voice echoing in the big room, "I've never heard of someone putting a Soul inside themselves, much less four of them."

"Yes, well that is why no one else is as successful as I have been," replied Veroci. "I would have used all five if I did not need to leave magic for the soldiers and the wealthy to draw from."

The woman set the tray beside the chair, and it hovered there by magic, as if sitting on an invisible table. She lifted the red vial and held it up to the light, gazing at it with wonder. "And to be imbued with the blood of a dragon," she said. "One can't even imagine the power that would give someone."

A grin broke Veroci's expression. "I can imagine it," he said.

The woman smiled at him, but he continued to stare forward unblinkingly.

"You understand that this may not work?"

"I understand," said Veroci. "I am willing to risk it."

"You would do anything for power, wouldn't you?" she asked, touching his face lightly with her long, black nails.

Veroci smirked. "Power is all that matters in this world, Anyela."

"Indeed, it seems so," said Anyela, returning her attention to the vials. "Now if all goes as planned, you know what to expect?"

"I'm either dead or more powerful than ever. I think I'll be able to tell the difference."

"Remember, though, that there will still be one with the power to destroy you."

"The blue-eyed boy," growled Veroci. "I know. But my powers will undoubtedly surpass his. He stands no chance."

Anyela flicked one of the vials and listened to the melodic ringing. "He already escaped you once," she said airily. "And that was before he had the dragon powers."

Veroci's hand flinched, as if he had considered hitting her, but then he relaxed again, and his arms stayed stoically on the chair's armrests.

"That won't happen again," said Veroci. "He is as good as dead."

"I think it's funny," said Anyela, pouring one of the white vials into her hand where it was suspended in a misty orb shape. "That the same boy you wanted dead before because he could have been your son is the same boy who was then imbued with incredible powers from the dragon."

Veroci's body was physically trembling, but he said nothing. Anyela continued to pour the other white vials into her hand, and the glowing orb gradually grew larger.

"Do you ever feel," she continued, "that you may have played an integral part in creating your own enemy? Isn't it ironic that you tried to kill your possible son just because I told you that he had the power to end you, and then he goes on and obtains a power that guarantees he can end you?"

Veroci did not respond. "That's okay, Master, you don't have to respond," she said lightly, leaning in and whispering in his ear. "I know you want to kill me, but you won't. You still need me, and you will continue to need me for a long time."

Anyela then poured the last white vial into her hand, and the orb shone brightly. She took the red vial in her other hand and began to pour it slowly over the white orb. The red swirled around the orb, looking as if hundreds of small snakes were slithering about it, and covered it completely. The orb in her hand was then glowing a bright red, tinting the room slightly.

"When this enters you," explained Anyela, "you will be able to use fire magic just like a dragon and, perhaps, even be able to transform into one. The four Callistonian Souls will not only amplify your own magic, but also protect you from the negative effects of the dragon blood. Then, the only being capable of ending your life will be one who also possesses dragon blood, which means you must end the Dragon's life and Jem's life if you wish to be truly unstoppable.

"You will, by no means, by invincible, however. You could still drown, you could still die in the vacuum of space, and you could still be crushed by a large enough boulder. But when this infusion of dragon's blood and Soul enters you, you will be the closest anyone has ever come to being invincible. Enjoy."

Clamps then extended from the chair, locking in Veroci's legs, arms, abdomen, and neck. Anyela pressed the orb against Veroci's chest, and it gently slipped inside of him. He screamed violently as she did this, and she cackled with delight. After the orb entered him completely and the room lost its red tint, Anyela backed away slowly, taking the tray with the empty vials with her.

Veroci howled in pain and thrashed about aggressively, but the clamps in the chair held him still. After a few moments, he stopped moving completely and just sat there, breathing heavily and staring forward.

"Did it work?" asked Anyela from a few yards away.

Veroci turned and looked at her for the first time. His eyes were literally glowing blue now. He smiled a wide, cruel smile.

Without warning, Anyela then went flying across the room and smacked into the wall. The tray went clashing about and the vials shattered, spraying broken glass across the room. The clamps on Veroci's chair exploded open, and he stood tall, gazing unemotionally at Anyela. She was still moving, and she looked up just in time to see Veroci's chair disintegrate into dust and the floor around him begin to crack.

"It worked," she muttered, smiling evilly.

Then the image that Jem was watching swirled away into a bunch of random colors and rearranged itself into a new scene.

Veroci was sitting at a slick black desk in his office, the same office that Jem remembered from when he and Sierra had been taken captive by the Regime. Metae, Veroci's brother, was standing in front of the desk and didn't seem very happy to be there.

"The portal is going to take several more months," he was saying apologetically. "There's just no way to build it faster, and the technology isn't quite there yet."

"Then I want everyone on this! The portal must be the first priority," spat Veroci. "This must get done before anything else. Hire poor people from outside the City if you must. Pay them close to nothing and tell them you're doing them a favor because at least they have jobs."

"Why not pay them a regular salary, like the rest of Veroci Corp's workers?" asked Metae. "It's not like their pay is that great anyway."

"Because then I have less money, brother, and I don't want that to happen. I deserve all the money; I earned it, I worked hard, and they were just lazy."

"But you hoard all this money and you do nothing with it!" cried Metae. "Most of the Xena Region starves while you live in luxury and the rest of Xena City barely scrapes by. It should be a crime to behave as you do."

"Well it isn't and it never will be because I have the money to ensure that. So stop your whining and finish that damn portal as soon as possible, or you'll be one of the poor people I employ to build my stuff. Now go."

Obviously very upset, Metae stormed from the room. Veroci put his feet up on the desk and smiled.

That image then dissolved away, and Ontam and Benya put their arms down. Neither of them spoke.

Jem breathed a heavy sigh. *I understand why I have to keep my dragon powers. All the pain I could ever experience would be worth it if I could save Callisto from that man. I have to do everything in my power to stop Veroci and the Regime once and for all. Thank you for showing me that. I now know what I have to do.*

Ontam and Benya both smiled, but they were weak smiles because while the two Or'lidi were proud, they saw the incredible pain that Jem was in and the burden he was taking upon himself.

"I'm glad you have made such an honorable decision, Jem," said Ontam. "But the second thing we showed you means that there is no time to waste. Veroci is preparing a portal that could be done within months. If the zombies need to be eradicated before the humans will focus on the Regime, then you must act quickly."

Jem nodded. *Are you always able to spy on Veroci like that?*

"Not exactly," explained Ontam. "We sent one Or'lidi to Callisto to spy for us about a week ago. The footage you just watched was everything that she was able to get for us. She was very weakened by the trip over there and never made it back. She is gone now, for good. She was our strongest Or'lidi, though, and it is doubtful any of us could even survive the trip there. We were meant for this planet, not space, nor Callisto. I wish we could help you extract more information, but what you just saw is everything we can provide you with. I'm sorry."

Don't be sorry. That was very useful information. Thank you.

"You're welcome," they both said.

Can I spend the night here? asked Jem. *I'm too tired to get back to the Fortress.*

"Of course," said Benya, petting his nose. "Take all the time you need."

Minosa then let go of Jem and went over to her parents. The three of them smiled and waved as they walked away. Jem, in dragon form, then curled up into a ball and tried to sleep, but the pain was too much.

He spent the night drifting in and out of sleep while nightmares barraged his mind and sharp pains jabbed at his torso and shoulder.

Justin Dennis

CHAPTER 20:
INJECTIONS

Farouche woke up in the morning before anyone else in building sixty-four. Dim light filtered inside signaling that the sun was about to rise. His headband was covering one of his eyes, so he pushed it back up onto his forehead and rubbed his eyes. Jem was still sound asleep, snoring loudly. Farouche got up quietly and tiptoed out of the room.

He passed by the room where Leo, Rimaya, and Sierra slept, but Rimaya didn't seem to be there. She must've stayed out last night partying. Farouche noticed that she tended to party even more than he did, and she often didn't come home. He envied her worry-free lifestyle. She didn't attend classes like some of the other refugees, she didn't play any sports, and she rarely helped ECKO with anything.

Sierra, on the other hand, had only recently started spending nights at building sixty-four. When Rabaiz had died a couple weeks ago, Sierra had spent a few straight days in her room. She hadn't really talked to anyone around building sixty-four at that point, but she had talked to those Nest Fenics when they came by to check up on her. Despite being a Fenic, Farouche had never really talked to those kids; he just hung out in a different group.

After her days of solitude, though, Sierra hadn't shown up for a couple days and Farouche had assumed that she had been staying at the Nest. Now she was back, apparently, but Farouche didn't really care. They never talked much, and her mourning over Rabaiz seemed a little overdone. Everything Farouche had heard about Rabaiz was bad. He had seemed like a real jerk.

Jem had explained to Farouche about what had happened to Rabaiz. Farouche had believed him, but unfortunately, not everyone did, and he got a lot of crap from some Fenics who had accused him of murdering Rabaiz.

189

It didn't help that he had fled the scene right after the shields went down. He had tried to explain to everyone about the Or'lidi, but no one had believed him, even though Farouche had backed him up. Everybody had seemed convinced that Jem and Farouche were making it up to further their own agenda. However, there was no proof that Jem murdered Rabaiz, so he was never arrested for it.

Farouche had been in the ECKO meeting when Jem had told everyone about the Phoenix Glove, but nobody had believed that it really existed or that they could obtain it. Jem had said that a Councilmember named Okka supported them, but nobody else from the Council or ECKO believed them. It seemed that they wouldn't be going after the Phoenix Glove anytime soon, which made Farouche sad because he desperately wanted it in his possession so that he could study it and the magic that went into engineering it.

When Farouche made it to the living room at the center of the building, a small amount of sunlight was trickling in from the main entrance. It looked like it was going to be a beautiful, sunny day. Farouche levitated some juice up from the refrigerator in the ground and got some bread and fresh fruit from the cupboard. The garden beside the building supplied them with delicious, fresh food every day. It had been Teek's idea, and it worked brilliantly. Farouche saw a lot of opportunity for small, local farms when they rebuilt Callisto, and he had a million ideas scribbled down about how to implement it.

After breakfast by himself, he headed out the front door and passed by Teek's family's room and Tachel's room. Farouche had a lot of respect for the feisty little girl and her parents, but the Reg was pretty weird. He hardly talked to anyone, and Farouche didn't know if he could ever trust a Reg. As far as he was concerned, they were all the same: heartless killers.

Farouche spent the day at the technician's building like he did most days. He was there before anyone else, so he started to work on the sylph weapon that he was helping to develop called an astra.

By the time his coworkers began to show up, he was already running tests on the small, black prototype. It was a cylinder with a rubberized hand grip around it and was transparent on one side. Inside the cylinder, the user's sylph was supposed to be stored, but they had been having trouble with a sylph leak on the prototype. Farouche was able to repair the sylph entry point so that sylph could enter upon demand but wouldn't leave until the user retracted it. It was a rather simple fix, and he palmed his face when he realized what he had done wrong.

Over the course of the day, all of the technicians took turns using the prototype to ensure that it was compatible with all of their different sylphs. Programmers were still designing different types of weapons that could be deployed from it. Currently, it could only launch bits of magic that would stun an opponent up to thirty yards away, but they were working on a longer range mode, a kill mode, a sword mode for close range, and Farouche was pushing hard for a defense mode that could deploy a shield. These astras were going to be the main weapon used to attack the zombies, so they had to be ready as soon as possible, and there was a lot of work to do.

After a long day of working diligently, Farouche felt like he had earned a good break. One of his coworkers, Cayo, was a Fenic who was just a couple years older than he was, and he invited Farouche to a party at his house that night. Farouche happily accepted.

Cayo lived on the top level of a building near the corner where the wall that separated the city from the Refugee District touched the wall that separated the Fortress from the rest of Kelados. Within an hour of Farouche's arrival, the sun had set and a bunch of different Fenics had arrived. Everybody was dressed in casual clothes: boots or canvas shoes, slim pants or shorts, t-shirts, and jackets for the most part. A lot of people wore Fenic colors, although not everybody did, but nobody wore Draig colors. That was just an unspoken rule that Farouche had picked up on since hanging around Fenics.

Farouche himself was decked out in nice clothes. He had big black boots, black pants, and a bright red t-shirt underneath his unbuttoned, light gray hoodie. He had his red headband on, a necklace with the two-pronged Fenic flame on it, and a fancy magic watch that he had designed. It connected to the digital magic server back in his office, which Jem had referred to as a "computer" for some reason, and allowed him to send messages and always be connected with ECKO. It worked somewhat like the mavs that the Keladonians had. He didn't go anywhere without it.

That night, however, he wasn't paying much attention to his watch at all. The music was loud and the house was buzzing with people. Farouche was playing a magic game called Soyu Shenanigans that functioned similarly to FI, allowing the users to control a virtual avatar.

In this game, Farouche and Cayo were on a team against two cute girls who they had both been flirting with for the entire party. Their small avatars went around a board and participated in mini games that consisted of random adventures ranging from racing sylphcycles to fighting with colorful paint bombs. The four of them were laughing and having a good time amongst all the other party-goers who were dancing, talking, or participating in games of their own.

"Want another hit?" the girl on the left asked Farouche.

"For sure," replied Farouche, taking the propo bottle that was being passed around. He took his needle from his pocket, plugged it into the bottle, and shot it into his arm. A wave of relaxation coursed through him immediately, and he handed the bottle to Cayo.

After they finished, Cayo had to use the bathroom and the two girls went to get more propo since the bottle was empty. Farouche was feeling a little lightheaded, so he headed for the balcony outside. The calm, crisp air felt refreshing. A few other people were standing out on the balcony talking, but he had his back to them as he leaned against the handrail and looked out towards the corner where the Fortress wall met the Refugee District wall. It seemed to zoom in and out repeatedly at first, but Farouche rubbed his eyes and things looked normal once again. His head was still spinning, though.

He breathed deeply in and out for a few minutes, trying to get himself together. He stared down at the ground below him for a bit, trying to figure out if it would kill him to jump that far. Maybe he should try to find out. No, no, that would be a bad idea. Bad idea.

When he looked back up again, he noticed a person sitting on the wall to the Refugee District. In the darkness of the night, it was difficult for Farouche to see who it was, especially since he couldn't tell if there was only one person or three or two or maybe five. No, wait, it was definitely just one, and he was looking over here now. He made eye contact with Farouche, and that's when Farouche realized that it was Tachel; light from the nearby buildings caught the Reg's hazel eyes precisely in a way that made them shine yellow. Farouche immediately had a flashback of being in Ilios.

He remembered sitting up on the roof of different local shops in Ilios City and staring out towards the horizon, wondering if he could ever make it in another region. He had only done that after his mother had beaten him, because on those nights, he couldn't stand to sleep in the same house as her; so he would find a shop that was closed and scale the side of the building and spend the night on the roof.

He could feel the sting of her hand on his face. He rubbed the side of his face to make it go away, but it wouldn't. Where could his mom be now? Dead? Enslaved by the Regime? Did she deserve that? Should he have tried to rescue her, bring her to Kelados, despite what she did to him? He could feel tears welling up in his eyes again, and he seriously considered jumping off the ledge now.

"Hey, Farouche," said Cayo, placing a hand on Farouche's shoulder and squashing any urge Farouche had to jump. "What're you doing out here?"

"Oh, just… clearing my head," replied Farouche.

"Hm, alright," said Cayo, leaning against the handrail beside him. "Who's that?" he asked, pointing towards Tachel.

"That's Tachel. He lives in my building in the Refugee District."

"Oh, should we invite him over here?"

Farouche thought about it for a moment. Tachel obviously hadn't made any friends since being here. Maybe he was lonely up there. Maybe he was as lost and hurt as Farouche had been in Ilios. Farouche shook the idea out of his head. *No, he's a Reg,* he told himself. *Regs are not good. Don't think about him like that.*

"No, don't invite him," said Farouche. "He's kind of a jerk."

"Okay, whatever you say, dude," said Cayo. "Well, come on then, let's get back in there; Bell and Reya and waiting for us. You good?"

"Yeah, yeah, I'm good. I'm good." Farouche ran his hands through his hair a few times trying to get his head to function properly. He glanced over his shoulder one last time at Tachel before he went back inside and saw him still sitting there, staring out at the emptiness of Kelados.

A few games and several bottles of propo later, Farouche was barely able to control his avatar and had trouble walking to the bathroom. While peeing, he couldn't figure out which toilet bowl to pee into, and he may or may not have flushed. He couldn't remember. He washed his hands and left the water running as he stumbled back out into the hallway.

Before he made it back to the living room, a deafening alarm sounded. At first, he thought it was just in his head, and he fell to the ground covering his ears, but when he looked up, people were running past him and disappearing down the fire escape. Within seconds, the entire building had been vacated, and Farouche was left stumbling helplessly through the living room trying to find an exit.

"Hey, everybody, where'd you go?" he called, half-expecting someone to pop up from behind the couch and yell, "Surprise!" But no one did. He couldn't deny it. This was definitely a zombie alarm. Maybe it could be a drill, though? That would be nice. Real zombies don't attack when it's a drill.

Suddenly, there was the sound of footsteps on the roof. *Footsteps?* thought Farouche. *That's weird. Who would be on the roof when zombies could be attacking? I better investigate.*

So he stumbled towards the balcony, ignoring his watch which was blinking, vibrating, and sounding its own alarm trying to tell him to stay inside. When he made it out to the balcony, he stood on a chair to see on the roof, and to his surprise, three giant Rastvo zombies were standing there wielding swords.

"Crap," he said aloud. The three Rastvo all turned and looked at him when he said this. One roared viciously, spraying saliva across the roof, and came charging at him. Farouche ducked and lost his footing on the chair, causing him to fall down and hit his head against the wall.

He then watched as the zombie came flying down from the roof onto the balcony. It was so large and moving so fast that it shattered the handrail and went sliding off the balcony, only staying on because it dug its sharp claws into the floor of the balcony.

Farouche rushed to get to his feet, but it was difficult because the whole building was spinning, and the chair kept getting in his way. By the time he finally got to his feet, the zombie had gotten to its feet as well. It charged straight for him, enormous gray sword in hand, and Farouche stumbled backwards through the doorway and fell on his butt.

This is it, he thought. *This zombie is going to kill me.*

But then an arm appeared around the zombie's neck, and it stopped running. Farouche watched as Tachel struggled with the zombie, clinging onto its back with his arm wrapped around its neck. Eventually, using his other arm, Tachel was able to hold a scepter up to the zombie's head, and the head exploded. The zombie's body fell to the ground, and Tachel stood there covered in pieces of green zombie flesh.

Farouche heard more zombie roars, and then two more zombies came jumping down onto the balcony. One swung its sword down at Tachel, and as he blocked it with his scepter, sparks flew. The zombie swung again, but Tachel ducked and took the zombie's legs out with his scepter. The second zombie stabbed at him, and he leaned to the side—narrowly avoiding the sharp blade. In one fluid movement, he whipped his scepter around and struck the zombie in the head, blowing it into a million pieces.

The other zombie then stood up from the ground, and Tachel just pointed his scepter in its face and shot a magical blue sphere at the zombie's head, exploding it. The alarms immediately stopped, but the shields remained up. Tachel walked into the building and reached out his hand to help up Farouche.

"Th-thanks," stammered Farouche, not knowing what else to say.

Tachel gave a slight smile and nodded. He then walked back out onto the balcony and Farouche followed him. They both stood there and stared towards the Fortress wall. It was a good thing that the shields were up because hundreds of zombies had scaled the wall and were standing on top of it, beating against the shield and stabbing it with various weapons. They roared with their mouths wide open, revealing their disgusting fangs, and climbed over each other to get as high on the shield as they could. There must have been hundreds, if not thousands, more zombies below the wall where they couldn't see.

"Good thing only three got in," said Tachel.

Farouche nodded.

CHAPTER 21:
PREPARATIONS

Jem sat in the conference room tapping his fingers against the table, waiting for everything to get started. Forenzi was still constructing the map of Kelados on the mav at the end of the room. Today, all the Councilmembers and ECKO leaders were gathered around a giant circular table in ECKO's main building. Apparently, a plan had already been made for their invasion of the zombie region. Jem hadn't been informed of this, as he was sure many of the people here weren't, and he was anxious to see what Forenzi was going to show them.

Also at the table were Afflatus, Tekkara, the other seven Councilmembers, Farouche, Tachel, Sam, Henry, Sierra, Rimaya, and Leo. Ever since Tachel had saved Farouche's life during the zombie invasion just over a month ago, the two of them had been very close friends, and today they were sitting side by side and whispering fervently. Jem knew that everyone else trusted Tachel now, but he still wasn't so sure.

Everybody had been preparing for this meeting for a long time. Ever since the Council had learned that the second Soul of Kelados was resting in the crown of the Leader of the Djimota, they had begun preparations for an invasion. Farouche, since he had traveled there with the Or'lidi, was able to supply them with an accurate map of the journey down there and the Leader's castle.

The last few weeks leading up to the meeting had been stressful for everybody. Jem knew that Farouche had been developing some kind of weapon with Sierra's help, Sam and Henry had been developing transportation, Afflatus and Tekkara had both been helping Jem develop his magic and dragon skills, Rimaya and Tachel had been developing armor, Leo had been preparing food and keeping everyone on a healthy diet, and the Councilmembers had developed the invasion plan.

Anxious to hear what everyone had been working on and what their plan was, Jem couldn't stop tapping away at the table. Forenzi had just finished poking around on the mav and was now using his hands to pull the 3D image of Kelados out of the mav and move it over to the table. The holographic Kelados was floating lightly in his hands as if it were made of pure light. He sent it out to the center of the table where it spun slowly.

"Welcome, everybody," began Forenzi, "to the first official meeting of the Zombie Invasion Squad. Everyone sitting in this room right now will be on one of the vimanas going to the zombie region when we attack in exactly three weeks. My fellow Councilmembers, you all will be in command of the others who are not here right now, and you will be responsible for informing them of everything that is discussed here. Seven other people have enlisted as soldiers and are currently undergoing tests to ensure that they are physically and mentally ready for what lies ahead. You will meet them later for training.

"Anyway, the map is displayed in front of all of you. As you can see, our Fortress is located on the northern tip of Kelados. We've learned recently that there are two different kinds of zombies: the Rastvo and the Djimota. The Rastvo populate the area around the center of Kelados represented by green on our map. The Djimota populate the southern tip of the planet represented by the purple. Our target, the second Soul of Kelados, rests in the center of the Djimota Kingdom.

"We will be coming down the east side of the planet in flying vehicles called vimanas." As Forenzi spoke, four virtual vehicles left the northern tip of the planet and began to follow a red arrow. They looked different from the vimanas that Jem remembered from Luria.

"The vimanas have been redesigned by Sam and Henry from an old blueprint from Farouche. They move slowly, but they are sturdy in the air and will be able to withstand a fair amount of attacks before crashing. They operate by a sylph turbine around the pilot's cabin; the pilot's sylph is inserted, and it spins around the cabin to power the thruster discs."

The vimanas were triangle-shaped aircraft, but instead of orbs on the three corners, there were giant rings. Nothing was inside the rings; there was just a dark blue, misty, waterfall-like stream being emitted downwards from the rim. That must've been how it stayed in the air. Other than that, it just looked like a giant piece of gray metal with sharp, jagged edges and a small circle protruding from the top of the center that looked like a place for a pilot to see.

"A few hours after leaving the Fortress," continued Forenzi as the virtual vimanas flew over the virtual planet, "we will reach zombie settlements just beyond the central river. We have been informed that these kinds of zombies, the large green kind we are familiar with, are called

Rastvo. It is likely that our ships will be under siege as soon as we enter. Our goal is to remain at a high enough altitude to be out of reach, but we don't know what kind of technology, magic, or weapons these zombies have, and we should be prepared for a fight.

"If we make it past the Rastvo, a new kind of zombie will be waiting for us: the Djimota. The Djimota are smaller, lighter zombies with purple skin and blades on their limbs. They can glide for short distances and will almost certainly be able to attack our vimanas. Jem, we're expecting you to protect the vimanas at this point in your dragon form."

Jem nodded. Forenzi spoke to him with a certain distain, but also with a note of respect. He knew what Jem was capable of, and he knew that Jem would be an invaluable asset during their invasion.

"Assuming all goes well up to this point, all four vimanas will hover above the golden dome located in the center of the Djimota Leader's castle. From there, we will descend down onto the dome and enter by blowing open the main entrance with magic since it is the only way to get inside. There will be four groups, one from each vimana, each led by one Draig and one Fenic Councilmember. The four pilots will stay in the vimanas to defend them and keep them out of the Djimota's reach."

As Forenzi spoke, small, faceless people descended from the virtual vimanas and cushioned their landing onto the castle with magic. The model then zoomed into the castle and followed the virtual people around.

"Once in the castle, two groups will circle around the back and the other two will hold out at the front. Then all four will open fire on the Leader who sits on a throne in the central room. The Soul is in a crown atop his head, and it will be Jem's duty to retrieve it. Once the Soul is in our possession, we get airlifted off the roof and head back for the Fortress. With both of the Keladonian Souls in our possession, a war against the zombies will be easily won in the near future. Questions?"

Jem raised his hand silently.

"Yes, Jem?"

"Yeah, what about the Dragon and the Phoenix?"

"What about them?" snapped Forenzi.

"How are we going to save them? Me and Farouche have told you and the whole Council multiple times that they are trapped and being held captive by the Djimota. Farouche even has a detailed map of where they are, just like he gave you a map of the castle."

Forenzi sighed heavily. "And I have told you multiple times, Jem, that no legendary could be contained by the zombies. Nothing can contain a legendary, not even something as purely evil as a zombie. The legendaries do not reveal themselves to us, but they are there, watching over us. They are most certainly not imprisoned, and therefore, we won't be wasting time, effort, and people to try and save them."

"But Farouche saw where they were kept," retorted Jem, "in a silver dome behind the castle, and Ontam told him about them. That is the same source of information that you have for knowing where the Leader and the Soul are. If you don't believe the Dragon and the Phoenix are in the silver dome, why do believe the Leader and the Soul are in the golden dome?"

"Because that is reliable information," snapped Forenzi, "but because of our systems, we know that the information about the Dragon and the Phoenix is unreliable."

"Your made-up systems don't count as evidence in the real world, Forenzi! The Dragon and the Phoenix are there and we need to save them!"

"That's enough, Jem," interjected Okka. Forenzi was red-faced and furious, hardly able to contain his anger. None of the other Councilmembers looked very pleased either.

"Other questions?" growled Forenzi through gritted teeth.

Jem raised his hand again, immediately drawing dirty looks from around the table.

"We are done discussing the Dragon and the Phoenix, Jem."

"My question isn't about that."

Forenzi glared at him for a moment. "Then what is it about?"

"The Sacred Portal," said Jem.

"Doesn't exist," spat Forenzi. "Any real questions?"

"Farouche saw it! He saw it right above the Leader! What is your excuse for that not existing?"

"The zombies did not come from a portal, Jem. They were spawned by the dra—I mean, the Evil One, in the absence of the Legendary One."

"No," barked Jem, ignoring the shut-up-right-now looks being shot at him from every person except for Farouche. "They come from a portal that is kept safe by the Leader, and if that portal is shut, they will die out because they need a constant flow of the virus. If we leave without shutting the portal, we won't be able to defeat them."

"I do not need a child to tell me how to protect my planet!"

"Well obviously you can't do it!"

"I am doing it just fine!"

"No, you're not!" cried Jem. "You're blatantly ignoring facts because of your beliefs. These systems are the stupidest things I've ever heard of; you all fight and argue just like the zombies. Those Rastvo and Djimota, they are fighting for control of the Sacred Portal just like you all fight over control of this city. You're no better than the zombies if you can't just put your beliefs aside, accept the facts, and work together for everyone's benefit."

"How dare you!" shouted Forenzi. "We are not zombies!"

"Enough!" shouted Ikuuno, standing to her feet and placing her arm in front of Forenzi. He seemed about ready to jump across the table and strangle Jem. "Jem, you are done with your questions," continued Ikuuno. "We are moving on now. Rimaya, Tachel, I believe you two have been developing armor. Go ahead with your presentation, please."

Rimaya and Tachel jumped to their feet anxiously as Forenzi and Ikuuno took their seats. Forenzi waved his hand angrily and the virtual model of Kelados disappeared. Tachel then took a small metal box from his pocket and tossed it into the center of the table, deploying a vivid hologram of a combat suit.

"These new combat suits," explained Tachel, "are made from a special combination of materials used in Regime suits and materials found only here in Kelados. The result is a very lightweight, flexible material which can deflect most magical lasers as well physical projectiles. Since we don't know what we will be facing, we don't know exactly how effective they will be. To account for that, the wrists of all the suits will be equipped with special magically powered shields that can be activated at will."

As Tachel spoke, the suit rotated slowly. It looked like it was made of a skintight black material with dark blue pieces of plastic around it. The dark blue pieces covered most of the suit in different shapes that contoured to the body except at the joints where there was just the regular black fabric. On the head of this virtual person was a matching dark blue helmet with a black visor.

When Tachel mentioned the shields, the suit knelt into a fighting position and two light blue, electric-looking shields shot out from the wrists. They wrapped around the suit and formed a perfect oval, protecting it from every direction.

"In the full-shield mode, the person will be completely protected from projectiles and limited physical attacks, but they will not be able to fire from their weapons. I believe Farouche has a presentation on the weapons prepared next, but for now, all you need to know is that weapons won't work in full-shield mode; it is a completely defensive position. It is also powered entirely by magic and will be difficult to sustain for long periods of time.

"A more practical option is single-shield mode," continued Tachel as the bubble around the suit dissipated and there was just a single, circular shield emanating from the suit's left wrist. "In this mode, the person's strong hand will be available to wield a weapon, but they will also be much more vulnerable to attacks from behind."

Tachel then nodded to Rimaya, who looked much more nervous.

"Oh, um, well I mainly helped with the materials and design and stuff," she said, motioning with her hands and causing the suit to throw a few kicks and punches, showing off the flexibility of the suit. "The black material forms to every curve of the wearer's body and stops at the neck, wrists, and ankles. The head is covered by a helmet which attaches to the neck of the suit and can only be attached and detached by magic.

"The gloves have a special sticky material on the palms that will allow the wearer to scale buildings and cling onto things with ease. That feature can be turned on and off with magic. The boots are thin and silent, allowing us to use stealth if we manage to get inside the golden dome. With magic, the user can get a higher jump through a special spring-like material in the bottom of the boots."

As she spoke, the suit demonstrated all the different uses with ease and skill. Jem was astounded by all of this, but he didn't know how he was going to learn to use the suit fully within the next three weeks.

"The dark blue panels across the suit's body offer greater protection than the black base, but are less flexible and that is why we didn't want to use it to cover the entire body. All of it should also be able to withstand an incredible amount of cold, heat, and stretching, meaning that your suit won't deteriorate over time, and Jem's suit—even the helmet—should stay intact when he transforms. And that, basically, is our suit."

"Daily training is mandatory for every person going on the invasion," added Tachel. "These suits will take a while to master, but it will be worth it. Farouche, Sierra, you're up."

Tachel reached out his hand, the suit disappeared back into the tiny metal box, and that box went flying back into his hand. Farouche and Sierra stood up as Tachel and Rimaya took their seats, Rimaya whispering to Tachel and hugging him happily.

"This is an astra," said Farouche, taking out a small, black cylinder from his messenger bag. "I didn't name it," he laughed, shrugging his shoulders. "I'd've called it a rendoblade, but—"

"But that names sucks," cut in Sierra, "and it's so much more than a blade. Can you demonstrate, Farouche?"

Farouche grinned. "Of course, Sierra." Everyone watched as his sylph left his hand and slipped into the top of the astra. The side of it then glowed blue with his sylph.

"To activate it," he explained, "you simply put your sylph into it and say a command to activate it. Each command is a word, but can be shortened into a letter, and hopefully we can train everyone to use it silently because it reacts much quicker when programmed verbal commands aren't needed. Let me demonstrate. Sword!"

A glowing, dark blue blade shot from the top of the cylinder and extended out maybe three or four feet.

"Off," said Farouche, and the blade disappeared back into the astra. "So it can be activated like that or by saying the first letter of the word: S." The sword extended out again. "Off," he said, and it retracted. "Once each of you masters the feeling of deploying the sword, hopefully you can deploy it without saying a word."

The sword then deployed again, and Farouche smiled. It disappeared without him saying anything.

"There are other modes, including several that fire projectiles," added Sierra. "Shooting, though, will take a large amount of energy because, after studying how zombies within the Fortress have been killed, we discovered that magic doesn't do it. Magic killing works by stopping the heart, but zombies have no heart. A physical projectile must be launched to kill a zombie, meaning that the user has to convert magic into physical matter.

"Normally, this would be draining enough to cause any regular person to pass out, but the astras make the conversion process much easier. It will still be very draining, but much less so than it would normally be."

"You'll also be training with the astras daily," said Farouche. "And we're going to be working on integrating the astras into the suit. You can expect a hip holster that locks the astra to it magically by the time we leave, as well as a personal tag on your astra so that only you can use it. That way, if your astra is lost or you are killed..."

Farouche's voice caught, and he cleared his throat. He readjusted his headband and continued. "Your, um, your astra will not be able to be used by any zombie. We don't know if they have sylph or anything similar to it, but we can't take any risks."

"So that's everything," said Sierra. "Thank you."

The two of them took their seats and Forenzi stood back up. "Thank you for your presentations, you four. We will be invading with the best technology available, and we are lucky to have you all to design it. Training begins immediately after this meeting at the stadium. The four assigned groups will be posted there, and the seven enlisted soldiers should be waiting there when we arrive. Any questions? Not you, Jem," he added, glaring at him.

The room was silent. Jem was biting his tongue.

"Perfect. Meeting dismissed then. See you all at training."

Everyone began to file out of the room, but Jem remained seated and so did Okka. When everyone else had left, Okka turned to Jem.

"You can't be so disrespectful to others' beliefs," said Okka.

"I wasn't being disrespectful," insisted Jem. "I was being factual. You believe me, don't you?"

"I... I believe you about the portal, Jem, but the Dragon cannot be contained by zombies. That's simply not possible."

"You—you're just as brainwashed as Forenzi!" cried Jem, horrified that his only ally had turned on him.

"I am not brainwashed, Jem, and watch your tongue. You cannot just spout off hateful words about Draigs or Fenics like that."

"I'm not being hateful. If your beliefs aren't open to criticism, then maybe they're wrong."

Okka looked away from Jem and shook his head. "You have disappointed me. I thought you were better than this."

Jem stood up. "You disappointed me, Okka. I'm going to free the Dragon and the Phoenix, and I'm going to shut the portal, no matter what you or Forenzi say."

"Don't be a fool," said Okka, standing up to face Jem. "You are flying in the face of thousands of years of tradition."

"Progress is inevitable; I'm only bringing it on a little quicker," said Jem, and he walked out of the room.

CHAPTER 22:
CONFLICTED

Teek wasn't enjoying dinner very much that night. The gozen—the Keladonian fake meat that was already bad enough to begin with—was overcooked to the point of practically being burnt, the vegetables were disgusting, and even the rice was worse than usual. Food within the Refugee District had never been exactly gourmet, but it had been tolerable. This wasn't. Teek picked up small bits of gozen to nibble on so that her parents wouldn't nag her to eat, and she simply listened to the adults' conversations.

It had been a little over a week since they had begun training with their fancy suits and weapons, but Teek still hadn't gotten to see what they were like. Her parents hadn't enlisted for the invasion and nobody was willing to sneak her into the stadium. She had a plan, though, and she would be a part of the invasion no matter what her parents said.

Across the table, Teek noticed that Jem and Sierra were sitting next to each other and actually talking. They had only started talking in the last week; maybe training had brought them closer together. Teek thought they were cute together, but she knew that Sierra didn't like that Avalon girl, and Jem hadn't been quiet about his dislike for Rabaiz.

Rumors had been circulating for a long time that Jem was going to be arrested for the murder of Rabaiz. Fortunately, a security camera on the wall that was used to detect incoming zombies had seen what had happened and cleared Jem's name. That was only a couple of days ago, though, and the conversation that Teek had eavesdropped on had taken place four or five days ago.

"I believe that you didn't kill Rabaiz," Sierra had said to Jem in the room next to Teek's in building sixty-four. "I know that you wouldn't do that. I know you're not like that."

"Thanks, Sierra, that's means a lot," Jem had said.

Teek thought that Sierra must really trust Jem, and she had heard that trust was important in relationships, even though she had never been in one herself. Maybe one day those two could end up in a good relationship.

Beside them was Farouche, and Teek had always thought that he was kind of weird. He didn't talk much at dinner, and when he did, he spoke fast and used big, confusing words. His headband always looked filthy too.

Afflatus and Tekkara led most of the conversation at the table. They were both lively and happy. Teek had noticed that most of the people around the Refugee District had been exceptionally sad during the course of their stay in Kelados, but not those two. They were always the smiling faces among the gloom, and it made Teek happy, especially since her own parents had been arguing and being sad more often. She didn't understand why everybody just couldn't be happy. She was happy, and her entire home planet was under the control of some evil Regime.

Rimaya wasn't at dinner. She didn't show up to dinner a lot. In fact, Teek had noticed that she wasn't even in the Refugee District that often. Leo didn't seem very happy about this, and Teek had heard him yelling at her once about being irresponsible, but it hadn't changed anything. If anything, she showed up less often. Teek assumed that it was because of this that Leo had been acting so sad lately. He looked sad right now as he pushed his food around his plate with his fingers. Shouldn't the chef at least eat his own food?

Then there was Tachel, that weird boy who had arrived at the same time as Leo. He was weirder than Farouche, and that was probably why the two of them got along so well. This evening, though, Tachel seemed exceptionally weird. His skin was paler than normal, and he hadn't eaten anything. His hands shook a little bit as he sipped on his water, and he kept glancing in the direction of Jem and Sierra. He wasn't even whispering to Farouche about some strange invention. Of all the people at the table, he had to be the weirdest, but also the saddest.

After dinner, Teek decided to follow Tachel. He didn't seem okay, and she thought that maybe she could help him. Weird or not, he was a person too, and he deserved to be happy just like everyone else.

He cleaned up his plate in a few seconds with magic and then hurried out of the room. Teek dropped her plates on the counter without cleaning them and scurried after him—she could deal with the plates later. Tachel was walking quickly and didn't head back to his room; instead, he went outside and disappeared down a street. Teek was running to keep up with him, and as she turned each corner, she just barely saw where Tachel was headed.

After only a few minutes, Tachel slowed down when he reached a pond. Teek stayed behind the building to watch what he was going to do. Why was he all the way out here by himself anyway? It was nighttime, and the Refugee District was silent aside from Tachel splashing his hands in the water. He was sitting on the edge of a large rock and splashing water into his face. It was freezing out; why in the world would he do that?

Tachel then began to cry. Teek could hear the sobs even though she could barely see him in the dim moonlight. He was hunched over, hugging his knees, and crying. Teek couldn't stand to watch anymore; she came out from behind the building and approached him.

"Tachel," she said. He jumped to his feet and pointed two fingers at her. "What are you doing out here?" she asked, unafraid.

"Oh, it's just you," he said, lowering his hand. "What are you doing here?"

"I followed you," said Teek. "You seemed upset."

"Hm," grunted Tachel. "Well, I'm fine. You can go." He sat back down and stared out at the pond, watching the moon's reflection in the water.

"You didn't sound fine. Were you crying?" Teek walked over and sat down beside Tachel.

"No," he sniffed, rubbing his eyes.

"You can talk to me," insisted Teek. "Maybe I can help. And if I can't, at least you can get it out."

"There's nothing to talk about, Teek. Go away."

"If I was sad, I would want someone to care."

There was silence for a moment.

"You wouldn't understand," said Tachel.

"I can try."

Teek watched Tachel's face as he bit his lip and rubbed his nose. He looked lost. She wondered what was going on in his head.

"I… I'm just confused," he said finally. "I have a lot going on, and I don't know what to do."

"What do you mean?"

"I can't explain it to you. I just… there's something I need to do. But I don't want to do it."

"Why don't you want to do it?" asked Teek.

"Because it's not a very nice thing to do."

"If it's not nice, why do you need to do it?"

Tachel ran his hands through his short blond hair that had grown out some since he had arrived. "Because doing it will help people I love."

"That's a tough one," replied Teek.

"Ha," laughed Tachel. "You're telling me." He picked up a small stone and threw it across the pond. "Sometimes there isn't always a clear right or wrong, Teek. And sometimes, your only option is to do wrong."

"That doesn't sound right," said Teek. "Everyone has the choice to do what is right."

"It's not that simple," groaned Tachel, shaking his head. "Some people are in worse positions than others. From your perspective, it might seem like you could always do the right thing, but some people don't have that option. Some people are just... unlucky, I guess."

Teek had to think about this for a minute. It didn't really make sense to her, but then again, she didn't know what was going on with Tachel.

"I'm sorry," she said. "I wish I could help more."

"That's okay," he replied. "It's my decision to make."

Teek nodded. "Yep. So what is your story?" she asked. "Where are you from in Callisto?"

"A region called Xena. I was, um... I was a soldier in the Regime before I came here. But I left them. I escaped with the Terellos and left the Regime."

"You were in the Regime? That must have been scary!"

"Not as scary as leaving the Regime," said Tachel. He squinted his eyes as if trying not to cry. "That's not something I recommend."

"Do you have family back home?" asked Teek.

He nodded.

"Are they in the Regime too?"

"Some of them," said Tachel. "My brothers and sisters. My parents are too old."

"Why did you all join?"

Tachel grinned a little bit. "I ask myself that every day," he said. "But when it comes down to it, it was hardly a choice. My family is incredibly poor, but if you join the Regime as a soldier, they pay you, feed you, house you. It's a great deal, and it's really the only deal for a lot of people. Me and all of my siblings would send most of our money back home to our parents so they could get by. It was a bad situation, but we did what we could."

"I'm sorry," said Teek, hugging Tachel's arm. "Maybe we can make things better when we go back. We're going to get Callisto back, and with the Regime gone, I bet Xena could be a better place."

Tachel gave a weak smile. "You make it sound so simple."

"I don't think it's simple," she replied, "but I think it's possible. If we work together, we're capable of so much. Just think about the invasion being planned. That's amazing, and if it works, we have a real shot at Callisto."

"If it works," said Tachel. "If it works..."

"It'll work," said Teek. "I don't know anything about it, 'cause no one will tell me anything, but I'm sure it'll work. It has to."

Tachel didn't reply.

"I wanna go," said Teek. "I wanna go on the invasion. You're going, right?"

"Yeah, I'm going," said Tachel. "But it's a good thing you're not. You're too young."

"That's not fair," whined Teek. "Age shouldn't matter."

"But it does."

"Can I at least see the suits and weapons?"

Tachel turned and looked at Teek for the first time. "No," he said firmly. "You'd hurt yourself."

"Would not!" cried Teek. "Come on, just show me. Pleaseee!"

"No."

"Come on," she whined, standing up and grabbing Tachel by the sleeve. "We're going to the stadium, and you're going to let me in."

"I'm not letting you in," said Tachel, although he allowed himself to be dragged by the sleeve all the way to the stadium.

They stood outside of the massive building, wedged awkwardly within city, and stared at the heavy metal entrance gates.

"Open it! Open it!" cried Teek.

"We shouldn't be here," said Tachel. "They told us to only train at the designated times."

"Hey, if rules don't make sense. Why follow them?"

Tachel glared at Teek who was smiling triumphantly. Tachel then approached the gates and pressed his hand against the center. They began to glow blue where he had pressed his hand, and then they swung open.

Teek went running in and found the suits in the locker room. She quickly changed and went running out to the center of the stadium. When she got there, Tachel was standing in the center holding a small black cylinder with long magic blades sticking out of both ends. He was twirling it around his head with incredible speed, and at one point, he launched one of the blades off the end of his weapon, and it embedded itself in the center of a target at least twenty yards away.

"Wow!" cried Teek. "How'd you do that?"

The sylph blade in the target dissolved away, and another one fizzled into existence on Tachel's weapon. "A lot of practice," he said.

The two of them were alone in the stadium, and their voices echoed every time they spoke. Empty seats lined the stadium, and bright lights shone down on them. Foldable walls, which were used to separate the stadium into different sections during training, were lined along the outside of the dirt ground they were standing on.

"So teach me," said Teek.

Tachel spent the next hour or two teaching Teek how to use the astra. She got the hang of it surprisingly quickly and was able to operate her suit with skill and fire the astra with great accuracy. She was even able to spar with Tachel a little bit.

"Alright, I'm beat," said Tachel, after they had briefly gone through everything he had learned. "We should go back and go to sleep."

"Aww, already?"

"We shouldn't even be here, Teek. Come on, let's go."

"Fine, but I want to keep the suit and the astra!"

"You can't keep those! That's stealing!"

"They won't notice. They made like a million of them."

Tachel glared at her, trying to think of a way to convince her not to take the suit an astra, but he had nothing. He didn't see any harm in letting her have them. "Why do you even want them?" he asked.

"Just for safety," she said. "If the zombies invade the Fortress again, I can throw on the suit and defend myself with the astra."

"Fine," said Tachel, remembering the three zombies he had saved Farouche from vividly in his mind. "But don't tell anyone, and don't get caught with it. Deal?"

"Deal," agreed Teek.

The two of them then left the stadium and began the walk back home to the Refugee District. The streets were completely deserted at this point, and the only sound was the occasional tweet of a bird.

"So you know about me," said Tachel. "But what about you? What's your story?"

"I don't have a story yet," said Teek. "But I'm going to make one."

This made Tachel smile. "You're not so bad, little one."

"Neither are you, big one," laughed Teek, nudging Tachel. "I think you'll make the right decision, by the way," she added. "You seem like a good person to me, and I'm sure that deep down, you really know what the right decision is."

"Thanks," grinned Tachel. "I guess we'll find out, won't we?"

"I guess so," said Teek.

CHAPTER 23:
THE HOSPITAL

"Come on! Hit me!"

"I'm trying!"

Their magic blades clashed together with a satisfying buzz. Jem swung again and again, but Farouche blocked every hit.

"You'll never get me!" taunted Farouche.

This only made Jem swing harder and faster, swiping at Farouche's legs and then bringing his astra up to go for his head—but Farouche blocked both by deploying a blade from the other end of his astra. The tip of his blade then bent and curved backwards like a fishing hook, and he used it to grab the handle of Jem's astra. In one swift movement, he ripped the weapon from Jem's grip. Farouche stood there, holding both astras and laughing.

"You're never gonna defeat the zombie Leader like that," he teased, taking off his helmet.

"I'm going to be in dragon form when I do it," snapped Jem, removing his helmet as well. "So this doesn't even matter."

Farouche retracted the blades and handed Jem his astra back before they both turned to face the targets. After almost three weeks of training, they had gotten used to a daily routine of training from when the sun rose to when it set—and occasionally longer than that.

Today, they were using about an eighth of the stadium field, since it was divided up by the foldable walls so that everyone had a separate area to train. The sun had just set, but the bright stadium lights meant that they could keep going if they wanted. The people in the other seven quadrants would probably be leaving soon. Jem and Farouche were both incredibly anxious since they would leave for the invasion tomorrow, and neither of them planned on sleeping much that night.

Farouche held his astra out at arm's length, and the top half bent at a ninety degree angle, resembling a gun. Dark blue, magic sights appeared on the top of the astra, allowing him to accurately aim at his target, and then he fired without saying a word. A small magic bullet landed in the center of the target with a *thud* before it dissolved, leaving the target unharmed.

Jem held his astra up and did the same, although he to say "N" out loud to activate his astra's near-shot capability.

"Do you think this could actually work?" Jem asked as they continued to pelt the target with magic bullets.

"'Course it'll work," said Farouche. "We've got a dragon on our side."

Jem smiled. "But what about the Dragon and the Phoenix?"

"It's all under control, dude. Remember that rendocom I had you put in your ear before you went up into space?"

"Yeah, what about it?"

"Well, I've worked out the bugs—mainly the excruciating pain upon installation thing—and I think we can use it to coordinate a plan separate from everyone else's. Before we go, I'll put one in and so will Afflatus, Tekkara, Sierra, Rimaya, Leo, Sam, and Henry. That's everyone we've got who believes that the Dragon and the Phoenix are trapped in the silver dome."

"Okay, so we can all talk to each other. Big deal."

"Jem, you're not getting this. Afflatus and Tekkara have agreed to go after the Dragon and the Phoenix to release them. I worked with Sam and Henry to install three miniature vimanas in the base of each regular vimana. They serve two purposes: if our thrusters are broken or disabled, we can use them to evacuate—there are six people aboard each vimana, and the minis will hold two people each—but for Afflatus and Tekkara, they will each take one of them to get to the silver dome."

Jem thought about this for a second. "If they each hold two people, why can't Afflatus and Tekkara just take one mini and leave the others in case we need to evacuate?"

"Because if one of them gets shot down, the other one can still have a chance."

Jem stopped shooting. He hadn't thought about that. They have to plan ahead in case people die. People were probably going to die. That seemed surreal to him.

"Got it," said Jem. "So why can't I go get the Dragon and the Phoenix? That way, Afflatus could charge the golden dome and close the portal."

"Because you need to stay and protect the rest of us," said Farouche, still firing his astra relentlessly. "If you go off to the silver dome, the rest of us are sitting ducks. This invasion will only work with you in your dragon form guarding us."

"But I've never closed a portal before!" objected Jem. "And I don't know if I could even do it in dragon form. Afflatus could easily shut the portal."

"We still need you to protect us, Jem. Afflatus is good, but not good enough to take on thousands of zombies. That's a job better saved for a dragon. I'm sorry, but you're going to have to close that portal. I believe in you."

"Thanks," grunted Jem. "Now can we go over the commands one last time?"

"Why? Like you said, you're going to be in dragon form—the astras shouldn't matter to you, and I already have them all memorized and can do them without verbal cues."

"I still want to know," said Jem. "Just in case."

Farouche sighed. "Fine. Face that dummy," he said, indicating a plastic, Rastvo-sized dummy. There were several of them lined up towards the outer edge of the stadium.

"Let's try your projectiles first. Long-shot."

"L," said Jem, and his already gun-like astra stretched out into a thinner barrel. A magic scope rose from the top, and Jem pressed his eye against it. *Fire,* he thought, and his astra delivered a hit right to the head of the dummy.

"Good," said Farouche. "Near-shot."

"N," said Jem, transforming his astra back into a smaller gun. He shot the dummy a few quick times rather inaccurately.

"Big-shot."

"B," said Jem, and his astra got significantly wider. When he fired, the dummy exploded, sending a cloud of dust into the air.

Farouche smiled. "Paralyze the dummy to the right."

"P," said Jem, and his astra shrunk back to a normal size. When he shot the dummy, what looked like a bolt of lightning struck it, rather than a magic bullet. The dummy had a clear burn where the electricity had struck it.

"Capture."

"C," said Jem, launching a dark blue net from his astra. It covered the dummy but dissolved away quickly.

"Sword, knife, double-ended knife, double-ended sword, hooked sword, hooked knife."

"S," said Jem, and his astra straightened out and deployed a long, magic blade from one end. "K." The blade shrunk to only about a foot long. "2K." A second short blade shot from the other end. "2S." Both blades grew in size. "HS." The second blade disappeared, and the first blade hooked as Farouche's had earlier. "HK." The hooked blade shrunk.

"And how do you throw a blade?" asked Farouche.

"R," replied Jem, swinging his hooked knife through the air. The blade detached from the astra and embedded itself in the dummy's chest. After a second, it dissolved. "For release," he added.

"And defend?"

"D," said Jem, and out of both ends of the astra spewed a light blue color much like the shields from the suits. It encapsulated Jem in a bubble, and then he released it.

"And how do you kill a zombie?"

"Shoot it in the head, or cut off its head," replied Jem.

"Very good," laughed Farouche, hugging Jem. "You'd make a good fighter as a human too."

"I'm kind of glad I'll be in dragon form," said Jem. "This stuff is hard."

"Really? Being a dragon seems kinda hard to me."

"It has its ups and downs," joked Jem.

"Alright," said Farouche. "Well, let's get one more spar in before we call it a night."

"Sure," said Jem. Farouche's sword immediately extended from his astra, and Jem said "TS" to activate his training sword.

The two of them put their helmets back on and went at it for at least an hour, hitting their blades together, throwing blades and deflecting them, even firing paralyzing shots at each other to practice evading. Jem worked up quite a sweat, but his suit wicked it all away from his body and kept him dry. The helmet was easy to see through and so light that Jem sometimes forgot that he was wearing it.

Before their duel had finished, one of the foldable walls was retracted, and Sierra came running into their part of the stadium.

"Guys," she said, panting hard and holding her helmet in one hand and her astra in the other. "Rimaya's in the hospital. We need to go see her."

"What? What happened?" asked Jem.

"I don't know, I was just sparring with Tekkara, and Afflatus came to tell us. They already left for the hospital, but I stayed to get you two."

"Okay then, let's go," said Jem, and the three of them took off across the stadium.

As they passed through the hallways underneath the seating, Jem heard a noise coming from the bathroom. He paused by the entrance to it and listened; it sounded like someone throwing up. He recalled the countless nights that he had spent throwing up from his pains when no one was around to help him, and he wanted to help whoever this was.

"Jem, come on," called Farouche from down the hallway. "What are you doing?"

"I'll catch up with ya'll in a minute," he said, and without any further explanation, he ducked into the bathroom.

The vomiting noise didn't stop as he passed by the sinks. The whole room was perfectly clean and spotless; it seemed out of place for someone to be sick in here. Jem passed by a few stalls, and it wasn't hard to tell where the noise was coming from. The doors opened outwards, and all of them were shut except for one that was cracked open slightly.

Jem pulled the door back to reveal a person in a combat suit lying on the floor with their head stuffed in the toilet and their helmet lying beside them.

"Tachel?" said Jem, surprised to see the Reg here.

Tachel looked up from the toilet, his eyes red and his skin white as snow. "What do you want?" he muttered.

"Are you okay?" asked Jem. "Do you need help?"

"I'm fine," coughed Tachel, wiping his mouth on his sleeve. "Just nervous about tomorrow is all."

"Hey, it'll be alright, man. We'll get the Soul and be one step closer to getting Callisto back."

"Hm," grunted Tachel, looking away from Jem and staring into the toilet.

Jem had never learned to trust this Reg, but in the position he was in now, Jem felt pretty bad for him. He knew what it was like to vomit uncontrollably, and he was incredibly nervous himself. Maybe Jem hadn't given him enough credit. Maybe Tachel really was a good guy, and Jem was just letting his preconceived notions get in the way of seeing that.

"Do you miss home?" asked Jem, sitting down in the stall beside Tachel.

"No. Home is worse than here. I'm glad to be far away from the Regime."

"Then why did you become a Reg?"

"I had no other choice. You saw the poverty in Xena, Jem. If you had to choose between starving and joining the Regime, I bet I know what you'd choose."

Jem nodded. "Do you have family?"

Tachel laughed a little bit, as if that was somehow funny. "Yeah, I do," he said. "Brothers and sisters… mom and dad."

"You'll see them again soon enough," said Jem, patting Tachel's leg. "There are a lot of people in Callisto we will save."

Tachel didn't say anything, just stared into the toilet. He threw up once more.

"Do you want me to take you to a hospital?" asked Jem.

"They can't do anything for me," moaned Tachel. "I'll stay here."

Jem nodded. "I'll see you tomorrow. We can do this."

He held out his hand to fist bump. Tachel looked him in the eyes for a second and returned the fist bump. Jem smiled and walked out of the stall.

After leaving the bathroom, Jem ran straight for the hospital. The receptionist told him which room Rimaya was in, and he got there as quickly as he could. Leo, Afflatus, Tekkara, Sierra, and Farouche were all gathered around her bed.

Jem walked up to the edge of her bed cautiously. She was awake but hooked up to several tubes and wires. There were bags around her eyes, and she looked as if she had been through quite a lot.

"Hi, Jem," she said, her voice rough and scratchy.

"Maya," he said. "What happened? Are you okay?"

"She overdosed on propo," said Leo solemnly. "But the doctors say that she is going to be fine."

Jem didn't know how to react. "Well, I'm glad you're okay," he said.

"Looks like I won't be going with you all on the invasion, though," said Rimaya, sadness apparent in her tone.

"No you won't," said Leo. "Maybe that'll teach you to be more responsible in the future."

"Oh, give it a rest, dad. All you've done is try to control me since we've been here."

"Control you? I've been looking out for you!"

"Hmph," grunted Rimaya, and she turned her attention away from him. "Well, you all better get that Soul. If you do, I'll be out there fighting right next to you when we go to take back Callisto."

"Deal," said Afflatus. "But you'll have to take better care of yourself in the future if you hope to be around to see Callisto."

Rimaya glared at him. "Mhm," she groaned. It was obvious that she had had enough of people telling her not to do propo. "Look, I'm going to try and sleep. Thanks, everyone, for coming to see me."

Everyone said their goodbyes and headed for the door.

"Wait, Sierra," said Rimaya. "Can you stay?"

"Sure," said Sierra, and after everyone else had left, she shut the door and sat on the edge of Rimaya's bed. "What's up, Maya?"

"You still gonna get the Phoenix Glove?"

"I don't know. I want to, but I was planning on having you with me."

"You could do it by yourself," reassured Rimaya. "As long as you keep your rendocom in, you'll still be able to contact anyone if you run into trouble. It's got a tracker in it too, so they'll be able to locate you if they need to."

Sierra nodded. "You're right. And we need the Glove if we want to get Callisto back. We can't keep relying on Jem for everything."

"I know," said Rimaya. "But hey, if you get the Glove, you and Jem will both have legendary powers. You'd make such a cute little dragon and phoenix couple."

Sierra shook her head. "No, Maya, that's not what this is about. This isn't about Jem; this is about me."

"So you don't want to be with him?"

"No, I don't know. I like him. I miss having him as a best friend. But

I'm not going to get the Phoenix Glove to impress him; I'm going to get it to save Callisto. I'm my own person, not Jem's."

Rimaya smiled. "You've always been the smart one," she said, laughing lightly. "I know we'll get Callisto back. I love you, Sierra."

"I love you too, Maya."

They hugged tightly and Sierra could feel tears welling up in her eyes. She realized that this could be the last time she ever saw her sister.

"You can do it," Rimaya whispered in Sierra's ear. "I believe in you."

"Thanks," whispered Sierra. She let go of her sister and stood up. "Feel better, okay?"

"I will," said Rimaya. "Don't worry about me, just get the Phoenix Glove."

"I will. Bye, Maya."

"Bye," said Rimaya, smiling.

Sierra left the hospital and walked out into the cold night air. She took a deep breath and allowed the chilly air to fill her lungs. It was so calm on the empty Fortress street. And in a few hours, they would all be boarding the vimanas and heading straight into zombie territory. Sierra would be leaving the others when they passed the central river, and the very thought of venturing into the underwater cave where the Phoenix Glove was hidden was enough to make her shiver.

She headed back to the Refugee District to try and get some sleep.

Justin Dennis

CHAPTER 24:
RICK'S SECRET

"We leave in the morning," said Jem, sitting at a small wooden table underneath a makeshift shack. Rain pattered down on the ceiling and splashed in the ocean a few yards away.

"I wish I could go with you," said Oliver, leaning forward on his elbows. "I hate not being able to help out with all that."

"I hate not having you here," said Jem. "We could really use your help."

"So you're not going after that Phoenix Glove thingy after all?"

"Nah, too risky. But we might try after the zombies are gone."

"Maybe I'll come grab it then," joked Oliver, leaning back and kicking his feet up on the table. "I could go for some cool Phoenix powers."

Jem laughed.

"So how are things with Avalon?" asked Oliver.

"I don't know, same old," replied Jem. "I just don't connect with her the way I did with Sierra, you know? I feel like me and Sierra had more in common and were able to talk about everything more openly. With Avalon, I feel like she sort of has a mask up, if that makes sense?"

"Yeah, yeah, I get you. So why not go be with Sierra instead?"

"Ha, you think Sierra would want to be with me? You remember that her partner—I mean her boyfriend—just died like two months ago, and for a while, everyone thought I did it! And ever since I've been with Avalon, Sierra hasn't wanted anything to do with me."

"But you guys started talking a few weeks ago, right?"

"Well, yeah, but just as friends. And she still gives me the cold shoulder if I mention Avalon."

"So break up with Avalon and go try to win her back."

"But you know how much Avalon has given up for me," protested Jem.

"Her whole life revolves around me now."

"Maybe that's the problem," said Oliver. "Maybe you need someone who's independent. It's not healthy to be attached to someone like that."

"You might be right," said Jem. "We'll see. For now, I just need to focus on the invasion. Relationship problems are second to world problems."

"True that," laughed Oliver, staring out at the ocean. "You know, it only started raining when you got here."

"Sorry to put a damper on your dream, your highness," joked Jem. Thunder roared, and a second later, a bolt of lightning cracked far out in the night sky above the ocean, and waves crashed against the shore. The only light came from a lantern hanging at the top of their shack that creaked as it swung back and forth in the wind.

"I think your dream is broken," said Jem. "I'm pretty sure you're supposed to see lightning before you hear the thunder."

"Oh, shut up," laughed Oliver. "It's a dream!"

"A poorly designed one…" murmured Jem.

Oliver laughed before asking, "How's Maya?"

"Oh, um, well actually… she ended up in the hospital last night."

"What? How?"

"She overdosed on propo, you remember that stuff, right?"

"Yeah, yeah, I remember it. And I knew Maya was doing it, but I didn't think she was stupid enough not to know her limit."

Jem shrugged. "What do you think about her injecting?"

"I don't think it's so bad," said Oliver. "As long as she's being safe, though, which she clearly wasn't. And recently she's been doing it more, so I was worrying that it was kinda consuming her life. But if she could do only a little bit and not so often, I don't see what's so wrong with that."

"I dunno," said Jem. "The whole thing just seems stupid to me. Why even do it at all?"

"For fun?" suggested Oliver.

"Isn't it possible to have fun without it, though? We've definitely had fun without it—most of Luria got along well without it."

"I dunno, dude. Some people are just gonna do it. I mean, why not?"

"'Cause you end up in the hospital, maybe?"

"Not if you do it safely."

"Farouche did it safely," said Jem. "But he almost died when the zombies attacked 'cause he couldn't defend himself properly."

"Alright, I don't think the in-case-zombies-attack argument is going to work."

Jem laughed. "I guess not. Oh well."

The two of them sat in silence for a while, just savoring their time together. Although they didn't say it, they both knew that this could be the last time that they ever saw each other, and it actually meant a lot to them.

"Well, you should go rest up for your big day tomorrow," said Oliver finally. "Let me enjoy some sunshine with my chimpanzee servants."

Jem laughed. "You have the strangest dreams."

The two of them stood up and hugged.

"When should I expect to hear back from you?" asked Oliver.

"Tomorrow night," said Jem. "The invasion shouldn't take more than a day. If you don't hear from me, well…"

"Nah, I'll hear from you," insisted Oliver. "I know you can do this."

"Thanks, Olive," smiled Jem.

Oliver smiled back. "See ya tomorrow."

"See ya," said Jem, and his body fizzled out of the dream.

***

Sierra stood outside in the largest courtyard in the entire Fortress, waiting for the vimanas to be ready to take off. These ships were smaller than the ones that she remembered from Luria, and all four fit snuggly within the courtyard. People in combat suits were running around like crazy.

Afflatus looked goofy without his usual robes. His big white beard billowed out as he attempted to tuck it into the neck of his combat suit. He also looked ridiculously scrawny in the skintight suit; it was as if a skeleton with a beard had tried to suit up for battle.

The sun was shining down on them, and the sky was a clear blue. The air was chilly for as early in the morning as it was, but it was beginning to get warmer. Only the sound of voices and cushioned combat suit boots echoed throughout the air.

Of the seven enlisted soldiers who hadn't been at the original meeting three weeks ago, Sierra didn't recognize four of them, strongly didn't like two of them, and was indifferent to one of them. Rick and Ella Dion were helping each other put their gloves on. Sierra didn't mind Ella, but she hated that Rick was there. Bert was standing silently off to the side, holding his helmet and staring back at the city. The creepy bartender had somehow passed all the tests and completed all the required training, although Sierra couldn't imagine what had compelled him to enlist in the first place. Sierra didn't think that he would actually be going on the trip, but apparently, he really was. Oh well, they could use all the help they could get.

Sierra was playing with the visor on her helmet, flipping it up and down. Inside her helmet, there was a white, mesh-looking lining. Nobody else had that. That was a water to air convertor material that she had swiped from ECKO's research lab. She didn't know how much it would take to keep her breathing underwater, but she didn't have much choice other than to just line her helmet with it and hope for the best.

She had done so much research on the Phoenix Glove, and she knew exactly what to expect once she dove into the river. After asking all of the most knowledgeable Fenics about the Glove, including Avalon's intimidating father, Fey had fessed up about a map that her grandmother had left her. Apparently, Fey had been there once but had been unable to retrieve the Glove. She told Sierra about it happily, hoping that someone could possess the Phoenix's powers and use them for good.

The map was a virtual one, stored on a digital magic server in Fey's home, and she had shown it to Sierra on a tablet. Sierra could remember the map exactly, and she had turned down Fey's offer to give her a physical copy. She didn't want any evidence lying around about her whereabouts. Rimaya and Fey were the only ones who knew, and it had to stay that way.

The only thing that worried her was the sea monster that Fey had warned her about. Fey had said that she had gotten by the monster using stealth and had never even woken it up, but she had also said that she had been lucky and that Sierra shouldn't expect the same result. Nevertheless, Sierra was determined to retrieve the Glove, and she figured that the astra would be a helpful weapon if need be.

"Hey, Sierra," said Jem, coming to sit beside her. "You ready?"

Sierra sighed. "As ready as I'll ever be."

"It'll be okay," he reassured her. "We've got the best people out here with the best technology. What could go wrong?"

Sierra smiled. *Well, I could get eaten by a sea monster, or zombies could kill you,* she thought.

"I'm just worried someone won't come back alive," she said.

"Me too," said Jem.

Sierra felt like she should hug him, and she started to, but then decided not to, and it really made the whole situation quite awkward as they both pretended to be incredibly fascinated in the helmets they were holding.

"Sierra, I just want to tell you that—"

"Attention, everybody," rang Forenzi's voice throughout the courtyard. "Please line up at the south side of the courtyard for briefing and loading the vimanas."

Jem and Sierra immediately stood up and joined the line of people standing before Forenzi. In his combat suit, the man looked even more intimidating. He was no longer wearing his crown, though. There was just short black hair on his head, and a helmet at his side. He looked up and down the row of people, as if trying to think of something to say.

"Thank you all for being here," he said finally. "And thank you to those of you, Keladonian and Refugee, who have volunteered to join this Zombie Invasion Squad. However, today, we are all on equal ground. Today we are not Fenics or Draigs, Keladonians or Refugees. Today, we are soldiers. And we appreciate each and every one of you, but you all must know that not everyone will come back alive today."

He took a pause where he seemed to be choked up.

"There are very few of us," he continued, "mainly due to a lack of volunteers, and that is just how it is going to be. The Council decided long ago that we would not require anyone to join us. But this means even more peril for those of us who are going. We believe that we have everything it will take to successfully infiltrate the zombie region and retrieve the Soul, but we can make no guarantees. If you are not prepared to sacrifice your life for this mission, please leave now."

He paused for a moment and scanned the row of people. Nobody flinched.

Forenzi smiled grimly. "Alright then. Please report to your assigned vimana. Vimana One is directly behind me, Two is to my right, Three is behind One, and Four is to my left. If you need to communicate with another vimana, each pilot's cabin is outfitted with a communication device to reach the other three. If all goes as planned, I will see you all at the entrance to the golden dome. Best of luck."

Everybody walked silently towards their assigned vimana. Jem was in the second vimana along with Farouche, but Sierra was in the first one. She watched as he boarded, and he glanced over at her, giving her one last look with his bright blue eyes before disappearing into the ship. Sierra swallowed hard and marched up the ramp onto Vimana One.

She sat down against a metal bench that was protruding from the wall. She knew that in case of an emergency, she was supposed to fold down the bench and open the hatch into the wing because that was where the mini-vimana was kept. To her left and to her right were two more sets of benches, each blocking the hatches to the other two mini-vimanas. Directly in front of her, in the center of the vimana, was an elevated platform where the pilot would sit. This central area was the only space they had—the spaces in between the benches were given to three large openings for entering and exiting the vimana.

Zenska and Lenro, the two councilmembers assigned to Vimana One, walked in behind Sierra, followed by Leo, Ella, and Rick. Sierra had known for the last three weeks that Rick was going to be on her ship, but the actual realization of being trapped in this tiny enclosure with him for hours was enough to make her want to vomit. There was nothing she could do, though. If she had requested to change ships, people would have asked why she wanted to change, and that wasn't something she wanted to tell anyone.

She stared at the floor as Ella and Rick passed by and took their seats on the other bench. Leo was talking to Zenska about something, and Lenro, the skinny, red-haired Draig woman, was climbing up into the pilot's cabin. Sierra pulled the straps down over both her shoulders and latched them in. She took a deep breath.

"Hey, sweetie," said Leo, sitting down beside her on the metal bench. His enormous physique barely fit on the tiny thing. "You know, you don't have to go on this if—"

"I'm going, dad," said Sierra emotionlessly. She glanced at him for half a second before returning her gaze straight forward.

"Alright," said Leo. "That's your decision."

"Everybody good?" called Zenska. He was already strapped in and had his helmet on. His astra was gripped firmly in his hand.

The four others nodded while putting on their helmets. "Alright then, let's roll, Len!" shouted Zenska, pounding his feet. The hatches to the outside lifted up and locked in place. A loud buzzing noise became audible, and Sierra recognized it as the noise the magic thruster rings made when they circulated air quickly enough to lift the vimana. In seconds, their ship was off the ground and headed straight up.

Each of the outside hatches had a wide window at about eye-level. Sierra stared at the one to her right so that she could have some idea of how high they were or where they were, and also so she didn't have to look over at Rick. The pilot's cabin rotated a little bit, and Sierra was just able to see Lenro's legs and lower body—the rest of her was protruding up into the top portion of the cabin.

Leo gripped Sierra's hand, and she gripped back. She was scared for sure, but not because of zombies, not even because of Rick. She was scared because when they would get to the central river, she had to jump out. And in this tiny cabin with her father, that wasn't looking like such a viable option, but it had to happen. The Phoenix Glove was her only hope of saving Callisto.

"We've reached maximum altitude," came Farouche's voice from the speaker system around the ship. "Fall into formation and do not break unless instructed otherwise."

Immediately, Sierra felt herself thrown backwards as they took off horizontally. Outside the window, she saw that the rings had rotated to propel them sideways.

They continued on like this for a while, no sounds except for the whirring of the thrusters. Zenska was stoic; he just sat there gripping his astra as if his life depended on it. Rick and Ella would whisper to each other once and a while, and every time Sierra glanced over, Ella was pushing him away. The sight of Rick made her feel sick, and the more she looked in that general direction the faster she felt herself begin to hyperventilate. So she tried not to.

Can you hear me? said a voice in Sierra's head. It definitely wasn't coming from the speaker system in the vimana; it sounded literally as if someone was speaking inside her head. It startled her pretty bad. *This is Farouche, pilot of Vimana Two. Just to recap, I've got Leo and Sierra on One, Jem here on Two,*

Afflatus and Henry on Three, and Tekkara and Sam on Four. Please acknowledge in order.

I'm here, said Leo, inside of Sierra's head. She was looking straight at him when he said it, but with his helmet on, it was impossible to tell that he had said anything.

Uh, me too, thought Sierra.

Here, said Jem. Sierra looked around the vimana trying to spot him, and then remembered that he was in another vimana. This communication inside her head was going to take some getting used to.

Afflatus, Henry, Tekkara, and Sam all acknowledged as well.

Perfect, said Farouche. *So use this line of communication when referring to missions "Save the Dragon and the Phoenix" or "Shut the Portal." Everybody should be all caught up on the plan, so I won't go over it again, but don't hesitate to communicate here. These missions are vital to the success of this invasion, even if most of our invasion squad doesn't realize it. Farouche out.*

Sierra's stomach clenched up in a tight ball. Too bad she wasn't going to be around to help any of them with the missions. She had a mission of her own called *Retrieve the Phoenix Glove without Dying,* and it was vital to saving Callisto, even if no one else thought so.

After a few minutes of nothing, Sierra began to cough. It was just a little bit at first, but then it became uncontrollable. Leo was next, coughing so hard that he removed his helmet and started gasping for air. Within seconds, everyone in the vimana was struggling to get enough air, and nobody could stop coughing. The ship began to swerve and dip as Lenro became unable to focus on the controls.

"Everybody," said Farouche over the speaker system. He was coughing between almost every word. "Air up… here is… poisonous…" Farouche stopped for a few seconds to have a coughing fit. "Descend," he coughed, "descend."

Sierra then felt her stomach rise up into her throat as they dropped altitude incredibly quickly. After they leveled off, she unlatched herself from the seat because she felt like it was choking her, and she fell on her hands and knees. Her helmet was already off and had rolled around somewhere in the vimana. She felt as if some kind of poison was glued to her throat and lungs, unable to come out.

Eventually, her coughing subsided, and she was able to stand up and look around. Leo was on the ground beside her, and he had thrown up. Ella and Rick were both also on the ground, still coughing violently, and Zenska was still strapped in his chair, although his coughing seemed to have subsided. Lenro was concentrating hard on flying the vimana, but she was still letting out a cough every few seconds.

Without saying anything, Sierra got back into her seat and strapped herself in. She saw that her helmet had rolled over by Rick, and suddenly, she didn't want it. Leo eventually stopped vomiting long enough to get seated again as well. He locked his helmet back on and asked, "What the hell was that?"

"I don't know," said Sierra, still coughing.

Ella finally overcame her coughing and got strapped back in to her seat, but Rick was up and walking towards Sierra with her helmet in his hand.

"I think you lost this," he said, handing it towards her. She snatched it out of his hands and put it on without saying a word. Rick walked back to his seat and sat beside Ella.

"Sierra," said Leo. "Don't be so rude."

Sierra scoffed at this, but said nothing.

"Sorry about that, ahem, folks," said Farouche over the speaker system. "It turns out that... the red sky you've all seen is actually poisonous gas." He broke out into a bunch of coughs for a second. "Looks like we'll need to maintain a low enough altitude to... ahem, stay out of the poison. Just follow me, pilots. Sorry, everyone."

"Wow," said Leo, unlatching himself and standing up to look out the window. "Looks like we're close enough to the ground for a zombie attack."

"I dare them," said Zenska, deploying the magic blade from his astra.

Sierra gulped.

It quickly became clear that their lower altitude left them vulnerable for attack. First, there were just a few *thuds* against the outside of the vimana. Then there was the undeniable scream of the zombies. Everybody except Lenro unlatched themselves and looked out the windows. A massive group of zombies was running at them from the south. Luckily, they didn't seem to have anything that could fly, but the persistent *thuds* on the vimana meant that they definitely had projectiles.

"Alright, team," called Lenro. "I'm going to keep the hatches up for as long as I can, but at our altitude we're easily in reach of those zombies. If we start taking too much fire, I'm gonna have to open them up and have you all start shooting. In the meantime, you all better latch in; there's gonna be some turbulence."

Great, thought Sierra. She hadn't planned on actually having to fight. She had thought that they wouldn't encounter zombies until well after the central river.

Everybody got back in their seats and latched in. Sierra was holding her astra tight with both hands, ready to spring up at any moment. She couldn't tell how her dad or anyone else was feeling since they all had their helmets on. All she saw were emotionless black visors staring back at her.

Lenro hadn't been kidding when she had said that there was going to be turbulence. The vimana was swinging back and forth, diving up and down, and vibrating intensely with every projectile that hit it. Sierra was barely able to see out of the window to her right—it was mostly just a blur.

"Oh, damn it, they can jump high!" yelled Lenro. Suddenly, a loud *thud* came from the bottom of the vimana, and it lurched downward.

"Vimana One, you've got a zombie on your bottom," said Henry, the pilot of Vimana Three, over the speaker system. "Repeat: you've got a zombie on your bottom. Pull up; I'm coming below you to shoot it off."

Just as the vimana began to climb upwards, another *thud* hit the bottom, and it lurched a bit lower.

"Open that door!" yelled Zenska, unlatching and standing up. "I'm taking it off myself!"

Lenro complied, and the door to Sierra's right dropped open. Zenska gripped onto a handrail running around the edge of the door and swung his body outside. His astra was in gun form in his other hand, and he opened fire on the zombies below.

Sierra could hear the zombies screaming and clawing into the bottom of the vimana. Luckily, the floor was so thick that their claws didn't penetrate through to the cabin, but it was doing heavy damage to the ship nonetheless.

"Enough of this," grumbled Leo, unlatching himself. "Len, open up all the doors! We're takin' 'em off!"

Without a second of hesitation, both the other doors dropped open as well. Leo gripped a handrail to their left and opened fire on the zombies. Rick had stood up as well and was at the third door, firing down at the zombies. Ella quickly joined him, and Sierra, being the last one sitting down, finally found the nerve to unlatch herself and join her dad at the open door.

Far below them, the ground was whooshing by at an alarming rate. Just looking at that made Sierra's head spin. But even more alarming were all the zombies that were leaping up and attacking them. To avoid the poisonous sky, they had descended into an easily reachable altitude for the massive zombies. Sierra watched helplessly as two zombies ran and jumped off the backs of their fellow zombies, launching them all the way to Vimana Three.

"They're on our back!" came Henry's voice from the speaker system. "Get 'em off, One!"

Sierra tried to transform her astra wordlessly, but nothing happened. "L," she spat nervously, and the astra bent and extended into a long-shot rifle. She tried to get a steady aim on one of the zombies atop Vimana Three, but the shaking and jerking of her own vimana was throwing her off. When she finally shot, her bullet missed and instead broke off a piece of one of Vimana Three's thruster rings.

"Damn it," she grumbled, lowering her astra. If her shots were going to hurt more than help, she might as well not shoot. She watched as Leo fired several shots as well, and all of them missed the zombies and the vimana entirely.

"Hang on, everyone," called Lenro. "I'm gonna knock those zombies off Three."

Suddenly, their vimana lurched and shot down towards the other vimana. They skimmed the top of it, successfully dislodging the zombies from their bottom, but the zombies that had been on top of Three were now clinging onto the wings of One. They quickly scurried to the top before anybody could get a shot at them.

"NO!" screamed Lenro. "Get them off NOW!"

"On it!" yelled Zenska as he whipped his body outside the vimana and climbed the side of it.

"Stay here," said Leo to Sierra before he did the same.

Petrified, Sierra looked around to see what Rick and Ella were doing.

"GET UP ON THE ROOF, WOMAN!" screamed Rick, grabbing Ella by the wrist.

"Vimanas Two, Three, and Four, we need assistance now—got two zombies on the roof," shouted Lenro through the speaker system.

"I'm not going up there!" yelled Ella, trying to slip her wrist out of Rick's grip.

"Negative, One, you're too high," replied Sam, the pilot of Vimana Four, over the speaker system. "Lower your altitude."

"I'm not going back down where those monsters can reach us!" barked Lenro.

"I SAID GET ON THE ROOF!" demanded Rick, throwing Ella against the wall and grabbing her by the neck.

"One, you need to come back down," said Farouche over the speakers. "You're getting up into the poisonous zone."

"Hey, leave her alone!" cried Sierra, running over to Rick and Ella.

"Back off, kid," spat Rick, shoving Sierra away with his free hand.

"You don't touch me!" screamed Sierra, brandishing a magic blade wordlessly.

Rick laughed. "What are you gonna do, kill me?" With his hand on the back of Ella's neck, he lifted her up and held her over the ledge. If he let go, or if Sierra attacked him now, Ella would die.

"Pull her back in," commanded Sierra. "Then don't touch her."

Rick glared at her, but he did as he was told. Above them, Sierra heard footsteps from the two zombies, her dad, and Zenska. The occasional buzzes and clanks meant that there was plenty of magic and metal fighting up there.

Once released, Ella backed away from the two of them, taking her helmet off and rubbing her neck. Her astra was still docked at her hip.

The ship dropped abruptly, and Sierra left the floor for half a second before crashing back down. Behind Rick, she saw two vimanas go by, each with zombies crawling all over them.

"What now?" asked Rick, pulling off his helmet with one hand. "What are you going to do?"

Sierra's hands were shaking violently, causing her astra to vibrate noticeably. She was beginning to hyperventilate. Her eyes darted around the scene, trying to discern what she should do next. Rick's hand was on his docked astra. Whatever she was going to do, Sierra knew that she couldn't lower her astra or allow him to draw his.

"Sierra, it's okay," said Ella weakly. "I'm fine."

"Does he hurt you?" demanded Sierra, taking off her helmet with one hand. She looked Ella directly in the eyes. "Does he hurt you?" she repeated.

Ella opened her mouth to speak, but no words came out. Instead, Rick interjected, "Shut up! Don't tell her anything. It's none of her business."

"If you're abusing her like you did me, it's my business!" screamed Sierra, pointing her magic blade directly at Rick's chest. Out of the corner of her eye, she saw Jem in dragon form flying upwards, one person on his back and one clinging from his tail. She didn't have time to worry about that now.

"What is she talking about, Rick?" asked Ella. "What did you do to her?"

"Tell her, Rick," said Sierra, red in the face and verging on tears. "Tell her what you did to me."

Rick looked between the two of them. "I haven't done anything wrong."

"LIAR!" shouted Sierra, tears now flowing freely down her face. She looked Ella in the eyes and said, "Seven years ago, Rick would come to stay at our house every once in a while—"

"Sierra, don't!" demanded Rick.

"You don't tell me what to do!" screamed Sierra, thrusting her blade closer to his face. She looked back to Ella. "And when he stayed with us... he... he raped me."

Sierra was barely able to say the words. It was the first time that she had ever said it aloud, and the weight of it leaving her lips was unimaginable. Ella looked between Sierra and Rick and gripped her head as if she had a massive headache. Her expression was a mixture of confusion and disgust.

"How dare you accuse me of that, you sl—" But Rick never finished his sentence. Sierra swiped with her blade as Rick raised his astra, and she cut it in half. As his face contorted with shock, Sierra shot a magic dagger from the backside of her astra. It struck Rick in the chest with such force that he fell backwards out of the vimana and was sent falling to the ground.

Sierra only heard her own breath. She looked to her left to see that Ella had taken a seat on the bench and had her head buried in her hands. She walked over and sat beside her, putting her arm over her.

"He… he…" mumbled Ella. "He raped me too." She put her head on Sierra's chest and cried harder, Sierra holding her and crying as well.

"He's gone now," said Sierra between gasps of breath. "He's gone."

Ella looked up at Sierra, but her eyes were no longer their strange brown color. They were a bright, shining blue. They looked shockingly like Jem's.

"After I s-saw Tulevik," spluttered Ella. "I knew there was m-more I couldn't remember. He had tried to hide it… with memory spells, but when you said that—when you said what he did to you—I remembered. Now, I remember everything he d-did to me. I remember… everything."

Ella cried, burying her face in Sierra's neck. The vimana was still swerving uncontrollably, and the fighting was still audible from the roof.

"I'm not from here," admitted Ella. "I'm from a place c-called Earth. I have a son, a husband. My name… my name is Swayella Surwae."

"Surwae," breathed Sierra, realization flooding her mind. "You're Jem's mom."

"Jem," said Swayella, as if the name was something foreign and unpronounceable. "That's his name. He's here, isn't he? Where is he?"

"He's in another vimana, Swayella, but you'll see him. We still have a mission to complete."

"That's right, we do," said Swayella, sitting up and rubbing her eyes. "We can talk more later."

Sierra nodded. The battle on the roof sounded as if it were over. There were no more zombie noises coming from up there, and the footsteps were quieter and headed towards the entrance hatch.

"Thank you, Sierra," said Swayella, giving a weak smile, "for being so strong, and for helping me to remember who I really am."

Sierra tried to smile back, but she had no words to say.

Leo and Zenska then came climbing back into the vimana. They were both covered in scratches and zombie blood, but otherwise, they seemed fine.

"We're past the worst of it," announced Lenro, "but the hatch doors are damaged, so we're going the rest of the way without them. Better strap in."

"Where's Rick?" asked Zenska, lifting his visor up and looking around.

Sierra took a deep breath. This was never something she had wanted to tell her dad, but now was the time.

"I killed him," said Sierra plainly.

"You did *what?*" cried Zenska. "Why would you do that?"

"He was hurting Ella," said Sierra, staring at the floor rather than Zenska or her dad, "and he almost killed her by trying to force her to go on the roof when she didn't want to. I tried to stop him, and he attacked me, so I attacked back, and he was knocked off the vimana."

"Is this true, Ella?" asked Zenska.

Ella nodded.

"But there's more you need to know about Rick," said Sierra, looking up at her dad.

"Dad, when we were younger, remember when Rick and Ella lived in Thysia, and Rick would come and visit every once and a while?"

"Yeah," said Leo, his tone full of fear for what may come next.

"Well, at night, or if you and Rimaya had both left the house, Rick would... he would... touch me. And he would have me touch him. He said that it was okay but that I couldn't tell anybody because it was our secret. So I didn't. But it got worse the more he came over, and one day, he... he raped me."

"No! Sweetie," said Leo, coming forward to hug Sierra. She backed away from his hug, and he stopped. But then, Sierra slowly reached out and hugged her dad, and he hugged her back. He was crying and squeezing her tight.

"He moved a couple months after that," said Sierra, her voice muffled in her dad's chest. "I thought that since he was gone I could just forget about it... but I couldn't. I don't think I can ever forget that..."

Leo hugged her closer. "It's okay, Sierra. You did the right thing. I just wish you would have told me; I would've done something about that horrible man a long time ago."

"In that situation, it's not something you can just tell people. It's too hard. But I wish I had." Sierra sniffled and wiped her nose on her sleeve. "I love you, dad."

"I love you too, Sierra, and nothing could ever change that, especially not this. You'll always be my special little girl."

Sierra smiled beneath her tears and pulled away from her dad's hug.

"I'm sorry, Sierra," said Zenska. "I didn't realize the circumstances. I didn't mean to accuse you of anything, and your actions seem completely justified."

Sierra gave a weak smile and nodded.

Leo looked over at Swayella. "Are you okay?"

She looked up at him from the bench and nodded. "I will be."

"Did he—I mean it's really not my place to ask..." stammered Leo, face turning red with embarrassment.

"It's okay," said Swayella, playing with the visor flap of her helmet. "But yes, he did rape me. I just didn't remember until Sierra told me what he had done to her. He must have been using memory spells to try and make me forget... but it was always in the back of my mind somewhere. Our entire relationship was abusive and unhealthy, but once you're caught in that cycle, it's near impossible to break it. Your daughter has brought back all of my memories, though—good and bad. And I am thankful for that because now I am free of that man, and I know who I really am: Swayella Surwae from Earth."

"You're..." said Leo, "you're not... Jem's mom, are you?"

"I am," she said, smiling.

"Attention, Invasion Squad," came Farouche's voice from the speaker system. "All four vimanas are now clear of that wave of zombies, but the worst is not behind us. We'll be reaching the central river in a few minutes, and after that, we'll be approaching the Rastvo cities. Prepare for the worst."

CHAPTER 25:
BETRAYAL

"We've reached maximum altitude," came Farouche's voice from the speaker system around the ship. "Fall into formation and do not break unless instructed otherwise."

Jem sat against the cool metal bench, listening to the whirr of the magical thrusters as they accelerated. Tachel was beside him, helmet on and latched in, but he seemed especially nervous. He was gripping his astra with both hands and trembling slightly. Jem could even hear him breathing heavily through his helmet.

Sitting on the bench to Jem's right was Ikuuno. To his left was Mualano along with one enlisted soldier named Yakoba, and Farouche was in the pilot's cabin. They were all in suits and helmets, though, so Jem wouldn't have known who they were if he hadn't seen them put their helmets on. Jem felt incredibly alone. He wished that Afflatus or Sierra were there—or anyone he was more familiar with, really. He had trained a little bit with these people, but he had preferred to train just with Farouche, Sierra, Afflatus, or Tekkara when possible.

A while passed as Jem stared out the window. Nobody said anything. Jem knew that Yakoba had grown close to Mualano during training, but even they weren't talking. The atmosphere inside the ship was rigid and tense; everybody was on the edge of their seats.

Can you hear me? said Farouche's voice inside of Jem's head. *This is Farouche, pilot of Vimana Two. Just to recap, I've got Leo and Sierra on One, Jem here on Two, Afflatus and Henry on Three, and Tekkara and Sam on Four. Please acknowledge in order.*

Everybody acknowledged that they had heard him.

Perfect, said Farouche. *So use this line of communication when referring to missions*

"Save the Dragon and the Phoenix" or *"Shut the Portal." Everybody should be all caught up on the plan, so I won't go over it again, but don't hesitate to communicate here. These missions are vital to the success of this invasion, even if most of our invasion squad doesn't realize it. Farouche out.*

Jem smiled. Luckily, nobody could see the smile beneath his helmet because it would've seemed very out of place. He felt less lonely, though, knowing that he was connected to his friends, and knowing that they were going to save the Dragon and the Phoenix after all this time.

After a while, Tachel began coughing violently for seemingly no reason. Jem stared at him, wondering what was wrong, but then Jem started coughing too. Within seconds, everyone else was coughing.

"Everybody," said Farouche over the speaker system. He was coughing between almost every word. "Air up… here is… poisonous…" Farouche stopped for a few seconds to have a coughing fit. "Descend," he coughed, "descend."

Jem's innards lurched as the vimana dropped quickly from the sky. Tachel took his helmet off and began vomiting between his knees without unlatching himself. Jem looked up to see that Mualano and Yakoba were also vomiting. Ikuuno was rigid as a post, gripping the edge of her bench.

Eventually, the ship leveled out and everyone stopped throwing up and coughing. "What the hell was that?" gasped Mualano between heavy breaths.

Nobody replied; they were all wondering the same thing.

"Sorry about that, ahem, folks," said Farouche over the speaker system. "It turns out that… the red sky you've all seen is actually poisonous gas." He broke out into a bunch of coughs for a second. "Looks like we'll need to maintain a low enough altitude to… ahem, stay out of the poison. Just follow me, pilots. Sorry, everyone."

Ikuuno stood up from her bench and approached a window to her right. "Looks like we've got trouble ahead," she announced. "And at this altitude we're sitting ducks. Jem, you ready?"

Jem unlatched himself and stood up; he felt like he had left his stomach back on the bench. He nodded to Ikuuno.

"Lower the hatches, Farouche," called Ikuuno. "We're sending out the silver dragon and opening fire on the approaching zombies."

The other three unlatched themselves, although it took Tachel a while because his shaking hands couldn't press the unlatch button. The hatch doors dropped open, and the sound of rushing wind filled the cabin.

Jem approached the door to his right and took a deep breath. *This is it,* he told himself. *Time to show everybody why you're here.* Below him, the ground was rushing by in a blur. Zombies were out in the distance but approaching fast. He prepared to jump, but just before his feet left the ground, something latched around his neck, sending painful electricity throughout his body.

He was completely unable to transform, try as he might. A strong arm wrapped around his torso, and he was forced to face back towards the cabin. Jem heard the *whiz* of an astra firing, and he saw blue flashes of magic strike Mualano, Yakoba, and Farouche, but Ikuuno deployed a single shield from her left wrist, and the shot that was aimed for her was deflected and struck the side of the vimana.

"Stand down!" shouted Tachel, hiding behind Jem's paralyzed body as a shield. "I don't want to hurt you!"

"Vimana One, you've got a zombie on your bottom," said Henry over the speaker system. "Repeat: you've got a zombie on your bottom. Pull up; I'm coming below you to shoot it off."

"What are you doing, Tachel?" shouted Ikuuno from behind her shield. "You can't paralyze our pilot! We'll crash!"

She was right; Jem could feel the ship losing altitude now that Farouche's sylph wasn't powering the turbine.

"Then let me paralyze you, and I'll fly this plane!" yelled Tachel.

A barrage of projectiles struck the vimana. Tachel held his ground well, but Ikuuno was knocked to the side and hit the wall. Mualano and Yakoba's bodies were thrown against the wall, but Ikuuno sent a spell from her hand to keep them tied to the benches. The ship was now tilted to the side and falling rapidly. Ikuuno quickly released sylph from her hand that went flying into the turbine around the pilot's cabin—Farouche's had disappeared when he had been paralyzed. This dramatically slowed down their descent, allowing them to remain in the air, but she still wasn't able to steer or take them any higher. Having her sylph power the ship while she had a shield deployed to protect her from Tachel and wielding her astra in a gun form must have been incredibly draining for her.

"What are you doing with Jem?" she cried.

"Jem has to die!" shouted Tachel. "It's the only way."

"What do you mean it's the only way?" asked Ikuuno. "Whatever it is, we can help you!"

"YOU CAN'T HELP ME!" screamed Tachel, almost breaking Jem's eardrums. "Nobody can help me! My family is dead if I don't do this! It's the only way I can save them!"

"They're on our back!" came Henry's voice from the speaker system. "Get 'em off, One!"

"Tachel," said Ikuuno, stepping closer and lowering her gun-formed astra while keeping her shield in front of her, "let us help you. We can save your family. You don't have to hurt Jem."

Tachel shook his head. "You can't do anything for me. STAY BACK! One more step and Jem goes off the edge."

Ikuuno stopped moving, but she was out of options. Jem was

completely paralyzed, the vimana was flying out of control without a pilot, and Tachel was clearly willing to die to kill Jem.

"Vimanas Two, Three, and Four, we need assistance now—got two zombies on the roof," shouted Lenro through the speaker system.

"Do what you know is right," said Ikuuno. "I can't force you. Only you can make this decision, Tachel. Don't let Veroci win. He wants this."

Tears were streaming down Tachel's face. "This is not my choice," he spluttered. "This is my duty to my family."

Tachel deployed a shield from his left wrist to protect him from Ikuuno and then turned so that Jem was hanging off the side of ledge. As soon as Tachel let go, Jem would plummet to his death, and there was nothing he could do about it.

"I'm sorry," uttered Tachel, but just before he could release Jem, something caught Tachel on the back, and he was jerked off the vimana. His shield dissipated, and he pulled Jem down with him; the two of them went plunging downwards.

"NO!" screamed Ikuuno, running to the ledge, but there was nothing she could do.

Completely paralyzed, Jem was helpless as Tachel clung to him and they fell to the ground. There was another pair of hands gripping at Jem, though, and something cut into the electric band around his neck.

"TRANSFORM!" screamed a high-pitched voice directly in his ear.

Jem didn't think twice about it; it was either transform or become a splatter on the Keladonian ground. He flexed every muscle he could, and immediately, his body formed into that of a dragon. He felt one small person clinging to his neck and another heavier person clinging to his tail as he flapped his wings hard.

He barely stopped their fall in time. They were only a few feet above the swarm of zombies, and some of them were leaping up to strike at Jem. He struck out with his feet, clawing several of them in the face as he flew back up. He whipped his tail about, but Tachel stayed attached to it.

Teek was holding onto Jem's neck for dear life, staring back down at Tachel as they ascended. Tachel was clinging onto Jem's scales and had his gun-formed astra pointed directly at Teek.

"Why, Tachel?" called Teek over the loud wind.

"I had no choice," he replied, his hand shaking ferociously.

Teek shook her head as her tears were blown away in the gust. "Don't do it," she cried. "I thought you had made the right decision."

"I made the decision to save my family!" burst Tachel. "Who are you to say that is wrong?"

With those words, Tachel let go of Jem's scales.

"NO!" screamed Teek, reaching out for him, but it was no use. Tachel tumbled downwards, falling to his death amongst the crowd of zombies.

Jem continued his flight up, and when he reached the entrance hatch, he tossed Teek from his neck into the vimana. There were four or five zombies on the roof of the vimana, and two on one of the thruster-wings. Jem flew effortlessly around the ship, knocking the zombies off with his tail and claws. Their arrows and swords bounced off his scales like they were toys.

After clearing the vimana of zombies, he transformed back into his human form and landed inside the vimana since his dragon form wouldn't have fit. Ikuuno had already unparalyzed everyone, and while Farouche was desperately trying to control the ship, the other three were shooting their astras out of the other hatches.

"Jem!" called Ikuuno, running over to them. "Who is this? And what happened to Tachel?"

"This is Teek," explained Jem, still trying to process everything that had just happened. "She must have snuck aboard the ship. Tachel fell; he's not coming back."

Ikuuno nodded grimly just as an arrow came shooting into their cabin and embedded itself in the roof. She turned back to the hatch and continued to fire down at the zombies.

"How did you get here?" Jem demanded of Teek. "What were you thinking?"

"I was thinking that I wanted to help!" defended Teek. "And I hid in the cargo wing with the mini-vimanas. When I heard what was going on with Tachel, I cut my way out with my astra and crawled across the roof. You're lucky I tackled Tachel; you'd be dead right now if I hadn't!"

Jem took a deep breath. "You're right," he said. "Thank you. But how did you get a combat suit and an astra?"

"Tachel gave them to me; he even taught me how to use them."

Jem nodded. "Come on, let's get you latched in."

As Jem latched Teek into the metal bench, the other three stopped firing spells and took their seats. One of the hatches rose back up, but the other two were clearly broken. Jem took his seat beside Teek as everyone got latched in, and they accelerated away from the wave of zombies.

"Attention, Invasion Squad," announced Farouche over the speaker system. "All four vimanas are now clear of that wave of zombies, but the worst is not behind us. We'll be reaching the central river in a few minutes, and after that, we'll be approaching the Rastvo cities. Prepare for the worst."

"Casualty report?" asked Sam over the speakers.

"We lost Rick," said Lenro.

"We lost Tachel," reported Farouche.

"We're good," said Henry.

"We're good as well," said Sam. "Resume formation and strap in, everyone; we're just getting started."

CHAPTER 26:
THE PHOENIX GLOVE

Sierra was sitting against the metal bench, trying to control her breath. She felt each metal ridge of the bench digging into her legs and lower back. Her dad was beside her, silent as a rock. She was trying to push out the memories, trying to focus on the task at hand, but it wasn't working. Her recollections of Rick were suddenly vivid and real. She was gripping her fists so tightly that she thought she might break through her suit's gloves.

She had thought that it had been her fault. Maybe she could have resisted more, maybe she should have said, "No," louder, maybe she should have told her dad as soon as it had happened the first time. But now she realized that it had not been her fault. She had been in shock, he had been much bigger and stronger than her, and she had been confused and afraid. He had threatened her and had said that she couldn't tell. It was his fault; not hers.

But now it was out in the open, and she intended to keep it that way. No more hiding. Silence meant that he was getting his way. When she returned to the Fortress—if she returned to the Fortress—it would no longer be a secret. She had had enough of keeping secrets. There would probably be insensitive, mean people, but all that mattered to her was that she knew that the people she loved would support her. Her dad was her greatest comfort at that moment, despite his stoic silence. She knew that he was there for her and that he would do anything for her.

She looked up and saw Ella through her visor. Zenska was sitting quietly beside her, and she was clearly crying although her visor covered her face. Sierra wanted to talk to her, she wanted to know what was going on in her mind, and she wanted to help her. Unfortunately, that would have to wait because they were approaching the central river, and she would have to leave soon. She certainly didn't feel prepared to face any giant sea monster, though.

The time it took to get to the river felt like days. Sierra felt like she was locked inside her own mind, unable to escape the nightmares which were there as well. A part of her just wanted to cry, a part of her wanted to punch something, a part of her wanted to talk to someone, and another part wanted never to talk to anyone again. Recognizing that it had not been her fault was a huge step, but nothing could erase the memories.

"Approaching the river," came Farouche's voice from over the speakers. "Will arrive at Rastvo cities momentarily. Get ready; the fun is about to begin."

Zenska stood up and walked over to the open hatch that was facing forward. Ella, Leo, and Sierra followed. They would be passing the massive river in seconds, and the cities were just on the end of the horizon. Sierra couldn't make out the buildings well, since they were so far away, but they didn't look too inviting.

She didn't have much time to prepare an exit. As the other three were staring out of the front hatch, she stepped quietly backwards to another hatch. Her legs were shaking, and she felt like her knees could give out at any moment. She glanced over the edge of the hatch and saw land be replaced by water. It was now or never.

She leapt off the vimana, arms and legs spread to slow her fall as much as possible. Her heart was pounding at a million beats per minute, and the wind was deafening, even through her helmet. The water was approaching fast, and Sierra only had one shot at the cushioning spell. As she came within feet of crashing violently into the water, she closed her legs, brought her arms to her sides, and performed the cushioning spell that she had practiced so many times before. It slowed her down just enough that she was able to dive headfirst into the water.

Cold was all she felt. The suit, being designed to keep out liquid and magically sealed at the neck, wrists, and ankles, kept her completely dry, but it was still astonishingly cold. Her ears began to throb with pain and she was flailing her arms and legs about in an attempt to generate some body heat.

Focus, she told herself. *You studied this. Water pressure. Calm down and stabilize yourself.*

She quit flailing and tried to breathe as steadily as possibly. She crossed her legs and gripped her hands together, focusing on the outer layer of her skin and the pressure it should be feeling. Gradually, over the course of a few minutes, her breathing slowed down, her ears felt better, and it felt like an enormous weight had been lifted from her body. But she was tired. She hadn't expected the pressure stabilizing spell to take so long or to take so much out of her. This wasn't a good start to her mission.

Oh well, she thought. *No turning back now.*

Sylph ejected from her palms and squeezed its way out of her gloves and into the water. That trick had taken her a while to master—getting her sylph to convert to a liquid, pushing it through the suit's material, and converting it back to its malleable solid form. She then broke the sylph into four thin, flipper-like pieces and attached one to each hand and foot. This allowed her to propel herself much more easily through the water.

Sierra, said her dad's voice through the rendocom. *Where are you? What happened? Are you okay?*

I'm fine, she replied. *Go shut the portal. I'll join you on the way back.*

There was a moment of silence before Leo replied, *I don't know what you're up to, Sierra, but you better be safe.*

Always, she replied, and she silenced her rendocom so that no one else could contact her.

Deep in the river, Kelados was a different world. Despite being dead and zombie-ridden on the surface, Kelados was a place thriving with underwater life. Bizarre fish of all sizes, shapes, and colors swam by Sierra. She saw one light gray creature that looked like a torpedo or a missile: it was just a grey cylinder with small fins on each side, big round eyes, and a propeller-like attachment on its back that was pushing it through the water.

Other than minor detours around sea animals, she was headed directly towards the island. From underwater, it looked like a towering mountain. The left side of the mountain was attached to the side of the river and was impassable from underwater. The right side of the island, however, dropped almost vertically like the edge of a cliff and descended all the way down to the bottom.

From what Fey had told her, the entrance to the cave should be on the other side near the bottom, so Sierra headed down at the same time that she swam towards the side of the underwater cliff. This meant that she had to readjust her pressure spell constantly just to stay comfortable inside the combat suit.

Her eyes kept darting around, examining all of the strange animals, half-expecting one of them to attack her. Maybe they were all guardians of the Phoenix Glove. Maybe if she tried to escape with it, they would all attack her. She swallowed hard. If that was the case, she wouldn't make it out alive.

The sea monster was nowhere to be seen, but Sierra wasn't expecting to see it. Fey had said that it slept inside the cave and only rarely emerged when it wanted a snack. Sierra didn't know what to expect once she got inside the cave, though. Fey had only described it as a big, horrible monster. She had also said that the Glove had been protected well in a ball of okori, a special kind of ice that was extraordinarily hard to break and was imbued with minerals that made it glow blue.

"Obviously, I am not a deserving Fenic," Fey had said, "for I could not retrieve the Glove from its okori encasing. It will be a test of your true devotion to saving your world that will determine if you can retrieve it. I merely wanted it for the power, but your cause is far more worthy."

"So once I find it, how do I get it out of the okori?" Sierra had asked.

Fey had smiled. "That is a question not only I, but none of my ancestors have been able to answer."

Sierra's swim was easy with her sylph flippers, and she was soon around the corner of the underwater cliff and looking straight at the cave entrance. It was nestled at the very bottom in the corner between the mountain and the river's wall. It looked big enough to drive a few sylphquads through, and it emanated a light blue glow that lit up the otherwise very dark river bottom.

Once inside the entrance, Sierra only had one path to follow. The tunnel dipped down and to the left, and then turned right and went upwards. The walls were glowing, illuminating the entire tunnel in a soft, azure light. Sierra skimmed her hand along the wall for a moment, and it felt like ice, freezing and smooth, but she knew that it had to be okori. The entire cave seemed to be made of the substance.

The tunnel seemed to go upwards for a long time. The very top looked to be the same light blue as the walls, and Sierra was starting to feel trapped. What if the tunnel just led to a dead end? What if the entrance had been sealed off? What if the cave had filled completely with water? She wouldn't be able to continue in the freezing water like she was, constantly readjusting her pressure spell. She was tired and needed to reach land, but it felt like she never would.

Finally, she broke the surface. She instantly released her sylph, removed her helmet, and threw it onto the piece of land beside her. The air was sharp, cold, and different here. She burst out into a fit of coughing, despite her best attempts to keep quiet. After a minute, her coughs subsided. She was just treading water and looking around to get a feel for where she was.

The tunnel stopped going straight up; instead, it leveled out and went off in one direction. There was a small bit of land in front of her and then a hill, all made of okori. The tunnel got noticeably wider, but Sierra couldn't see what was beyond the hill. She coughed a couple more times, ran her hands through her hair, rubbed her eyes, and headed for the shore. It was then that she noticed two helmets sitting there.

Sierra got out of the water slowly and stayed close to the ground. She picked up the other helmet and examined it. It was definitely a standard issue combat helmet. One of the other people in the vimanas must've had the same plan that she did. Oh well, maybe they could help her then.

Sierra stood up and walked cautiously towards the top of the small hill. Whoever was there must've heard her already and be waiting for her, unless they had traveled deeper into the cave already.

But as soon as she poked her head above the hill and saw someone standing there, the okori exploded in front of her. She dropped to the ground and covered her head as bits of the okori fell around her. The person she had seen—it couldn't be her. Could it?

Another blast hit the ceiling and large, jagged chunks of okori rained down upon Sierra. She rolled to the side, dodging a couple of big pieces, and used a spell to knock another one away. She took her astra from its holster and prepared to fire back. She leapt to her feet and shot paralyzing beams at her attacker over the hill.

Avalon deflected the beams by deploying the shield on her astra. She then stood there perfectly still, shield out at arms-length, wet blond hair tussled about.

"What are you doing here?" she demanded.

"What are *you* doing here?" retorted Sierra, breathing hard. The air in the cave felt thin and difficult to inhale.

Avalon smirked. "I think you know. And if you get in my way, Sierra, I won't be afraid to kill you."

"Are you crazy?" spat Sierra. "There is a sea monster in here; we can't be fighting each other!"

Right on cue, a roar erupted throughout the cave, shaking the walls and causing ripples in the various puddles around them.

Avalon looked shaken for an instant, but then that expression was gone, and she looked as angry and intimidating as ever. "Don't follow me," she said. "That glove is mine and mine only."

Before Sierra could protest, Avalon turned her suit's full shield on, docked her astra, and ran away. There were three tunnels ahead of them, and she took the one to the left. Somewhere in the cave, Sierra could hear the sound of a giant creature moving, and she didn't hesitate to take off running for the tunnel to the right.

According to the map that Fey had showed her, all three of these tunnels would lead to a large, dome-shaped room with a massive lake in the center where the monster dwelled. From there, the Glove would be in a small room accessible by a tunnel on the other end of the lake. All Sierra had to do was get there before Avalon and not get eaten by the sea monster. Sounded easy enough.

Traversing the tunnel system turned out to be harder than it looked. The tunnel that Sierra had chosen went up at first and then curved to the left, and running up the slick okori proved to be about as difficult as running on ice. The grip on her combat boots did a pretty good job, but it took a lot of concentration and effort for her to stay on her feet.

When the tunnel began to curve downwards again, Sierra sat down and simply slid the rest of the way. She started off slow but began to pick up speed and was holding her astra with both hands as she went, just in case. The monster must have taken a different tunnel because she could hear it somewhere far off.

Eventually, the tunnel did let out into a vast open space. Sierra put her boots to the ground and stopped sliding. A strip of land ran around the lake, which was at least a couple hundred yards in diameter, and hundreds of tunnels were branching out from around it. The water sparkled a mystical light blue, like the walls around them, but it was entrancing just to look at. Sierra stepped forward slowly and dipped her hand into it.

The water was so clear that Sierra could see straight through the bottom. Deep down there, something was sparkling brightly, and that must've been what caused the water to shine the way it did. The entire lake floor twinkled like it was covered in some kind of expensive stone. Maybe she could just swim down there really quickly and get some of it to bring home…

"AHHH!" screamed Avalon as she came running into the main cave. She fell on her side as she tried to turn sharply and slid all the way to the edge of the water. She jumped back up to her feet and took off running away from Sierra. An ominous sliding noise told Sierra that the monster wasn't far behind.

Forgetting the shiny gems at the bottom of the lake, Sierra took off running in the opposite direction around the lake. Within seconds, she heard the monster screeching a shrill call, and she looked over her shoulder. An enormous beast, bigger than the Dragon and the Phoenix combined, came sliding out of the same tunnel that Avalon had.

It had dark green, slimy-looking skin, and a grey underbelly. It had four huge fins, a stubby tail that was barely there, and a long neck. It was only visible for a second before it slid effortlessly into the lake. Suddenly, the cave was silent except for the breathing of Sierra and Avalon, who were both on opposite sides of the lake.

Sierra watched as Avalon turned down a tunnel and disappeared. Either she didn't know where she was going, or she just didn't want to be in the same part of the cave as the sea monster. Sierra had been counting tunnel entrances as she ran, and the one she needed to get to was only about ten away. Maybe she could actually make it.

But then the monster came sliding up out of the water and stopped in front of Sierra, blocking her path completely. It didn't attack; it just extended its neck and roared loudly at her. She pointed her astra at it and stood still, but she couldn't fight it. Instead, she went sprinting down the tunnel to her right and shot the ceiling, causing large pieces of okori to fall and block the entrance behind her. The monster roared, and she could hear it take a different tunnel.

She continued down the tunnel for a while, hoping to find some sort of clue pointing her to the Phoenix Glove. She shivered violently as she passed different tunnel connections, but she didn't turn down any of them. She could get lost very quickly doing that, and she wanted to know how to get back to the main cave if she needed to.

The tunnel went upwards for a long while, but then it turned and curved sharply downwards. Sierra ran and slid down on her back, keeping her astra out in gun form, ready to paralyze. Intersection after intersection whooshed by in a blur. Sierra could hear the monster sliding somewhere in one of the other tunnels, but she did not see it. Then she heard Avalon's screams.

As Sierra passed by another tunnel intersection, she looked to her right and saw Avalon sliding down that tunnel, followed closely by the monster. Sierra shot a sylph rope from her hand and wrapped it around Avalon, tugging her towards her. Instead of continuing by into the same tunnel, Avalon was forced to descend along with Sierra. The monster was able to react quickly enough, and it turned to follow them, smacking against the side of the wall and causing the whole place to shake.

As they shot down the tunnel, Sierra released her sylph and deployed her full shield, afraid that Avalon might attack her. But it became apparent pretty quickly that Avalon wasn't paying any attention to her. Instead, she was firing her astra back at the monster, and it was howling in pain as the magic beams struck it.

"Don't hurt it!" screamed Sierra, and she lowered her shield long enough to shoot a paralyzing beam at Avalon's astra. It hit the astra and knocked it out of her hands, but it continued to slide down the tunnel with them.

"What the hell do you think you're doing?" yelled Avalon. "You're gonna get us killed!"

"And what's your plan? Just piss it off more?"

Avalon didn't have a chance to reply before their tunnel reached the main cave again. The two of them went sliding uncontrollably into the water with a *splash*, but the monster leapt over them and dove quietly into the depths of the lake. Both of the girls swam rapidly for the shore.

Avalon summoned her astra and had it pointed at the lake, ready to fire. Sierra, on the other hand, was trying to figure out where in the cave they were because all the tunnels looked the same. She glanced around, trying to find some hint, and then she saw the tunnel that she had collapsed before. That meant that the tunnel they needed to go in was only two to their left.

The monster shot up out of the water, roaring viciously and flapping its fins. While Avalon immediately started shooting at it, Sierra's reaction, again, was to shoot the astra out of her hand; only this time, she used a regular beam, and it shattered the astra upon contact.

Howling in pain, the monster zipped straight towards them, skimming just on the surface of the water. Sierra fired the capture rounds from her astra, sending multiple giant nets at the creature. One caught it over the face and the others subdued the fins. It squirmed and fought but it was no longer able to swim, and it sunk below the water.

"Come on," said Sierra, not wasting any time. "We have to get to the Glove."

Avalon followed Sierra towards the tunnel to their left. "Why'd you do that?" asked Avalon as they ventured through the winding tunnel. "We could have killed it!"

"Why should we kill it, Avalon? It hasn't done anything to us. We invaded its home and are trying to steal something from it. The least we could do is not kill it."

"But it tried to kill us! Haven't you ever heard of self-defense? When that thing breaks out of those nets, it'll come right back after us."

"By then, we'll have the Glove," said Sierra. "And we'll be able to figure a way out. Besides, it had plenty of opportunities to kill us, and it didn't. When we fell into the water we were easy targets, but it jumped over us instead of eating us right then. I don't think it's bad."

"Are you kidding me? It's been attacking us this entire time; it just hasn't had the chance to bite one of our heads off yet!"

"Still, we shouldn't kill it if we can avoid it. It's not right to kill it for doing nothing. We just need to get the Glove, get out, and let it be."

"You're gonna get us killed," grunted Avalon. Both of them were still shivering fiercely, and their breath was clearly visible as they ran through the tunnel. Sierra kept her distance from Avalon but made sure not to let her out of her sight because even without her astra, Avalon would still be able to shoot spells at Sierra. And while Sierra was mostly protected by her combat suit, she didn't have her helmet, so a well-placed shot from Avalon could potentially end her.

Soon, they reached a small room which had several other tunnels connected to it. In the center was a floating orb of okori, about the size of a kiorah ball—or what Jem would've called a soccer ball. Suspended in the okori was a red, fingerless glove that seemed to flicker with flames, despite being frozen in the okori. A yellow, two-pronged flame was visible on the back of it.

"That's it!" cried Avalon, running up to the Glove. "I got it!" She tried to grab the okori orb, but it didn't budge. She pushed, pulled, and put her entire body weight onto it, but it didn't give at all. She took a step back and began shooting spell after spell at it from her fingertips, but it was immovable.

"Give me your astra!" she demanded of Sierra, holding her hand out.

Sierra took a step away from her. "You can't use it. It's calibrated to me."

"Then you blast open this orb, and let's get the hell out of there!"

Sierra glared at her but then turned to the okori orb and did as she was told. She fired an explosive big-shot round at it, draining her of precious energy and causing a minor explosion, but the orb didn't budge.

"How do we get it out?" asked Avalon worriedly. "I need this. I need this!"

"What do you need it so bad for anyway?" asked Sierra.

"To impress Jem, of course," Avalon spat back, running her hands over the orb as if looking for a seam to break open.

"To impress Jem? What are you, his servant?"

Avalon stopped examining the orb and stepped close to Sierra. Sierra held her ground, though, and they stood nose to nose.

"I'm more to him than you'll ever be, that's for sure," said Avalon.

"If he chooses a power-hungry psycho over me, then that is his loss," retorted Sierra. "I don't need him."

"Ha, what a lie. Don't pretend that you aren't jealous of me and him. I know you think I stole him from you, but you never had him in the first place. You saw our kiss—you saw our love. He loved me more than he could ever love you."

Sierra felt her heart drop a little bit. "We had months together in Luria where I took care of him, and he never kissed me…"

"That's because he never loved you," taunted Avalon. "He loves me, and when we get back to the Fortress, and he sees the power that I possess, and he learns of your failure, he'll choose me over you in an instant."

"This isn't a competition for a boy," insisted Sierra, although her voice was weak and quiet. "This is about saving my home."

"Jem isn't just any boy. You must know of the power he has… his unique ability."

"So?"

"So," continued Avalon, "ever since I met him and saw that scar on his hand, I knew he was powerful, and when I have the Phoenix Glove, the two of us will be unstoppable."

"That's not what having the Glove is about! You shouldn't get it just to impress Jem or to have power; you should want it to do some good in the world!"

"Who cares about doing good if you're doing it alone, Sierra? Let's be real. I need Jem, and he will love me if I get this."

"You don't need anybody," said Sierra, staring hard into Avalon's grey-green eyes. "You're pathetic. All you are is an attachment on Jem's side. He doesn't need you. He's independent and worth something without you, but without him, you're nothing."

"That's a lie!" screamed Avalon. "He loves me, and he needs me!"

"You know," said Sierra, eyes watering slightly. "I would like to be with Jem—we used to be great friends—but if he doesn't want to be with me, then that's fine, and if he wants to be with you, then that's fine too. But you will never be happy living your life for someone else. Because while you kiss the ground he walks on, I'll be living my own life, doing what makes me happy, and all you'll ever be is what he wants you to be."

"Stop it!" shouted Avalon, pushing Sierra back and beginning to cry. "I love him!"

The creature roared from somewhere distant. They didn't have much time left.

"It's one thing to love; it's another thing to be obsessive and dependent," said Sierra, walking by Avalon without touching her. She stood in front of the orb and took a deep breath. There had to be some trick to this thing, some failsafe that the Phoenix enacted so that only a worthy person could retrieve the Glove.

It will be a test of your true devotion to saving your world that will determine if you can retrieve it, Sierra remembered Fey telling her. *I merely wanted it for the power, but your cause is far more worthy.*

Sierra carefully took the combat glove off one of her hands and pressed it against the okori orb. She felt the freezing, icy feeling against her skin, and she closed her eyes to try and interact with it. It felt like magic similar to how she formed sylph or performed any spell—she had to focus on what she wanted to do and work out the correct feeling.

The monster continued to roar in the background, and it was obviously getting closer. Avalon was breathing heavily and sniffling, but Sierra was completely focused on the task at hand. It felt like the orb was beginning to get smaller, and when she opened her eyes, she saw that it was starting to melt, and water was dripping down it. She continued to work with the magic to warm up the okori—a slow and delicate process.

Avalon came closer and was staring over Sierra's shoulder, watching as she got closer and closer to the Glove. Avalon's breathing got faster and faster, but Sierra maintained her composure. As Sierra finally revealed a bit of the Glove, Avalon knocked her to the ground with her arm. Sierra watched as Avalon reached for the Glove but immediately jumped back in pain.

"It burned me!" yelped Avalon, clenching one of her hands with the other. "It burned me..." she said more drowsily, and then she fell to the floor. Sierra got back up, worried that the Glove may have been enchanted to knock out anyone who tried to get it, but she had to keep trying.

She continued the melting process, despite the roars that were almost into their room. When the ice was completely gone, the Phoenix Glove hovered in the air and spun around so that the wrist was pointed at Sierra.

You have to do this, she told herself. *The Regime needs to be stopped.*

Slowly, she slipped her shaking hand into the Phoenix Glove. She winced, expecting it to burn, but it didn't. She managed to get her entire hand in, and then the Glove caught fire—but it didn't burn. She examined her hand, twisting it around and looking at it from every angle. Contentment flooded her body, but that was quickly squelched by the appearance of the monster's head in the tunnel to her right.

Sierra backed up and stood in front of Avalon's body, holding out her hand with the Glove on it. She didn't know what the Glove could do, but if the monster tried to attack either one of them, she was going to find out. She really hoped that there would be a peaceful way out of the situation, though.

The monster barely fit inside the room. It poked its long neck in and about half of its body before it filled most of the room, and its face was only a few feet from Sierra's. Its big black eyes looked right into hers, and it breathed heavily out of its nostrils.

You have done well, a gentle voice said inside her head. *Congratulations on retrieving the Glove.*

Sierra was confused, and she looked around for the source of the voice.

It's me, continued the voice. The sea creature did not break eye contact with her. *My name is Tylas. Quetzalus had asked me to guard nir Glove for nem. You have obviously proven yourself worthy to possess such a power.*

"W-who's Quetzalus? And h-how did I prove I w-was w-worthy?" stuttered Sierra, freezing cold and still trying to understand how she was communicating with this creature.

Quetzalus? The Phoenix? Big fiery bird, flaps nir wings like this.

Tylas then reared up on its hind fins and began to flap its front fins as if it could fly.

And your intentions are good; I can sense that much. No one with bad intentions would have been able to melt the ice. That is why your friend is in her current state— because she tried to take that which was not hers to take.

"Is sh-she going to b-be okay?"

Of course. She will awaken soon. You were very brave to stand up to her. You easily could have allowed her to attack me while you searched for the Glove.

"I didn't think it w-would be fair to kill you when you h-hadn't done anything to us, and I w-wanted her to be safe t-too."

Why would you protect someone in competition with you to obtain the Glove? What if she had gotten it first?

"I had to p-protect her. Maybe one d-day she can change and she c-can look back on this and think how s-stupid she was."

Tylas' lips pulled back in what could only be a large, awkward smile. *Your restraint and your compassion are admirable. I see why Quetzalus has chosen you to be the bearer of the Glove. Wear it wisely, young one.*

"I w-will."

Let me take you out of this place. You must be freezing, and you need to return to your other humans. Climb on my back, and I will assist your friend.

Sierra did as she was told, jumping up onto Tylas' slippery fin and then making her way onto its back. The suit helped her cling onto it, and the Phoenix Glove, despite its fiery appearance, didn't burn it or damper when pressed against its wet skin. Avalon then began to levitate and floated over to Tylas' back where she was placed delicately in front of Sierra.

Hold onto her, don't let her fall, said Tylas.

"I won't," replied Sierra. "You can do magic?"

Of course. Humans are not the only magical species, young one. Don't let your apparent dominance go to your head; we are all inhabitants of this universe.

With that, Tylas took off through the tunnel system. Avalon and Sierra stayed attached to its back somehow; Sierra assumed that it must've had some spell on them to keep them in place since its back was otherwise very slippery. As big as it was, it barely fit through the tunnels, and the roof of the tunnels came within inches of hitting the two girls.

Rather quickly, they came shooting out of the tunnel and skimmed weightlessly across the water of the lake in the main cave. After going through another tunnel, they arrived at the exit to the river, and Tylas levitated their helmets back onto their heads.

I'll keep an air bubble around you, but you're probably safer wearing the helmets anyway.

"Got it," said Sierra, latching her own helmet on and latching Avalon's as well. Tylas then dove into the tunnel that descended straight downwards, and an air bubble appeared around Sierra and Avalon.

They popped out into the river, and all the wildlife was still there. All the fish and other animals seemed to get out of the way as Tylas approached.

Are there more like you? Sierra asked Tylas in her head, wondering if the mental communication went both ways.

No, replied Tylas sadly. *I am an elasmorus, and the last of them. But I have known both Quetzalus and Hazeryx for a long time.*

Hazeryx? repeated Sierra.

The Dragon. You know, like the Phoenix but not so on fire.

Oh, okay. I didn't know they had names.

I see. Well, the three of us have been around for a while, but unfortunately, each of us are the last of our kind.

That must get lonely.

Sometimes, admitted Tylas. *But for the most part, I am just fine.*

Tylas then took them up to the surface and levitated them off its back and onto the north side of the shore.

I can sense that the zombies are preoccupied in the south, it explained, just its head sticking up out of the water. *You will be best off just walking to the north back to your human city.*

Thanks, Tylas, said Sierra. *Oh, one last thing. Can you wake her up so I don't have to carry her?*

Ah, yes of course, of course. Without Tylas making any apparent movements,

Avalon then began to wake up.

"What—what's going on?" asked Avalon, sitting up and looking first at Sierra and then at Tylas. She scampered backwards quickly. "What's *that* doing here!?"

"Calm down," said Sierra. "This is Tylas. It's on our side."

Avalon stared at Tylas for a minute, squinting her eyes. "Are you…" she began, "are you like the Dragon and the Phoenix? Are you a legendary?"

Tylas nodded its big green head.

"So you're on our side?" asked Avalon.

Tylas nodded again.

Avalon grinned. "Well, thanks for not killing me. I'm sorry I attacked you."

All is forgiven, said Tylas inside both Sierra and Avalon's heads.

"Did—did you just talk inside my head?" asked Avalon.

I did, said Tylas.

"But… but Jem told me that the Dragon could only talk to him because of his dragon DNA. How can you talk to us?"

My situation is unique. You see, when the Souls were first created by humans, they took all the magic from the three worlds and put it into a physical form. One Soul was given to each planet. The Earth Soul, to the extent of my knowledge, remains hidden and intact, but the other two were divided. Callisto's was divided into six, one for each region, and Kelados' was divided into two, one for the north and one for the south.

When the spell happened that robbed the worlds of their magic, trapping it in a physical form, my cave was unaffected. My cave is made of a special material called okori, which is impervious to magical attacks from the outside. It withstood the thievery, and my cave and I remain naturally magical, allowing me to communicate with non-legendary species such as humans. The Dragon and the Phoenix, however, weren't as lucky as I. Their lands were robbed of magic, and it greatly limited their natural abilities. While they can still perform magic in the absence of a Soul, their magic is much less powerful than it could be.

"Wow," uttered both Sierra and Avalon.

It won't stay that way forever, though, continued Tylas. *People can only be greedy with magic for so long, and soon it will return to its natural state. Now you two must go back to your Fortress and be safe before the zombies return. If you ever need anything, you know where to find me. What are your names, by the way?*

They both introduced themselves, and Tylas smiled. *Pleasure to meet you both. I wish you the best of luck in returning the three worlds to their natural order. Take care.*

Tylas then ducked under the water and disappeared. Avalon's eyes flickered to Sierra's hand with the Phoenix Glove on it.

"So…" said Avalon, "you got the Glove."

"I did," said Sierra, trying to determine if Avalon was a threat anymore or not. "Because I deserved it. I'm trying to do what's right, Avalon."

Avalon stared at Sierra for a minute, as if thinking over everything she had just experienced. She looked halfway between being very angry or very confused.

"I know," she said finally. "You deserved it. Not me."

Sierra's jaw dropped in shock. That wasn't the answer she had been expecting.

"But I'm going to be better, Sierra, I am," insisted Avalon. "Come on, let's go home."

Sierra smiled. Together, the two of them began the long walk back to the Fortress.

CHAPTER 27:
THE SACRED PORTAL

Jem sat against the metal bench, breathing deeply. He was very conscious of each breath: the air going in… the air going out. Any one of those breaths, he thought, could be his last.

He had both his hands clasping the latch that would release him from the bench. At any moment, he had to be ready to transform. The only noise was the wind rushing in through the broken hatches. Jem thought about Tachel and what his life must have been like growing up as a soldier in the Regime. They had grown up so differently, though, and Jem couldn't imagine it. He felt bad for Tachel. He shouldn't have had to die.

"Approaching the river," came Farouche's voice from over the speakers. "Will arrive at Rastvo cities momentarily. Get ready; the fun is about to begin."

Fun, thought Jem. *If that's what you want to call it.*

He looked over at Teek beside him. He couldn't allow her to die, not after she had saved his life. The instant that the zombies began to attack, he would transform and protect all the vimanas, but especially this one.

"Teek," he said quietly, so that only she could hear. "I know you don't like to listen to your parents—or any authority for that matter—and I'm glad because otherwise I'd be dead, but while we're out here, you have to work as a team with these guys. Don't go off on your own. Listen to Ikuuno and Mualano, please."

Teek nodded her head. The severity of the situation seemed to be sinking in for her finally. "War is scarier than I thought, Jem."

Jem gripped her hand tightly. "That's why we have to end it."

"Invasion squad, this is Vimana One," said Lenro over the speaker system. "We've just lost Sierra, anybody see what happened?"

Jem's heart almost stopped as he strained his ears to hear more.

"It… it looked like she just jumped off," said Sam, the pilot of Vimana Four. "It looked intentional."

The Phoenix Glove, thought Jem. *We just passed the river. She's going for it.*

"Vimana Three, you just lost someone too," said Farouche over the speakers. "Who was that?"

"What are you talking about, Two?" replied Henry. "We didn't lose anyone."

"Then you might want to check your cargo bays because I definitely just watched a body fall from your vimana," said Farouche. "You may have had a stowaway."

"On it."

I really hope that wasn't Avalon, thought Jem. She had been determined to get the Glove, but Jem had thought that she had given that up when her dad wouldn't allow her to come with the invasion squad. Guess not.

"Why would anybody do that?" asked Teek. "Just jump off the vimana?"

"Why would anyone sneak aboard a vimana going to war?" replied Jem.

Teek didn't laugh. "Will Sierra and the other person be okay?"

Jem looked away from her. "I sure hope so."

Hey, said Leo over the rendocom. *I've gotten word from Sierra that she's okay. I don't know what she's doing, but we'll have to trust her and worry about that later. Continue with the plan as scheduled.*

Within minutes, they were above the Rastvo cities. Jem unlatched himself and held onto the edge of the ship, looking outside. The city that they were approaching was bustling with zombies. The air around them was thick and grey, and the sharp, jagged buildings jutted up at them as if they were going to attack the vimanas.

"Jem, you're up," said Farouche, crouching down and peering at him from the pilot's cabin. "Good luck."

Jem looked over his shoulder and gave a weak smile and nod. He flexed his hands and shut the visor on his helmet. He put his toes over the ledge, and his stomach dropped as he stared down at the city below. Zombies were climbing buildings and beginning to leap high into the air. Jem didn't have any more time.

He stepped off with one foot and then the next, allowing himself to tumble headfirst off the vimana. He transformed as he fell, pulling up from his dive by extending his giant wings.

A Rastvo jumped from the nearby building and took a swipe at him, but he swerved to the left and avoided it. As he came back up, one jumped off a skyscraper and fell straight towards him, but he rolled sideways and avoided it. Three more Rastvo attacked him before he got back up to where the vimanas were, but only one of them was able to hit him, scratching him pretty well down his right leg.

Zombies were already clinging onto the ledges of two vimanas. Jem swooped by and knocked them off with his head; one leapt from the vimana and grabbed onto his tail, but he was able to throw it off with enough whipping around. A few of the skyscrapers were so high up that the vimanas had to swerve to avoid them. One zombie jumped from the tip of a skyscraper, but Jem swatted it down with his claw before it could touch a vimana.

Jem swooped back around, diving in between vimanas as magic beams shot out in every direction. Jem breathed fire over a group of zombies huddled on the roof of a tall building and then pulled one off the bottom of a vimana, throwing it down to the ground. They seemed to be attacking from everywhere, and no matter how many he fought, they just kept coming.

This persisted for what seemed like forever. Many of the pilots had to turn off course to avoid tall buildings and to shake zombies. Jem swiped countless zombies off the roofs of vimanas and knocked even more out of the sky. Every once in a while, though, one of the zombies would sink its claws into him and he would howl in pain, breathing fire wherever his mouth was pointed.

The Rastvo also seemed to be armed with arrows and a catapult-like weapon that launched giant boulders. The arrows just glanced off Jem's scales, but the catapult boulders were harder to stop. One was launched at Vimana Two, Farouche's vimana, and Jem threw himself at in a desperate attempt to save Farouche, Teek, and the others onboard. He managed to redirect it by smacking into it from the side, and it barely missed the vimana, but it gave Jem a sharp headache and made the whole left side of his body sore.

Ya'll will have to dodge those projectiles yourself, said Jem over the rendocom. *I can't take any more of them.*

Like I was trying to get hit by them, right? replied Farouche. Jem snorted a bit of fire out of his nose in a suppressed laugh.

His dragon vision, thankfully, was incredibly adept at picking up movement. He could see zombies out of the corner of his eye and attack in an instant. Things seemed to be going relatively well. Even though the wave of zombies didn't seem to end, Jem and the others were able to keep them at bay for the most part. They were definitely more prepared now than they had been before the river.

A few got inside Vimanas One and Three, but they didn't stand a chance. Jem witnessed Afflatus perform a power spell that sent three zombies shooting out of Vimana Three—one through each hatch. Leo took on two zombies with his sword-formed astra, dealing a deadly blow to each before knocking them out of Vimana One.

Eventually, they escaped the challenge that was the high buildings and were above the wasteland in between Rastvo and Djimota territory. The ground was desolated, covered in craters and scattered debris, and the Rastvo were too busy fighting the Djimota to be occupied with the vimanas. It seemed like crossing the wasteland would be a piece of cake— that is, until multiple catapults started firing at them from both sides.

The Rastvo were yet again firing giant boulders, causing all four vimanas to swerve erratically and almost hit each other. From the other side, the Djimota were launching smaller projectiles, but those projectiles were on fire. Jem smashed into those and they broke apart into much smaller pieces easily. So he focused on the attacks from the south and didn't see the boulder coming from the north.

BAM!

A Rastvo's boulder nailed Jem in the back and sent him plummeting to the ground. Jem crashed hard on his stomach, all four limbs stretched out and the boulder on his back. He created quite a crater, and he didn't know if he had the strength to push the boulder off his back. As he strained to get to up, though, the boulder just flew off his back as if by magic.

When he stood back up on his hind legs, Afflatus was gently floating down beside him, his astra in its holster and his hands glowing blue with magic. He landed with his back to Jem as zombies of all kinds, Rastvo and Djimota, began to surround them. In an attempt at intimidation, Jem roared as loudly as he could, fire shooting out of his mouth and covering everything ahead of him. Behind him, Afflatus launched a similar attack with what looked like several blue lightning bolts.

Neither of their attacks slowed the onslaught of zombies, however, and both of them fought with skill as hundreds of zombies rushed them. Djimota were gliding overhead, and Jem would breathe fire at them while clawing at Rastvo on the ground. He heard Afflatus' grunts and yells as the old man performed spell after spell, knocking zombies back in a powerful display of magic.

Swing your tail and turn, said Afflatus. Jem, breathing fire as he turned, did as he was told. He whipped his tail around, and Afflatus leapt into the air, just barely dodging it. Jem's tail knocked out multiple zombies, and he took out several more with his breath as he turned. Afflatus ran up Jem's back and jumped into the air, sending out more spells as he went. They were now back to back again, but fighting on the opposite side.

Despite their maneuvering, the zombies just kept coming.

We're going back up, commanded Jem. *Hold on.*

Without waiting, Jem began to flap his wings and take off. He felt Afflatus leap onto his back and grab him by the joints of his wings as he took off. They flew through the sky, and Jem headed straight for Vimana Three to place Afflatus back on it.

As they passed by Vimana Four, Jem saw a person fall from the ship, entangled with a Djimota, and he heard Okka's voice yell, "HELP!"

Jem immediately turned and dove towards him, but he was not nearly close enough to reach him in time. Out of the corner of his eye, he saw someone diving from Vimana Four, and he watched as that person shot the Djimota with their astra. The Djimota let go of Okka and fell off to the side. The diving person then sent a net from their astra and caught Okka. The bottom of the person then began to glow blue, like a meteor entering the atmosphere, and they slowed down. Jem flew by them and circled around.

As he made his way back around, the diver had retracted their net and was holding Okka beside them, hovering just a few yards above the ground. Jem flew under them and allowed them to both drop down on his back. The weight of three people was far too much for him to bear, but he would have to get them back to their vimanas safely—he had no other options.

"Forenzi, you saved me," Jem heard Okka say.

"I told you," replied Forenzi in his suave, deep voice, "today we are not divided by our systems. Today we are one."

Jem grinned a toothy dragon grin as he ascended slowly into the sky, but his grin faded quickly when a Djimota flew up from under him and struck him in the gut. He swatted it off quickly, but a dozen others began attacking. Afflatus, Okka, and Forenzi were all shooting spells at the surrounding zombies, but it was much more difficult for Jem to fly evasively with all the weight on him.

As they passed by the Holy Tower, the zombies stopped attacking them and started attacking themselves instead. Jem flew higher unabated, watching the Djimota dive down at the Rastvo, and the Rastvo shoot arrows at the Djimota. Some of the Rastvo had climbed the Tower and would jump off and attack the Djimota; it was a zombie bloodbath around the Tower. In fact, the Tower seemed to be the center of the entire war. They were directly in the center of the battlefield now.

Jem found it amazing how quickly the zombies forgot about the invading humans when they approached the Holy Tower. It was as if the Djimota and Rastvo were so consumed with their own hatred that they spent more time fighting themselves than fighting their real enemy—Jem and the other humans. It worked well for him, though, allowing him to get enough altitude to deliver Forenzi, Okka, and Afflatus to their respective vimanas.

What's the point of fighting over that stupid tower anyway? thought Jem. *It doesn't even do anything, and they're killing each other over it. I don't get it.*

He didn't have much time to think it over; soon he was being assaulted by hundreds of Djimota fighting their way towards the Holy Tower. He breathed fire as he flew and swatted a bunch out of the sky, but his main priority was to protect the vimanas. He circled around the four vimanas, knocking Djimota off when they would land on the roofs and trying to prevent them from even landing there in the first place. There were just too many flying zombies for him to keep track of.

The soldiers in the vimanas were incredibly accurate. As Jem flew around, he could see dark blue, magic beams shooting out from all four vimanas and striking down individual Djimota. However, the Djimota seemed to have their own projectiles—thin, sharp, arrow-like things that they shot from their wrists. They couldn't penetrate Jem's scales, but they hurt significantly more than the Rastvo's arrows, and they pierced the vimanas pretty easily.

The next thing Jem knew, they were flying over the Djimota cities. They contrasted starkly against the jagged, rough buildings of the Rastvo cities. Here, most of the buildings were skinny, smooth, and rounded. The vimanas each took a different path around the buildings, and this made it a lot harder for Jem to protect all of them. Djimota were popping out from every building and gliding around at every altitude. The vimanas wouldn't be able stay in the air long here, Jem suspected; the Djimota were much more dangerous in the air than the Rastvo had been.

As Jem dove through the sky and clawed one Djimota before it could enter the hatch of Vimana Two, he saw an explosion out of the corner of his eye.

We've got a thruster out, Henry said over the rendocom. *This ship ain't stayin' up much longer.*

Jem turned sharply and flew down to Vimana Three. Sure enough, one of the three ring thrusters was missing a giant chunk and was no longer propelling dark blue magic. Jem let loose a giant puff of fire that scared away most of the Djimota from that vimana, and he used his head to bash away the remaining ones.

We're almost there, he said to Henry. *Keep it up just a little longer; I can see the Leader's castle.*

Far out in the distance, Jem could see the giant golden dome approaching. Even though it wasn't that far away, there were hordes of flying zombies in the way that were definitely going to slow them down. Jem charged forward, breathing fire and swiping at anything that got close to him. He even broke through some of the thinner towers as he soared by.

We lost soldier Himay, said Sam. *Repeat, we've lost soldier Himay, and we're taking heavy fire.*

Jem spun around, caught in a storm of fire, smoke, and the debris of collapsing towers. He tried to locate Vimana Four with his sharp eyesight, and it took him a moment. By the time he had gotten his bearings and was flying for Vimana Four, he saw a group of three or four Djimota dive into the edge of one of the thruster rings, shattering it completely.

Thruster out! Thruster out! called Sam. *Initiating mini-vimana evac.*

An evacuation in these circumstances didn't seem like a smart move to Jem. With all the enemies around, the mini-vimanas would be incredibly exposed—but they didn't have much further to go. Jem would just have to clear a path.

He swooped down ahead of Vimana Four as its surviving soldiers shot out from the three wings of the vimana riding the mini-vimanas. He let loose an inferno of flames to burrow a path ahead for Sam and the others. He didn't spend much more time there, though, because he had other vimanas to save. He turned and flew past another tower, headed for Vimana One.

As he reached them, however, he watched Vimana One smash into the side of a tower. One of the wings was crushed completely and the thrusters were all immediately rendered useless. The tower toppled over, and Jem had to swerve quickly to avoid it, but it still smashed against his back, knocking him down closer to the ground. As he came back up, he saw two mini-vimanas escape from Vimana One, but there were only two people on one and one on the other—someone was still in the falling vimana.

Jem dove for the vimana but was cut off by a flock of Djimota that sliced him across the face and neck with their blades. He lost control of his wings and fell. Through his blood-specked vision, he saw the mini-vimana with only one person diving down towards the vimana. The pilot of Vimana One, Lenro, broke open the top of the pilot's cabin and leapt out just as the mini-vimana swooped down, and she landed on the back of it swiftly.

Deploying decoys, said Farouche, and Jem whipped his head around to locate Vimana Two. By the time he found it, three empty mini-vimanas were falling from it, and the swarm of Djimota around Vimana Two were diving down to attack the minis.

Brilliant, thought Jem. He flew by the falling mini-vimanas and shot a wall of fire as he went, destroying all the Djimota that had pursued the decoys.

All thrusters out—we're evac'ing too, said Henry. Jem saw Vimana Three below and saw that two of its thrusters were missing completely, and the third was broken in half. It was flying crooked, the broken thruster higher than the destroyed thrusters; and when the mini-vimanas deployed, one was launched straight up, and the other two were launched downwards. The two that were launched downwards didn't stand a chance—they crashed into different towers and burst into flames.

Land, commanded Afflatus, apparently still alive. He must have been in the one surviving mini from Vimana Three. *Land at the base by the main entrance—I'll get us inside. Farouche, stay as high as you can so we have a way out.*

You got it, captain, replied Farouche.

The tall city towers disappeared just before they reached the castle. Jem watched the six mini-vimanas crash into the dirt and skid. Vimana Two flew overhead, and four people jumped from it, magically cushioning their falls before hitting the ground. Jem landed behind everyone else and turned to face the Djimota that were pursuing them.

Go in! he shouted in his rendocom as he unleashed an enormous firestorm upon their pursuing zombies. The fire expanded in all directions and intertwined like thousands of flaming vines encapsulating everything within their reach.

Jem heard an explosion and then Afflatus yelling, 'Go go go!' As soon as Jem felt he had thoroughly roasted everything behind them, he turned and ran on all fours into the building. Afflatus and Tekkara were standing on either side of the broken entranceway, and as Jem passed by, they both began to glow blue around their feet and hands. They both nodded their heads and took off like they had rockets attached to them.

We'll save the legendaries; you shut the portal, said Afflatus through the rendocom. *Good luck.*

You too, replied Jem.

His dragon body was too big to fit through the entrance, so he transformed as he entered. As soon as he got in, a massive wall that Afflatus and Tekkara must have summoned shot up from the ground, blocking the entrance completely. It was eerily silent inside, and everyone was staring at Jem.

He panted heavily for a moment. "Well, what are ya'll waiting for?" he snapped. "Let's go."

He closed the visor on his helmet and began to storm down the hallway, but Forenzi called after him. "Half of us should be going the opposite way; the plan is to surround the Leader, remember?"

"Right," said Jem. "Then half of you follow me."

Six of the soldiers followed Forenzi, and the other six followed Jem. Jem was trying to pull up a mental picture of the plan they had gone over, but he couldn't focus at all. He just kept seeing the two mini-vimanas from Vimana Three crashing into the towers. There were people in those vimanas—people who were dead now. He saw the crashes again and again.

Jem, I can still see what you see, Farouche said over the rendocom. *Send three people down further and leave the other three where you are standing. They can enter the throne room through that doorway.*

Jem finally looked up from the ground and stopped walking. Everyone stopped around him and lifted their visors.

"Why'd you stop?" asked Okka. "Should three of us go around to the back?"

"Yeah—yeah," stuttered Jem. He looked around at who was with him: Okka, Bert, Ella, Teek, Ikuuno, and Mualano. That left Zenska, Lenro, Leo,

Sam, Henry, and Yakoba with Forenzi. Okay, he could do this. They had a lot of people still alive. But also a lot dead…

"Come on," said Okka, motioning towards Bert and Ella. "We're going around the back. Ikuuno, Mualano, take care of Teek. Jem, find yourself a way to get at the Leader."

Okka went walking off, followed by Bert. Ella glanced over at Bert and hesitated. She looked like she was about to say something to Jem, but then she shut her visor and went off behind Bert and Okka. For a second, Jem thought that her eyes had looked blue, but he knew that that couldn't have been possible.

"Alright, you three breach the throne room here," said Jem, indicating a large oval doorway to their side. "Wait for my signal."

"What's the signal?" asked Mualano.

"Oh, you'll know," replied Jem.

He then left them as he headed back to the main entrance. He had seen a staircase that could possibly give him a better vantage point to attack from. The hallway around him had a large ceiling and was lit by several torches running along the walls. Everything shone a dull gold, and there were various stairways and hallways jutting off in all directions, but the main hallway wrapped around the throne room in a circle.

Jem couldn't help but wonder why everything was so quiet and why the halls were empty. They hadn't met any resistance since getting into the castle, and it was definitely starting to feel like a trap. He didn't have much choice, though, other than to proceed with the plan.

When he made it back to the front entrance, he could hear a horde of zombies outside pounding and hacking away at the wall of ground that Afflatus and Tekkara had summoned. They sounded dull and far away—a dream compared to what Jem was about to face. He snapped his visor shut and proceeded up a steep staircase.

Much higher up, the staircase branched off in three directions, and Jem figured that he had to go right to get to the throne room based on what he could remember. He turned out to be right; the thin hallway passed directly by a large window that overlooked the throne room. Jem crouched down and peered through it.

The Leader, Loph, was sitting on its decorative golden throne, staring down at its feet. It wore heavy-looking golden armor that covered most of its body aside from the bladed arms and legs. It looked much bigger than the other Djimota, and it had a threatening, spiky tail. Jem saw the Soul sparkling from the top of its intricate crown, and his heart began beating at breakneck speeds.

Above Loph was the Sacred Portal, which Jem still didn't know how he was going to close. Hopefully, something would come to him. His first priority had to be to get the Soul; that was why they came here after all.

He tried searching around the throne room for signs of other Djimota, but there were none. Was Loph really the only one here? It seemed suspicious to Jem, but he had to spring on the opportunity while he had it. He tensed every muscle in his body and prepared to jump.

Jem, you're not going to do that, are you? asked Farouche over the rendocom. *It's clearly a trap.*

No other choice, replied Jem.

He then leapt forward and crashed through the glass window. He landed on a balcony that ran around the interior of the circular room, rolled, and got back onto his feet. He jumped off the edge of the upper-floor and dove at Loph as he transformed. He could feel his claws extending, the wings protruding from his back, the flames licking at his lips, but Loph was staring up at him... and smiling.

Before Jem could reach Loph, chains wrapped around each of his four limbs, delivering powerful electric shocks throughout his body. He immediately stopped transforming and fell out of the air, landing hard on his stomach in human form. The shocks kept coming, though, and he writhed in pain as the chains stretched all his limbs in opposite directions.

Jem heard Loph stand up and walk over to him, its metallic, golden boots clinking against the shiny floor with every step. It laughed an insidious, disgusting laughter. Jem heard explosions, the sound of magic beams being shot, and then silence. The electric chains stopped shocking him and pulling his limbs outwards, but they remained attached around his wrists and ankles. His limbs fell uselessly beside him.

"Fools," said Loph loudly, placing its foot under Jem's shoulder and pushing up to turn him over onto his back. "You think you can walk into my kingdom and kill me so easily?"

Jem's vision was blurry, but above him, he saw zombies lining a third-floor balcony, their wrists all aimed at him. Four of them were holding the chains that were connected to his limbs. Jem sat up, ignoring the pain that that caused him, and saw multiple zombies beside each group of three humans that had tried to enter. They all had their wrists pointed at the humans, keeping them from moving.

"I could kill your friends now," said Loph, pacing back to its throne. "But then they couldn't watch their hero die."

Jem rolled over and crouched on his knees. He coughed violently and spit up blood, coating the inside of his helmet with it.

"I'm not going to die," said Jem, ripping off his helmet and throwing it to the side. It was useless in this situation anyway, especially with the visor covered in blood.

"Oh, really?" laughed Loph, stepping slowly towards Jem. "And how do you plan to escape here with your life?"

Jem stared up at the giant zombie with no answer. He was going to die.

There was no way out of this. Any magic or transformation would immediately be halted by the electricity in the chains. All he could think to do was stall long enough for Afflatus and Tekkara to release the legendaries, but what could he say to keep Loph from killing him?

Challenge him to an Unekai, said Farouche over the rendocom.

What is that? asked Jem.

"Exactly as I thought," taunted Loph, raising its wrist to Jem's forehead. "You cannot escape. I hope your friends enjoy your death.

Just do it! screamed Farouche

"I challenge you to an Unekai!" burst Jem, shutting his eyes and clenching his teeth. The silence that followed seemed to be a good sign, since he wasn't dead yet.

"You?" laughed Loph finally. "A human? Wish to challenge me? Why should I accept when I could kill you now?"

Call him a coward, said Farouche.

"Because only a coward turns down an Unekai," said Jem, trying to get to his feet but falling back down to one knee.

"I am no coward! I am Loph, Leader of all the Djimota!" It roared a ferocious roar, spraying Jem with saliva. All the other Djimota cheered as well.

"Prove it," spat Jem. *What the hell am I getting myself into, Farouche?* he asked through the rendocom.

A one-on-one duel to the death, replied Farouche.

Loph seemed to be considering this proposal, and it only took it a few seconds to decide. "I shall accept your Unekai. Release the chains."

I hope this works, said Jem.

Me too, replied Farouche. *But I'm putting the vimana on auto-pilot 'cause I gotta fight some of the zombies coming aboard. Get to the roof when you're done. Good luck.*

You too, replied Jem. They were going to need it.

The chains gently released Jem and slunk back to their owners. Jem stood up unsteadily and put one foot behind the other in a fighting position. Loph, towering above him, did the same.

"Ready, human?"

"Ready," grunted Jem.

The golden plates covering Loph's forearms then swung forward and formed swords projecting from each of its arms. With its left arm, it swung forcefully at Jem, roaring as it did so. Jem activated the shields on his suit, but they didn't stand a chance. Loph's golden sword sent Jem flying across the room and smashing into the wall, disabling his suit's shields completely.

Before Jem could get his head together, Loph came charging at him. With hardly any time to react, Jem tried to transform, but he was still too weak. His eyes transformed, though, and he watched Loph's blades as if they were in slow motion. He leaned to the right, and Loph's first blade slashed the wall behind him; he jumped out of the way, and Loph's second blade sunk deep into the wall. While Loph struggled to pull out its blade, Jem made a run for it, his dragon eyesight flickering away.

"You call me a coward, and then you run from a fight?" called Loph, just as it took its blade from the wall. "Face me with dignity, human scum."

Jem was running straight for the Sacred Portal, and just as he activated his dragon-hearing, he heard a projectile coming directly at his head. He ducked, the projectile skimming his hair, and turned around to face Loph.

"There is no dignity in fighting," he said, concentrating hard on transforming. Unfortunately, he didn't have many options but to fight, and that would probably be easier as a dragon.

"There is only dignity in fighting," spat Loph, brandishing its blades.

Jem jumped into the air and transformed, the full length of his wing span taking up almost half of the room. He flapped several times and was already hitting his wings against the walls and his head against the ceiling. Clumsily flapping around, Loph was able to slice away easily at his tail, leaving Jem with a few deep gashes as he roared in pain. He fell back to the floor, and as he did so, he breathed fire down upon Loph. Obviously, though, being a dragon wouldn't work in the tiny room.

Immediately after unleashing his flames on Loph, he transformed back into a human, and the pain in his tail disappeared as his tail did. He looked up to see that Loph was positioned on one knee, its arms over its head in a protective position. It stood up and grinned, its fangs hanging from its mouth and dripping saliva.

"Gonna have to do better than that to kill me, filthy human," it yelled.

You got this, you got this, Jem told himself. *Partial transformations. Get the crown. Shut the Portal. Easy enough.*

Jem stood there breathing heavily, waiting for Loph to make a move. The Sacred Portal was directly behind it, and Jem would need some time to focus on shutting it. He didn't know how this was going to work out. He looked around the room and saw the other soldiers all being held captive by the surrounding Djimota. Everything was riding on him.

This time, as Loph charged, Jem tried a different approach. He transformed his eyes and ears so that he could see and hear the attacks coming and dodge them preemptively. For the ones that he couldn't dodge, he would transform a piece of his arm into hard dragon scales and deflect the blades with that, although that still hurt incredibly badly and left his bones shaking.

That went on for what felt like an eternity to Jem as he ducked, dodged, and blocked. He was draining himself quickly, though, with all the transforming, and he wasn't getting any nearer to the portal, so he eventually took out his astra. At first, he used it as a sword, swinging it against Loph's arm-blades and taking a few swings at its legs from time to time.

However, Loph was much more skilled with a blade, and Jem was forced to transform his astra to its gun form. Shooting at Loph did nothing with regular near-shots, but the big-shots actually seemed to have some impact. With each hit that Jem sank, Loph was pushed back further, and it even seemed to dent its armor. With a quick burst of shots to the face, Jem was able to subdue Loph long enough for him to run over and stand on the Leader's throne.

"How dare you stand on my throne, you inferior being!" cried Loph, firing projectiles at Jem that he easily deflected with magic so that they passed by him and hit the wall.

"I'm inferior?" teased Jem, an idea suddenly coming to him. "You're just a disease that killed thousands of humans and used their bodies for your own gain. You're nothing but a parasite on the human existence."

"We improved upon the human condition!" shouted Loph. "We are faster, stronger, better in every way."

"You're also more violent. We have a shot at peace, but you will always be at war, always killing, always fighting."

"You are just as violent as us! And besides, peace is a myth—something humans dream of that will never be reality."

"I will make it a reality," declared Jem, "and that starts by getting rid of you."

"Do you not see that by killing me, you will only anger the rest of my Djimota who will then come after you? You cannot escape the reality of war, human."

Jem grinned. "But I'm not going to kill you. I'm going to shut your portal."

On that note, Jem jumped onto the back of the chair directly below the portal and reached his hands out as if he was going to shut the portal. He didn't, though, and he heard Loph come lunging at him, roaring in fury. Instead of focusing on the portal, Jem waited until Loph was diving in midair directly behind him. Then, he jumped and flew up high into the air with magic. As he did this, he flipped backwards and his head went just above Loph's head. With one hand, he snatched the crown from the Leader's head.

As he came back down to the ground, he saw Loph getting sucked into the Sacred Portal, since Loph had been unable to change its direction in mid-dive.

"NOOO!" came an angry voice from the depths of the portal as Loph disappeared. It sounded as if it were underwater and very far away.

Immediately, Jem heard the sound of the Djimota firing their wrist projectiles. He expected to be covered in them in an instant, but he felt nothing. He looked around and saw that he was surrounded by a giant magic shield. All the soldiers were shooting their astras together to collectively form a giant shield for him. He had no time to waste.

Jem tucked the crown into the neck of his suit, ran back up to the throne, stood on top of it, and placed a hand on each side of the portal. He deployed one dragon claw for each hand and sunk them into the corners. With those firmly secured, he began to zip the Sacred Portal shut like a zipper. Just before it had shut completely, though, a large purple hand came jutting out of it. Refusing to lose concentration, Jem continued shutting the portal, and the purple hand was cut clean off. It fell to the throne lifelessly, its fingers twitching slightly.

Sweat pouring down his face, Jem completed the closing of the portal. As soon as it was done, he transformed his fingers back to human form and stepped down onto the throne beside Loph's severed hand. He crouched next to it and watched it dissolve into the air as if it were evaporating.

Jem looked around, and all the Djimota that had been holding the humans captive began to dissolve away just like the hand had. Closing the Sacred Portal did it; the zombies were dying out almost instantaneously. But something more sinister was happening as well. The ground began to shake like an earthquake, and a noise like a muffled explosion sounded beneath them.

"To the roof!" yelled Jem, grabbing the crown from his neck and holding it as tightly as he could.

Their exit was anything but organized. Everybody scrambled for a way out of the throne room and headed back to the main entrance. By the time that Jem was about halfway up the stairs by the main entrance, some people were already way ahead of him while others were still behind him. The building was shaking harder and bits of the walls were beginning to fall, torches crashing to the ground. Jem didn't think that this building was going to stay up much longer.

"This way!" he heard Okka calling from the base of the staircase. "Everybody up here! This castle is going down!"

As several people ran by Jem, he waited on the stairs for Okka to come by.

"What's going on?" Jem asked Okka as they continued up the stairs.

"I think that the death of the Leader triggered a failsafe," explained Okka, breathing heavily. "This building is self-destructing, and we don't have long."

They continued to run up the stairs, avoiding the steps that were breaking apart and dodging the falling chunks of ceiling. Jem tied the crown around his waist with a string of silver sylph. After a couple of floors, the stairs turned and went above the throne room, leading to a large, empty room with a curved ceiling. A massive hole was blown open at the center of the ceiling, and some of the other soldiers were already crawling through it when Jem and Okka got there. They were the last two out.

Up on the roof, all of them stood on the curved, slippery surface trying to stay on their feet as the dome shook. The sky was blood red, and Djimota were surrounding the dome and gliding around the sky freely. As Jem watched, though, they began to evaporate into the air just like he had seen the others do. They were dying out now that the Sacred Portal was shut.

Then Jem's jaw dropped and his heart stopped as he saw the Dragon and the Phoenix fly above him. The Dragon roared, and the Phoenix screeched, both of them breathing fire over any zombies that got in their way. Tekkara was on the back of the Dragon, while Afflatus was on the back of the Phoenix, but both of them jumped off and landed on the dome as their legendaries flew by.

Directly above them was the vimana that Farouche had been piloting, but the last Jem remembered hearing from him was that he had left the pilot's cabin to fight zombies that were boarding.

Bring us up, Farouche, Afflatus demanded through the rendocom, gathering everyone together on the roof.

"How do we get up there?" yelled Forenzi. "What is Farouche doing?"

"Wait for him!" Afflatus shot back. "He'll get us."

But nothing came over the rendocom. The Dragon and the Phoenix flew circles around the dome, incinerating all the zombies that were holding out a little longer without the Zombie Virus. The dome shook violently, and Jem could hear large pieces inside begin to fall apart.

"Afflatus, we need to act now!" shouted Okka. "This castle could crash at any instant!"

Afflatus seemed conflicted as he looked around at the soldiers and then stared up at the vimana. "Fine," he said finally. "Everyone get together. Councilmembers, Kara, hovering launch on three."

Everyone huddled together closely, the Councilmembers and Elders in a circle on the outside. From Jem's count, everybody was there.

"One, two, THREE!"

Immediately, Jem felt his entire body squished down as if he were shooting off on a roller coaster straight up. In an instant, the accelerating feeling left him, and he felt weightless. All of them were flying through the air, reaching their maximum altitude just at the height of the vimana. Some of them maneuvered themselves into the vimana while Jem and a few others grabbed onto the ledge and pulled themselves up.

Inside, dozens of Djimota bodies were lying on the ground. Most of them were unmoving, but some of their limbs were twitching and others were squirming as if they were in pain. The soldiers stood around the edge of the vimana, staring at the scene. Jem was searching for Farouche.

And then he found him. At the center, just beside the entrance to the pilot's cabin, Farouche was lying on the ground, astra in hand. Jem walked across zombie bodies as they began to dissolve away and crouched beside Farouche's body.

"Farouche, what happened?" asked Jem. Farouche's eyes were barely open, and as Jem examined his chest, he saw that a Djimota's projectile was sticking out from the center of his chest.

"Everything's gonna be alright," called Henry as he ran passed Jem and Farouche to get into the pilot's cabin. "But we gotta get out of here. Hang on!"

The vimana lurched and took off, the zombie bodies sliding to the rear as they dissolved away completely. Some of the soldiers latched into chairs while Jem, Sam, Tekkara, and Afflatus knelt beside Farouche.

"I…I killed them all," stammered Farouche in between bloody coughs. "I kept it in the air. You can go… home."

"You'll be fine," said Tekkara, her and Afflatus hovering their hands over his chest trying to magically heal it. The projectile had dissolved away like the zombies had. "We can heal you."

Farouche laughed painfully. "No… no, I've lost too much blood. I know that. Even magic can't put blood back in my body."

"You've never seen us heal," said Afflatus, pulling blood from the pools around Farouche and directing it back into his chest.

Farouche grinned weakly. "Magic really can do anything."

Jem looked over his shoulder. Outside the hatch, he could see the castle imploding on itself. The golden dome crumbled like a pile of sand, falling in on itself before exploding outward. The explosion shook the vimana and blew them forward, forcing Jem to grab onto the edge of the pilot's cabin so that he wouldn't slide away. Behind them, the explosion seemed to be following them, but their vimana was just fast enough to stay ahead.

"You saved us all," Jem said to Farouche. "We wouldn't have made it without you."

"You got the Soul?" asked Farouche.

Jem detached the crown from the sylph rope he had around his waist and held it in front of Farouche. Farouche's brown eyes sparkled with the light of the Soul.

"We stand a chance now," he mumbled, looking Jem in the eyes. "You need to stop them. Create a better world… a world where people can be safe."

Jem nodded, tears welling up in his eyes.

"It isn't working," said Tekkara. "The spike must have had a special poison because I can't figure out why it isn't working."

Afflatus said nothing; he merely furrowed his brow and concentrated harder on his complicated hand motions.

"I know…" continued Farouche. "I know I was caught up in my

inventions a lot… but our friendship meant a lot to me, Jem. I love you."

"I love you too, Farouche," spluttered Jem, tears cascading down his cheeks and splashing against the ground. He watched as Farouche's facial expression lightened, and his eyes glazed over. His breathing became incredibly slow and then stopped entirely. Afflatus and Tekkara stopped attempting to heal him.

"I'm sorry, Jem," said Tekkara, tears in her eyes as she looked at Jem. "We did what we could."

Afflatus looked at Jem too, the most extreme agony on his face that Jem had ever seen from him.

Behind them, the explosion was now far in the distance: a giant cloud of dust billowing into the red sky. Their vimana continued on, unobstructed by zombies because they were all dying off due to their lack of Zombie Virus.

Hey, Invasion Squad, came Sierra's voice over the rendocom. *Ya'll on your way back yet?*

Justin Dennis

CHAPTER 28:
HOSTAGE

Sierra and Avalon walked several miles in silence. It was awkward as they marched on over the dry dirt of Kelados. Sierra kept flexing her hand with the Phoenix Glove on it, trying to get a feel for it. She still didn't know exactly what it did, but she didn't feel like testing it out quite yet; she was exhausted from all the magic she had used in the river.

She had thought about trying to use the Glove to fight her way south into zombie territory and find the rest of the Invasion Squad, but she didn't think that that was possible, especially with Avalon; and she figured it would just be safer to go back to the Fortress. She felt drained of all her energy and useless despite the immense power contained in the Glove.

"Hey," said Avalon, not looking Sierra in the eyes, "do you think they're okay?"

Sierra looked over at Avalon. The Council Spokesperson's daughter kept her head down, her wet hair falling over her eyes. Her helmet was in her hand, and she was slouching her shoulders; she looked absolutely defeated.

"I hope so," said Sierra, thinking of all her friends and her dad.

"I wish we had a way to reach them," grumbled Avalon.

Sierra perked up at this, remembering the rendocom. She had completely forgotten about it until then.

Hey, Invasion Squad, she said in her head. *Ya'll on your way back yet?*

There was a moment of silence in which Sierra held her breath, waiting for a response. It felt like her heartbeat stopped too. If no one replied, what did that mean? Could they all have been killed?

Sierra, said her dad. *Are you okay? Where are you?*

Sierra exhaled, immensely relieved.

I'm great, dad. North of the river, headed back to the Fortress. What's the status there?

We've lost people, but we got the Soul, shut the Portal, and saved the legendaries. We're headed north as we speak.

Sierra wanted to smile, but she couldn't knowing that some of them had died in their invasion.

I'm so glad you're okay, dad, she said.

I'm glad you're okay, Sierra, he replied. *What did you do at the river?*

I got the Glove—the Phoenix Glove.

You... you did what? gasped Leo. *You have it?*

I do, she said, a grin barely surfacing on her face. *And I'm going to use it to save Callisto.*

You should have told me what you were doing, said Leo, although she could hear the joy in his voice from the news. *But I look forward to taking back our home. I'm very proud of you, sweetie. Did someone else jump off the vimanas at the river?*

Avalon did, Forenzi's daughter. But she's fine too.

Good, good, said Leo. *Well, we'll pick you up on the way. I don't think we can miss two girls in the middle of the nothingness here.*

Sounds good. See you soon, dad.

Bye, honey. I love you.

I love you too.

Sierra glanced over at Avalon, trying to think of something to say, but she had nothing. She used to hate her, but as she thought about why, she didn't have any good reasons. It had been jealousy, really—the fact that Avalon had taken Jem from her. But that didn't matter. Having Jem or not having Jem didn't define her, and either way, she couldn't blame Avalon for Jem's choice.

She felt bad for the girl, though. She had gone through a lot for Jem, even if she had only wanted him initially because of his power. Sierra wondered if maybe Avalon could learn the same lesson that she had: that a partner doesn't make a person whole. She felt confident and capable by herself, and she hoped that Avalon could experience that eventually too.

Nothing showed over the horizon in any direction. There were some boulders and dead-looking trees but not much else. Sierra gently put her arm around Avalon and squeezed her in an awkward side-hug. Avalon remained stiff at first, but then rested her head against Sierra's shoulder.

"I'm sorry," said Avalon quietly, her voice shaking. "I'm glad you got the Glove. I don't deserve it."

Sierra rested her head against Avalon's. "You were just motivated by the wrong things. I believe in you, Avalon."

Avalon sniffled and nodded; Sierra could hear her crying. The two of them continued on in silence, Sierra keeping an eye out for a vimana in the sky.

***

Jem sat next to Farouche's body, arms wrapped around his legs, staring out the hatch door. He couldn't believe everything that had happened. He wanted to feel happy that they had achieved their goal, but he couldn't feel happy knowing so many had died. Farouche's lifeless body was a constant reminder during their flight, and the image of the mini-vimanas crashing into the buildings kept replaying in Jem's mind.

He had heard Sierra and Leo's conversation and was relieved to know that Sierra was safe but surprised that Avalon had been the other one who had jumped off at the river. He didn't understand why Avalon would have done that, and he couldn't imagine what must have happened if they had both been fighting for the Phoenix Glove. Obviously, Sierra had won, and Jem thought that that was probably for the better. He didn't know if he trusted Avalon with that much power, but he trusted Sierra without a doubt.

Thinking of what would happen when they got Sierra and Avalon, Jem stood up and walked over to the rear hatch. Behind them, the sky was changing from red to blue, and the blue was expanding, staying just a couple miles behind them. The clouds in the sky were swirling and moving in erratic patterns.

Jem's thoughts weren't on the landscape, though. He felt like he had to decide between Avalon and Sierra, but he didn't know if Sierra would even want to be with him. If he wanted to be with Avalon as he had been before they had left for the invasion, he could probably do that, but he hadn't really been happy then. He had missed Sierra, and while Avalon was a great person, he hadn't connected with her in the same way that he had with Sierra.

Trying to ignore which of them would take him back, he thought about the situation again, and his decision was easy. He loved Sierra. She was more than a girlfriend or partner, she was a friend. He connected with her on more levels than Avalon, but he didn't want Avalon to hate him for his decision, although he felt like it would be inevitable.

If Sierra didn't want to be with him, though, that was her decision and he would respect it. He may have made a mistake being with Avalon for their time here in Kelados, but it had happened, and he couldn't take it back. Besides, he had enjoyed being with Avalon and grown a lot in his time with her. He still wanted to be friends with her, but he didn't know if that would ever be possible.

On the edge of a cloud outside, he thought he saw something moving. Upon closer inspection, he saw the blurry outline of Minosa floating towards him. As he made eye contact with her, she smiled, giggled, and flew back into the cloud.

Jem turned back to the group at large and said, "I'll be right back. I'm going to visit the Or'lidi."

Those who heard him acknowledged him. He approached Afflatus and held out the crown. "Can you hang onto this for me? I think we're going to need it."

Afflatus grinned weakly. "You got it."

Jem returned an attempt at a smile and then turned back to the hatch. He took a deep breath and leapt off the edge, transforming as he did. Below him, the Rastvo cities were in chaos. Zombies were running around and dissolving into the air before Jem's eyes. He swooped back up into the sky and headed for the cloud. Luckily, the poison in the red sky didn't affect him in his dragon form. In the distance behind the vimana, he could see the Holy Tower shining brightly.

When he broke through the clouds, there were familiar faces there. Ontam, Benya, and Minosa stood on the clouds, smiling.

"Hi, Jem," said Ontam. "Congratulations on your success."

Jem sat down in his dragon form, looking around the sky. Behind the Or'lidi, the sky was blue, and the blue was approaching fast, erasing the red as it went.

Thanks, said Jem. *But what is happening?*

"The Zombie Virus which tainted our world has run out of supply," explained Benya, "and the planet is returning to its natural state."

"We will disappear too, as the Virus does," said Ontam. "We are only suspended here as long as the zombies are. But that is okay; our presence is no longer needed."

Jem nodded. *Thank you for everything. We couldn't have done this without you.*

Ontam nodded and smiled widely. "I have been waiting for a long time to see the zombies destroyed. We should be thanking you."

"Before we go," interjected Benya, removing a necklace from her neck, "I must give you this. It is a key to the Holy Tower. I sealed the Tower when the zombies came. I didn't have much time, but I cast my strongest spell on the building, and they have never been able to break it.

"Inside, you will find something you must take good care of. It will be of great help to you in your war to take back your home. I didn't want to give you this earlier because the Tower was the center of the zombies' battlefield, and you couldn't have gotten there safely. But now that the zombies are gone, you may safely retrieve it."

Jem leaned his long dragon neck down, and Benya placed the key around his neck. It felt light as air and began to glow an electric blue as it touched his scales.

"Good luck to you," continued Benya.

Thank you, said Jem.

Before Jem's eyes, the three of them began to dissipate like the zombies had, bits of their cloud-like bodies drifting away in the wind. The blue sky had finally caught up to them and was sweeping over them. The air felt cold and clean as it breezed across Jem's scales.

"Bye," whispered Ontam, Benya, and Minosa, their voices intertwining with the sound of the wind.

Bye, said Jem, and within seconds, he was left sitting in the clouds alone. He admired the beauty of the sky, now a thousand times shinier and bluer, before he dove back down through the clouds and made for the vimana.

The Dragon and the Phoenix were circling the vimana, both looking absolutely jubilant; after all, they had finally escaped the small silver dome that the Djimota had kept them in for so long. Jem flew up beside the Dragon, feeling tiny in his smaller dragon form.

Glad to have you back, he said telepathically.

Thank you for rescuing us, Jem, replied the Dragon. *We were foolish to have rushed in and put ourselves in that position. We are fortunate that you humans were so clever in your invasion.*

I don't know if clever is the word, laughed Jem. *Maybe lucky.*

The Dragon grinned. *Whatever it was, we are thankful.*

Jem looked over at the Phoenix who had just come to fly beside them. Even it seemed to be smiling, and it made an appreciative clicking noise like a dolphin.

Well, I'm gonna go back inside, said Jem. *I'm exhausted, and I don't think I could continue to fly much longer. I will see you two back at the Fortress.*

Bye then, said the Dragon, and Jem flew back to the vimana.

Despite their victory, the atmosphere inside the vimana was depressing. Farouche's body was still there, and many people were crying over the loss of the many soldiers who had died. After taking a headcount, Jem realized that eight people had died: Rick, Tachel, Farouche, Fey, Harcos, Himay, and two other soldiers that had been aboard Vimana Three named Ischia and Elsa. It was difficult to celebrate when so many lives had been lost.

Soon they were passing over Sierra and Avalon. Henry took the vimana down and landed softly beside them. They came aboard, and Avalon walked straight to her father, embracing him in a tight hug. Sierra glanced at Farouche's body and began to cry. She said, "Hello," to Afflatus and the others as she went, but she walked towards her dad. Jem noticed the Phoenix Glove on her hand that looked as if it was on fire.

After hugging her dad, saying a few words to him, and controlling her tears, she walked over to Jem who was standing alone towards the rear of the vimana.

"Hi," said Jem, not sure of where to put his hands as he spoke.

"Hi," replied Sierra, gripping one of her forearms with the other hand.

"You got the Glove," said Jem, his eyes flickering towards it.

"Congratulations."

Sierra smiled. "You got the Soul, and you shut the Portal. I think I should be congratulating you."

"Well, we both did pretty great," said Jem.

Sierra laughed nervously. "Yeah."

They both stood there awkwardly for a moment, their eyes darting around the ship but not making contact with each other.

"I, um… I was thinking a lot during the invasion," stammered Jem. "And I… I want to be with you. I miss you, Sierra, and I miss how things were back in Luria. There's nothing wrong with Avalon, she's great, but I feel like I connect better with you. And I haven't stopped thinking about you since we've been in Kelados. I just don't want to spend the rest of my life wishing I'd told you how I felt. But if you don't want to be with me, I totally understand—"

But Jem was cut short as Sierra gripped his face and kissed him on the lips. The left side of his face felt warm from the Phoenix Glove, but his lips tingled, and his heart leapt out of his chest. He put his arms around her and pulled her in closely.

"I want to be with you, Jem," she said after pulling back from the kiss. "Because you're more than a partner to me—you're my best friend."

Jem smiled, and they kissed again. Behind him, Jem heard the Dragon purring and the clicking noise that the Phoenix had made. Sierra and Jem pulled out of their kiss and looked out the hatch to see the two legendaries leaning their heads down to peer into the vimana. Sierra perked up as if she had heard something and then walked out of the vimana, Jem following behind her.

Sierra stood before the Phoenix as the massive bird lowered its head for her to pet. As she stroked the Phoenix's head with her gloved hand, the Phoenix Glove changed from its red and yellow flames to blue flames. The Phoenix retracted its head and looked Sierra in the eyes. It took Jem a second to realize what was going on, but then he assumed that they must have been talking telepathically, much like he and the Dragon could do.

The Phoenix then spread its wings wide and breathed fire from its mouth. As it did so, the fire across its body grew in intensity, and Jem could feel the heat radiating from it. In response, Sierra threw her arms back and the Glove erupted in an explosion of blue flames. The flames licked around her hand and arm, soon swallowing her body completely. She grew in size as this happened, and within seconds, she was a large, fiery blue phoenix.

Jem stepped back, the heat from the two phoenixes being too much for him. "Wow," he said aloud, marveling at Sierra's transformation. She was a little smaller than the Phoenix, just as Jem was a little smaller than the Dragon, and the tip of her right wing was red instead of blue like the rest of her body. All the rest of her feathers flickered like flames and shone all different shades of blue. She threw her head back and expelled bright blue flames from her beak.

Then she returned to her human form. "Thanks, Quetzalus," she said aloud.

"Quetzalus?" repeated Jem.

"That's nir name," said Sierra. "The Dragon is Hazeryx."

"How do you know that?" asked Jem, still a little thrown off by the weird pronoun.

"I can explain it to you later," said Sierra. "Come on, let's go back to the Fortress." She extended her hand, and Jem took it.

Jem looked back over his shoulder at the Dragon and smiled.

See you soon, Hazeryx, he said.

Likewise, Jem, replied Hazeryx the Dragon.

The Dragon and the Phoenix rubbed their heads together and then took off into the sky. Jem and Sierra sat down in the very crowded vimana as Henry took off again.

The trip back was very quiet. Everyone was still mourning. Sierra played with her Glove and her new fire powers, and Jem fiddled with the key around his neck. Thankfully, nobody asked what it was because he wasn't in the mood to explain. He didn't really know what kind of mood he was in.

He looked over at Avalon. She avoided his gaze at first but then gave a weak smile. He smiled back. She looked in pain, though, and he felt horrible that he wasn't able to comfort her. He really didn't want to lose her as a friend; he still cared about her. But there was no way to relay that to her now. He would have to remember to talk to her later.

Jem couldn't decipher his emotions for the entire ride back. He was overwhelming sad that Farouche and the others had died; he was mad at himself for leaving Avalon; he was happy that he was with Sierra; he was ecstatic that they had the Soul in their possession and that the zombies were gone forever. Overall, he was optimistic about the future since they now stood a much better chance against Veroci and the Regime, but that didn't stop the pain that he felt in that moment.

As his eyes wandered around the vimana, he made eye contact with Ella. She was sitting on one of the benches, and she looked as if she had been crying for days. When she looked at Jem, she started to cry again. Why, though, Jem didn't know. Something was different about her, and it took Jem a minute to realize why, but then it struck him: she really did have blue eyes.

He stood up and walked over to her; Sierra followed behind him.

"Ella," said Jem, "are you okay?"

She looked up at him and shook her head. "No, but I will be."

"Your... your eyes," said Jem. "They're blue, like mine."

She smiled a little bit. "I know."

"Are you… are you related to me? Or to Veroci?"

Ella stood up and hugged him tightly. At first, he was incredibly confused.

"I'm your mom, Jem," she said softly into his ear. "I didn't remember until I was on the ship with Sierra, and she helped me to remember. My real name is Swayella Surwae."

She pulled back from their hug and looked Jem in the eyes, blinking the tears from her own. Jem couldn't believe what was going on. It felt like a dream—his mom, back from the dead.

"Rick had put spells on me to make me forget and had even enchanted my eye color, but when Sierra stood up to him, it broke the spells, and I remembered."

"Sierra, you stood up to him?" Jem asked, turning to face her. "What happened on your vimana?"

Sierra took a deep breath and gripped Jem's hand tightly. "When I was younger, Rick used to come and stay at our house a lot, and one day, he raped me. That's why I've never liked him, and it's why I didn't want to stay at his place in Radeon except as a last resort. But he didn't touch me in Radeon—don't worry. I never told anyone, though, or confronted him about it, until we were on that vimana.

"He was pushing Ella around, abusing her, and I couldn't bear to watch it. I attacked him and admitted out loud what had happened to me. That's when Swayella began to remember that he had done the same thing to her. Then Rick raised his astra to fight me, but I knocked him off the ship."

Sierra was in tears by the end of that, and Jem was holding her close. He had no idea what to say, so he just held her as tightly as he could. He couldn't imagine being in her position, and he just wanted her to know that he supported her and would do anything he could to help her. He had so much respect and admiration for her.

"Jem," said Swayella, "there is something I need you for. Could you come with me?" She smiled and held her hand out, and Jem took it. She led him to the other side of the vimana where Bert was sitting beside a metal bench, just at the edge of the hatch. When he saw them coming, he didn't react much; he continued to stare out the hatch.

"Robert," said Swayella. Bert perked up at this name and turned to face her.

"How do you know my name?" he asked suspiciously, but Jem already knew. The pieces were starting to fall together.

"Do you remember me?" asked Swayella. "Because I remember you now."

"No," said Robert immediately, turning back to stare out the hatch. "Now leave me alone."

"No, Robert," said Swayella more firmly. "I need answers, and I think you're the only person who can confirm what is going on in my mind right now. Tell me what you know about us."

Robert turned back to her. He looked as if he was putting a lot of thought into it.

"We were married," he said finally, "back on Earth. We went skydiving for our belated honeymoon, and as we fell, you transported us to Callisto. We crash landed in an ECKO building. I blamed you and yelled at you for stranding us in some new world, and I left. When I later heard that the building had been bombed, I thought you were dead. I lived with that misery for thirteen years, knowing that I had wrongly blamed you for something that wasn't your fault and believing that you were dead because of it. It wasn't until I arrived here and saw you that I knew you were alive. I couldn't tell you this before because you wouldn't have remembered. I'm surprised that you remember now."

"Oh my gosh…" muttered Swayella. "So it is true. It's all true."

"It is," said Robert, standing up to look Swayella in the eyes. He seemed much more serious and composed than he had back in Callisto when he had been injecting. His beard was shaven and his brown hair was cut short. Jem looked at his father's face and finally saw some of his own features in there.

"This is too much for me to process," said Swayella, backing away. "I need time."

"That's fine," said Robert calmly. "Take all the time you need."

"But in Callisto," interjected Sierra. "You had Jem and Oliver banished from Eltaes because you wouldn't testify that you saw us in your café! They could have been executed!"

"And we all would have been executed had I testified on your side," explained Robert. "The system was rigged to work against anyone who opposed the Regime. I was saving myself in that act, but I also saved Jem's life. You remember that I pointed out that his eyes were blue, yes?"

"Well, yeah, but how does that—"

"When the Eltaean Elder realized that Jem had blue eyes, and therefore could be the son of Veroci, he dared not to lay a hand on him. If he killed Jem, and it later turned out that Veroci wanted his son alive, the Elder would have been killed. He didn't want to involve himself in that, so he was forced to banish Jem and have nothing to do with him."

"He still could've killed Oliver!" protested Sierra.

"No. It would have been seen as an unfair and arbitrary punishment to execute Oliver and banish Jem. The Elder would not have done that. Besides, had I testified in your defense, it's likely that all five of us could have been executed, or at least Jem, Oliver, and I."

Sierra opened her mouth to talk, pointing her finger at him, but couldn't seem to think of anything else to say.

"So… you saved me?" asked Jem. "And that whole time I thought you were crazy…"

Robert grinned slightly. "I was crazy, at least to some extent. In my despair, I injected a lot. I earned a reputation around the city for that. But since I've been lucky enough to survive the Regime takeover and make it to Kelados, I've pulled myself together and realized that I can do better than who I was."

Jem's head was spinning. His mother and his father were here, two people who he had thought to be dead. He couldn't believe it. He was running through his mind pulling up every memory of Ella and Bert and trying to convert those two people into his parents: Swayella and Robert.

"Your voice," said Jem. "It sounds so familiar… did you—were you there when Rabaiz died? Did you save me then too?"

Robert looked shocked that Jem had figured that out. "Well, I, uh…" he stammered. "Yes. Yes, I was the one who brought you within the walls and told you to stay put while I got medical attention. Unfortunately, you didn't listen to me."

"I know," said Jem, almost laughing because it was so unbelievable. "So you've saved my life twice now, and I didn't even know it."

Robert nodded, smiling slightly. Jem hugged him tightly. "Dad," he muttered. The feelings inside of him were indescribable. Both of his parents were alive, and not only that, but they were here with him in Kelados and had fought alongside him to defeat the zombies.

He released his dad and hugged his mom, completely at a loss for words. He just cried into her shoulder.

At that moment, they began their descent into the Fortress. Jem released his mom and all four of them stepped away from the hatch. When they landed back in the same courtyard they had left from, hundreds of people were gathered around to greet them. Families of the soldiers rushed to meet them, and Jem was quickly able to spot the families of those who had died. Many people were in tears around him, and others were hugging their loved ones tight. It was a strange feeling where extreme sadness met joyous relief, and Jem was in the middle of it all.

The Dragon and the Phoenix flew down and landed softly beside the vimana. A few people screamed, but most just watched them in awe. There were lots of gasps, pointing, and chatter about the legendaries. Jem knew that the arrival of those two would cause a big stir with the systems, since the Draigs worshipped the Dragon and despised the Phoenix, while the Fenics had it the other way around. To Jem, the legendaries looked majestic; the Phoenix's flaming feathers rippled with the wind, and the Dragon's red scales shone brightly. He didn't understand all the hatred and division that had sprung up around them. Maybe that could be a thing of the past now.

Jem watched as Afflatus detached the Soul from the crown and held it above his head. Without saying anything, he released it, and it began to float high above them. Everyone in the crowd went quiet as the Soul floated through the sky and combined with the other two at the tip of the tower of the Council Center. The three combined Souls shone brighter than ever, instilling a small amount of hope in Jem.

"Sir," said a young woman who was facing Forenzi. She was dressed in business robes and holding a small black box. "A small ship crashed into the city while you were away. This was all it was carrying. It appears to be a message transmitter, but upon trying to activate it, it kept asking for a Jem Surwae."

Jem's heart sank and the entire crowd turned to look at him. Forenzi silently took the device from the woman's hand and walked over to Jem. The people around Jem dispersed to give him room, and Forenzi set the black box on the ground before him.

A holographic image of Veroci then expanded from the top of the device. His black hair was slicked back, he had a faint beard covering his large jaw, and he was wearing a suit much like a business suit on Earth, except with more detail and complexity to it. His hologram stood tall, towering above everyone else, and it stared directly at Jem.

"We have your friend, Oliver Pautelle," said Veroci's hologram. "He was recently taken from a planet which will soon be under my control. I believe you are familiar with Earth? Turn yourself into me, Jem Surwae, and give me the Dragon and all of ECKO's Souls, or Oliver will die a slow and painful death. Would you like to say hello to him?"

Veroci's hologram then disappeared, only to be replaced by the image of Oliver tied to a metal chair. His eyes looked swollen and red, and he had gashes and bruises across his body.

"Jem…" he said quietly. "Don't come for me… it's a trap…"

Oliver then disappeared from the hologram and Veroci returned. "If the Dragon and all of ECKO's Souls are not delivered to me by you, Jem, within the next three days, Oliver dies. If that is not enough motivation for you, then be aware that my takeover of Earth will begin immediately following your friend's death. The choice is yours, Jem. Choose wisely."

The hologram then clicked off, and the black box sat silently before Jem.

THE END OF BOOK TWO.

DON'T MISS THE FINAL BOOK
IN THE TRILOGY: **SWITCHING**

Find it on Amazon.com or Amazon.co.uk

ABOUT THE AUTHOR

Justin Dennis is from the rainy state of Washington but is going to college in sunny California. Soccer, which he used to play in high school, is his favorite sport, and he has in interest in creative writing, anthropology, and physics. He is a huge tech nerd who is obsessed with the newest and shiniest phones, tablets, and computers.

Writing occupies almost all of his time. The Through the Portal trilogy is his effort to inspire good morals in an entertaining and exciting way. Through fantasy, he believes that important real world lessons can be conveyed effectively.

To keep in contact with Justin and stay updated on his future writings:

Visit **www.JustinDennis.com**

"Like" **Justin Dennis (Author)** on Facebook

Follow **@JustinDennis4** on Twitter

Printed in Great Britain
by Amazon.co.uk, Ltd.,
Marston Gate.